A Prince

by C...

❮...

And then he kissed her.

Just one kiss. One kiss that lasted a minute, an
hour, an eternity. A kiss that shook Lise to her
foundation. A kiss like none she'd ever had.
His hands moved down her arms to her hips. He
pulled her close to him, closer and closer until
she felt the muscles in his thighs through her sheer
dress. Breathless and shaken, she pressed her face
against his shirt and inhaled the intoxicating scent
of his skin, his soap, his clothes. Her pulse was
racing…

And it was then, after she somehow managed to
pull away, to lift her head and gaze into Charles's
deep brown eyes, that she knew she would accept
his proposal of marriage.

* * *

Praise for Carol Grace

'Ms Grace provides romance fans with
heartwarming entertainment.'
—*Romantic Times*

A Prince at Last!
by Cathie Linz

ฉ ᚱᚱ ฏ

A familiar fire smouldered within him.

It wasn't the kind of flame that flared to life the instant he saw her, but it was the kind that grew in intensity each time he and Juliet were together. Instant lust Luc could deal with, but this overwhelmingly powerful attraction was something else entirely.

'I should have worn black leather,' he heard her mutter and almost groaned aloud at the sexy fantasy of her dressed like a biker babe— her thighs barely covered by a short skirt, her breasts pushing against a tight T-shirt. His body responded to the hot images, forcing him to shift position on the motorcycle, which only made her thighs rub against his even more.

When had his sweet innocent Juliet turned into such a sultry sex kitten?

Available in June 2003 from Silhouette Desire

Plain Jane & Doctor Dad
by Kate Little
and
And the Winner Gets…Married!
by Metsy Hingle
(Dynasties: The Connellys)

Her Lone Star Protector
by Peggy Moreland
and
Tall, Dark…and Framed?
by Cathleen Galitz
(The Millionaire's Club)

A Princess in Waiting
by Carol Grace
and
A Prince at Last!
by Cathie Linz
(Royally Wed)

A Princess in Waiting
CAROL GRACE

A Prince at Last!
CATHIE LINZ

SILHOUETTE®
DESIRE™

*Silhouette, Silhouette Desire and Colophon
are registered trademarks of Harlequin Books S.A.,
used under licence.*

*First published in Great Britain 2003
Silhouette Books, Eton House, 18-24 Paradise Road,
Richmond, Surrey TW9 1SR*

The publisher acknowledges the copyright holders of the
individual works as follows:

A Princess in Waiting © Harlequin Books S.A. 2002
A Prince at Last! © Harlequin Books S.A. 2002

*Special thanks and acknowledgement are given to Carol Grace
and Cathie Linz for their contributions to the
Royally Wed: The Missing Heir series.*

ISBN 0 373 04869 6

51-0603

*Printed and bound in Spain
by Litografía Rosés S.A., Barcelona*

A PRINCESS IN WAITING
by
Carol Grace

CAROL GRACE

has always been interested in travel and living abroad.
She spent her first year of university in France and
toured the world working on the hospital ship *HOPE*.
She and her husband spent the first year and a half of
their marriage in Iran, where they both taught English.
She has studied Arabic and Persian languages. Then,
with their toddler daughter, they lived in Algeria for
two years.

Carol says that writing is another way of making her
life exciting. Her office is her mountain-top home,
which overlooks the Pacific Ocean and which she
shares with her inventor husband, their daughter,
who's just graduated from university, and their teenage
son.

Special thanks to my wonderful daughter Nora for taking the family to Europe so I could research this book.

Chapter One

Once upon a time in a small country called St. Michel, wedged between France and Rhineland, lived a beautiful ex-princess named Lise de Bergeron. The former princess didn't live in the stately palace with its turrets and ballroom and bevy of servants. She lived in a small cottage on the palace grounds. This gave her the independence she wanted and suited the present queen—her father's fourth wife— and her grandmother, the dowager queen. Lise had no crown and no legitimacy since her parents' marriage had been declared invalid. She was not surrounded by maids who waited on her hand and foot. She was attended by her former nanny, the woman who had raised her when her mother had deserted her and her sisters. Nanny was old now and afflicted by arthritis and Princess Lise was more caregiver than pampered princess.

A lack of royal trappings did not bother the princess. What did bother her was that her father the king had just died, she'd been deserted by her husband, Wilhelm, of neighboring Rhineland, and she was three months pregnant.

All in all, this past year had been a difficult one. The future was unclear. What was in store for her and her unborn child? She pushed the question to the back of her mind and concentrated on the problems at hand. Number one was stopping the leak in the roof of the cottage.

"Nanny, who said April was the cruelest month?" she asked the old woman in the rocking chair.

"One of those poets you're always reading, I suppose," said Gertrude, smoothing the afghan over her knees. "Perhaps the same one who said April showers bring May flowers."

"It can't happen soon enough," Lise said, gazing out the small leaded window at rain pelting the vast green acres surrounding the palace.

"Ah, *ma pauvre,* is it really the weather that is making you melancholy or is it everything else?" the old lady asked with a worried frown.

"I'm fine really," Lise said hastily. It wouldn't do to make Nanny worry about her. "Let's have tea. I must confess I'm ravenous. You know, if I keep eating like this for the next six months, I'll be as big as a blimp."

"Nonsense," said the old woman. "You're eating for two."

Lise placed one hand over her still-flat stomach. It was amazing how much she looked forward to having this child. No matter how uncertain the future.

"When I was up at the castle this morning, the cook sneaked me some of her chocolate gateaux, so today we feast." Smiling, Lise held the basket out so her old nanny could see the delicate frosted cakes.

Keep smiling, she told herself. Though inside she was in turmoil, she couldn't let it show. Not to Nanny, who'd suffer for her, not to Queen Celeste who would think she deserved it, and not to her sisters who would feel sorry for her. No one must know the pain she felt at being deserted and divorced by her husband, the shame of being disinherited, of coming back alone to be at the mercy of the current occupants of the palace.

Today. She would think only of today, not tomorrow, not six months from now. She would take it one day at a time. At least she had a roof over her head, leaky though it was. The palace repairman said he couldn't fix it while it was raining, he'd get to it when the sun came out and when it was convenient. She told herself she was lucky to have a job of sorts and she had her dear old nanny. Things could be worse.

Things *had* been worse when she was married to Wilhelm. Yes, they'd lived splendidly in Rhineland, where he, as a member of the royal family, had money and power. But he was a cold, arrogant, ambitious man who'd been chosen for her by her father for political reasons. If she had one thing to be thankful for, it was that she was rid of the scoundrel. She'd endure any amount of shame if she never had to see him again.

After handing Nanny a tray with her tea and cake, Lise sat down at the polished pine table in the kitchen and gratefully inhaled the steam from the fragrant brew.

"What news from the palace?" Gertrude asked. "Did you see the queen by chance?"

"No, I hear she's keeping to her bed, preparing for the birth of her son."

"Son? It's going to be a son, then?" the old woman asked, setting her cup down with a clatter.

"So she says. But no one really knows. Not even the queen because she refuses to have a test to determine the baby's sex. It seems talk of a boy is just wishful thinking. Because if it isn't a son, she'll lose everything—her power, her status…well, you know as well as I do, as well as the whole kingdom does, how desperate she is to bear a son." What everyone knew was that according to the ancient law, the monarchy of St. Michel passes only through the male line.

Nanny nodded thoughtfully. "I guess everyone in the country is feeling desperate for an heir. Because if there is no heir, our beloved country will be absorbed by Rhineland."

Lise shivered involuntarily at the thought. She and her husband had lived royally in Rhineland during the brief months of her marriage, but she had no happy memories of him or of his country.

"Now, child, don't fret," her nanny said when her sharp eyes noted Lise's distress. "Isn't it true that the dowager queen has sent the head of the security force, Luc Dumont, to find the missing heir? Perhaps he will find him."

"Yes, maybe."

"Ah well, something will save us, it always has," Gertrude said. "In the meantime, if you'll hand me my knitting, I must get busy on the sweater for your baby."

Lise took away her tray and handed Nanny her knitting basket full of pale yellow yarn. After getting her settled next to the ornate cast-iron stove that gave off a comforting glow, Lise put on her smock over a turtleneck sweater and leggings and went to the adjacent greenhouse. It was there she did her best work as restorer of priceless artifacts of the Kingdom of St. Michel. Today she was painting an old cracked frame she'd restored.

Besides the peace and quiet, Lise appreciated the natural light that poured through the slanted windows of the greenhouse even on a rainy day. There were only a few leggy green plants left by a long-ago gardener, leaving the shelves free for her collection of glass mosaics, jars of acrylic water-based paint and a selection of bristle brushes and tools.

The smell of the damp earth and paint pigment melded together in a heady blend that soothed and inspired her.

If there was any place she could forget her troubles, it was here. Mixing and blending the paint, she hummed to herself. The work was challenging, but her studies in London with a master craftsman had prepared her well.

An hour later she heard a car pull up in front of the cottage. She was still immersed in her work and hated interruptions when it was going as well as it was today.

"Nanny will take care of it," she murmured to herself. She hoped it would be the delivery of her belongings from Rhineland. She'd left so suddenly, she'd taken only a small suitcase. Whatever it was, whoever it was, Gertrude knew enough not to bother her when she was at work.

However *someone* didn't know enough There was a knock on the door of the greenhouse Lise pushed an errant strand of hair back from her face.

"Yes?"

"Lise?" It was a deep voice. Vaguely familiar. "It's Charles. Charles Rodin."

"Charles?" Charles, her husband's twin brother? What on earth was he doing here. Anything, anyone connected with her ex-husband was upsetting and an intrusion in her new life. She'd left Wilhelm and wanted no reminders of the biggest mistake of her life.

"May I come in?" he asked.

As annoyed as she was, she couldn't help but notice the difference. Wilhelm would have barged in. His brother waited to be invited.

She opened the door. And stared at the man who stood there. He looked disturbingly like her ex-husband and yet the expression on his face was nothing like Wilhelm's arrogance. She barely remembered Charles from her wedding at which he had been the best man; she hadn't seen him since that fateful day, but she knew this was a man who was self-confident but not arrogant. Maybe it was the way his rain-dampened hair fell across his forehead or the way he'd stuffed his hands into the pockets of his cashmere coat, still, the resemblance bothered her and brought back unpleasant memories. She wanted nothing to do with Wilhelm or any member of his family. She was doing her best to forget all of them. And now this....

"May I come in?" he asked again.

What was wrong with her? She'd been raised with better manners than to let a guest stand in the doorway. But he was so big, so broad-shouldered, so startlingly like his brother, she'd thought he *was* in.

"Of course," she said briskly.

He stepped into the small greenhouse with the earthen floor and suddenly the glassed-in room was crowded to overflowing. She had no space, no room to breathe or think. There was a fluttery feeling in the pit of her stomach. She tried to think of something to say, but her mind was blank. All she could do was to stand there and wait for him to say something.

After a long silence during which he looked her up and down with a shade too much intimacy and she continued to stare at him, she finally found her voice.

"What is it, Charles? What do you want?"

He frowned at her lack of civility. What did he expect, that she'd welcome him with open arms, after what his brother had done to her?

"I came when I heard the news, about the divorce...to see if...to see what I could do."

"Nothing. You can do nothing. You can't stop your brother from divorcing me, you can't make my parents' marriage valid, you can't find an heir for our country, and you can't bring my father back to life. So go back to your country and tell your brother I don't need him or any of his family."

Charles looked surprised at her angry words. "I haven't been in my country for months nor have I seen much of my family. Perhaps you aren't aware, but my brother and I have never been close. And now we are hardly on speaking terms," he said stiffly. "We lead separate lives, both professionally and personally. I'm in charge of the wine business of Rhineland and Wilhelm is managing the family's investments abroad. I've been in the U.S. for the past six months. When I ran into Wilhelm last week in Los Angeles he told me about the divorce. I couldn't believe it. It's only been, what ?"

"Eight months," Lise said. "Eight months that I am doing my best to forget. So if you don't mind, I'll get back to work." She pivoted on her heel and turned back to her frame. If only she'd been wearing a gown and a tiara, she might have pulled off this obvious dismissal and he would have left. She used the imperial tone. She had the movements down pat. Those years of training came in useful at times. But not today. He didn't leave. He did just the opposite. He stepped forward. He was right behind her, leaning over her left shoulder.

"What are you doing?" he asked in a deep voice, so much like his brother's she shivered involuntarily. And yet, the tone was altogether different. Wilhelm gave orders. Charles had asked a question as if he was interested. Wilhelm never asked about her work. Never wondered if she missed it or how she would fill the empty hours in Rhineland while he was working.

She sighed. "I'm doing some restoration work on an eighteenth-century frame for the palace archives," she said. She couldn't help it. She should have said it was none of his business, but she had so few people to share her enthusiasm for her work. Not that he cared. Of course he didn't. He was just making conversation.

"I would guess it held a portrait at one time," he said coming even closer, so close he brushed her shoulder with his arm. She felt a wave of heat sweep through her body.

"A portrait," she repeated. "Yes, it did." She wished he would move away. His warm breath fanned the back of her neck and made her knees weak. It was difficult to concentrate on the subject of the painting. "It was one of my royal ancestors. Frederic the Second."

"Frederic the Bold, I believe they called him, for his acquisition of the lowlands," Charles said.

Lise nodded slowly. She was impressed by his knowledge of history. It wasn't even *his* history. She'd thought she was the only one who could keep the ancestors straight. How did he know?

"And for his wooing of *my* royal ancestor, Princess Gabrielle," Charles added. Though she couldn't see his face, she thought his voice held the hint of a smile.

"Which resulted in a royal scandal, because she was affianced to someone else. How do you know all this?" she asked, turning to face him. He was so close she could see that though his eyes were the same color as his brother's, they were a softer brown, almost velvety. Wilhelm had the coldest eyes she'd ever seen, as cold as the stones from the river. She couldn't drag her gaze away. She couldn't stop comparing the two brothers. They looked so much alike, but acted so differently. Or was this just an act? He really hadn't explained why he was here.

He shrugged. "My grandfather used to tell me stories. My parents were too busy with their own lives to pay much attention to me or my brother. Wilhelm had other interests, but I was fascinated by the history of my country. And Grandfather was a great storyteller. He'd walk me through the portrait gallery at the palace and tell me about the people in the paintings. Before he died, he wrote a history of Rhineland, which includes quite a bit about St. Michel. One can't study one without getting involved with the other, as you know. We can't ignore each other, whether we want to or not. We're too close, have too much in common, too many ties going back over the centuries.''

The way he said it, the way he looked at her, with such warmth in his gaze, she felt the heat. Lise wondered if he was talking about their countries or themselves. She didn't dare ask. Why was he here? If he wondered if she'd been devastated by the divorce, he could see she hadn't been.

When she didn't say anything, he continued. ''History is your field, isn't it?''

She was surprised he knew. Wilhelm had thought it a useless hobby, but it was her passion, along with art. ''History and art restoration. I've been criticized more than once for living in the past.''

Get your nose out of that book, her mother had said.

You'll never find a man in a museum, her father had cautioned.

What are you doing in the library all day? her husband Wilhelm had demanded.

''That's ridiculous. Who was it who said if we don't study history, we're doomed to repeat it?''

She smiled. ''It's true, but you didn't come here to discuss history,'' she said. If he did, she could go on all day, having no one else to talk to about it, and neither of them wanted that. As much as she enjoyed sharing her love of the past with someone, even him, his presence disturbed her more than it should have. He looked like his brother, but didn't act like him. He was tall and handsome and well-bred, but lacked the pretension of other members of his family.

She wasn't quite sure what to make of him. Or why he was there in the first place. She didn't know how to get rid of him. Or if she really wanted to. There were questions she wanted answers to: How many minds had his brother poisoned against her? How did his parents feel about her? What stories was his brother spreading about her? And yes, she had to admit she wanted to know, how did he, Charles, feel about her?

"No, I didn't come here to discuss history. Although it's an interesting topic and since Grandfather died I've had no one..." He paused as if he was unwilling to admit he'd had no one to talk to. "No, not history," he continued.

Charles leaned back against a stone countertop and studied her for a long moment. He was trying to collect his thoughts, but just looking at the lovely princess caused his mind to wander and his heart to pound erratically. The last time he'd seen Lise de Bergeron had been on her wedding day.

He'd thought at the time that in her white satin gown and diamond tiara she was the most beautiful thing he'd ever seen. He'd been filled with an unbecoming rush of envy for his older twin. As usual, Wilhelm had succeeded in snatching the prize before Charles had had a chance to compete. He couldn't help but wonder, even then, if his brother would be as careless with this prize as he'd been with all the others he'd won. The silver cup for polo, the gold medal for fencing—all tossed aside as soon as he'd gotten them. The contest forgotten, except for the bragging and the gloating that continued long afterward.

Marriage to Lise was a prize Wilhelm hadn't even competed for. It had been handed to him by an official arrangement. Her father wanted to strengthen the ties between their countries; Wilhelm wanted the marriage because it would advance his claim to some of the Micheline royal lands, should the country revert to Rhineland control. Wilhelm was the elder brother by thirty minutes. In this case, those thirty minutes made all the difference between Charles's loss and his brother's success.

When his brother had found out Lise was illegitimate and would inherit neither her title nor royal land, he immediately divorced her. When Charles had heard that, straight from his brother's mouth, he'd been stunned. His brother was not known for his kindness or compassion, he'd always had a ruthless streak, pushing aside anyone and anything that got in his way, but this time he'd gone too far. Charles was not only stunned, but he was ashamed on behalf of the family honor. Charles felt as if his brother had put a sword through his chest. He'd left the U.S. on the next plane and here he was, determined to do something to make things right.

Seeing the princess today, attired in the garb of a peasant with a smudge of paint on her cheek, her silky blond hair twisted in a knot at the nape of her neck, he found her even more beautiful than the last time he'd seen her in her wedding finery. He felt a rush of emotion he hadn't expected. He'd thought he'd feel pity. But that wasn't what he was feeling at that moment. Lise de Bergeron did not inspire pity. She was too confident and self-assured. What he felt for her was a much stronger emotion he dared not name.

He knew she needed help whether she'd admit it or not. Living in this humble cottage with only her faithful nanny was not suitable for a princess. Especially one pregnant with his brother's child. Being deserted by his scoundrel of a brother was something that had to be righted. He was the one who could do it. He wanted to sweep her off her feet and carry her away to the kind of life she deserved. However, she didn't look as if she'd permit him or anyone else to sweep her off her feet.

She didn't know why he was there, but he did. He'd planned his speech. He knew what he had to say, but now that he was there and she was looking at him with those incredible blue eyes, he could only stand and stare.

She'd changed. It had only been eight months, but she was not the same demure princess who'd so dazzled him on her wedding day. It wasn't only her clothing, it was her manner. He'd thought she'd be meek and mild and jump at the chance he was going to offer her. Now he wasn't so sure. She had a stubborn tilt to her chin, a proud look in her eyes and a certain tone to her voice. If he'd been infatuated with her before, he was fascinated now. He didn't know what she was going to say next. He decided to put off his declaration.

He was saved by the entrance of her nanny.

"Lise," Gertrude said, opening the greenhouse door just a crack. "Won't you ask Monsieur Rodin in for some tea? I fear it's chilly out there."

Lise looked annoyed, but her manners didn't fail her. "Of course," she said. "Won't you come in, Charles?"

He nodded. He was relieved, unwilling to leave without saying what he'd come to say, but not ready to say it. Not without some hope she'd agree to his plan.

In the cozy parlor a fire was blazing, the silver tea service was on the table and Gertrude was nowhere to be seen. Lise motioned to him to take a seat across from her on a chintz-covered love seat. He watched her pour the tea into two delicate china cups.

"Sugar, lemon?" she asked.

He shook his head. Though she was dressed like an artisan, she had the manners of a princess, and she always would. She'd grown up in a palace, but she seemed completely at home in this modest cottage. He wondered how much sorrow, how much disillusion she was hiding. He wondered if she still loved his brother. Or if she'd ever loved him. He knew it had been only a political match on his brother's part, but what if he'd broken Lise's heart? If he had, Charles would never forgive him.

"What are your plans?" he asked.

"Plans?" she asked.

"For the future."

"Ah, the future. Good question. First I will call the repairman again about the leaky roof. When it rains, he's always too busy, and when it stops and the sun shines, he goes fishing."

He glanced at the ceiling.

"It's in the kitchen."

"Let me handle it for you. I know a man I can send. You shouldn't have to live like this, you know."

"I live very well," she said so swiftly, he knew he'd said the wrong thing. Her blue eyes were cool and distant. "Much better than I lived in Rhineland. I have my nanny, my work and the freedom to do what I please, be what I please."

"What about the baby?" He couldn't help letting his gaze stray to her stomach. There was no sign of maternity there. Not yet. Yet he thought he noticed a slight rounding of her cheeks, a smoothing of her brow. But maybe he was just imagining the effects of pregnancy, of which he knew nothing. He'd always hoped to find someone, a woman to share his life with, to bear his children. But he'd always known he'd never find anyone as lovely as Lise de Bergeron.

"The baby will fit in to my life. I have a large bedroom." She gestured toward a pair of French doors to her left. "Plenty of room for a cradle."

He almost told her that babies grew up and needed rooms

of their own, but he didn't. She knew that and it was none of his business.

"Whatever happened to our star-crossed ancestors?" he asked, changing the subject to something safer and less personal. "Frederic the Bold and Princess Gabrielle. I don't remember the end of the story. Or maybe I never heard it. Sometimes Grandfather got distracted or confused."

"I don't believe Frederic ever married," Lise said. "He resisted all royal efforts to marry him off to one European princess or another. It's too bad I didn't follow his example." Though her tone was light, a shadow fell over her pale face.

"Don't blame yourself," he said frowning. "There were reasons."

"Of course," she said. "There always are. Being small and defenseless, St. Michel has always needed alliances with foreign powers. Believe me, I've heard it over and over from my father and grandmother."

"But it's wrong to use humans as pawns in these games," he said.

She didn't answer. Instead, she refilled his cup. "And the beautiful Gabrielle?" she asked. "What became of her? Did she marry her fiancé?"

"I'm not sure. I'll have to do some research and get back to you on that. If Grandfather were here…"

"You miss him," she said simply, her expression softening.

Yes, he missed the old man in many ways. Someone he could go to with his troubles. Someone who'd listen with a sympathetic ear. Someone who cared about him when no one else seemed to.

"Yes. He was the one person…" He stopped abruptly. Why go into family matters? She'd presumably had her fill of the dysfunctional Rodin family while living in Rhineland with his brother. Talking about the distant past was safer and allowed him to keep the dialog going, to keep the connection between them. Maybe it happened a long time ago, maybe it was history repeating itself. Whatever it was, he knew he'd do anything to forge a bond between Lise and himself. A bond that had nothing to do with his brother.

"I mustn't keep you any longer, Charles," she said, glancing at the door. It was plain she was dismissing him before he'd said what he'd come to say.

He'd hoped to establish a mood and set up the appropriate atmosphere. He'd planned to lead up to it gradually, but he no longer had time. It was clear it had to be now. He stood and looked down at her. The silence in the room was deafening. It was now or never. He took a deep breath

"I came today to offer you my hand in marriage," he said.

Chapter Two

There, it was out.

Lise turned pale. She braced herself with her hands on the seat cushion of her chair. Her mouth fell open in surprise. Good thing she was sitting down, because he was afraid she was going to faint. He went down on his knees next to her and held out his hand, but she ignored the gesture and leaned back against the cushions. Her eyelids fluttered.

He cursed himself for being so blunt. He'd obviously said it all wrong. How did he know? He'd never proposed to anyone before. Never wanted to settle down with any woman he'd ever met. Only one. And she was taken. Now she was free.

His view of marriage had always been shaped by that of his parents. He wanted no part of any institution that was designed to bring together suitable mates to ensure political stability. His parents were polite to each other, but he'd never witnessed much warmth or affection between them. But this was a different situation. There was no doubt in his mind this was his obligation, his duty. If it were only that, he could explain it to her rationally. But there was nothing rational about the way he felt about her. Nothing rational about the way the desire surged through his veins.

"I've taken you by surprise," he said, getting to his feet and clasping his hands together behind his back. He couldn't tell her he loved her or that he desired her, that would only frighten her and she surely wouldn't believe him. He had to present it from another angle. "I didn't mean to startle you, but surely you see the logic of it. How advantageous it would be."

"Oh yes," she said, leaning forward, the color rising in her face. "Because I married for political advantage the last time, it seems obvious to you I should do so again. But I'm not the same woman I was. I'm on my own now. My father is dead, God rest his soul, and from now on, I make my own decisions. I have learned many painful lessons in these past eight months. One is this: I will never marry again. Not for any reason." Her blue eyes shot sparks of determination. He stared fascinated. This was not what he expected. An inner strength forged by what had happened to her.

"My brother has done this to you," Charles said. His brother had turned a sweet young girl into a stubborn young woman. He'd never forgive him for destroying her innocence. It was up to him to make it up to her. To show her all men were not like his brother.

"I agreed to the match so I bear some responsibility," she said. "Yes, I did it to please my father, but I could have resisted. I didn't. He was very strong-willed."

"It seems to run in the family," he said. He had to admit he admired her willpower, in spite of the fact that she was using it against him.

"Perhaps," she said with a rueful half smile.

"If you won't think of yourself, think of the child. I want to give it a home, a father."

Her smile faded. "You want to be the father of my child," she said flatly, in obvious disbelief.

"Yes." He couldn't stop his gaze from resting on the striped smock that covered her stomach, imagining the life underneath, imagining the swell of her belly, the transformation that maternity would make on her hips and her breasts. A jolt of desire hit him along with a fistful of doubts. What kind of a father would he be, he who'd grown up with parents who were more concerned with their image than their children? What was his real motive here, was it to take his brother's bride and make her his or to take care of her because his brother didn't? Or did it have something to do with the irrational desire to take her away and make love to her so passionately she'd forget anyone else had ever touched her?

"Because you feel sorry for me," she said.

"Because I feel responsible for you," he said. Say it. Tell her. *Because I desire you. Because you're the most exquisite thing I've ever seen. Because I've wanted you from the first moment I saw you.*

"I'm sorry, but that's not good enough. I appreciate the thought, but the answer is no."

"Won't you think it over?" he asked.

"I don't need to think it over," she said. "I have more important things to think about."

Brave words. She was a brave woman. And a stubborn one. He knew he couldn't push her any further. If she decided to marry him, she would have to come to that decision on her own. He had to admit, her summary refusal hurt him more than he'd thought it would. If his brother had plunged a knife in his chest, Lise had just twisted it with her refusal. He wasn't sure what he'd pictured, perhaps tears of gratitude, perhaps joy and happiness at being rescued, but not this.

"Very well," he said brusquely. "I'm sorry to have bothered you." He turned to go.

"Charles, wait." She stepped forward and put her hand on his arm as he reached for the door. "Don't think I'm not grateful to you. I appreciate your concern for my welfare. My answer has nothing to do with you personally. It would be the same no matter who you were. I don't expect you to understand, but I've been through a very bad period and I need time to recover."

He turned to face her. A surge of hope sprang from her words. Of course, she needed time to recover. He'd spent a lifetime recovering from his brother's oppressive presence. He wanted to smooth the tiny worry lines in her forehead and tuck a stray curl of hair behind her ear. He wanted to trace the outline of her soft cheek with the pad of his thumb. He wanted to hold her close and tell her she would recover and that she needed him. He wanted to feel her body pressed close to his. But he knew she wasn't ready for that. Maybe she never would be. Why couldn't he have been the one to marry her in the first place? He knew the answer to that one. Wilhelm was the oldest, the fair-haired boy. The boy who always got everything he'd ever wanted.

"Take all the time you need," he said. He could only hope she would come around, she had to. For her sake. For the baby's sake. For his sake.

"All the time in the world will not convince me to marry again," she said firmly and his hopes went down just as fast as they'd risen a moment ago.

"I understand," he said. "I won't trouble you again." He opened the front door and stepped out into the rain while Lise stood in the doorway. "But if there's anything

I can do for you, please let me know. I am determined to make amends for my brother's grievous behavior.''

''The only things I want from your family are my belongings. I left Rhineland so precipitously, I brought with me only a small suitcase.'' She looked down at her leggings, knowing she could get by perfectly well if she could only stay in her workshop all day, but unfortunately, one of these days, she hoped later rather than sooner, she'd be forced to take her place in the world again and attend some social functions, and then she'd need all those dresses, shoes, riding outfits and sailing garb. On the other hand, she wondered how much longer her clothes would fit.

''Consider it done,'' he said soberly.

''Thank you. Good-bye,'' she said. ''Bon voyage.''

''Bon voyage?'' he said, his eyebrows raised in surprise. ''I'm not going anywhere.''

''But I thought you'd be going back—''

''Not to Rhineland. Or to the U.S. Not now. It is not only you but my work that has brought me back to Europe and to St. Michel in particular. I am setting up a joint venture with the vintners of your country, producing wine under our label. I have an office here and I'm looking for a place to live.''

''Oh.'' She paused for a long moment, trying to digest this news. Charles was staying in St. Michel. It was a small country, an even smaller city on the banks of the river. If he was here, she didn't know how she could avoid seeing him, even though she was currently leading the life of a hermit. It could be awkward. She felt awkward at that moment, not knowing what to say.

She didn't dare give him hope she'd change her mind, because she had no intention of doing that. Perhaps he was hoping she'd be pleased at this news, but she couldn't feign any emotion at all.

He seemed just as awkward as she did. The silence hung as heavily as the leaden skies above them.

"Well, then," she said at last, "please ignore everything I said. I don't need my things I left behind in Rhineland very much after all. I won't say good-bye, just au revoir."

He leaned forward and kissed her cheek, and then he was gone.

Lise stood in the doorway until his car disappeared from sight. Then she went back to the kitchen, sat down at the kitchen table and buried her head in her hands.

What kind of a man was he to accept her refusal so graciously? No temper tantrums, no rages or threats. No reminders of what her future held as a single mother in St. Michel without a husband or a father or protection from the palace. He looked so much like Wilhelm, it frightened and confused her. And yet he didn't talk or act like Wilhelm. He seemed nothing like his brother, but how could she be sure? She was just recovering from the worst mistake of her life and was not about to make another. If only she could erase the memory of the look on his face and the kiss on her cheek that lingered no matter how long she sat there.

Her instincts told her she could trust him. But her brain told her not to take a chance. She would be just fine on her own. Marriage was risky. Marriage to another Rodin brother was the riskiest of all.

For the next two weeks she tried to put Charles and his surprising offer of marriage out of her mind. She might have succeeded, if a whole crew of workmen hadn't arrived one clear, sunny day to fix her roof. When she tried to pay them, the chief said it had been taken care of by Monsieur Rodin.

Charles. Charles was as good as his word. But she didn't

want to accept charity from him. She was too leery of taking favors from anyone in his family. She'd been fooled once and she refused to be fooled again. But she didn't know quite how to get in touch with Charles to repay him for his repairmen's work, and she didn't really want to see him again. She might have forgotten the favor he'd done her, if it weren't for Nanny.

"Wasn't that kind of Monsieur Rodin?" she exclaimed at least once a day, gazing upward at the repaired roof.

"Yes, Nanny, he is undoubtedly a kind and wonderful man," Lise answered, trying to hide the cynicism in her voice.

"Nothing like his brother," she said.

"No, not at all," Lise agreed.

"It's not everyone who can be counted on these days," the old woman said sagely.

"I know, I know," Lise agreed. There was no point in disagreeing with Nanny. Gertrude had a habit of being right about these matters, and who could deny the man was as good as his word. Lise ended the discussion by going back to work on the picture frame so she didn't have to continue talking about Charles. It was obvious that Nanny was quite taken with the man. Lise had been careful to keep his offer of marriage to herself, but Nanny had a look in her eye that made Lise wonder how much she'd overheard that day. Fortunately her beloved nanny was much too tactful to ever bring up the subject of marriage or the future.

When Lise had finished painting the frame, it was time for the frosting on the cake of her restoration project. With the light coming through the windows onto her work bench, she installed the portrait of Frederic the Bold back where it belonged. It had been stashed in the archives at the palace for many years. Lise felt the thrill of accomplishment.

In the natural light from the bright spring sunshine, Lise

studied the portrait. No doubt about it, Frederic was a handsome man. But there was something about his eyes, a certain sadness that caught her attention. Was this painted after he lost his Princess Gabrielle? Or did he really lose her at all? Now that the portrait was framed, she wished she had someone to show it to. Sharing it with the queen was out of the question. She was consumed with hopes of producing an heir, the dowager queen was involved in the search for the missing heir. There was Nanny, of course, who never failed to support her work, but it was obvious the only other person who'd care, who would appreciate the work she'd done, was Charles.

It was too bad. They might have been friends. If he wasn't the brother of her ex-husband. If he hadn't asked her to marry him. If he hadn't had such a disturbing effect on her.

Ah, well. If her work didn't give her pleasure and satisfaction on its own, she wouldn't be doing it. She refused to worry about the future. She was just happy to be home in St. Michel again, with her divorce final and the memories of her brief, disastrous marriage behind her. Next weekend was the dowager queen's official seventy-fifth birthday party. Though her real birthday was in October, it was always celebrated in May when the weather was usually nice enough for a garden party.

Lise hoped everyone would be too busy scrutinizing the dowager queen at the party, wondering if she'd had yet another face-lift, and debating whether the reigning pregnant queen would even put in an appearance, or gossiping about the missing heir to the throne, to pay any attention to her. She wanted to stay out of the limelight, avoiding questions about her marriage, her pregnancy, her illegitimacy and more condolences on the death of her father. She was looking forward to a reunion with her two sisters: Marie-Claire, who'd been traveling abroad with her new husband, Sebastian, and Ariane, who was living in Rhineland with her husband, Prince Etienne. But after she'd had a chance to see them, she planned to slip away, back to the solace of her cottage.

The problem was she had nothing to wear to the party. Ideally, no one would notice her at all. But if they did, she didn't want them to feel sorry for her. She wanted to look her best in a quiet, subdued, unobtrusive way, though without her wardrobe left behind in Rhineland, she didn't know how she was going to pull that off.

"Maybe I won't go to the party," she said to Nanny very casually over dinner one evening. Though Nanny insisted on serving Lise, Lise insisted they eat together. How ridiculous to have the old woman eating alone in the kitchen. Besides, Lise was grateful for her company.

Gertrude laid her fork down. "What? Not attend the queen's birthday party?"

"Well, you know, I don't think I'd be missed."

"You would most certainly be missed. You've forgotten how many friends you have here at home."

Home. Yes, this was her home. Home, the place where no matter what you've done, whether they want to or not, they have to take you back again. They'd taken her back, however reluctantly, and she'd better make the best of it.

"All right. But what will I wear? I scarcely have any dresses and the ones I have are getting a little tight."

Nanny suggested altering one of Lise's few dresses or making her a new one, but Lise didn't want the old woman to take on yet another task, so she assured her she'd make do somehow and put it out of her mind.

But the morning of the party, she stood in her small bedroom staring at herself critically in the full-length mirror. Yes, her pants were getting a little snug in the hips.

Though she was still not quite ready for maternity clothes, it wouldn't be long before her regular clothes didn't fit at all. She opened her armoire and frowned at the meager selection of dresses in her closet. There was absolutely nothing appropriate for a garden party. She sat on the edge of her bed and sighed. How ridiculous she was, worrying about a dress when she had so many other things to worry about. Her future. Her baby. Her country's future if the heir wasn't found.

When she heard the sound of a vehicle arriving in front of the cottage, she jumped up and peered down through the second-floor window and saw a large pickup truck piled high with trunks she recognized. Her things. Her personal belongings had arrived. At last. Just in the nick of time. Surely there'd be something she could wear to this party.

Not only did the men bring the trunks into the house, they carried them upstairs to the extra bedroom. When she offered them a generous tip, they waved her efforts aside, saying they'd already been paid. She didn't ask, but the words buzzed in her brain. By whom? Who had paid the delivery men? Who had arranged the transfer of the trunks when all her efforts to recover her things had gone unanswered? She knew the answer. It was Charles.

The only things I want from your family are my belongings.

Consider it done.

He was as good as his word. But how to thank him? She was not about to start asking questions about him, such as where she could find him, thus raising suspicions of why she needed to know. This was no time to dwell on the hows and whys and wheres regarding her personal belongings. She unlocked the trunks and began her search through the piles of silk, satin, wool and leather. Her trousseau clothes. All reminders of a life that was gone. The life of a princess.

A legitimate princess with a bright future as the wife of a prominent Rhinelander embarking on a life of ease and luxury.

The memories came flooding back as she sifted through the clothes—parties, balls, dinners. The memories of Wilhelm, who viewed her, not as a person with feelings or needs or desires, but as a trophy to be shown off in her matching shoes, her hand-painted scarves and her designer dresses. The memories brought her nothing but sadness. Where was that young, naive princess with her whole life ahead of her? Lise stood up and paced back and forth in the small bedroom. That princess was gone forever. In her place was an older, wiser woman who would not dwell in the past. Who would learn from her past mistakes. Who would allow no one to force her into another marriage of convenience.

She told herself she was better off now than before. Anything was better than being married to Wilhelm. She would wear one of these dresses—hopefully one still fit—and not think of anything but the present. She would go to the party and face the future with her head high and show the world she was not ashamed of what had happened. After all, it was not her fault her marriage was over and she'd been cast out and returned home.

But when she stood on the flagstone path that led to the formal gardens of the palace, her nerves almost failed her. The figures in the garden, women in flowered dresses, men in black tie, the rows of willow trees planted hundreds of years ago and the vibrant green of the sweeping lawn looked like a painting. A painting that was beautiful to observe, but not to be a part of.

But she had no choice. Her sisters Ariane and Marie-Claire spotted her and came rushing across the vast lawn to hug her and demand to know how she was and where she'd been. She felt a surge of love for the two people she cared most about in the world. Being deserted by their mother and largely ignored by their father, the three of them had been exceptionally close growing up together. It was so good to see them again, her eyes filled with happy tears.

"I've missed you both so much," she said. "I'm so glad you're both here."

"As if we could miss the queen's birthday. But honestly, we came to see you," Ariane said, squeezing her hand. "You don't look as though you're pregnant." She dropped her hand and walked around her sister, looking at her from all angles and beaming her approval.

"Doesn't she look wonderful?" Marie-Claire enthused. "You were the first to marry, and the first to get pregnant."

"And the first to get divorced," Lise said lightly.

Marie-Claire frowned. Divorce was nothing new in the family. Still, Lise's situation was especially painful for her sisters to accept. "How are you, really?" she asked. "I can't believe that horrible Wilhelm divorced you."

"Believe it," Lise said soberly. "And believe that it's for the best. I'm so happy it's over, and I'm back where I belong." As she said the words she realized she *was* back where she belonged. Despite the fact that the country's future was up in the air and that she had no real place to call home, St. Michel was where she belonged. The three princesses stopped at the edge of the formal English gardens and surveyed the scene. The murmur of polite voices, the burble of the fountains, the soft music from a string quartet came wafting across the ancient stone walkways.

"I think everyone agrees," Ariane said with a glance in the direction of the dowager queen who was seated in a chair that was not quite a throne, but close to it, surrounded by loyal sycophants, "she knows how to celebrate her birthday."

"How does she treat you?" Marie-Claire asked Lise.

Lise shrugged. "As well as can be expected. I have the run of the palace archives and the attics. I come and go as I please and she doesn't stop me. I'm working on some interesting restoration projects. And of course she's given me the use of the cottage. Me and Nanny. Other than that, she pays no attention to me. So I can't complain."

"You never did," Ariane said. "You haven't even said a bad word about Wilhelm."

Lise held a finger up to her lips. "Not here I won't. I'm doing my best to put the past in the past."

"She's amazing," Ariane said to Marie-Claire. "I told you we wouldn't get a word of complaint out of her. If my husband had..."

"But he didn't. How is Etienne?" Lise asked, anxious to change the subject.

"See for yourself. Here he is now."

Lise felt slightly nervous seeing her brother-in-law, a Rhinelander prince, not knowing what or how he felt about her divorce from Wilhelm. But Etienne greeted her warmly and her fears were dispelled. Whatever he'd heard, he obviously had no hard feelings against her, and Lise was relieved. She could see immediately how happy the young recently married couple was. She stifled a pang of envy. When Marie-Claire's husband, Sebastian, joined them she knew she had no worries on that side either. Neither sister had made the kind of mistake she had. Sebastian was charming and clearly adored her sister. No, she was the only one who'd made the wrong choice of a husband.

Admittedly the choice had not been hers. It had been her father's. But, as she'd told Charles, she could have protested more strongly. When the men left the sisters to refill their champagne glasses, the three women found seats under a magnificent oak tree on the edge of the garden. Ariane turned to look at Lise again and regarded her sister carefully.

"How do you feel?" Ariane asked with concern. "You look sensational, by the way. Pregnancy agrees with you. Don't you think, Marie-Claire? I don't remember that dress. How is my niece-or nephew-to-be doing?"

Before Lise could answer, Marie-Claire leaned forward and asked under her breath, "Where is Wilhelm?"

"I hear he's in America, but I really don't know," Lise said. And prayed that was the end of that discussion.

"What are your plans?" Marie-Claire asked. "We've missed you so much. I hope you'll never leave here again. Ariane has moved way over to Rhineland, but that can't be helped. Now that I'm back from my honeymoon, I want us to get together as much as possible. Is that clear?"

"All clear," Lise said with a smile. "As usual, you two have asked so many questions I don't know where to start. And you've scarcely given me a chance to say a word. I'm fine and I've been right here, in the gardener's cottage where I plan to remain as long as the powers on the throne are willing," Lise said. "I wrote you both, but our paths haven't crossed lately. With both of you married, I didn't expect to see as much of you. But here we are, together again. Now, tell me, besides honeymooning, what have you two been up to?" Lise asked, deftly switching the subject from herself to them.

"We arrived only yesterday from Rhineland," Ariane said. "For the party—and to see you, of course—then we're off again on a business trip."

"I suppose there are rumors in Rhineland," Lise suggested hesitantly. She didn't really want to know about any rumors having to do with her.

"Of course, what would life be like without rumors?" Ariane said lightly. "Rumors about a takeover of St.

Michel, about a missing heir to the throne. These are nothing new. But rumors concerning you? Believe me, no one would dare say a word against my sister in my presence.''

Lise nodded gratefully. What else would she expect from her little newly-wed sister?

''Speaking of rumors,'' Marie-Claire said, looking over her shoulder to be sure she couldn't be overheard. ''What's this I hear about Charles Rodin?''

Lise felt her cheeks burn. ''I…I don't know. I haven't heard anything.''

''Are you sure?'' Marie-Claire persisted. ''Are you sure you haven't seen him?''

''Seen him? Yes, I saw him. He came to pay his respects.''

''Is that all he paid?'' Marie-Claire asked. ''I thought maybe he asked you to marry him.''

''Why would you think that?'' Lise asked, startled. ''Don't tell me it's on the Internet,'' she said, in an attempt at levity. But she should have known she couldn't fool her sisters.

''Oh no. It's more like ESP or just common sense. He's available, you're available. You know, he's nothing like his brother. That's what everyone says,'' Marie-Claire said. ''So if he did ask you to marry him…''

''I would refuse, of course,'' Lise said firmly.

''But why?'' Ariane asked. ''You mustn't let Wilhelm put you off marriage forever. You just heard, Charles is nothing like his brother.''

''I don't know that for sure. I don't know anything about him. I met the man once at my wedding. Then he stopped by to see me. We had a nice conversation, but that's hardly the basis for getting married again. They're twins. How different can they be?'' Lise asked. But in her heart she knew they were as different as night and day.

"What about the baby?" Marie-Claire asked softly, her green eyes wide. "Don't you want a father for your baby?"

"Of course I do. But there are more important things. Like a warm, loving home. I think a child is better off with one good parent than with two parents who are at odds with each other. The three of us know a little bit about that."

Her sisters nodded in agreement. There was a long moment of silence while they were each lost in their own thoughts.

"But what about security?" Ariane asked.

"I guess you mean financial security," Lise said. "That's a worry, of course. I still have the jewels mother left us. I can always sell them if it comes to that. But I'll tell you this. I'd rather live in the most humble cottage with Nanny and my baby than the biggest palace with a man I didn't love."

"You mean you couldn't love Charles?" Ariane asked. "He's really very nice. Nothing like his brother. Except in looks, of course. They're both handsome devils."

Lise sighed. As if looks mattered. "When I was your age, Ariane, and young and naive, I might have fallen in love again and jumped into another marriage, but…"

"Young and naive," Ariane sputtered. "Did you hear that, Marie-Claire? I'm an old married woman now and I demand to be treated with respect." Her blue eyes twinkled and the three of them burst into laughter. The idea of Ariane as an old married woman at the age of twenty-three sent them into helpless giggles. Lise realized she hadn't laughed for months. It was so wonderful to be with her sisters again. She'd been hungry for the warmth and affection they shared. After they'd calmed down, Lise gazed off into the distance for a long moment.

"If only life was that simple," she said quietly. "Loving

someone because they're nice." Even as she spoke the words, she wondered if she'd know love when she found it. Chills up and down the spine, goosebumps on the skin, an erratic heartbeat. What did those things mean? A heightened sexual awareness, due to living a celibate life. That was all. Love was something else entirely.

"So tell me, you two, are you both happy? Are you sure you've made the right choices?"

Their spontaneous bursts of joy told Lise all she needed to know. They were both deliriously happy. After breathless assurances Ariane went back to the subject of Charles.

It was clear Ariane hadn't given up and that her goal was to see her sister as happily married as she was. "In Rhineland I heard there was hell to pay when Charles learned your belongings hadn't been sent," she said. "I tell you, one phone call from him and the servants dropped everything to make sure your trunks got packed and returned to you."

"I see," Lise said thoughtfully. "Then I have Charles to thank. Because if he hadn't come through, you wouldn't see me in this dress today. I'd be wearing an old bedsheet."

"You'd look good in a bedsheet," Marie-Claire declared with a grin. "Especially one with lace around the hem."

"Thank you, dear sister. It won't be long before bedsheets are the only thing that will fit me. But I haven't been reduced to that yet. I can still squeeze into some of my trousseau dresses. Believe me, before my trunks came, I had nothing suitable for a queen's birthday party." She stood up. "Which reminds me, I'd better go wish her majesty a happy birthday."

"We've already done our duty," Ariane said. "We'll see you later."

Lise took a deep breath and set out down a stone walkway in her strapped sandals, her sheer voile dress brushing against her bare legs. Her sisters only wanted what was best for her and her baby. But she was tired of hearing how different Charles was from his brother. That didn't automatically make him good husband material. If and when she ever married again, it would be for love.

Before she got to the queen, she was stopped by various old friends and acquaintances, all of them too polite to mention the scandal that had brought her back to St. Michel. She was thankful that not one mention was made of her former husband or her illegitimacy. She did receive condolences on the death of her father, for which she was grateful.

She was just congratulating herself on her poise in the face of this situation she'd been dreading, when she spotted Charles standing at the side of a fountain where white marble cherubs spouted water into a circular pond. He was wearing a dark suit and gazing at her thoughtfully across the grass. She hesitated. She didn't want to be rude, but what was her response supposed to be? What was the protocol in greeting a man whose offer of marriage you'd recently turned down? She managed a small smile and he must have taken that as an encouraging sign, because he quickly joined her.

"I was wondering if you'd come today," he said, his dark eyes traveling up and down her pale blue dress.

She felt slightly dizzy in his presence. His intense gaze unnerved her. When he glanced at the rounded neckline of her dress, she was conscious of her breasts swelling, of the fabric tightly stretched across the bodice and of her nipples budding. She felt the color rise to her cheeks. If only she'd kept walking. Talking to the queen would be a piece of cake compared to dealing with Charles. Yes, he was clearly the handsomest man here today. And the memory of his words hung in the air between them.

Take all the time you need... I'm not going anywhere.

"It's a bit of a command performance," she said, proud of her composure in the face of the man who looked so much like her ex-husband. "Being my grandmother's birthday. But I didn't know you..."

"She was kind enough to invite me."

"I see," she said. "I was just on my way to wish her a happy birthday."

"I was hoping to have a few words with you."

"Well, now you have," Lise said. But she should have known she wasn't going to get off so easily.

Charles smiled briefly at her attempt to dismiss him. "When you have a moment, won't you join me for something to eat and drink?"

"Well, I..." she said. She knew she needed some sustenance soon if she was to continue to engage in social discourse with him or anyone. If not for herself, for her baby. She needed to eat frequently and to stay hydrated.

"You look a little pale," he said. "I won't keep you and I won't distress you by bringing up anything unpleasant. I'll be waiting at the table under the big oak."

"Very well," Lise said. How could she refuse? There was a look in his eyes that told her he was sincere. Her sister's words came back to remind her.

He's nothing like his brother.

She turned to leave then turned back. "I almost forgot to thank you for fixing my roof," she said.

"I merely made a phone call," he said.

"You made another to get me my trunks."

He shrugged. "It was no trouble. If there's anything else, please let me know. It must be difficult being a woman alone."

"I'm not alone," she said stiffly. "I'm surrounded by family. Not only my sisters, but my grandmother, my stepmother, stepsister…'' She could have gone on and on, but the truth was that aside from her sisters, who now had their own lives, and her dear nanny, she *was* alone. Her grandmother cared, she knew, but Queen Simone's priority right now was locating the missing heir.

Charles frowned at her response. ''I didn't mean to imply you were in any way helpless. Of course you have family and friends. I just meant…''

''I know what you meant,'' she said, suddenly contrite. ''I'm sorry I took it the wrong way. I don't know what's wrong with me these days. I get upset at the slightest thing. One minute I'm in tears, the next minute I'm laughing. My doctor says it's hormones.'' The concerned look on Charles's face told her it was time to stop this conversation. She'd gone on way too long about herself and her condition. No man wanted to hear about a pregnant woman's emotions or hormonal problems.

What was she thinking? She finally managed to murmur something about the queen and her duty and left him standing there. As she walked across the lawn she felt his gaze on her. He was probably wondering what on earth had gotten into her. Probably happy she'd turned him down. Who wants to marry an emotional basket case?

She kissed the queen on both cheeks, wished her a happy birthday and said something about how young she looked. At seventy-five, her face was unlined, and her eyes were still bright and alive with the spirit of someone half her age.

Lise retained her composure under the queen's piercing gaze, answered her polite questions about her family, her work and her situation as best she could.

''How unfortunate it is that you're divorced,'' the queen said, tiny lines etched between her eyebrows. ''Your father, if he were still alive, would be very displeased. He arranged this marriage for you with your future in mind. And now…''

Lise knew what she was going to say. *And now, you have no future.*

''Yes, Grandmama. Most unfortunate. But life is full of unfortunate events.'' As if her grandmother didn't know that. Everyone in the kingdom knew what she'd been through in the past fifty years—with more than one unfortunate marriage in the family. And now she was fighting to keep the country from reverting to Rhineland's control by coming up with a missing heir. Missing because of her interference in her son's affairs.

''What are your plans?'' the old woman asked.

Plans. If only people would stop asking her about her plans. Wasn't it enough to plan for the birth of her child? Lise smiled sweetly. ''For the moment I am quite content in the cottage. I have Nanny…''

''She can't be much help,'' the dowager queen sniffed. ''At her age.''

''Oh, but she is,'' Lise said. ''A great help.''

''And when the baby comes?''

''There's plenty of room for the baby. The baby will fit in nicely.''

The dowager queen looked as displeased as if Lise had suggested putting the baby in a dresser drawer. ''I was not referring to the square footage of the cottage,'' she said stringently. ''The best thing for you would be to marry again. As soon as possible. You can't go on forever in a gardeners' cottage. It isn't suitable. It is most regrettable this situation has occurred.''

Lise fought off the urge to tell her to mind her own business. That another marriage was the last thing she wanted. But she knew better than to cross her grandmother. She needed all the support from the palace she could get.

"Yes, Grandmama," she murmured.

"As you know we are searching for the missing heir to the throne. If we do not find him…" The queen broke off, but Lise knew what she was going to say.

If we do not find him, you will be without a home, money, protection from the palace, family or friends.

Out of the corner of her eye, Lise noticed that Luc Dumont, the man in charge of the St. Michel security force, whom Queen Simone had summoned to give the latest report on his search for the missing heir, was waiting for an audience with her. Lise knew anything she had to say paled in comparison to Luc's information, so she excused herself.

All of St. Michel was consumed with this project. If the heir wasn't found, and if Queen Celeste didn't give birth to a boy, then Rhineland would absorb their country. As much as she hated to admit it, her grandmother had a point. Her future was uncertain. But so was her grandmother's. In any case, that was not enough reason to consider marrying again.

With these sobering thoughts in her mind, she turned toward the ancient oak tree where Charles was waiting. From fifty meters away she knew he was looking at her. She felt the heat of his gaze even at this distance. She had an overwhelming desire to bolt. To disappear behind the palace and sneak through the servants' entrance into the cool marble halls where she had once lived. How tempting it was to slip away into her childhood, when her father was king and her mother was queen. Before her mother had deserted them; before her father had remarried. When she didn't have to worry about the future. When talk of weddings and royal alliances were far in the future.

She feared meeting Charles. She didn't want to have the same conversation all over again. She knew this was not a meeting to enjoy refreshments and small talk. Charles was not the bully his brother was, but he had a determined look in his eyes that told her he hadn't given up on her.

But she too had a determined streak. She would not let herself be talked into another disastrous marriage. No matter how many people told her it was a good idea. No matter who tried to frighten her into marrying for "security." She squared her shoulders and walked steadily in his direction, repeating these words to herself.

Don't give in.

You are in charge of your own life.

You are strong.

You don't need a man in your life.

Don't let him get to you.

You were married to his twin brother.

He only asked you out of a sense of duty. Yes, duty is important, but where marriage is concerned, next time, look for love.

You have lived as a princess. Your father was king. Royal blood flows through your veins. No one can tell you what to do.

Chapter Three

Charles watched her walk toward him. Her head was held high, her blond hair shiny and full. She looked like every man's dream of a princess. In the dappled sunlight he could see how her dress clung to her body, so lush, so ripe, so beautiful. He felt the desire flood his body. His heart was in his throat. He didn't know what he was going to say when she got there. He only knew that if she turned him down again, he wouldn't give up.

But if he couldn't convince her this time, he didn't know what more he could say. He didn't expect her to love him. He didn't expect to love her. He'd never been in love before. Love, if it existed outside story and song, was immensely overvalued. That wasn't what this was about. This was about redemption, about honor and respect. A voice inside his head asked what about desire? What about revenge? Was that really what this was about?

"You came," he said simply. "Sit down. You look as if you could use something to eat and drink." She looked fragile and pale. Again, that overwhelming desire to take care of her. To take care of her baby. His brother's baby. A bitter taste filled his mouth as he forced himself to remember—she had been his brother's wife. She was pregnant with his brother's baby.

She nodded and sat down at the small table spread with a white linen cloth. He'd filled two plates with every kind of delicacy from the buffet tables and poured her a glass of fruit juice. Her hand shook just a little as she picked up her glass. He wanted to take her smooth hand in his, to calm her nerves, to soothe her fears. But that wasn't what she wanted.

"How did it go?" he asked. "I noticed you had quite a chat with your grandmother."

Lise set her glass down. "Yes, she's as stubborn and determined as ever. But so am I." She paused. "I am hungry," she admitted. "And tired too. I don't know why. Sometimes my relatives wear me out. Just talking to them. I'm so much alone these days, working in my greenhouse, that making small talk in a social situation is almost too much of an effort."

"I know what you mean," Charles said. "I have a feeling that everyone here has some kind of agenda. There's intrigue behind the small talk, behind the smiles and the black ties."

"How did you know?" Lise asked. "I guess I shouldn't be surprised. There is so much gossip around. It's the same in Rhineland."

"Yes," he said. He didn't tell her that rumor was rife, both here and in Rhineland, about matters that could affect her situation. Speculation about political factions who were making trouble, both in his country and hers. "Your family must be worried about the future. That doesn't mean you have to worry too." He bit his tongue to keep from telling her that if she married him, she would have no such worries. Her future and her child's future would be secure.

"No, of course not," she said. "I'm *not* worried."

Brave words, he thought. That was one thing he admired about her. Her courage.

"Relax," he said. "You don't have to make small talk anymore, especially not with me. I'm sure everyone else just wants to say hello and welcome you back."

"And give me advice," she said with a wry smile.

He wanted to ask what kind of advice, but didn't. If she wanted him to know, she'd tell him. He was very conscious of not pushing her. He had no idea how to convince her to marry him. He only knew that she couldn't be rushed or forced into such a serious decision.

"I saw you with your sisters," he said. "I envy you the close ties you have with them."

Lise gave him a quick look that made him wish he hadn't said anything. He should have kept his feelings to himself. He had no wish to give her any reason to suspect how bitter were his relations with his brother. He didn't want to open a crack in the wall he'd built up around himself. It had taken too long to put it up. It was common knowledge he'd never been close to his brother, but no one knew that he'd always felt like second best to his outgoing, extroverted brother. Or that he'd always picked up the pieces from Wilhelm's mistakes, the mistakes no one even knew about. The engagements he'd broken, the promises he'd never kept, the business decisions that had backfired.

Fortunately Lise made no comment at all about the contrast of her situation with his. "I feel very lucky having the girls back in my life now. Of course they refuse to think of themselves as girls. Now that they're old married women." She smiled and he felt as if the sun had burst through the clouds and was shining only on her. He thought he'd never seen her face any lovelier, not on her wedding day, not that day in her greenhouse. He wished he could make her smile like that. Maybe some day....

"For a while back in Rhineland I didn't feel like seeing anyone," she said soberly. "I was afraid Marie-Claire and Ariane would think I'd shut them out of my life. I worried about them making the same mistake I had. But they went ahead and fell in love, got engaged—all without my help— and now they're married. It seems they've both made good choices and found the happiness I missed...with the men they've married."

Charles wanted to blurt out that she could be as happy as her sisters were. That he could make her as happy if she gave him a chance. But he didn't know that. He wasn't sure he could. She deserved so much. What would it take to erase the memory of his brother's treachery? "I know both Etienne and Sebastian quite well. We play polo together. You're right. Your sisters have made good choices. They're fine men."

She nodded, picked up her fork and started eating. He unfolded his napkin and joined her. He was happy to see her eating, to see the color return to her cheeks. He was careful not to appear to be studying her. He only looked at her when she didn't notice. It wouldn't do to scare her off just when she was starting to confide in him.

When she finished, she put her napkin down on the table and thanked him. He was afraid that was it. She was going to leave or go back to the party or rejoin her sisters.

"How is your picture frame coming along?" he asked, desperately searching for a topic of conversation before she could go anywhere.

"I've finished it and the portrait is back where it belongs," she said. "Would you like to see it?"

He couldn't believe his luck. Just when he was searching

his brain for an excuse to stay with her, to continue the conversation, she had done it for him. He pictured going back to the cottage with her. And again asking her to marry him. She seemed so much different today, more relaxed and so much more receptive. Maybe today she'd say yes. She had to say yes. Why not today?

"I'd very much like to see it," he said. "And in return, I have some information on Princess Gabrielle for you."

"Really?" Her eyes sparkled. "Tell me."

"I have to show you. I found her diary, or at least part of it."

"But that's thrilling. I can't wait."

"I'm afraid you'll have to. I don't have it with me."

"But you know what it says," she said.

"Not really. I merely leafed through it to be sure it was hers. I saved it for you. I'll bring it the next time I see you. Now, what about the portrait?"

"Come with me," she said. She stood and brushed off her dress. He tried to avert his gaze from the sheer material of the bodice. Her breasts seemed to have swollen since the last time he'd seen her, but her waist was as small as ever. Her stomach might be slightly rounded under the filmy skirt, but he couldn't tell. He was having a hard time keeping his eyes from her body, from picturing the curves underneath the dress, from imagining her without that dress, picturing her bare legs and her smooth hips. They were halfway to the servants' entrance to the palace before he realized they weren't going to her cottage.

"I put it back where it belongs," she explained, as he opened the back door for her. In the servants' kitchen, she stopped to say hello to her favorite baker, the one who'd given her the chocolate cakes.

"You've outdone yourself, Blanche," she said. "The queen's birthday cake is a work of art."

Blanche's round cheeks reddened and she beamed at the compliment from her favorite princess. "All in the line of duty. Birthdays, feast days, all weddings all call for special cakes," she said.

Lise blushed at the mention of weddings. Now she wished she hadn't brought Charles here at all. Perhaps Blanche wasn't referring to her. But there was danger at every turn. Marriage was on everyone's mind. She didn't know what to say. Fortunately, she didn't have to say anything. Charles had taken over, complimenting the baker and her assistants, and charming them all in the process. Once again, he'd bailed her out.

When they left the kitchen, Lise led the way upstairs to the hall of portraits. It was dark and musty, the velvet curtains drawn against the sun, so the light wouldn't fade the tapestries on the walls or destroy the priceless works of art. She didn't know why, but she tiptoed across the marble-tiled floor and spoke softly as if she was afraid to wake the dead ancestors.

"I thought this would be where he belongs," she whispered, as she found the place where she'd had the workmen hang the picture. "Between his sister, Princess Charlotte, and his parents, the king and queen. With no wife, as far as I know." Together they looked up at the handsome face of Frederic the Bold.

"You've done a fine job," Charles said. "The fabric of his robes looks as rich and vibrant as the day he wore them."

"Do you really think so?" she asked, pleased and proud of her work. "I worked hard at it. I did it before I left St. Michel, before I…I…" She didn't want to even say the words *before I married your brother*. She hurried on. "And I wanted to do him proud. I became very fond of him while

working on him. Which is why I wanted to fix the frame.
He deserved a frame to match his portrait.''

They walked down the hall past portraits of other ancestors. She could have told the story behind every one of
them, but she didn't want to bore Charles. Yes, he was
interested in history, but this was her history.

"I suppose you have many suits of armor in Rhineland,"
she said. "But I want to show you ours anyway."

"Please do," Charles said.

At the end of the portrait gallery, they stepped into a
small alcove full of chain mail and complete sets of armor.

"This was our favorite place to play when we were children," she said. "When our tutor was looking for us, we'd
each hide inside a suit of armor and clank around. The tutor
was completely spooked. Needless to say he didn't last very
long. Poor mother, no wonder we drove her to leave and
never come back.''

"Is that what happened?" Charles asked.

"I don't suppose it was that simple," Lise said. "We
never really knew why she left. Of course we blamed ourselves for being naughty and father blamed us too. But
Nanny said mother never was cut out for motherhood. She
was restless, unhappy. Actually, even before she left for
good, she was never around. Always off gambling in Monte
Carlo or skiing in Gstaad. Now that I'm grown up, I realize
how stifling life can be in a palace and I think I understand
a little. But not the part about leaving us. Even though my
baby isn't born yet, I don't think I could ever leave it, even
for a day, no matter how stifling the palace atmosphere.''

Lise stood there with Charles. He didn't say anything,
neither did she. She felt the silence close around them, en-
velop them in a kind of cocoon. She didn't know what had
made her confide in him like that. She rarely spoke of her
mother. She and her sisters found it a painful topic. She

barely knew Charles. Maybe that was why she'd opened up to him. There was something about his presence that was calming and comforting. Although he looked so much like his brother, there had been nothing calming or comforting about Wilhelm.

She'd almost forgotten what Charles wanted from her. She'd almost forgotten to be on her guard, to keep up her defenses, lest he talk her into something she'd be sorry for later. She told herself it was just a tour of the palace, one that she, as the unofficial palace historian, had given many times to many people. Yes, he was more interested in it than most, but there was nothing to worry about. Or was there?

Suddenly there were voices. A door opened and a shaft of light fell across the floor of the portrait gallery. Lise's heart rate doubled. Without thinking, she grabbed Charles by the arm and wedged herself back into the corner in the shadows next to him.

"But what..." he said.

Lise pressed her finger against his lips. And instantly regretted it. The touch of his lips against her finger sent arcs of awareness shooting through her body. She didn't know why she'd done it. It wasn't as if they had to hide or keep quiet. She had a perfect right to be there. The portrait gallery had always been her own territory. She had acted on pure instinct. She could take her finger away, but didn't, even though Charles had clearly gotten the message. But she didn't want him to get the wrong message.

The voices grew louder. One voice belonged to Queen Celeste, the widowed pregnant queen no one had seen much of the last few weeks.

"We can trust no one," she was saying. "Especially anyone from Rhineland."

Lise felt Charles's body tense next to her. She dropped

her finger from his lips and instinctively reached for his hand.

"My dearest queen, there is no need to worry. Rhineland is our ally, our friend."

Lise recognized the voice of the palace chauffeur, a smooth, ambitious, oily schemer. She couldn't believe Celeste would allow him to call her *my dearest queen,* unless...

"I will continue to worry until we have a legitimate heir to the throne. Until my son is born."

Their voices were getting closer. Lise held her breath. Yes, it was all right for her to be here, but to be found hiding and eavesdropping was another matter.

She pressed herself closer to Charles. His arm went around her and held her tightly. Her heart was pounding so loudly she was afraid the queen would hear it. Whether it was fear of being caught in the palace or fear of being caught in the arms of her former brother-in-law, she didn't know. She just knew she felt confused and excited and breathless.

Celeste spoke again. "Let's get out of here," she said. "I'm allergic to dust and I can't stand these old pictures. That wretched de Bergeron girl comes in and cleans them up. Why, I don't know. I thought we were rid of her, but she's back. These paintings are part of the past. So is she. As soon as Simone dies I'll have them all put into storage, or auctioned off. These old relics mean nothing to me. Nothing."

Lise gasped. She knew Celeste didn't like her. Celeste didn't like anyone who reminded her that her dead husband had had other wives, other children. But she thought they'd reached a kind of understanding. She'd stay in the cottage. She'd stay out of the way.

Now Lise realized Celeste wanted to auction off her heritage. The footsteps faded in the distance. She turned to face Charles. Her mind was in turmoil. Her knees were shaking. If Charles hadn't held her by the shoulders, she might have fallen to the hard, cold floor. His face was hidden in the shadows. She had no idea what he was thinking or feeling. She only knew he was so close she could feel his warm breath on her cheek. He lowered his head until his lips were only a whisper away from hers. She couldn't breathe, couldn't think. If she lifted her head, if she angled her mouth...anything could happen.

"Charles," she whispered.

"Shhh," he said. "Don't say anything." And then he kissed her. Just one kiss. One kiss that lasted a minute, an hour, an eternity. A kiss that shook her to her foundations. A kiss like none she'd ever had. There was no mistaking him for his brother, not after that kiss. His hands moved down her arms to her hips. He pulled her close to him, closer and closer until she felt the muscles in his thighs through her sheer dress. Breathless and shaken, she pressed her face against his shirt and inhaled the intoxicating scent of his skin, his soap, his clothes. Her pulse was racing. She lifted her head and gazed into his dark, fathomless eyes.

"Lise," he said hoarsely.

"Yes," she whispered. Then she came to her senses and pulled back. "We must get out of here." She was surprised she could speak at all. Her mouth was dry, her lips swollen. She was grateful for the darkness, hoping he couldn't see how the kiss had affected her. The question was, how had it affected him? Had he kissed so many women, it meant nothing to him? She didn't know. She didn't know anything about his past.

Even when they'd gone down the stairs and back through the kitchen and outside again, she was too embarrassed to look him in the eye. What must he think of her, allowing him to kiss her like that? She walked briskly through the small palace kitchen garden with its rows of beans and peas and herbs and chattered on about the picture gallery, spouting facts about the history of the palace itself until he stopped under a grape arbor and grabbed her by the arm. She stopped talking and stared at him. Would he apologize? Was he sorry he'd kissed her?

"I'm sorry you had to hear those unkind words back there."

"It's all right. I shouldn't be surprised. I knew she didn't like me. And I knew she didn't appreciate the pictures either. It's just... Never mind."

"I hope I didn't frighten you," he said. "I gave in to an impulse. I can't say I'm sorry I kissed you. I've wanted to kiss you...for a long time."

"I see," she said as calmly as she could with her stomach doing flip-flops and her cheeks burning. What did he mean by a long time? How long was a long time?

"I haven't changed my mind," he said, staring into her eyes. "I still want to marry you. Now more than ever."

"Please, Charles..." Why did he persist? Why didn't he realize she couldn't marry again, especially not the brother of her ex-husband? "If you're referring to that kiss, it was just a kiss, no matter how...how..."

"Earth-shattering, mind-blowing it was?" he suggested seriously.

"Yes...no...I mean...." Now she was caught. How could she deny the kiss was everything he said and more? She had the sinking feeling he could see into her mind, maybe even into her heart. If he did, he'd know how vulnerable she was. She'd never given her heart to anyone. She was waiting...hoping she'd find the man of her dreams. But maybe that wasn't practical. Maybe he'd never come along. And if he did, maybe he wouldn't want an impoverished, divorced princess with a baby, but without a home. Charles was offering her a home for her baby, a father for her baby. Would anyone else do the same?

"I hope you'll reconsider your decision," he said. "I hope you'll realize marrying me is the only sensible thing to do."

"Do you always do what's sensible?" she asked. It shouldn't offend her that he only wanted to do what was right instead of what was desirable, but it did.

"I try," he said. But there was a look in his eye that told her the kiss was not part of his plan. There was nothing sensible about it at all.

"Yes, all right I...I'll reconsider. I'll think about it." Her sisters' words echoed in her head.

He's nothing like his brother.

What about security?

You mean you couldn't love Charles?

She didn't know the answers to these questions. She only knew she didn't love Charles now. He didn't love her either. As if he'd read her thoughts, he spoke on that very subject.

"I don't expect you to love me," he said.

"What *do* you expect?" she asked with a shiver.

"Just what I have to give you. Loyalty, respect, fidelity. And security. That is what I have to offer. Financial security for you and your child."

How cold it sounded. She wondered if he'd rehearsed it. Well, what did she expect? She was no longer a young, virginal princess. She was used goods. She'd been disinherited when it was discovered that her parents' marriage was invalid because her father's previous marriage had never been legally dissolved. Then the divorce. Who would marry someone like her? A woman without a home, protection, family or friends?

She wanted to ask, what about sex? Do you expect us to share a marriage bed? If that kiss was any example, there was something there between them. Something she'd never experienced before. Something even he acknowledged. So she wasn't the only one whose pulse was racing. Again he read her mind.

"As for our sleeping arrangements..." he paused and let his gaze wander intimately over her body. She felt the heat from those dark eyes and wondered how it would feel if he made love to her. What kind of lover would he be? She refused to compare him to Wilhelm, who'd treated sex as a duty, taken what he wanted from her and left her bedroom immediately afterward. She'd experienced no pleasure and she doubted she'd given any. There were whispers of Wilhelm's mistresses, but he never told her anything. She sensed Charles would be a much different lover than his brother.

Charles continued his leisurely tour of her body with his eyes. If his hands and lips followed the same intimate trail, moving from her engorged breasts to her slightly rounded belly to the apex of her thighs...then she didn't know how she'd respond. She put her hand against her chest as if she could stop the rapid beating of her heart.

A small, ironic smile quirked one corner of his mouth. "As for our sleeping arrangements...I will let you decide when and where and if.... I would never force you to do anything you didn't want to do. Naturally I would like a wife in every sense of the word, but I respect you too much, Lise, to ask you to share my bed, unless you... But I'm getting ahead of myself. You wanted some time to think it over. Take all the time you need."

"Thank you." The breath rushed out of her lungs. He'd said that before, but here he was asking her again today. He said she had time, all the time she needed. Did she have weeks, months, years? Or would he call tomorrow and ask her again?

"Would five minutes be enough?" he asked lightly.

"Charles," she said.

"I want to take care of you," he said. "I want to start now."

"Because it's your duty," she said grimly.

He didn't answer. How could he deny it? He knew it was true. She told herself she couldn't expect any more than that. He was offering her everything he had to give. His name, his money, his support. Not just for her, but for her baby. He wasn't offering love, because he didn't love her. At least he was honest about that. There would be no surprises. He already knew she was illegitimate. He already knew she'd been divorced. He knew she was pregnant. Still he wanted to marry her and raise her child.

But what did she know about him? The best thing he had going for him was that he was *not* his brother.

Charles felt a breeze blow through the arbor and heard it rustle the broad grape leaves. He didn't realize he was holding his breath waiting for her answer. He'd told her to take her time because he couldn't bear to be turned down again. As long as she was thinking it over he could still hope she'd say yes. It was too painful to watch her struggle with her emotions, knowing he could make her life easier and better and more comfortable if she'd only say yes. It was the right thing to do. Why couldn't she see that?

He told himself that's what he was doing here, fulfilling his duty, as she'd correctly said. But what about himself? What did he really expect from her? What did he want? He knew the answer to that. He wanted her to be his wife in every sense of the word. The memory of that kiss came back and he knew it would haunt him for days. He hadn't intended doing anything like it.

Something had happened to him when she'd put her finger on his lips. It had set off a reaction he didn't know how to deal with. He was so intensely aware of the scent of her skin, the brush of her hair on his cheek, that no one could blame him for not thinking clearly. He didn't pretend to be thinking at all, he was only conscious of her finger, his lips and then her lips. She could have stopped him. She could have pulled away. But she hadn't. That was a good sign. He wanted her. He wanted to make love to her. He wanted her to be his wife, his lover, his companion. What did she want from him? He was afraid she wanted nothing.

Shadows were falling over the vast lawns. Waiters were carrying trays of empty champagne glasses. A few small groups of guests still gathered under huge blue-and-white umbrellas. The quartet had packed their instruments and gone home. The queen was no longer on her faux throne.

"I'm going home now," she said.

His spirits fell. He didn't really expect her to give him an answer in five minutes, but he didn't know how much longer he could wait.

He had only one more ace up his sleeve. Now was the time to play it. "I've found a house in St. Michel. Perhaps you know it, the Château Beau Rivage on the river."

"Of course I know it. It was built in the eighteenth century. I've been in it only once, but…"

"The architect was the same one who built several of the châteaux in the Loire Valley. I don't know if you remember, but it has spacious rooms, views of the river and the surrounding countryside, and spectacular gardens."

"Do you mean you've actually bought it?" she asked incredulously.

"I've made an offer on it. The estate agent tells me the owner is bound to accept."

"But isn't it rather large?"

"For a single man, yes. But I need a place where I can do business and entertain. Being in the wine industry, I want to be able to show off my products. And this particular house appealed to my sense of history. It seemed I came along at the right time. The absentee owners are anxious to sell. It needs work because it's been neglected, but there is no dearth of craftsmen here. I would, of course, be grateful for your advice on furnishings, decorating…"

He would be even more grateful if she would agree to live there with him, to be his wife. He didn't tell her, but she must suspect that he'd done it with her in mind. Of course it was too large for a single man, no matter what business he was in. But for a family with servants, with children running through the marble halls and playing in the gardens…it was close to ideal.

He told himself he was dreaming. He should not get his hopes up. If Lise didn't agree to marry him, he would not marry at all. There was no woman who could compare to her. If he couldn't have her, he would have no one. There would be no children's footsteps echoing in the halls, no shouting from the garden, no ponies pulling carts filled with laughing children along dirt paths bordered with flowers. Only himself. Alone.

He didn't know why the thought bothered him so much. He'd been alone most of his life. Or at least he'd felt alone. Now that he'd proposed marriage, and the possibility of another kind of life was within his grasp, his outlook had changed.

"Of course, I'll be happy to help you, if I can," she said. But if he expected her to jump at the chance, to agree to accept his offer of marriage just so she could live in a historic château, he was mistaken.

"I'll walk you back to your cottage," he said. There was no more to say.

They walked in silence. When they reached the thatch-roofed cottage, Nanny was waiting at the door. Charles greeted her with a smile and asked after her health. The old woman looked worried. He wanted to ask what was wrong, but Lise said good-bye to him abruptly, and he had run out of excuses to prolong the visit.

"I hope to hear from you soon," he said to Lise. He reached into his pocket. "Here is my new business card with my office number. You can find me in the old parliament building where I have a corner office."

"Yes, thank you," she said briskly. Then she was gone. She hadn't shut the door in his face, but she hadn't exactly kissed him good-bye or given him any reason to hope she'd change her mind or even call him. He walked back to get his car at the palace, staring off into the distance, wondering...worrying... He would have given much to hear the conversation inside the cottage.

Chapter Four

Lise slipped off her shoes and collapsed on the couch. She'd talked and laughed and eaten, flattered and been flattered, kissed and been kissed and eavesdropped, and now she was exhausted. She'd had enough social interaction to last her months. She was looking forward to spending the next six months confined to her cottage and her workshop. She was tired of talking, tired of thinking and tired of worrying about the future. Despite her brave words to her grandmother and her sisters and especially to Charles, she was worried sick about her future and that of her baby. Her mind was spinning, her lips still stinging from that kiss she couldn't forget and couldn't understand. Nanny handed her a cup of tea.

"How was the party?" she asked.

"Just what one would expect. Lovely food, fine music and the gardens in full flower."

"And the queen?"

"Looking younger than ever."

"Did she say anything?" Nanny asked.

"Not much. She regrets my divorce, of course."

"I have bad news," Nanny said.

Lise's eyes widened. Just when she thought she couldn't take any more bad news today. "Tell me," she said, sitting up straight.

"A messenger brought this." Nanny held out a white envelope. "It's addressed to you. It's from the palace. I haven't read it, but I know what it says. The messenger couldn't keep from spilling the beans."

Lise felt the color drain from her face as she ripped the envelope open.

The queen regrets that the gardener's cottage will no longer be available for the use of family members. It is to be renovated and refurbished for the new head gardener. The queen requests that her stepdaughter and her servant vacate the premises within the week.

It was signed with the royal seal and a simple initial— C.

So much for the love and compassion of a stepmother.

"I should have known," Lise said, as a feeling of gloom settled over her. "The only surprise is how fast she did it. Or did she have it all ready before the party?"

"What shall we do?" Nanny asked, her forehead lined with wrinkles.

"Do?" Lise said taking a deep breath and facing the inevitable. She had run out of time and of choices. There was no longer any doubt as to what she must do. "I shall get married and we—you, me and the baby-to-be—shall move into the Château Beau Rivage."

Lise spent a sleepless night during which images of a cold, empty château matched a cold, loveless marriage to yet another Rodin brother. But in the morning she was just as determined to do what was best for her and the baby, no matter what the personal cost to her. She dressed carefully in a pale yellow dress with a high neckline and a dropped waist.

Nanny gave her a worried look when she left the house in a taxi. But she didn't ask where Lise was going. Her reaction to Lise's announcement the night before had surprised her, but pleased her also. For some reason, the old woman had taken a liking to Charles and was most relieved to hear that Lise would have what she needed—a home and security for herself and her baby. As for Nanny, even this morning, she was still protesting being included in the marriage package.

"You won't need me," she said. "You'll have new servants, younger and more spry than me."

"I will always need you, Nanny," Lise said firmly. "If you won't come, I won't marry him. I can't get along without you. Not now, not ever."

Nanny's eyes filled with tears. Lise kissed her on the cheek, got into the taxi and gave the driver the address on Charles's card. She didn't call first. She didn't want to talk to him on the telephone. She didn't trust her voice.

What would Charles say when he heard she was only marrying him because she had no place to live? Would he still want to marry her? She thought he would. After all, though his reasons for marrying her were honorable, they had nothing to do with her personally. He would offer his hand to anyone who'd had the misfortune to have been divorced by his brother.

The old parliament building was located behind an iron fence at the end of the main, wide, tree-lined avenue of St. Michel. Parliament had been dissolved long ago when her grandfather had been alive, when he'd disagreed with it over some legal matter. He'd solved the problem by simply declaring parliament nonexistent. Since then, the offices had been used by various business and government agencies.

Lise paused at the door with Consolidated Vintners on it in gold letters before knocking. A secretary came to the door and she entered a small anteroom with a large desk.

"Is Monsieur Rodin in?"

The secretary looked her over. Lise had no idea if the woman knew who she was.

"He's in a meeting," she said, with a nod toward the door to his office. In the background she could hear the murmur of voices.

"Oh." Lise was relieved and disappointed at the same time. She had to tell him soon before she lost her nerve. She had to know if he was really willing to go through with his plan. If his offer was still good.

"Is he expecting you?"

"No, but perhaps I could wait?" she asked. "My name is Lise de Bergeron."

"Of course, madame. Won't you sit down?"

Lise was too nervous to sit down. She walked around the office, probably making the secretary as nervous as she was. On one wall was a painting of lush, green vineyards. Whether they were in St. Michel or Rhineland or France she didn't know. In a glass case were several bottles of wine and above them several framed awards for the company's wine. Another frame held a photograph of Charles accepting a medal. She stared at the picture. He looked so serious, so stern. She started to worry. Maybe this wasn't the right thing to do. Maybe there was another way out. Move in with one of her sisters. Leave the country. Emigrate to France or America.

A moment later Charles opened the door to the small office.

"Chantal," he said, "get me the file on Mondavi." He stopped abruptly when he saw Lise and stared at her. "Why didn't you tell me you were here?" he asked.

"I...I didn't want to interrupt..."

"I'll be right with you," he said. A moment later four or five people filed out of his office, casting curious glances in her direction.

"Come in," Charles said, his eyes never leaving her face. "Sit down."

Lise wiped her damp palms against her skirt. Her mouth was so dry she didn't think she'd be able to say a word. She'd have to write him a note. What would it say? Just one word ought to do it. Yes.

As if he knew, Charles offered her a glass of water. "Or would you prefer wine?" he asked. "We were just tasting our latest varietal."

She shook her head. "Not while I'm pregnant. You have a lovely view," she said at last, glancing out the window but not seeing anything.

"Yes." He seemed as tongue-tied as she was.

She set the water down. "I came," she said.

"Yes, I see," he said. He didn't sound impatient, which he had every right to be. His eyes never left her face.

She swallowed hard. "I came to tell you I will marry you."

He sat down in the chair behind his desk and tented his fingers together. She hadn't expected him to jump for joy, but she'd expected something other than silence. Had he changed his mind? She wouldn't blame him if he had. He was not getting any bargain marrying a pregnant princess with no dowry.

"You must wonder why I've changed my mind." If he

wasn't going to say anything, she would. She owed him an explanation at least. If she didn't tell him, he'd find out somehow.

"It doesn't matter," he said.

"But it does. The queen has evicted me from my cottage."

"And that's the only reason?" he asked, raising his eyebrows.

"No. As you and everyone else I know has pointed out to me, I am in a very vulnerable position with no home, no security and no future. The obvious solution is to get married again. You were kind enough to offer your hand to me, I accept, unless…"

"Unless?" he said, leaning forward and fixing his dark gaze on her.

"Unless you've changed your mind."

"No." He stood up. "When I give my word, I do not retract it. I'm only sorry you had to be forced into this decision. Even though it's the right thing to do, I would have preferred… Never mind. You've made the right decision. If you don't know that now, I think you will in the future. I confess I don't know exactly how, but I intend to be the best husband I can be. I've had no real examples of a good marriage in my life. One thing I know, you deserve the best, Lise, and I will try to give you that."

"Thank you," she said. Her voice shook. The reality of it all was hitting her like a hammer. Marrying again. Marrying again for all the wrong reasons. For security. This time she'd have no one to blame but herself. No one was forcing her to do this.

"How soon can we have the wedding?" he asked.

"I was thinking perhaps next week. I haven't asked anyone, but there is the small chapel on the palace grounds. I don't think anyone's ever been married there, but if it's only our families..."

"*Your* family," he said. He held out his hand to help her to her feet. Then he bent and kissed her hand. His lips were warm. The memory of his kiss in the palace came back and left her feeling light-headed.

She'd done it. She'd committed herself to a man she barely knew. A man who looked so much like her former husband it sent shivers up her spine. He was different. Everyone agreed he was different. She knew he was different. She was still worried. Very worried.

Charles stood at the window of his office watching his future bride walk away from the large parliament building. Her hair was gilded by the sun and shone so brightly it hurt his eyes to look at her. She walked gracefully, her skirt molded to her body by the breeze. He couldn't get it through his head that she was really going to marry him after all. Lise de Bergeron would be his bride, to love and to cherish for as long as they both would live. His wife. His heart banged against his ribs. He clenched his hands into fists as the reality sunk in.

He wanted to shout it from the rooftops. He wanted to tell the world. She said yes! She's going to marry me!

Maybe it was a dream. Just another dream like the ones he'd had before. No, this time it was real. She'd stood there in his office and promised to be his wife. He smiled to himself, picturing the wedding. This time it would be different. This time it would be him and not his brother waiting at the altar. He'd make her happy, but not as happy as he was right now. Right now he was the happiest man in the kingdom, maybe the whole world. Lise de Bergeron was going to marry him!

His life would change radically with a wife. Not just any

wife, a beautiful, intelligent, charming wife, one he had secretly coveted since the first time he'd seen her. She would never know that. It was his secret. He knew she'd never forget her unfortunate marriage to his brother, but maybe in time it would fade to a distant memory. If only he could forget it too.

If some day she agreed to become his wife in every way, physically and emotionally as well as legally, he would never ask for more out of life. His cup would truly run over. But if she didn't, he would still have more than he'd ever imagined. He'd have Lise. He didn't realize he was holding his breath until he saw her turn the corner and disappear from view. Then he took a bottle of rare, vintage champagne from the cabinet behind his desk and put it in his briefcase. He didn't want anything to drink now. He was drunk with joy.

Ariane and Marie-Claire could scarcely contain their glee when they heard the news. When Lise called them, they rushed to the cottage to hear the news in person. Ariane jumped up and down just as she used to do as a child when excited. She threw her arms around Lise.

"He's a wonderful man. You won't be sorry."

"You'll wear *the dress*, of course," Marie-Claire said.

"I wore mother's dress the last time. It didn't exactly bring me good luck. Besides, I hardly think white is an appropriate color for a pregnant bride," Lise said wryly.

"What about a cream-colored *peau de soie* dress with an empire waist?" Marie-Claire asked.

"It sounds lovely. But I don't have one."

"I don't either, but I have the cloth. I bought it in Thailand on our honeymoon. Maybe Nanny...."

"In one week?" Lise said. "I don't see how."

As if she'd been listening outside the door, Nanny poked her head in.

"Nanny, dear," Marie-Claire said, "can you sew a wedding dress in a week?"

"For my girl?" the old lady said. "Of course. Didn't I make you girls matching dresses for your father's fiftieth birthday?"

"But that was years ago," Lise said. "We're bigger now, or at least I am."

"We'll help," Ariane said. "We'll do all the hand work, the hems and the lace trim and the little beads. We have nothing else to do this week, do we Marie-Claire?"

Lise felt her eyes fill with tears. The women in this room were giving up this week to make her a wedding dress. The love and gratitude she felt for them filled her heart.

"Uh…no tears," Ariane cautioned. "Tears will spot the fabric. Think happy thoughts, Lise."

"I am happy," she said, unwilling to give her sisters the wrong impression. She was worried, she was nervous, but she was happy too. So happy the tears spilled down her cheeks. "These are happy tears."

Queen Celeste gave her permission for the wedding to be held in the small stone chapel on the palace grounds. She even consented to be present at the wedding, no doubt because she was so happy to be rid of her stepdaughter. It was certain she'd felt the shame of Lise's divorce and the burden of her presence living there without prospects. Certainly she must feel proud she'd been successful in nudging Lise into a hasty marriage by denying her any further use of the cottage.

Lise knew her stepmother wouldn't approve of her inviting the cook and Nanny along with her sisters and their husbands, but she did it anyway. She decided against a florist or a photographer. This was going to be a simple ceremony in a simple setting.

As she pinned up her long hair that morning and soaked in the clawfoot porcelain bathtub for the last time, she realized how different her last wedding had been. She'd been made up and dressed by servants, then transported in a horse-drawn carriage to the cathedral where hundreds of Europe's royal and not-so-royal guests were waiting. The church was filled with expensive floral displays. She'd carried white roses and her attendants had bouquets of baby pink roses. Her father had walked her down the long aisle, beaming at friends and relatives. She could tell how proud he was. She was marrying the man he'd chosen for her. He'd gotten one daughter off his hands. It was fortunate he'd died before she was sent home from Rhineland in disgrace. If his heart attack hadn't killed him, the shame would have.

The reception had been a formal affair in the mirrored ballroom at the palace. A photographer had taken endless pictures of everyone. The popping flashbulbs had given her a headache. The reception line had been at least fifty meters long. Lise knew almost immediately she'd made the wrong choice when she saw Wilhelm using the occasion to further his business interests, making contacts, exchanging business cards.

And there was Charles. She remembered him standing next to his brother in the church with a somber face and brooding eyes. Charles had been in the background watching her with an inscrutable look on his face. What had he been thinking? Did he know what a terrible mistake she was making? Did he ever dream that one day in the not-too-distant future, he'd be standing in his brother's place, taking his brother's place in her life?

No one could have known. Not that day. No one could

have predicted that her father would die, that his marriage to her mother would be declared invalid and that Wilhelm would divorce her. Or that Charles would be the sort of man who would step into the void and take care of his brother's pregnant ex-wife. She owed him a debt of gratitude.

This time she dressed at home in her homemade dress. Her sisters curled her hair and pulled the dress over her head. When they'd finished she stood in her bedroom and stared at herself in the full-length mirror. The dress was beautiful. It fit her like a glove. They'd worked so hard on it. She looked eons older than she had at her last wedding. She'd been through so much. She wanted to believe it had made her stronger, wiser and more understanding. The face that stared back at her in the mirror was not the innocent girl who'd married Wilhelm. That girl was gone forever.

Her closets were empty. The trunks had been transported to the château. Nanny was going to spend three weeks with her sister after the wedding, then join her mistress in her new home. Everything was in order. Charles had put his business on hold this week and devoted himself to making arrangements.

The subject of a honeymoon had come up only once—but not between Charles and Lise. Only her sisters had suggested it.

"Where will you go?" Ariane asked. "I suggest Bali. It's the most beautiful island, palm trees swaying in the wind, waves lapping against the sand. There's the most romantic little hotel, right on the beach. If you hang a Do Not Disturb sign on your door, they leave the breakfast on a tray and—"

"I don't think so," Lise said, feeling a wave of heat rush to her face. The picture she conjured up of her and Charles in Bali sequestered in a hotel room was more than she could handle. It was clear her sisters had no idea about the true nature of her forthcoming marriage. Although she hated to mislead them, she couldn't tell them the truth either. They didn't really want to hear it. "We can't go anywhere. Charles has too much work to do right now."

"Later then," Marie-Claire said. "When you do go, let me know. Sebastian and I went to the most charming place on Crete in the Greek islands. White buildings, blue waters, romantic candlelight dinners for two. You'd love it."

"I'll be sure to let you know," Lise said.

The truth was, there would be no honeymoon. It was completely inappropriate for a marriage of convenience. They weren't in love and they weren't going to make love. The purpose of this marriage was clear. Lise was getting a secure future and Charles was getting the satisfaction of redeeming his family's honor. They were both doing the right thing. But romance? That was not part of the bargain.

"We've packed your trousseau bag," Ariane said with an impish grin. "Don't open it until you arrive at the château."

"We didn't think your long flannel nightgown and cotton underwear were really appropriate for a honeymoon, and there wasn't time to throw you a lingerie shower, so we took some liberties…"

"I told you…" Lise said.

"You don't have to be shy with us, Lise," Ariane said. "We're old married women, you know. Women of the world. We know what goes on on honeymoons. We know what to wear and what not to wear."

"*Do* you?" Lise asked. "You'll have to tell me all about it."

Marie-Claire and Ariane giggled helplessly then stepped back to admire the dress.

"You look gorgeous," Marie-Claire said and she smoothed the *peau de soie* fabric.

"Thanks to you two and Nanny," Lise said. "I still can't believe you got it done in time."

"It's the last wedding. It makes me kind of sad." She sniffed dramatically and they all laughed. Even Lise. It was the last wedding. And her last chance at happiness.

Charles arrived at the small stone chapel an hour in advance. He'd been working day and night getting their quarters in order at the château. He wanted Lise to have input into the refurbishing of the old place, but he didn't want her to walk into totally bare and unfinished living rooms. He didn't know what to do about the bedroom. His? Hers? Theirs? Finally he put a large bed with matching chaise lounge and dresser into a bedroom facing the garden. He left the curtains and other fabrics for her to choose. His own bedroom adjoined it. Dare he call it theirs? No. Not unless she agreed. Not unless she initiated the change.

These thoughts ran through his mind as he stood at the door of the chapel. The priest arrived and they went over the short ceremony. Charles took advantage of some powerful connections to make sure Lise and his brother's marriage was officially annulled so there was no problem having another religious ceremony. He and Lise had agreed they would have no attendants.

Lise had asked a musician friend to play the traditional wedding music and she arrived with her violin and began to tune up. Queen Simone, wearing a regal purple gown, was driven up by two attendants who then waited for her outside the chapel. Charles kissed her hand and she acknowledged him with a brief nod and took a seat in the front row with a little smile. Lise's sisters rushed in with their husbands and hugged him tightly.

He took his place at the altar. He remembered the last wedding. He'd stood next to Wilhelm as his best man and handed him the ring. He remembered how Lise had looked, her face pale beneath her veil. His heart had gone out to her. He wondered if she knew what she was getting into. It turned out she didn't. If only he'd spoken when the priest asked if anyone objected. But no one would have listened to him if he had. They would have chalked it off to jealousy. Who was to say they would have been wrong? He was fortunate now to be able to spend the rest of his life making it up to her.

A hush fell over the small group in the chapel. The violinist struck up the wedding march and suddenly she was there, framed like a painting in the stone arch of the old church. She stood there for a long moment looking straight at him. For one terrible moment he was afraid she'd changed her mind. He half expected her to turn and leave.

But she didn't. He breathed a sigh of relief as she began the excruciatingly slow journey to the altar. She was so beautiful it made his heart ache. She was wearing a floor-length gown, and she carried a small bouquet of wild roses as she walked up the narrow aisle by herself. How fitting it was she should walk by herself. She was her own person now. No father to force her into a marriage she didn't want. Her steady gaze never left his. Instead of the pale cheeks he remembered from the last wedding, today her cheeks were rosy. She was glowing with health. Yes, pregnancy became her. He must remember to tell her that.

He heard himself promise to love, honor and obey. He heard her do the same. He bent to kiss her. Her lips were soft and sweet. He didn't dare kiss her the way he wanted to. The way he had in the palace. Not with all these people watching. But oh, how he wanted to. He wondered if she wanted him to.

The priest pronounced them man and wife. He took her hand and they walked back down the short aisle together. Man and wife. For as long as they both shall live. There would be no more divorces. She knew it as well as he did. They would stick it out no matter what happened. The two of them and the baby. The faces in the church were a blur. So was the luncheon that followed at Marie-Claire's house. He only remembered the laughter floating around him as the sisters teased each other. It seemed as if everyone there made a toast with the fine champagne he'd provided. Even Nanny got to her feet and raised her glass.

"Here's to my mistress. My princess has finally found her prince." Everyone clapped and Nanny sat down quickly as if she was surprised she'd even had the nerve to speak.

At the end of the afternoon, he noticed that Lise looked tired. He thanked everyone and took her hand.

"We must leave now. My wife is getting tired." *My wife*. He wanted to say it over and over. My wife is pregnant. My wife and I have to go home. My wife. Lise de Bergeron was his wife.

When he carried her over the threshold of the château he felt the satisfaction of being home at last. Strange, the château had been legally his for a week or two, but it wasn't until that moment, with Lise in his arms, that he'd felt this was really his home.

She gasped in surprise when he lifted her off her feet. "You'll hurt your back. I'm getting heavy."

Her face was pressed into the front of his shirt. She smelled like the spring flowers that had decorated the church and her hair brushed his cheek. He wanted to carry her straight up the stairs to his bedroom and make love to her all night long. That's what everyone thought they were going to do. He'd seen the looks her sisters exchanged as they said good-bye. He'd seen the knowing smiles on the faces of his brothers-in-law. But they didn't know why she was marrying him. He did. He knew she didn't love him. He didn't expect her to.

"Put me down, Charles," Lise said softly. "I can walk." Of course she could walk, but the truth was, she didn't want to. She wanted to stay in his arms. She'd never felt so safe and so cared for. It was only an illusion. She was married. Charles would support her financially. He'd give her the respect and devotion and loyalty she expected, but emotionally she was on her own.

But tonight, just one night, her wedding night, was it so wrong to cling to him? To give in to the impulse, to the illusion that this was a real marriage? If it was, then she was guilty. She put her arms around his neck and sighed.

He stood in the middle of the great room and lowered her to her feet. Her knees buckled and he put his arm around her to support her. This was the first time she'd seen the château. He wanted to surprise her. He said she'd have plenty of time to redo it.

"It's beautiful the way it is," she said, taking in the large open windows and the beautiful old inlaid oak floors, and the high ceilings with carved moldings.

She sat down on the velvet cushion of a high-backed cherry-wood chair. "Ouch," she said. "I must take these shoes off." He knelt in front of her and took them off for her. Then he began to massage her feet with his strong hands. She was surprised by the pleasure that coursed through her body. She leaned back in the chair and gave in to the sensations. She was scarcely aware that she was making small sounds of pleasure in the back of her throat. Her whole body began to unwind and relax.

"That feels...so...good," she said as he concentrated on her toes, stroking, tugging, rubbing until she was out of breath. Every stroke, every caress sent a shaft of pure, exquisite pleasure ricocheting through her entire body. She'd never felt this way, almost as if she were on the verge of a climax. With Wilhelm she'd never even come close. He was a man only interested in his own pleasure. Charles was different. But she was still afraid. Afraid to let go. Afraid to let down her defenses.

With a huge effort, she forced herself to sit up straight. He got to his feet, his eyes shuttered. Did he know, did he guess, what he'd done to her? She looked around the room with a curious gaze. She'd almost forgotten where she was, who she was. Soft lights illuminated the high ceilings with the ornate molding. There was not much furniture. Only a few high-backed chairs and a library table. But it had potential. Possibilities. Fires were burning in the fireplaces, taking the chill from the night air. The servants, now invisible, had been busy.

"It's a wonderful house," she said. Although she was not thinking of the house, but only of how Charles had made her feel. "I want to see it all."

"You'll see it all tomorrow. Come to bed now. You're tired."

He'd said *come to bed*. Not *go to bed*. She didn't know what that meant or what he wanted. She didn't know what he expected. She was married. He was her husband. She looked into his eyes and saw beyond the curtain he'd put up to hide his feelings. She saw flames of desire flicker in the depths. She knew then that he wanted her, and God help her, she wanted him. She wanted to feel his clever, capable hands all over her body. It wasn't just the way he'd handled her feet. It was the memory of his kiss. It was the way he'd carried her in. The way he'd treated her and her family. The magic of his hands on her tender, sensitive feet. Her heart thudded in her chest. She felt like a virgin. She'd had so little experience. She was afraid he'd be disappointed in her.

She put her hands on his shoulders and met his gaze. "I want to see your bedroom." She scarcely recognized her own voice.

He didn't answer. He just scooped her up in his arms again. He took the marble stairs two at a time, took a right turn at the top of the landing and walked into the master bedroom. He pushed the door shut behind him. Then he put her down on the edge of the bed. His bed.

A fire blazed in the fireplace here too. But that had nothing to do with the way she was on fire. She had to get that dress off or burst into flames. She reached for the zipper. He watched with eyes glowing like hot coals while she let the dress fall off her shoulders. Underneath she wore a silk teddy and matching bikini panties her sisters had bought her. She let her dress slide to the floor. He sank to his knees on the floor.

"You are so beautiful," he said, his voice as rough as sandpaper.

She reached down and undid the top button of his formal shirt. She wanted to see him, to see his body by firelight. Impatiently, he ripped the shirt open and tossed it aside. His chest was dusted with dark hair, his shoulders broad and bronzed. He stood and kicked off his shoes and peeled off his socks. Next came the black pants, and finally his boxer shorts.

She stood and stared, unable to move, unable to breathe. He was magnificent. For just a second she thought of Wilhelm, his twin, equally handsome. But this was Charles, so utterly gorgeous she was shaking like a leaf. All the air left her lungs. Now that he'd done what she wanted him to without her asking, she was stunned at the perfection of the clearly aroused male who was her husband. She staggered backward toward the bed. Even though what she was wearing consisted of a few pieces of fabric that barely covered her, she felt overdressed. She paused and lifted the straps and the teddy slithered to the floor.

She could hear him breathing hard. She let her bikinis go next. She thought she'd feel awkward and shy, but she didn't. She felt wanton, free and a little wild. She, who'd always been the good girl, felt decidedly bad. If he didn't take her to bed now she would have to do something rash. She'd have to take his face in her hands and press it against her breasts.

He was so close. So close she could smell his skin, and the wine on his breath. She could feel the heat from his beautiful, rock-hard body. When he reached for her she went into his arms. His mouth covered hers and claimed her. With that kiss he said everything she wanted to hear. I want you. I need you. You're mine. He didn't say anything about love, but love wasn't part of the bargain.

She kissed him back. Telling him without words that she was his. Not just for tonight, but forever. She wanted him to know that she'd decided "when and where and if...." The answer was here and now. She didn't know if *decided* was the right word. She wasn't conscious of making a decision. She only knew she had to make love with him, her husband. Now.

He held her by the shoulders and looked into her eyes, asking again without words if this was the time. If this was the place and if he was the man.

"Do you know how much I want you?" he asked. "How many nights I've lain awake and dreamed about you? How much it hurt me knowing you belonged to someone else? You're mine now. Tell me now if you want what I want. Tell me you feel the same."

Now was not the time to be sensible. To remind him this

was not a marriage made in heaven, but a marriage of convenience. For her convenience, for his family honor. Even if she'd wanted to, she couldn't say those words. Her throat was dry and clogged with emotion. She put her arms around him and murmured in his ear.

"Yes," she said. "Yes, yes, yes."

Chapter Five

He laid her in his bed on the smooth Egyptian cotton sheets. She closed her eyes and smelled leather and wood smoke and felt from the open window a welcome breeze off the river that helped to cool her overheated body. She was in his bed. She was in bed with her husband. The same hands that had almost brought her to a climax when stroking her feet downstairs were now stroking the insides of her thighs, making her break out in goosebumps. Her skin was cold, but inside her body was feverish. As his hands reached the apex of her thighs, she heard herself cry out in ecstasy as she teetered on the verge of abandon. She arched her back to get close, closer and then it happened. Just when his fingers found the core of her existence, she shattered.

She threw her arms around him and the tears came coursing down her cheeks. She couldn't believe what had just happened. She finally understood what all the shouting was about. No wonder wars were fought over it, kingdoms lost or won. She'd never known, never understood. Now it was his turn. He entered her, hard and hot and heavy. So heavy she didn't think she could take him in, but she did, deeper and deeper and faster. So fast she had to gasp to catch her breath. Her fingernails dug into his skin as she gripped his shoulders.

He pushed into her again and again as the pressure built in her own body. Then his mouth came down on hers and his tongue met hers in a dance that matched the one going on between her legs. She didn't know how much more she could take. She had no experience, nothing to help her know what to do, what to expect. When she opened her eyes and looked into his, she saw a look of wonder and realized he might be just as amazed as she was. Just as stunned by the experience.

When he convulsed into her she cried aloud and shattered again. They'd ridden the wildest ride of her life, together. He lay on top of her in the darkness with their arms entwined. Their bodies were welded together. He was heavy, but she didn't ever want him to move. She'd never known it could be like that. The give and take, the feeling of unity, of belonging, of becoming whole. She had no idea if he felt the same. She just knew she'd never forget this moment or this night. She could no longer think or reason or wonder or do anything but sleep.

The next morning she woke up in Charles's bed, but Charles was not there. Slowly, carefully she sat up in his bed and looked around the room. Every muscle in her body ached. And the memories came flooding back. She and Charles. Her wedding night. There was her wedding dress on a chair in the corner. Her underwear was still in a pool on the floor. And her? She was wearing nothing at all. She pulled the sheet up and held it tight against her chest with trembling fingers. She'd made love to her husband. That was all. It had been her decision. She could have stopped him. But she hadn't. She couldn't have. Now what? Where would they go from here?

She'd spoiled what could have been a perfect arrangement. He got to make amends for his brother's actions and she was getting the support she needed. They'd almost become friends. Now they both had to deal with a new situation. Unless they pretended it had never happened. Lise was good at pretending. She'd pretended her last marriage was happy. She'd pretended she could take care of herself and her baby without help. But could she pretend last night had never happened or that it had meant nothing to her? Was she in danger of losing a friend, the best friend she could ever hope to have?

"Good morning."

She was so startled to see Charles enter the room she almost dropped the sheet she was clutching in her hand. He was carrying a tray with a pitcher of café au lait and a fresh croissant. The rich smell of pastry and the dark roast of the coffee filled the air.

She studied his face, but had no clue as to how he was feeling. She didn't know what to do or how to act. If she accepted breakfast in bed, how would she eat while holding a sheet above her breasts? If she got up to dress, she'd have to walk across the floor naked. Never mind that he'd already seen her that way. Never mind that they'd been as intimate as people could be.

"I…I'll just be a minute," she said, leaping out of bed and walking rapidly to the spacious bathroom gleaming with gold fixtures. She caught a glimpse of his face as she passed him, seeing a slight smile twitch at the corner of his mouth.

She stared at herself in his mirror, stunned to find her lips swollen and her face flushed. She brushed her teeth and thankfully found a terry-cloth robe hanging from a hook. As she snuggled into it, she was enveloped by his masculine scent. Her skin tingled. A spiral of desire started in the very core of her body. Not again, she thought. It was too soon. But he'd started something. Or was she the one who'd started it? She couldn't remember. All she knew was that she wanted more.

Back in the bedroom he'd set her breakfast on her bed-side table.

"I hope you don't mind," she said, running her hand over the soft terry cloth.

"It looks better on you than on me," he said.

She blushed and fought the urge to take the robe off. He might be shocked. He might not be prepared for her new self. She had better take her cue from him. She turned to the breakfast he'd so thoughtfully brought her. She sat on the edge of the bed and sipped her coffee. When she looked up he was standing there, looking down at her. She didn't know what to say. Sooner or later they would have to discuss what had happened. Decide what to do next. But she wasn't ready for that kind of a discussion.

"Have you eaten?" she asked.

He nodded. "The cook has arrived. She's waiting to meet you."

"I'm sorry I overslept. I don't know what..." She blushed. "I don't know why..."

He shrugged. "Don't worry about it." He sat next to her on the edge of the bed and slanted a glance at her. "And don't worry about what happened last night. We both got carried away."

That was one way to put it. Another would be they'd both given in to passions they'd never experienced before. At least she hadn't. She had no idea what Charles's past love life had been and she had no intention of asking him.

She felt a surge of jealousy thinking he'd ever made love to anyone else like that. But if he had, maybe he felt nothing about last night. Just another night with a woman. Only this time the woman was his wife.

"Carried away," she repeated. "Yes, that's all it was. We can't let it spoil our marriage or our friendship." She was afraid he was going to laugh at the idea of sex spoiling a marriage. He didn't. He was probably just as worried as she was.

"No," he said, standing. "Definitely not. When you get dressed, come on downstairs. I'll give you a tour of the house before I go to work."

Work. Of course he had work to do. She was a distraction. He'd given up last week to prepare for the wedding and now that it was over, he could go back to his real life. She must try not to get in the way. Fortunately she had her own work. Besides the furnishing of this house, and preparing a nursery for the baby, she was still the unofficial palace historian and she had a lifetime of work restoring royal art and jewelry. Until Celeste sold it all off, of course. Charles had promised her a large, well-heated, well-lighted work room. It was up to her to get back to work. She couldn't sit around waiting for the baby to be born. Waiting for Charles to make love to her again. Yes, she was married now. Yes, she'd had sex with her husband, but now it was back to real life.

"Thank you," she said politely. As if he was still her brother-in-law instead of her husband. "I'll be down promptly."

"You'll find your clothes in your bedroom." He gestured toward an open door down the hall.

He left and she went to her bedroom and reached into the armoire for her jeans then realized she wasn't a craftswoman living in a cottage anymore. She was the wife of a prominent businessman and she had to start dressing like one. She went to find her new walk-in closet, adjacent to her new bedroom and found the servants had unpacked her trunks. She chose a pair of gabardine slacks and a silk blouse. The blouse was a little snug leaving a gap between the buttons. Sooner or later she'd have to have a maternity wardrobe. Then she went downstairs, feeling like somebody else. Feeling like the wife of a successful businessman. A role she would have to get used to.

Charles looked at her as if she was someone else. Someone he scarcely knew. That made them even. Today he was someone she scarcely knew. She saw his eyes fall on the gap in her blouse between her breasts, then he looked away, and led her on a tour around the château. There were so many rooms she got confused.

"You'll have to give me a map," she said jokingly, "or I'll get lost."

"We don't need all this space," he admitted. "Not for the three of us, or rather the four of us including Nanny. But I couldn't find another house I liked as much as this one. This is one of the reasons." He opened the French doors of a drawing room that looked out on several acres of vineyards.

She gasped at the sight of the vines, planted in orderly rows, brilliant green in the sunlight. "I had no idea. Now I understand why you wanted this house."

He smiled. "I confess, living in a vineyard has always been my dream. The river on one side, the vines on the other. Beyond the vines are the formal gardens. They were designed by Bertrand de Guigne in the eighteenth century to go with the château. When I come home this evening I'll take you through them." He looked at his watch. "I must be off now. Will you be all right by yourself?"

"Of course. I'm a big girl, Charles. I'm quite accustomed to being by myself. I like it."

"All right then."

She followed him to the front door. He gave her a brief glance, then he left her there. No kiss, no sign of affection. No reminder of what had happened last night. She lingered at the doorway, she even followed him down the steps to the circular driveway where his car was waiting. She wanted to say something to him. She wanted him to say something to her. Something important, something profound. Something about the events of yesterday and last night. But it didn't happen. He drove away while she stood in the driveway and watched him go. She felt empty and depleted. If she'd expected more from him, she was bound to be disappointed. It was time to lower her expectations. This was marriage. She'd better get used to it.

Charles watched her in his rearview mirror. He had an overwhelming desire to turn around, go back and carry her up to his bedroom. But that would shock her and where would that lead? To more confusion about their marriage. He could see the confusion on her face this morning.

At least he could have kissed her good-bye. Or said something about how he felt. If he could express in words how he felt. That was the problem. After the most amazing night of his life, he was in a daze. He didn't know what to say. He had no words to describe how she'd made him feel. He'd made love to his wife. Ordinarily that would not be front-page news. But in their situation, it most certainly was. It was something he hadn't expected and he didn't think she had either.

But it had happened. She had been so responsive, so warm, so giving. Her cries rang in his ears long afterward. The memory of her soft skin, the sight of her silken hair spread out on the pillow made his body respond once again. He'd lain on the cool sheets replaying their extraordinary lovemaking while he watched her sleep. She was curled up next to him with a small smile on her lips. He'd brushed a lock of hair from her forehead. It was as if every dream he'd ever had had come true. The woman of his dreams was his now. She'd stepped out of his dreams and into his bed, into his house and into his life.

When he came home today, she would be there waiting for him. The thought filled him with indescribable joy. As for his bed, he had to get used to the idea that last night was special. Their wedding night was just one night and there would never be another one like it. Not unless she wanted it to happen. From now on it was back to being friends. There was nothing wrong with that. He'd never had a friend like Lise. He'd never thought he would. If he was careful and respected her, their friendship would grow and bloom like the roses in the formal gardens. If he tried to push her into a different kind of relationship, it would spoil everything.

For now he would take his cues from her. She'd said nothing about their wedding night. He too would say nothing. She would move into her own bedroom and he would occupy his. If she wanted more…but she didn't. He could tell by the look on her face this morning. By the way she'd almost run past him into the bathroom.

He had a hard time concentrating on business. Everyone he saw congratulated him on his marriage. Some said they didn't expect to see him in so early. Others asked him about his honeymoon. He said he and Lise were postponing it until after the grape harvest. He felt the heat creep up the back of his neck as he realized they expected him to be at home behind the closed bedroom door making love to his wife. The idea caused him to forget to call the people on his list, to lose a portfolio and to forget the name of the dealer in California he'd seen last month.

He even forgot he'd scheduled a wine-tasting for the following week. His secretary reminded him.

"We have firm answers from about seventy-five people," she said.

"What? What day was that again?" Lise would want to know if seventy-five people were coming to the château. He'd have it catered and the servants would take care of the hard work, but she would act as his hostess. At last he had a home and a wife. And what a wife. His home wasn't bad either. Yes, he was going to be proud to show them both off.

His secretary came back into his office. "I got the book you asked for," she said, put it on his desk as if it was a hot potato and left the room.

He unwrapped it quickly. *The Pregnancy Handbook From A to Z.* Ignoring the stack of phone messages on his desk, he opened the book to the chapter on the first trimester.

These words leapt out at him. *Well-balanced diet... protein, minerals, calcium and vitamins. No alcohol, limited caffeine...moderate exercise... Chest and abdomen fully formed...lungs...heart has four chambers and beats...* Fascinated, he read on and on.

Suddenly he could no longer stay in his office. Not with Lise at home alone. He had no idea how many things could go wrong with a pregnancy. He couldn't keep his mind on business anyway, so it was useless to pretend he was accomplishing anything.

When he arrived at the château and saw Lise in the great room, looking more like herself, wearing blue jeans with her hair fastened in a knot at the base of her neck, he breathed a sigh of relief. It reminded him of the day he'd gone to see her in her workroom. She no longer looked like the wife of a businessman; she looked like herself.

"You're home early," she said with a glance at the tall clock in the corner that looked as if it had been standing there for centuries.

"Since I am my own boss, I sent myself home early. Any employee of mine with a wife who's three months pregnant should take every afternoon off."

"What a generous boss you must be," she said with a smile.

"Not excessively generous, just sensible. And perhaps a little worried. Tell me, have you had a nap today?" he asked.

"No, why?" she asked, looking puzzled.

"I bought a book about pregnancy. In it, I read that you may be very tired." He took the book from his briefcase and showed it to her. "And have mood swings."

"Really," she said with a half smile. "I was tired at first, and I took lots of naps, but I'm feeling fine these days. And I had plenty of mood swings. But then my whole life was up in the air. Anybody in my position would have had mood swings. I didn't know you knew so much about it."

"I didn't until today. Did you know that your baby's face is very developed now, except for the jaw of course," he said.

"No, I didn't know that," she said. "But did you know that right about now his head is disproportionately large for his body?"

"His?" he said. "Do you think it's a boy?"

"I don't know why I said that. I really have no idea."

"But do you want a boy?"

"I don't care. Coming from a family of girls, I don't know anything about boys. Do you want a boy?"

He stared at her. She'd asked him what he wanted as if

it mattered. She cared what he thought. "I don't care either, as long as it's healthy," he said.

"That's how I feel."

"I stopped by the store and bought you some cheese—Camembert, St. Andre, Roquefort...I was afraid you weren't getting enough calcium. I also bought a bunch of spinach—iron, you know."

She smothered a smile. "Yes, I know. How thoughtful. I believe the cook has already got the menu for tonight, but we could always have a spinach salad in addition to the veal paupiettes."

"Good. When I was reading this book I suddenly got worried about all the things that could go wrong."

"But they won't," she said. "I'm very healthy. You were probably reading about women who had problems before they got pregnant. My doctor says I should sail right through my pregnancy."

"Who is your doctor?" he asked.

"Doctor Duverger. He's new. The doctor who delivered me and my sisters has retired. I won't be having my baby in the palace as my mother did. I prefer the hospital, the one my grandfather founded and supported."

"I would like to go with you the next time you see your doctor. I have some questions I'd like to ask."

"I see," she said. "All right." She looked surprised that he was that interested, but she didn't protest.

"By the way," she said, "we received a wedding present." She held up a large package for him to see. "It was just delivered from the palace. I can't believe the queen...no, it must be from my grandmother. Even so, I didn't expect...."

A wedding present. He realized he was supposed to give her a present. Of course she didn't expect one. She was the least acquisitive, the least demanding person he'd ever met.

Still, he ought to have thought of giving her something himself.

He reached into the drawer of the ornate table for a knife and cut the brown paper wrapping. Lise tore the paper and then stood back and stared at the painting inside the frame.

"It's Frederic. She's given us his portrait. I don't know what to say."

"You want him, don't you?"

"Of course, but I thought he belonged with his family. However if they're going to sell off the rest of the collection…"

"Perhaps he belongs with his beloved Gabrielle," he said.

"Do you have a painting of her?" Lise asked.

"There is one back in Rhineland. I'll send for it. We'll find a place for them here."

"United at last. You haven't forgotten her diary, have you?" she asked.

"No, it's upstairs. I meant to give it to you yesterday, but in the excitement…" He didn't finish his sentence. The excitement he was referring to was their wedding night. A night like that not only made him forget the diary, but almost made him forget his own name. But he was not going to embarrass her by mentioning it. Instead he looked around the great hall. "It already looks more like home in here. What have you done?"

"Just moved a few pieces of furniture and taken down those heavy drapes."

"Not by yourself," he said, alarmed. "You're only supposed to have moderate exercise."

"No, no. The servants did all the work. I merely gave orders. I must say I'm out of the habit of telling people what to do. But they're all very understanding. They seem to know what I want even before I've told them. Even the flowers. They've filled every vase in the house." She buried her face in a bowl of sweet peas and sniffed appreciatively.

He smiled at her enthusiasm. It took so little to make her happy. He wanted to shower her with flowers and gifts. But he didn't know what to give her.

"Have you been to the garden yet?" he asked.

"No, I was waiting for you to show it to me."

He'd admired the stately elms and the rows of boxwood trees before he bought the house. He'd walked down the pathways through shady copses, but he hadn't really enjoyed the garden until he strolled down the lanes with Lise. She admired every colorful bird in the aviary. She crushed leaves from the oregano plants in the herb garden and held them up for him to smell. She almost skipped down the path.

"This is wonderful, Charles," she said, her face glowing. "Even without the gardens, the house is a treasure, but with the vineyard and the gardens…I can't believe how lucky I am."

"I'm the one who's lucky," he said. "To have found the house, to have married you."

She blushed and looked away. He didn't expect her to say anything else, but he wondered how she felt about him. Especially after last night.

For the first time in his life he felt sorry for his brother. Wilhelm had a good job, money, and a house in Rhineland that rivaled the castle, but he didn't have Lise. He could have had her, but he let her go. Of course it was unlucky for Lise that she'd been disinherited, but Charles hoped she would be content in her marriage to him. But was contentment enough for her? He hoped so, because love and passion were not likely to be part of their lives together. A wedding night like theirs was something he'd never forget, but dared not hope it would be repeated.

He reached for her hand. She laced her slender fingers through his. He felt a sense of peace and harmony with her and with nature. This is what it was like to have a home. A home and a wife. Soon they'd have a child too. A boy or a girl. It didn't matter to him. It didn't matter to her.

They paused at a grassy meadow and listened to the twittering of a guinea hen sitting on her nest.

"I know how she feels," Lise said. "Waiting for the birth of her baby." She put one hand protectively against her stomach.

He wanted to put his hand there too, but he refrained. If it was his baby...but it wasn't. He would raise the baby, but he didn't know if he would ever feel that he was the father. Would he always think of it as Wilhelm's child? Would she?

He had to know. "What will we tell the baby about his father?"

She didn't answer for several minutes. Before she spoke they strolled together until she sat down on a wrought-iron bench facing a pond fringed with willows. "The truth, I suppose. When he's old enough to understand. But...you, if you really want to...you will be his father. Or her father. Wilhelm has made it quite clear he wants nothing to do with this baby. I know you said you'd take care of us, me and the baby, but I'm not sure how much you really want to be a father...."

He sat next to her, resting his arm along the back of the bench. "I want to be the best father I can be. I told you once I didn't know how to be a husband. The truth is I haven't had a very good example of a happy marriage or of how to raise a child. But there are books I can study. I can learn."

Lise brushed a tear from her eye. "Thank you, Charles. I can't ask for any more than you've given me…us. I know how you feel. My own parents were hardly good examples. As you know, my father wanted a boy. Of course, he loved us, but I always sensed we were a disappointment to him. And my mother…she didn't really want children at all. The only reason she had any was to try to provide my father with an heir. The whole thing was a mess. Mother took off, father was determined to produce a son. If it hadn't been for Nanny, I don't know what we would have done. If anyone needs to learn to be a parent, it's me."

They sat in silence for a long while watching a pair of swans glide across the pond.

"They mate for life, you know," Charles said. "I admire that."

"So do I," she said. No matter what happens, she thought, we will stay together. She knew she couldn't afford to go through another divorce. She knew Charles would never put her through one, no matter what happened. She would never be able to repay him for what he'd done for her. She was greedy if she asked for more than that.

But that night as she lay alone in her bed in the pale pink silk negligee her sisters had picked out and packed in her bag before the wedding, she knew that there *was* more she could ask for. She could ask for a husband to make love to her at night. She was angry with herself for even thinking it. After all he'd done for her. She should be grateful. She was grateful. But what a waste all those filmy, slinky, formfitting slips and nightgowns and teddies and panties were.

She sighed and picked up Princess Gabrielle's small, leather-bound diary Charles had given her to read. The first few pages were written neatly in pale blue ink in her fine penmanship. They told of her engagement to a Greek prince, an admiral in the navy who was some twenty years older than her. She wrote of parties and gowns and her forthcoming royal wedding to be held in the cathedral of Rhineland, but in between the lines Lise recognized how unhappy she was. She never wrote of love, only of duty.

Lise knew exactly how she felt, engaged to a man selected for her by her father for political and financial reasons. As the days grew short before the royal wedding, Gabrielle seemed more and more distraught. Her diary entries were incomplete sentences. She mentioned a man with only one initial—F. Lise thought it had to be Frederic.

She talked of sitting for a portrait in her wedding gown. Of trying to sit still, but fidgeting as the wedding date grew closer. She mentioned commissioning the artist to duplicate the picture on a small porcelain plaque, but she didn't want her parents to know about it. She had to find a way to pay the artist. Lise sat up in bed. She had seen a collection of porcelain plaques in the museum. How she would love to see this one. Or the portrait itself.

Without thinking, she got out of bed wearing only her nightgown and went to Charles's bedroom.

"Do you know anything about a plaque?" she asked. He turned to look at her from where he was seated at his desk wearing well-pressed blue jeans and nothing else.

He stood and looked at her. "What plaque?" he asked.

She'd never seen him in casual clothes before. She'd seen him in suits and in his wedding tuxedo and she'd seen him without any clothes, but seeing him in snug Levis made her stomach do a series of flip-flops. Suddenly she was intensely aware of his broad shoulders and his washboard stomach. Her eyes drifted downward to the apex of his well-fitting jeans. Then, aware of what she was looking at and what she was thinking, she forgot what she'd come in there for.

"What is it?" he asked.

"I…nothing. It's just…I haven't seen you in casual clothes before. Only suits and…I didn't even know you had any blue jeans." Or that you filled them out so well.

He gave her a half smile. "I guess there are many things we don't know about each other. For instance, I prefer casual clothes. I bought these jeans in California. But my job requires I look the part of a successful businessman so I only wear them at home. I wasn't expecting any guests. If I'd known you were coming I'd at least have put on a shirt."

"Oh, no, don't do that," she said. If he did, she'd be deprived of seeing his bare chest. Heaven only knew when she'd have another chance. "I'm sorry, I shouldn't have barged in like that."

"Lise, you can barge in any time you want. I don't consider you a guest. This is your house now. Our house. And I'm your husband."

"Yes, I know, but…" But why didn't he act like a husband and take her to bed right now? Why couldn't he see that was the real reason she was here? Not about a plaque, not about anything but him and her.

"Did you say something about a plaque?" he asked when she didn't finish her sentence. Now it was his turn to look her over. She'd been so excited she'd forgotten what she was wearing, or not wearing. Her nightgown came with a matching pink silk peignoir, thanks to her sisters, but she was so eager to find out about the princess's portraits—at least that was what she'd told herself—she hadn't taken the time to slip into it. She knew that was just an excuse, for she had really come to his room for another purpose altogether.

She felt his gaze linger on her breasts, which made them swell even larger than they were. They felt so heavy she longed to feel his hands cup them, hold them, caress them. But all he did was look. Couldn't he tell how much she wanted him to cross the room and take her nightgown off and make love to her the way he'd done last night? Her whole body ached with need. She needed him. She needed him now.

What was wrong with her? Last night was an anomaly. He had not married her because he loved her or couldn't keep his hands off her. He had married her to make amends for the past. The sooner she got that through her head the happier she'd be with her fate.

"Yes," she said, frantically gathering her thoughts. "A plaque. It's in the diary Gabrielle was engaged to someone she didn't love. A marriage arranged by her family. She asked the artist who was doing her portrait to duplicate the portrait on a porcelain plaque. Hand-painted plaques were all the rage in those days, so that's not unusual. What's strange is that she wanted it kept a secret. I wonder if she planned to give it to Frederic."

A cool breeze blew in the window of Charles's bedroom, the same breeze had cooled her feverish skin last night. Tonight she shivered.

"Sit down," Charles said. "Let me get you a robe."

She sat on the edge of his bed and he put his robe over her shoulders. His broad fingers grazed her bare shoulders and she shivered again.

"So you're finding the diary interesting?" he asked, moving back to lean against his dresser, still halfdressed, still barefoot, still so sexy she could barely keep her mind on the princess's mysterious picture or keep her eyes off his jeans.

"Yes, oh yes. It's fascinating. I just wondered if you'd ever seen the portrait or the plaque?"

"The portrait is in the portrait gallery back in Rhineland.

I've sent for it. I doubt anyone will miss it. Only grand-father and I really ever appreciated the paintings. As for a plaque, I don't believe I've ever seen one. But if she gave it to Frederic, maybe we can track it down,'' he suggested. ''It must be here in St. Michel, unless he took it with him on his battles.''

''I intend to look for it just as soon as I can. I'd planned to go to the palace tomorrow anyway. There are trunks and trunks full of what the queen calls 'these old relics.' I can hardly wait to see if I can find the plaque or anything else that will shed light on Frederic and Gabrielle.'' She clasped her hands together. Now that she was back in his bedroom, she didn't want to leave. But she couldn't think of any reason to prolong this nighttime visit. If he wanted her to stay, he'd surely say or do something. But he didn't. He just looked at her. If there was desire in his gaze she couldn't tell in the dim light from his desk lamp. She told herself to get up and go.

''Are you working on something?'' she asked with a glance at his desk.

''Yes, the reception to celebrate a new vintage we're producing. It will be held here next week.''

''Here? Next week? But Charles...''

''I'm sorry I completely forgot to tell you. With the wed-ding, I almost forgot about it myself. Until my secretary reminded me. Don't worry. It's being catered. The servants are prepared. All you have to do is to show up looking beautiful.''

''Beautiful? Charles, I'm three months pregnant.''

''And you are more beautiful now than ever.'' He gave her an unmistakably admiring glance that made her cheeks redden.

''But I'll have to have a new dress.''

''Call a dressmaker.''

"That gets expensive," she cautioned.

"Money is not a problem," he said. "The wine business is flourishing. The move to St. Michel was a good idea in more ways than one. Have the dressmaker make you a whole new wardrobe for your pregnancy." He stuffed his hands into his back pockets, straining the fabric and outlining his masculinity.

"All right," she said tearing her eyes away from where she shouldn't be looking. She stood up. She really had to go back to her own bedroom. If she stayed any longer, he'd begin to wonder what was wrong with her. What *was* wrong with her? She was behaving like a lovesick guinea hen sitting on an egg. She was experiencing pure and un- adulterated lust for the first time in her life. The irony was, she was lusting after her own husband. Was this why she couldn't concentrate on her work, her house and her new role as hostess? She had a husband who was kind and gen- erous. Surely she didn't need him to be a lover too.

The robe slipped off her shoulders onto the floor. He crossed the floor and picked it up and put it back on her shoulders. His face was so close she could look deep into his eyes. She was looking for something, a sign that he felt something for her besides care and consideration and con- cern for her welfare. But his gaze was deliberately blank and told her nothing.

"Good night, Charles," she said and went back to her bedroom. Her feet were as heavy as lead as she shuffled out in her pink satin mules. She might as well be wearing a granny gown for all her husband noticed.

When she got back into bed she couldn't do anything but think about him. She'd been fascinated by the diary, but it lay open to the page she'd already read. She should reach for the pad of paper on her nightstand and sketch out a dress for the dressmaker. She should turn off her light and close her eyes. She did none of these things. She lay there staring at the wall, not seeing the mural painted there long ago, depicting a landscape. All she saw was Charles's face, his broad chest with the dark hair tapering down below his jeans. Her body was suffused with heat, wishing, wondering—

There was a knock on her bedroom door. She froze. Had he read her mind? Was he feeling the same frustration as she was? Had he come to seduce her? She let one strap fall carelessly over her shoulder. She ran her hand through her hair, hoping for a tousled, sexy look.

"Come in," she called.

"I forgot one thing," he said.

She leaned forward and knocked the diary to the floor. "Yes?"

"I didn't give you the guest list."

"Oh." Her heart fell. Her shoulders sagged. She felt like a balloon that had just been punctured. She readjusted her strap. "Just put it on the bureau."

"Is there anything I can get you?" he asked. "A glass of milk or a vitamin pill?"

She shook her head and tried to hide her disappointment. She didn't need a glass of milk or a vitamin pill. She needed her husband to make love to her. If it ruined their budding friendship, it was worth it. If it made things awkward, so be it. She'd trade his respect and consideration for another night of passion. But that was not her choice to make. Respect, consideration, milk and vitamins. That was what he was offering. She had no choice. It ought to be enough. He left the list, said good-night and left her room.

Back at the desk in his room, Charles sat staring at the contents of his briefcase without seeing them. He had work to do. The wine business was booming, as he'd told Lise, but it meant more work for him. He'd taken the afternoon off, but the work was still there, lying in front of him. It was work that he was interested in, work that he was good at, work that he loved. But he couldn't do it. Couldn't think about wine when his wife was in the next room wearing the sexiest nightgown he'd ever seen. A nightgown with straps that begged him to put his thumbs under them and let the garment fall from her body. She had skin that begged to be stroked, a body that begged to be kissed from head to toe while spread out beneath him on his sheets.

But he didn't dare risk spoiling a beautiful relationship. For all he knew she was still mourning the loss of Wilhelm. She'd never said anything bad about him even after what he'd done to her. It wasn't his place to bad-mouth his brother. If Lise wanted him to make love to her as he'd done last night, she'd give some indication. For one crazy moment when she'd come to his room in that nightgown that clung to her breasts, brushing against her budding nipples and her rounded hips, he'd thought that was why she was there.

Then he found out it was about the diary and a painting. He couldn't even remember the details. He was having trouble paying attention with her in his room. He'd had to clench his hands together to keep from framing her face in his hands, looking deep into her eyes and asking the questions that were constantly on his mind.

Do you want me? Could you love me? Will you ever make love to me again?

If he did, he might scare her off forever. She was so fragile, he didn't want to upset her in any way. Not now, not when she was pregnant. Finally he gave up and closed his briefcase and paced back and forth in front of his window. He'd thought that one night with Lise would be enough to get her out from under his skin. He'd always thought that wanting her the way he did was a reaction to the fact that his brother had seen her first. Now, he realized it went deeper than that. He was getting to know her, to know what she liked, and to discover what she wanted. What he really wanted to know was—did she want him?

Chapter Six

The next day Lise went to the palace in a chauffeured car that Charles insisted she use. He said he'd buy her a car after the baby came, but now he felt better knowing she wasn't alone in case something happened. She appreciated his concern, but she longed to be independent again.

As usual, she entered the palace by the servants' entrance and went straight to the kitchen where the cooks made her sit down and drink tea and eat buttery almond cakes.

"She's looking a little peaked," Blanche said, refilling Lise's cup. "We'd better pack up some goodies for her to take home. Who's cooking for you?"

"Her name is Marceline," Lise said. "She's really very good. But not as good as you all."

The three women in white starched aprons beamed at her praise.

"What's it like being married to a Rhinelander?" Genevieve asked, forgetting that Lise had been married to one before.

"Very nice," Lise said primly.

"I take it he's not one of those that's trying to take us over," Genevieve said.

"No, of course not," Lise said. "Who's trying to take us over?"

"Nobody," Lucette said. "She's talking off the top of her head."

"I'm not either," Genevieve said indignantly. "Don't think I don't keep my ears open when I'm upstairs. Maybe the princess better hear it from us than someone else."

"I don't hear anything," Lise said. "That's why I'm here, to find out what's going on."

Genevieve's eyes widened and she leaned down to whisper into Lise's ear. "They say there's trouble brewing in Rhineland. Not everyone, mind you, just one group talking about making their move. Just you stay away from there, and tell your husband the same."

"Surely you don't think it's dangerous?" Lise said.

"I'm just saying…" Genevieve said.

"Just saying nonsense," Lucette continued. "Now how about a slice of brioche hot out of the oven?"

Lise couldn't say no. She let the cooks fuss over her and feed her and gossip and regale her with stories of their own pregnancies and deliveries until she finally excused herself and climbed up to the attic, which was really a storeroom under the eaves on the top floor. She opened the high narrow windows to let in some fresh air and looked out on the turrets and an ancient gargoyle that she and her sisters had always thought looked like their grandmother. They'd played up here, dragging dresses and shawls and furs out of the trunks and teetering around in the borrowed high-heeled boots and shoes.

If they'd ever been caught, there would have been the devil to pay, Lise thought. Some of the clothes had no doubt been worn by revered royal ancestors. And could be worn again if tight corsets and décolletage ever came back into style. But they'd been careful and as quiet as three little girls could be and their clandestine activities had remained their secret. She hadn't been back up here in years. It seemed no one else had either. The dust was now another inch thick at least.

Lise looked around at the crates and boxes and trunks and sighed. She didn't know where to start looking for a plaque that might or might not have been given to Frederic the Bold by a lovelorn princess.

"Frederic," she said softly. "Why did you never marry? Was it because of Gabrielle? Did she give you her heart and then marry someone else? Did she give you a plaque with her picture on it? And if so, where did you put it?"

Her words hung in the dust-filled air. There was no answer. Not from Frederic. There were, however, voices drifting up from the balcony below her. She stepped up onto a wooden crate and poked her head out the window again, but couldn't see anyone. She didn't dare lean out any further without risking losing her balance and bouncing off the railing below and careening to certain death or dismemberment. She could just imagine the headlines in the St. Michel daily newspaper:

> Princess Falls Out of Palace Window
> into Royal Greenery.
>
> Queen regrets accident but disclaims any
> responsibility.
>   "Lise de Bergeron had no business in the attic,"
> she says.

But she did have business there. She was trying to solve a royal mystery. Not that anyone else would care. Besides her and Charles, no one would be interested. That was why Queen Celeste had given her Frederic's portrait. She didn't want it.

The voices below were closer now and clearer.

"Weddings and funerals. That's all we have around here. The oldest one has married again," a high feminine voice said. "The queen must be relieved to have those three girls off her hands. The way the three of them used to prance around as if they were heiresses to the throne when everyone knew they were illegitimate."

Lise winced. She recognized the voice of one of the ladies-in-waiting. Had they really pranced around that way? Had everyone known they were illegitimate when they didn't even know themselves? She'd never thought of herself as an heiress and neither did her sisters.

"The poor queen has enough problems finding an heir for the throne without a divorced, destitute, pregnant princess around."

Lise bit her lip. She hated to be talked about that way. She wondered who was gossiping about her like that?

"Who did she marry?" asked a vaguely familiar voice that belonged to one of the maids.

"Her ex-husband's brother."

"So it's all in the family, is it? How did that happen?"

"He felt sorry for her, of course. Then there was the family honor to uphold, though who could blame his brother for divorcing her once he heard that her parents' marriage was invalid? I don't know who else would have married her. I hope she knows how fortunate she is. Did you see her at the party? She's so aloof, so proud of herself. And for what reason? No money, no title. Yes, she's lucky she found someone to marry her. Poor Charles. He's got his hands full, I can tell you."

Lise closed the window and stepped off the crate. She'd heard enough. She didn't want to hear any more and she didn't want to know who was talking about her like that. She wished she'd never listened to their conversation. It only confirmed what she thought in her darkest moments. Charles had only married her because he felt sorry for her.

Why that should make her feel queasy and sick to her stomach she didn't know. She knew he cared about her. She knew he wanted to take care of her and the baby. Surely she didn't believe he could ever love her. Why should he? She was damaged goods. It was time for her to give up any romantic fantasies about him desiring her for herself or wanting to make her his wife in every sense of the word. She'd better get used to sleeping alone in her trousseau finery, because no amount of flirtation, of seduction was going to change the way he felt about her. Yes, she was lucky he'd married her. They were right about that, whoever they were.

She sat in the middle of the attic floor for a long time, listlessly sorting through piles of men's clothing, trying to forget what she'd just heard. She uncovered breeches, tights, gloves, capes, scarves and shoes. They were the right era for Frederic the Bold, she could tell because she'd studied fashions of the seventeenth, eighteenth and nineteenth centuries and had a collection of books she could refer to if she couldn't place a certain cravat or a pair of knickers. The question was, how would she be able to tell if an item had actually belonged to Frederic? Would his name be on the label? Hardly.

Then she found a white silk scarf, fringed and yellowed with age, with a large letter F embroidered on it. She pressed the warm silk to her cheek. The excitement of finding something that might have been his almost made her forget the disturbing conversation she'd overheard.

She chastised herself for being so self-centered. She told herself the people gossiping about her were just jealous, underpaid servants. But in her heart she knew what they said was true. Charles had only married her out of pity. Nothing she could do would change that. She was fortunate he had a good heart. That in itself was a rare commodity these days. Even better, he was committed to raising her child with her. Together they would provide a good, loving home.

Suddenly she was terribly tired. So tired she had to leave the trunk open in the middle of the floor and stumble down the narrow staircase. Outside at the gate, Charles's driver was waiting for her in the comfort of the air-conditioned car. She leaned back against the leather seat and closed her eyes until they arrived at the château.

She was so tired she could barely stay awake during dinner. Charles watched her lack of interest in the excellent *pommes frites* the cook had prepared with the steak and sauce for dinner with alarm.

"What have you been doing today?" he asked. "You're not supposed to get overtired."

"I went to the palace and looked through some old trunks. Nothing that strenuous," she said. "I don't know what's wrong with me." But she knew. She knew her fatigue was more psychological than physical. "I did find one thing, an old scarf with the initial F on it. Of course I can't be sure it's Frederic's, but I was happy to find it anyway."

"Did you see anyone while you were there?" he asked, peeling a peach for her and cutting it in quarters.

"My old friends, the cooks. They fussed and fidgeted over me and hinted at some gossip coming from Rhineland."

"The old stories of factions plotting against St. Michel?" he asked. "I can't believe there's anything to them."

"Neither can I," she said, gratefully accepting the peach. It was easier for fruit to slide down her throat than an entrecôte, however delicious the bordelaise sauce that covered it. "But you know how it is, gossip is rife within the walls of the palace." If only that were really all it was that she'd heard in the attic, harmless gossip. But as so often is the case, there was truth at the heart of the gossip. And the truth hurt.

"Within and without," he commented. "Maybe you ought to take some time off," he said. "Stay home and enjoy the gardens. Invite your sisters to lunch or tea. And if you're not up to hosting the reception next week, I can postpone it or move it to another venue."

"Oh, no, you mustn't even think it. I'm looking forward to showing off the house. This place is meant for parties and receptions."

"And for just us, just the family too. I don't want us to live in a fishbowl," Charles said. "I want to fill the house and gardens with our friends and relatives and with the voices and activities of our children. Can't you see them running down the paths and fishing in the river and picking grapes? I can." He had a faraway look on his face, and she knew he was visualizing the scene. She could see how much the house and his family meant to him.

That didn't mean he loved his wife or ever would, it just meant that who she was wasn't all that important to him. It was the whole package. It was the wife and the house and the children he longed for. A wife and house and children that would make up for his own unhappy childhood, his dysfunctional parents and his overbearing brother.

Lise blinked and realized he'd said, "our children." But how could they have more than one child unless…? Was that a slip of the tongue or did Charles foresee a time when they'd create more children, him and her? He went on eating as if nothing had happened. But it had. He'd said *children*. Not *child—children*. He'd said *them*.

"Yes, it's a wonderful place for children," she agreed. She bit her tongue to keep from asking what he'd meant. To keep from asking how many children he planned on having, how many he pictured fishing in the river and racing down the garden paths. But she was afraid he'd take it back, say he'd misspoken. That he hadn't meant it at all. She couldn't bear it if he did. She'd had her illusions destroyed once today. She couldn't risk having all her hopes destroyed as well.

"If you'll excuse me, Charles," she said, setting her napkin down, "I'll retire to my room. I guess you're right. I overdid it today. I'll take it easy tomorrow, though, you know, I'd give anything to find that plaque. Maybe the diary will yield a clue if I keep reading."

He walked up the stairs with her and said good-night to her at her bedroom door. His expression was solemn and there were worry lines in his forehead. Before she went in, he kissed her on the cheek. She should have been reassured, she should have been happy. She should have been downright ecstatic that she had the kind of husband whose hopes and dreams centered around home and family. Who could care less about her royal heritage.

She had the distinct feeling that if Wilhelm had married the scullery maid and gotten her pregnant and then divorced her for whatever reason, Charles would have come and asked for her hand just as he'd done for Lise's. He was that honorable.

Charles went to his room and changed into his casual clothes. He sat at his desk in his jeans, hoping against hope that she'd burst in on him again, excited about something she'd read in the diary. Or come in for any reason at all. As long as she wore her satin gown. He'd never seen anything as lovely as she was last night. He felt his temperature rise just thinking about how her lush body looked covered only by a few yards of satin. He'd hated to let her leave his room. He'd wanted to follow her back to her room. He had followed her but stopped before he overstepped the boundaries she'd set up. He would have known if she'd wanted him to stay. She didn't.

He was worried about Lise tonight. She looked tired and, even worse, she looked sad. Her lovely blue eyes had shadows under them and her face was pale. When they went to the doctor, he'd ask him what he could do for her. In the meantime he would wait for her to make the next move.

He opened his portable computer and went to the Internet. He was searching for something to give her for a wedding present. Something special. Something he knew she wanted. He started by searching *antiques*. Then he narrowed his search. If he could find what he was looking for, if he could bridge the gap between Frederic and Gabrielle, it might bridge the gap between Lise and himself. He certainly didn't know how to do it on his own.

A week later, Charles accompanied Lise to the doctor, whose office was located in a modern building near the hospital. Charles was shocked to see how young the doctor looked. He'd expected to see an old, fatherly figure in a white jacket with a stethoscope hanging around his neck. Dr. Duverger appeared to be about his own age, and although he wore the traditional white jacket, under it were a casual shirt, khaki pants and running shoes. But if Charles had any doubts as to his competence, they were soon dispelled by the man's confident manner and sensible advice.

"Always glad to meet the father," Dr. Duverger said, shaking Charles's hand with a firm grip. "It's never to soon for you to get involved."

Charles didn't know what Lise had told the doctor about who the baby's father was, but from now on he wanted the whole world to know it was him. He was proud to take over this role. Proud to be the father-to-be of Lise's baby. The biological father was out of the picture. He was irrelevant and unnecessary. The sooner he was totally forgotten, the better.

"Your wife has expressed interest in our childbirth classes," the doctor continued. "Can I assume you'll be attending with her and will be available to assist her in the delivery of your baby?"

He caught Lise's eye. She looked anxious as if she didn't know how he'd feel about that. Some men were probably squeamish about witnessing the birth of their child.

"Of course," he said. "I want to be there every step of the way."

Lise smiled. The doctor made notes on her chart.

"Now, what about nutrition. Are you eating a well-balanced diet?" the doctor asked.

"I haven't been hungry lately," Lise admitted.

"That's normal for the first trimester. But your appetite should pick up now that you're in your fourth month. Get plenty of calcium and iron."

Lise slanted a glance at Charles, no doubt remembering his advice, his insistence that she eat the spinach and the cheese he'd brought her. She reached for his hand and his heart banged against his ribs. At times like this he felt so close to her and he sensed she felt the same.

"Any headaches, altered vision, abdominal pain, vomiting?" the doctor asked.

Charles gripped her hand tightly. She shook her head and he breathed a sigh of relief. Surely she'd tell him if she had any of these symptoms, but he couldn't be sure of that. Sometimes he thought she kept too much to herself. Take

the other day when she'd come home from the palace looking pale and upset and gone to bed early. He knew something had upset her. He didn't know if it was physical or
emotional. She seemed to have improved since that day,
but not as much as he'd have liked. A sparkle was gone
from her eyes and a sadness crept into her voice no matter
what he did to cheer her up. He'd brought flowers, candy
and sent his secretary out for fancy imported soaps and
lotions. He knew she was pleased by the gifts, but underneath there was a deep-seated melancholy buried beneath
her calm exterior and he couldn't get to the cause nor could
he find a cure.

"What about insomnia? Any trouble sleeping?"

Lise shook her head but she didn't look at him or the
doctor. He wondered if she was telling the truth and if not,
why not?

"If you do have any sudden pain or bleeding," the doctor said, "call the hospital at any time of night or day. They
will page me. Now, if you'll go into the examining room,
we'll do a checkup and then we'll have your husband come
in for a few minutes."

Charles paced back and forth in the waiting room. What
if they found out she was anemic, or the baby was upside
down or… This was no time to worry. And if he did worry,
he must not let Lise know. But how could he help it? The
two of them, Lise and the baby, were his family. His first
family, the parents who'd raised him and his brother who'd
tormented him were fading into the background and the
memories of the past could no longer haunt him. He had
Lise and the baby now. He'd been given a second chance
at having the family he'd always wanted. He'd meant it
when he told her he was looking forward to their children
running through the gardens, hearing their laughter waft
toward the château.

Children. Did Lise want more children? He would have to wait and see. He couldn't push her into sharing his bed with him. After their wedding night she'd given no indication she wanted more of the same. Obviously it hadn't meant as much to her as it had to him. Even if they never made love again, he thought he'd got the best of the bargain. He'd got her.

The nurse beckoned him to go into the examining room. Lise was flat on her back on the table covered with a blue sheet. She looked small and helpless, but she gave a little smile when she saw him.

"Good," the doctor said with a welcoming smile for Charles. "Just in time to hear your baby's heartbeat." He pulled back the sheet to expose Lise's gently curved stomach and laid the sensor of the Doppler machine over her taut skin. The booming sound of a rapid heartbeat filled the small room thanks to the amplifier. Charles stared at the machine, then at the doctor, then his gaze found Lise's.

It was real. Their baby was alive and well. He felt tears sting the back of his eyes and he fought off the urge to cry. He hadn't cried since he was five years old and his brother had broken a valuable vase and blamed it on him. Then the tears were of rage and fury. Today his tears sprang from somewhere deep within him, so deep he felt shaken. What shook him even more was that Lise's eyes were glistening. He couldn't tear his gaze from hers. He stood transfixed for seconds, maybe minutes while the sounds of their baby's heart filled the air.

Something passed between them during that time. He didn't know what to call it, a kind of understanding, an agreement or a pact. He wasn't sure what it meant but he felt bound to her in a way he never had before. Not at their engagement or at their wedding or even on their wedding night. He went to stand next to her and put his cool hand on her warm forehead.

The doctor turned off the machine and the room was suddenly still. "What do you think of your son or daughter?" the doctor asked Charles.

Charles was so choked up he couldn't speak.

"Everything seems to be in order," the doctor continued without waiting for an answer. "I'll see you both next month. In the meantime your wife needs to increase her calcium and iron, as I mentioned earlier. I've given her some pills to take, but keep an eye on her diet."

"He does that," Lise said, sitting up on the table. "He's always after me to eat something healthy."

"You're very fortunate to have such an attentive husband," the doctor said.

Lise nodded. On the way back to the car she asked Charles if he really wanted to be present for the birth.

"Of course I do. I've been reading in my book about the role of the coach, that's me, in our case."

"What have you learned?" she asked.

"A lot. I'm to pack your bag weeks ahead of your delivery date. Use baking soda for massaging your muscles, take ice chips for you to chew on during labor. Time your contractions. I've ordered a stopwatch."

"You're amazing," she said, turning in her seat belt to gaze at him with admiration. "You've read the book and you're taking the class with me. What's left for me to do?"

"Just relax and enjoy yourself," he said. "Let me and the doctor take care of the details."

"Relax and enjoy myself. Apparently you haven't been talking to the cooks at the palace. They've got stories that would curl your hair."

He reached over and took a strand of her smooth straight hair between his fingers. "Don't listen to them," he said.

"Let the cooks stick to their cooking. And you stick to preparing for one of the great moments of your life."

"By taking those vitamin pills he gave me."

"That and relaxing. I don't want you to tire yourself or worry about anything. If something's bothering you I will deal with it. But I can't deal with it if I don't know what it is."

Just a glance at his stern profile told her how serious he was.

She didn't know what to say. She couldn't very well tell him that she was worried he'd only married her out of pity. That was something he couldn't deal with. He was too honest to deny it and she'd see right through him if he did. She'd have to be more careful about letting him see she was worried. He was much too perceptive.

"I'm not worried," she said. "Not now that I have you." It was true. She'd imagined she could go through this pregnancy by herself. She'd even looked forward to it, because the alternative was to have Wilhelm with her. But now she had Charles and she knew she had a partner she could count on for support when she needed it. And she would need it. She knew that now.

"When I heard the baby's heartbeat…" she said, "I thought it was a miracle. It was like seeing into the future. Our baby. Alive and well."

Our baby. The words struck a chord in his heart. He was going to have a baby. In less than six months he'd be holding their baby in his arms.

"Have you thought about what you'll name it?" he asked.

"Have you thought about what *we'll* name it?" she asked.

"What about Frederic if it's a boy?"

"And if it's a girl?"

He smiled. "You choose."

She returned his smile. If it was a girl, they both knew what they would name her.

Chapter Seven

The night of the wine-tasting party Lise was wearing a new black velvet dress with a long skirt and a red chiffon scarf to toss around her neck. She was pleased with the style she'd designed herself and with the way the dressmaker had followed her drawings, making a drawstring waist she could expand as she needed it. She had to ask Charles to help her with her zipper. She went to his room not knowing if she should knock or not. With Wilhelm there had been no question. She always knocked and hoped he wasn't there.

But with Charles...it almost seemed like an insult to knock on his door. She hadn't knocked that night he was wearing his jeans and nothing else. He'd looked pleased to see her. And she was more than pleased to see him only half-dressed. The memory still made her whole body heat up with the desire for her husband to make love to her again.

But nothing she did seemed to work. No amount of dreaming about it or scheming to make it happen. Just as she'd get up her nerve to go to see him at night in one of her new nightgowns, the memory of that day at the palace when she'd overheard that fateful conversation came rushing back and filled her with uncertainty and melancholy and caused her to stay in her own bed, tossing and turning.

After reading through Charles's book on pregnancy, she realized her mood swings were normal and due to hormonal changes. But there was nothing normal about the physical side of their marriage. Of course, what did she know about normal? She'd been married twice and each time there was something wrong. She knew she wasn't enjoying an ordinary conjugal life because her sisters were given to making remarks like:

"I'll bet Charles loved seeing you in the white lace gown we got you."

"Or did he prefer seeing you out of it?"

"You're looking tired, Lise, not getting much sleep? Too busy doing other things in your beautiful boudoir?"

"When are you going on your honeymoon, Lise, or is every day a honeymoon at the château?"

"Etienne went to see Charles, but they said he'd left for the day. At noon? Can't he wait until night to see you?"

Lise didn't know how to answer these questions so she merely smiled enigmatically and let her sisters' imaginations continue to work overtime—which only fueled their speculations that she and Charles were engaged in sexual activities night and day. If only half of it were true.

She stood in Charles's bedroom with her back to him as he zipped her dress.

"You look beautiful tonight," he said huskily, and kissed the back of her neck. Shivers ran up and down her spine. She wished he'd unzip her dress and then they'd skip the party and make mad passionate love in his room all night. But he didn't.

"Thanks to the dressmaker," she said, proud of how even her voice was. "She's doing marvels."

"It's not the dress," he said, his breath warm against her skin. "It's you. You look beautiful in anything you wear."

Her knees went weak. If he got any closer, if he nibbled on her ear, she wouldn't be able to support herself. She'd be on the floor in a puddle.

If she had the strength, or the nerve she'd ask, *What about when I'm not wearing anything?* But she didn't.

"I have a surprise for you," he said. "It's downstairs."

She turned to face him. She had to say something, anything, before they went downstairs. She had to know how he felt about her, and why he didn't make love to her. She was prepared for the worst but hoped at least for some clue into what he was thinking.

"Charles..." she said, her voice trembling.

There was a loud knock on the door. It was Ariane.

"Hello, you two. Your guests are here. Come on out."

Lise sighed. She might never get up her nerve again. "All right, we're coming." Lise opened the door and hugged her sister.

"I hope I'm not interrupting anything," Ariane said, with a knowing smile.

"Not at all. Charles was just helping me get dressed," she said. She knew that ought to please her sister. She could take that any way she wanted.

"This is no time for any hanky-panky," Ariane said, wagging her finger at her sister.

"Are there really guests here already?" Lise asked.

"Just Etienne and I. But we helped ourselves to some champagne. I must say, Charles, it's delicious," she said, holding her glass up. "You won't have any trouble marketing it."

"Glad you like it," he said.

Lise shot a quick look at him, wondering if he guessed that her sister had interrupted an important moment. Or a moment that could have been important if he'd only told her what, if anything, was wrong. Maybe Charles didn't want to talk about it. Maybe he was completely happy with their situation. He certainly looked happy. He acted happy. Maybe she was the only one with unreasonable expectations. Yes, that was probably true. She'd better count her blessings and stop wanting more than she had.

By the time they got downstairs and greeted Etienne, other guests had started arriving. Charles took them on a tour of the château. Lise could hear the pride in his voice as he described various pieces of Louis XVI furniture and architectural details such as the hand-carved molding around the doors that led to the garden. He introduced her to many people she didn't know, businessmen from Rhineland and St. Michel. She could hear the same pride in his voice when he said, *This is my wife, Lise.*

She smiled and shook hands or kissed some old friends on both cheeks. It made her happy to see Charles in his element. Everyone admired his house, his fine wines and, she hoped, his wife too. The way he beamed at her from across the room told her he was pleased with his party and with her.

"Have you had something to eat?" he asked a while later, coming up to her with a full plate.

"Not yet," she said. The food looked wonderful. He'd spared no expense, hiring the best caterer in St. Michel. She hadn't realized how hungry she was until she saw the plate in his hands.

"This is for you. Come into the library with me. That's where the surprise is. You've been on your feet all evening."

"I don't mind," she said. "It's a wonderful party. I can say that because you planned the whole thing. I feel as though I'm a guest."

"I'm glad," he said simply. "I was worried you'd get too tired." He carried her food in one hand and rested the other on the small of her back as they walked to the library where he opened the double doors, which had been closed all evening. The portrait of Frederic hung above the fireplace. Next to it Charles had hung the portrait of the lovely Princess Gabrielle.

Lise stood transfixed. "Oh, Charles," she said and kissed him on the cheek. "You found her."

Lise stared at the face of his beautiful ancestor. She had cascades of dark curls falling over her shoulders, fastened by a pink ribbon. Her dress was made of pink silk, so soft and shiny Lise wanted to reach out and touch it. It was low-cut with short sleeves revealing creamy skin. But it was her eyes that claimed Lise's attention. They were dark and deep-set and held depths of sadness Lise could only wonder at. Her small rosebud mouth was set in a firm line as if she was holding back her feelings and her protests. Lise could almost hear her begging her father not to force her to marry against her wishes. What was wrong with Frederic anyway?

"I'm still looking for the porcelain," he said. "I haven't given up. But in the meantime, they're back together again."

David Duval, one of Charles's partners, came up behind them. "Who are these handsome people?" he asked Lise and Charles. "I don't know her, but I have a strange feeling I've seen him before."

"Not likely," Charles said. "He died some two hundred years ago. He's one of my wife's ancestors, Frederic the Bold. Quite a warrior in his day."

And quite a lover, Lise thought.

"I've seen him before. It's those eyes, so sad and yet so penetrating. I have seen him somewhere and I don't mean in person. I've seen his picture. I couldn't forget a face like that. Was he ever in Rhineland?"

"Good question," Charles said. "We have reason to believe he was madly in love with my ancestor, the lovely Princess Gabrielle who's hanging next to him."

"I don't blame him," David said. "She's a beauty." He stood staring at the two paintings for a long moment. "Now I know where I've seen him. It was at a small shop in Rhineland that specializes in antiques. I was looking for a snuff box for my mother. She collects them."

"There was a painting of Frederic in the store?" Lise asked, amazed.

"Just a small one, not very well done, almost amateurish in technique, but interesting nonetheless. Not good enough to hang in the museum, not at all like this one, but rather charming. I don't know where it came from or how much they wanted for it, but I could swear it's the same man," he said. "It's something about the eyes."

Lise and Charles looked at one another. Was he thinking what she was thinking? Was it possible Gabrielle had painted it herself, from memory, to remember her lost love? But what had happened to it when she married someone else? Or did she marry someone else? Where had it been all these years? Wherever it had been, whoever had had it, however much it cost, she had to have it.

"Do you have the name of the shop?" Charles asked his partner. "My wife would like to have the painting. We're starting our own collection with these portraits. Some day we'll have our own gallery. Then we'll take our children through it and tell them stories of their ancestors the way my grandfather did with me."

Lise blinked back a tear. There she went again, getting emotional over the thought of having more children with Charles and bringing them up together.

"I don't know the name," David said. "But I can tell you where it is, on a small back street behind the cathedral. You can't miss it. The man that owns it must be at least one hundred years old. He located several snuff boxes for me and I selected one. He knows his business, no doubt about that. I'm surprised you've never been there."

After David drew them a map of the location of the store, he wandered off and they were left alone for a few moments, Charles asked Lise if she would like to go back to Rhineland with him to look for the painting. He was afraid it would bring back unhappy memories of her life there with his brother at the palace, but he knew she wanted the painting.

She hesitated a moment. "Yes, let's go," she said. "I only wish Ariane was there, but they're traveling. When I left I said I'd never go back, but we wouldn't stay long, would we?" she asked anxiously.

"Only overnight. We could drive across the border and I wouldn't tell my parents we were there. We could stay in a hotel under a different name." The more he thought about it the better he liked the idea. He and Lise on a trip together. He liked the whole clandestine nature of it. The secrecy. The goal of tracking down a lost painting. "Of course, we may not find it. Someone else may have bought it or we'll find it isn't Frederic at all. Was there anything in the diary about Gabrielle doing a painting of anyone?" he asked.

"Not that I've read. But in those days every well-bred woman knew how to paint and draw and play the piano-forte. So I wouldn't be surprised if she'd painted it. The problem I have is that part of her diary is in some language

I don't know. It's a kind of shorthand. Maybe she was afraid someone would find it and find out she didn't want to marry the prince she was betrothed to. Then at the end there are pages ripped out. I was very disappointed. Finding a painting of him she'd actually painted for herself or whoever…that would be thrilling.''

"As thrilling as finding the plaque she supposedly gave him?'' he asked.

"Well, no. I still haven't given up on that. I plan to go back to the attic at the palace and continue my search.''

Lise went off to talk to her sister and Charles went to the garden for a breath of fresh air. The pathways were illuminated by overhead lights in the trees, turning the whole place into a fairyland. He strolled out to find a quiet spot behind a hedge of oleander.

On the other side of the bushes he heard voices. He didn't recognize them, but that wasn't surprising. He'd invited many people he didn't know well—or even at all—just because they were prominent businessmen from St. Michel or Rhineland. Waiters were pouring his company's wines and he'd heard nothing but praise for his latest pinot noir and his vintage burgundy. So far he'd have to say his party was a definite success. The voices behind the bushes became louder and clearer. He wasn't trying to eavesdrop, but he couldn't help hearing them. The man spoke first.

"How well do you know Charles, Guillaume?''

"He's a business acquaintance. Nice place he's got here.''

"Nice wife too. I heard she's pregnant,'' a woman said.

"Already? They just got married.''

"Oh, it's not his. It's his brother's.''

"Where did you hear that?''

"A friend was telling me Wilhelm divorced her because she was disinherited when the palace found out she was illegitimate. She had to find somebody to marry. Charles came along and she snared him just like she did his brother.''

''You mean she married him for his money?''

''What do you think? Can't blame her. What would you do? Pregnant and poor and homeless? Where would you rather live, in a hovel or here in the château? How would you raise a child without support? I guess she looked around and decided if she couldn't have brother number one she'd take what she could get—Charles. He's a good man and they say he's crazy about her, but you can't help feeling he's been taken.''

Charles froze. He was stunned. He didn't know who these two were and he didn't want to know. At the same time he wanted to confront them and make them take back their words. He clenched his hands into fists. How would it look if he made a scene at his own party? A moment later he heard their footsteps crunch on the gravel pathway and they were gone. He let out a huge sigh. They might be gone but their words lingered in his brain until the last guest was gone and he could finally stop circulating and stop smiling.

When he'd seen how tired Lise looked a while ago, he'd sent her upstairs. He went up and knocked on her bedroom door and offered to unzip her dress for her. It was the best excuse he could come up with.

She nodded and turned around. Once unzipped, the dress slid off her body and fell to the floor. She made no effort to stop it or to pick it up. She was wearing a black lace half-bra and matching panties. He put his hands on her shoulders and turned her around slowly to face him. Her eyes were half-closed, either from fatigue or desire, he didn't know which. He wanted so desperately to ask her if she'd only married him for his money. He was afraid he knew the answer, but there was a slim chance she'd deny it.

He knew she hadn't married Wilhelm for his money. She'd married him because her father arranged it. But her father had arranged it because of Wilhelm's money and connections, so it all boiled down to the same thing, didn't it? He didn't know what to think. He only knew that he'd learned nothing new tonight, he'd only had the ugly truth articulated. The best thing he could do was to forget what he'd heard. To pretend he'd never heard it. And to proceed with his life, his life with Lise. He had pledged to support her and care for her. Love, honor and obey. That's what he'd pledged. But how could he love a woman who'd married him because she needed someone? Not him, just someone.

Love was never the problem. He didn't expect her to love him and he didn't expect to love her. Then why did it hurt so much to hear what he already knew? But she hadn't "snared" him. He'd pursued her. She didn't consider him number two. She'd despised Wilhelm as much as he did. At least that's what he thought.

What was the truth? Had he been taken? It wasn't possible. He'd known from the start how she felt about him. Even if he had any doubts, he couldn't ask her. Not now when she was so vulnerable. Not now when he wanted her so badly his whole body ached. It didn't matter what she thought of him, or why she'd married him. It was true, he was crazy about her. If he ever loved anybody it would be Lise, but if he did, his love wouldn't be returned. Because the sad truth was, she'd married him so she could have a father and a home for her child. The sooner he got used to that, the better off he'd be.

It had been a long evening during which he'd played the role of the genial host. Even overhearing a disturbing conversation, he had retained his composure—with great effort. Now at last he could finally relax and play the part he really wanted to play. The role of passionate husband. He'd watched her throughout the evening being the perfect hostess. Now he wanted her to be nothing more than his wife. He knew he couldn't force her to make love to him. He would never do that. He would have to wait for her to make the first move as he'd promised her.

But he couldn't resist circling her breasts with the pads of his thumbs. She gasped. He cupped them with his palms and felt them swell to fill his hands. He touched her nipples with his fingers and sucked in a sharp breath. She stood there with her eyes closed, either in ecstasy or agony. Despite his vows to forget what he'd heard tonight, the words came back again.

She had to find somebody to marry…married him for his money.

No matter how hard he tried to forget them, the words had the effect of a cold rain falling on his head. He dropped his hands and backed out of the room, still staring at her, still wanting her so badly his whole body throbbed.

They went to Rhineland two days later. He told no one except his secretary where he was going and instructed her only to call him on his cell phone if something urgent happened. Even she thought it was a business trip. If all went well, Charles would avoid seeing his parents or anyone else who'd ask questions about his marriage or his brother's divorce.

He'd notified his parents about his marriage. They'd expressed surprise and disbelief. No doubt they couldn't understand why their son would marry the woman their other son had divorced. He knew what their attitude would be. Who would want a princess with no fortune or claim to the throne? Better get rid of her as soon as possible. Which was just what Wilhelm had done. The divorce had caused Lise the pain of rejection, but though she'd never discussed it with him, she had to believe it had also saved her a lifetime of grief through living with his brother. No one knew him as well as Charles did. No one despised him as much as he did, either, for what he'd done to Lise and for what he was and had always been.

"Do you want the air conditioning on?" he asked Lise as she adjusted the front seat of his car so she could recline.

"No, the air smells so sweet." She smiled at him. She looked young and carefree with her hair blowing in the breeze. He smiled back. He felt as young as she looked. It was one of those rare times when no one knew where they were. They were free and carefree as any newlyweds, off on their first trip together. Anything could happen. They might find a painting or a plaque from two lost lovers out of the past or they might find themselves, two lost lovers in the present.

Lise suggested a picnic and Charles agreed. He had a bottle of wine in his trunk, but since Lise couldn't drink alcohol, he'd brought bottled spring water, too. They stopped in a small village and bought cheese and meat at a small shop then followed their noses to a bakery where they bought a baguette. They strolled a little farther to an open-air fruit stand where they selected ripe tomatoes, a melon, juicy strawberries and a kilo of sweet cherries. On the way to the car Lise couldn't wait to sample the cherries and tear off a chunk of the fresh bread.

"I'm glad to see your appetite has improved," he said with an approving glance.

"Improved? I'm ravenous all the time. I'm going to weigh one hundred kilos before this baby comes. Then what will you do?"

"I'll have a special bed made for you of sturdy oak. I'll put in an elevator so you don't have to climb the stairs. I'll buy a draft horse to carry you around the grounds."

She laughed. "I believe you would. You pamper me, Charles."

He loved to hear her laugh. It lifted his spirits. She did it too seldom. Maybe it was his fault. He was too serious. He'd been told more than once in his life to lighten up. Maybe now was a good time to do it. He'd done a pretty good job of putting the unfortunate conversation he'd overheard out of his mind. If he was going to listen to gossip, he was bound to have a life of disappointment. No, he was determined to face the future with hope and optimism.

They drove for a few kilometers until they found a grassy field by the side of a lake. He pulled off the road and carried their supplies along with a blanket he kept in the back of his car. Lise tried to help, but he took the bags out of her hand.

"I'm strong as an ox, Charles. I can at least carry the blanket."

He shook his head. "Most women would be happy to be pampered."

"I'm not most women."

"No, you're not."

"Would you have married me, no matter who I was?" Lise asked, stopping in the shade of a weeping willow at the edge of the lake. Suddenly the answer was very important to her. She thought she knew the answer, but she wanted to hear him say it. She knew he was honest, but she also knew he wouldn't want to hurt her feelings.

He spread the blanket and laid the bags of groceries on it. "Sit down," he said. "I know you're hungry." It was as if he hadn't heard her. Well, that was one way to avoid telling the truth and hurting her feelings. Just ignore her question and pretend she'd never said anything. She wouldn't ask him again. Instead she used his knife to cut the bread and the cheese. She made him a sandwich of meat and cheese and ripe tomatoes and handed it to him.

"Now who's pampering whom?" he asked, taking the sandwich.

"Most men would be happy to be pampered. And don't say you're not most men, Charles. I know that. How many men would marry a pregnant woman with no means of support, with a questionable family tree? Which brings me back to my question. I know why you married me, Charles. I have no illusions. You acted out of honor and responsibility. And I admire that in you. I just wondered if…if…"

"I might ask you the same thing," he said. "I know why you married me. I have no illusions either. You needed a father for your child, a home and a future for both of you. There's nothing wrong with that. In fact I was the one who urged you to consider your needs. Perhaps I forced you into this marriage. I don't know."

There was a long silence broken only by the buzz of bees and the whirring of dragonflies in the distance. Lise gazed at the glassy surface of the lake, broken by tiny ripples. They both had questions. Neither had answers, or if they did, they were reluctant to give them. What could she say? I know you married me out of honor and duty. Maybe it was more pity. I understood it and I thought I'd accepted it. But now I want more. I want love. I want to love and be loved. I want to make love. She swallowed hard and said nothing. Instead she turned her attention to the food and cut some more bread.

They ate in companionable silence, each determined to make the best of their marriage. Each determined not to give anything away, not to hurt the other. Lise decided not to ask any more questions that had no answers. Perhaps

Charles had decided the same. He looked happy enough, his back braced against the smooth bark of the willow tree while he ate cherries and tossed the pits into the tall grass.

He caught her looking at him and he smiled. "We should take more time off," he said. "I don't know when I last had a vacation."

"When I was young, we used to have picnics at the palace," Lise said, slicing the melon. "Not that we were allowed to. We had a governess who was determined to teach us manners. Normally we'd have to sit at our table in the nursery and she'd rap our knuckles if we used the wrong fork. In the summer, when she wasn't there, we'd sneak into the kitchen and grab whatever we could find and take it out to some far corner of the garden, sit on the ground, use no forks whatsoever, eat with our fingers like monkeys and get as dirty as possible. It was heaven." She smiled dreamily.

"So what will you do if your children decide to forego learning manners to picnic in our garden?"

"I'll probably go with them," she said. "Of course the fun of it is to do something that's forbidden. So I guess I'll have to give them a chance to sneak away on their own too." Suddenly she realized the subject of more children had come up again. This time she had to ask and she had to have an answer.

"Charles," she said, laying her knife on the blanket. "Are we going to have more children? More than this one, that is."

"Would you like that?" he asked.

Once again, he was avoiding the question.

"Yes," she said, "I would. I don't know when I would have done without my sisters. I can't imagine a lonelier life than being an only child. Especially the way we were brought up, by nannies and governesses with an absentee mother and a distracted father. As it happened, it brought the three of us closer together. Of course, our children will have our undivided attention. I won't be off hang-gliding in the Alps or skiing in Gstaad, unless they go with me, so…''

If she'd finished her sentence she would have said, so how will we have more children if we don't make love? Of course the answer was that they'd wait until the baby was born. But she didn't want to wait. She wanted him to make love to her now, under this tree, with the grass beneath her and the smell of clover in the air. What did she have to do for him to get the message?

"What about you?" she asked.

"Me? I would have preferred being an only child to growing up with a brother like Wilhelm. But in answer to your question, I'd like to have a big family, to make up for the loneliness I felt as a child. That's one reason I wanted a big house and a garden.''

Instead of showing his desire to have more children by making love to her under the tree, Charles strolled off to the lake, saying he wanted to pick some wildflowers for her. Lise watched him go, admiring the way he walked, the way the sunlight shone on his dark hair, not knowing what more she could do to show him what she wanted. He seemed to have made up his mind about the sequence of events. Did that mean he only wanted to make love to her in order to have more children?

These thoughts were a jumble in her mind. Lately she'd become accustomed to taking an afternoon nap and was finding it hard to stay awake or alert. She yawned and lay down on the blanket and promptly fell asleep. When she woke up she was disoriented. There were shadows falling across the grass. Charles was leaning against the tree, observing her. If only she knew what he was thinking.

"Charles," she said, sitting up and blinking her eyes. "You shouldn't have let me sleep. Are we going to be late getting to Rhineland?"

"We have no schedule. I made a reservation under a different name at the inn in the old section of town. With any luck we should be able to avoid my parents or anyone else we know and don't want to see. If the antique store is closed when we get there, we can go tomorrow."

Charles had packed up the remnants of their picnic and they made their way slowly back to the car. He had been noncommittal about his relationship with his parents and with Wilhelm too for that matter. She knew there were bad feelings there and she didn't blame him. She knew from first-hand experience what kind of people they were.

Lise didn't know how she'd feel crossing the border into Rhineland. When she'd left in disgrace she'd vowed never to return. But she was a different person now, with confidence to face life again. Thanks to Charles, who'd boosted her confidence by marrying her and giving her his name and his protection, she was free to admire the scenery and even the capital city itself. It had a certain charm that St. Michel didn't. It was older, consisting of a medieval section of town with a cathedral and the charming old inn where they were staying. It had become a tourist destination for travelers looking for old-world charm and spectacular scenery in the mountains.

Charles apologized for not getting separate rooms, he'd thought the suite would be more comfortable. Her heart thudded wildly. Did this mean he intended them to sleep together? She looked around the high-ceilinged living room, killing time while admiring the frescoes on the ceiling. She deliberately refrained from entering the bedroom for fear she'd see two beds there.

"It's lovely," she said peering out the windows overlooking the slate roofs of the old buildings and the spires of the gothic cathedral. "Don't you ever miss your country?" She was half afraid he'd say yes, that he intended to come back one day. As much as she admired Rhineland, she would never want to live there again. But if Charles wanted to...

"No, not at all. Do you think I would have bought the château if I'd intended to return here? I also would have told you if that was my intention. You don't think I'd make you live here, do you?"

"No," she said, and crossed the room to kiss him on the cheek. "You've been up-front with me about everything." Everything except how he really felt about her. If it was only pity, then she didn't want to know. But if it was anything else...

"Lise," he said, taking her hands in his. "Our marriage means so much to me. I can't tell you how much."

That was the problem. He couldn't tell her. Maybe if she asked him... No, she feared knowing the truth. So his words hung in the air for a long moment. She waited, hoping maybe he'd find a way to tell her, but he didn't.

Lise changed into comfortable walking shoes for the cobblestone streets, and they went out to find the antique shop where they hoped to find the portrait of Frederic. The area was closed off to cars, which made it possible to stroll down the narrow streets looking into small shops.

"I've never been here before," Lise said. "I lived here for eight months and I never knew about this charming old quarter." Other people knew, she noted. The streets were full of locals and tourists alike, out strolling in the early summer evening.

"Rhineland has its assets," Charles said, giving her a

sideways glance. ''But I confess I've never appreciated them as much as today.''

Lise stopped to look in the window of a crepe shop where a woman wearing a huge white apron and a chef's hat stood in the window and poured batter on a hot griddle. The most wonderful smell came wafting out the door and made her mouth water. The list of choices on a blackboard was endless—savories like ham and cheese, sweets like bananas, fresh strawberries and honey.

''You're not hungry again, are you?'' Charles asked with a teasing smile.

''I'm always hungry these days,'' she confessed.

''Then let's get you a crepe. What will it be, fresh raspberries with creme chantilly or cinnamon and sugar?''

Lise and Charles shared a raspberry crepe while perched on stools at the counter of the tiny shop. She felt young and carefree and happier than she'd been in months. The miracle was that she felt this way in the country where she'd spent her least happy days. The change in her attitude was because of Charles. He seemed happy and carefree too. She reached over to wipe a smear of red raspberry from the corner of his mouth and his gaze honed in on hers. She thought he was going to say something or do something, but he didn't. He just looked at her as if she was as appetizing as a fresh raspberry.

They finished their snack and continued down a small alleyway behind the cathedral. Lise looked up at the imposing gothic spire of the church, which must have been twice the size of the one in St. Michel. Everything was bigger and more imposing than in her country. She'd attended services there with Wilhelm and his parents when she was married. All she could remember were the cold stone walls and the feeling of isolation. How she'd missed the small chapel in St. Michel where her family sat in the front pew.

Rhineland had seemed overwhelming to her when she'd lived here, not to mention cold and inhospitable. That must have been because she was so unhappy with Wilhelm, because all she felt now was that it was a friendly, warm place to visit. They strolled hand-in-hand past boutiques filled with stylish clothes, the same boutiques also found in St. Moritz and Biarritz. They peered into shops that sold handmade ceramic bowls and others that featured jewelry made of amber from the Baltic. But they couldn't find the antiques shop they were looking for. They studied their handdrawn map and asked everyone, but no one seemed to know where it was.

Finally they stumbled on it by chance down a narrow street, but it was closed. Lise felt almost sick with disappointment. "Oh, Charles," she said, her eyes filling with tears. "We shouldn't have dallied like that." She hadn't realized just how much she was counting on finding the painting. She peered in the window, pressing her face against the glass. "If we hadn't stopped for crepes…if we'd only hurried and not taken our time…"

Charles knocked on the door. If there was anyone inside, he'd make it worth their while to open up. He couldn't stand to see the look on Lise's face. He knew how much she'd been counting on finding the painting. Even though they'd come back tomorrow, he shouldn't have let her stop and linger. He banged on the door, but instead of a response from inside, someone called his name.

"Charles, is that you?"

Chapter Eight

It was his father. Of all places, this was the one place he'd least expect to find the suave, silver-haired older man, dressed, as usual, in an Italian suit that fit him as if it had been made for him—and it probably was. His parents liked to dress, eat and live well. Jacques Rodin had always dismissed this part of town as a tourist trap, discouraging the family from venturing there and rubbing elbows with hoi polloi. If they wanted something from one of the shops, they'd send a servant to get it.

"What are you doing here?" his father asked, with a swift surprised glance at Lise.

Charles bit his tongue to keep from asking his father the same thing. "I'm here on business…with my wife," he added, emphasizing *my wife*.

"Ah, yes, so I see. How are you, Lise?" Jacques Rodin said, shaking her hand.

Lise murmured something polite, but Charles felt her stiffen. He didn't know exactly what their relationship had been when she'd been married to Wilhelm, but he knew his parents had not objected to the divorce. In fact, he suspected they might have been behind it. He wondered if his father would ask why he hadn't called them or told them he was in town. Maybe he knew Charles was angry at them for their role in the shameful matter of Wilhelm's divorce.

Finally Charles asked the question he'd been wanting to ask. "What are you doing in this district, Father?"

"It's not something I can discuss in public," his father said, clutching a large bundle to his side. "But if you come back to the house with me I can tell you there. Because of your interest in antiques, you might find it interesting."

Charles shot an inquiring glance at Lise. He suspected it would be painful for her to revisit his family's estate, but his father had piqued his curiosity, and perhaps Lise's too. She gave a very slight shrug of her slender shoulders and he made a decision.

"Very well," he said, "but only for a short visit. We have dinner reservations."

They rode in his father's black Mercedes to the house. Even in the car, his father said nothing about what was in the bundle or what he was going to divulge when they arrived. Charles was pleasantly surprised at how congenial his father appeared to be, making as polite conversation as could be expected from the man who'd never been the kind of father he'd wished for. Maybe his father had never known how to treat children. Maybe he was only at ease with adults. He was definitely an astute businessman.

Jacques surprised Charles by inquiring into his wine business and the older man seemed pleased by Charles's success. One name that was not mentioned—Wilhelm. While driving toward the house, his father telephoned to his mother.

"I got it," he said cryptically. "Everything." Then he

told Marianne that he was bringing Charles and his wife to the house for drinks.

Charles couldn't hear his mother's response, though he assumed she must be surprised. But was she pleased? He didn't know. He hadn't seen his parents for months. He might have happily gone for years without seeing them if left to his own devices. He looked at Lise. She gave him a wan smile and he wondered how upset she was at having to face her in-laws once again. What would his father have to tell them that would make up for it?

His mother was waiting in the drawing room, looking regal and composed as ever. She was dressed as if she were expecting foreign royalty, but he knew it was only her normal evening attire and he doubted she'd changed especially for them. He was grateful for Lise's lack of formality, her cotton shirt and slacks and her sturdy shoes. She seemed so much more real, so natural, compared to his family. He remembered the pleasant shock of seeing her in her leggings in the greenhouse the day he'd gone to propose to her. He'd known then he wasn't proposing to a spoiled princess.

His mother greeted him with a smile. Only spots of color high on her cheekbones gave a sign that anything was out of the ordinary—that she was facing an unexpected and possibly awkward meeting with her son and daughter-in-law.

He kissed his mother on the cheek and was surprised and pleased to see Lise do the same. His mother handed him his favorite drink, a claret, but her hand was shaking slightly, possibly indicating her unease at this unexpected visit. She offered Lise the same and when she demurred, poured her a glass of mineral water.

"You're looking well, Charles," his mother said, taking in his casual slacks and open-necked shirt. "Your father says you're here on business." She, too, refrained from asking why he hadn't called them. If she did, he might have to tell her the truth. Something she wouldn't want to hear. Perhaps that was why she didn't ask.

"That's right. I have some calls to make." It was true, he did have calls to make. But that wasn't the reason he'd come. He could have made them from St. Michel on the phone. He probably would make them from St. Michel when he got home. This was his honeymoon, as much of a honeymoon as he was likely to get and he wasn't about to spoil it by making business calls. "As you may know I have a joint venture with the vintners in St. Michel and Rhineland. Lise was good enough to come with me. We were doing some shopping in the old town when Father saw us."

Charles was getting impatient. He wanted to see what was in his father's bundle and he wanted to hear what his father couldn't tell them in the street. But his mother turned to Lise and inquired about her health, and she and Lise managed to have a cordial conversation about their château and her family. He was proud of his wife for the way she was dealing with this unexpected situation. He hoped that it wasn't causing her undue stress to keep up the facade of calm and serenity when in fact being here, with his parents must have brought back unpleasant memories.

His father tilted his head in his direction and with his drink in one hand and the mysterious package in the other, beckoned him to his study. Charles hadn't been in that room very often. He remembered the rule. When his father was there and the door was closed, it was understood there would be no interruptions. When he'd been called to the book-lined study, his heart would pound with fear. His father was a strict disciplinarian. He never raised his hand to Charles, but one look from that stern countenance and a few harsh words and a small boy would feel the sting as if he'd been struck.

Things were different now that he was grown. But walking into the study with the smell of cigar smoke in the air, Charles still remembered the fear and trepidation he'd felt many years ago.

His father set the package on his huge walnut desk. "A most unfortunate incident occurred some weeks ago," he said, setting his drink on the corner of his desk. "One I wish to keep from leaking outside of the family. One of the servants was caught stealing artifacts from the estate. Instead of reporting it to the police, and receiving unwanted notice from the press, I decided to investigate on my own. As you know, I follow the rule that a gentleman's name appears only twice in the newspaper—when he's born and when he dies. So naturally I was eager to avoid any adverse publicity that might affect the family in any way."

Charles raised his eyebrows and his gaze fell on the package.

"Yes," his father answered his unspoken question. "These are the stolen items which I just recovered from an antique shop in the old quarter. The one where I saw you knocking on the door. It has taken me some weeks to track them down and only today was I able to buy them back, which was why you saw me leaving from the back exit. Which is also why you found the shop closed."

Charles stared at the package. His father ripped it open and held up a small landscape by a famous painter of the French school of landscape artists. He was sure it must be worth a great deal. But Charles felt a sense of loss. He should have known his father wouldn't want an amateurish painting done by a remote and forgotten princess.

"Very beautiful," Charles murmured.

"And very valuable," his father said. "The other things

are not so valuable, but since they belong to us, I bought them back too.''

Charles went to the desk and pulled back the brown paper. There, staring up at him was the small portrait of Frederic. Was it the one they were searching for? It didn't matter. He wanted it. He had to have it.

"May I buy this from you, Father?'' he asked calmly.

"No, you may not,'' his father said gruffly.

Charles's heart sank. What would Lise say when she found it had slipped between their fingers?

"It's worthless. Strictly amateurish. I don't know who did it. But if you want it, say so,'' his father continued. "It's yours. There are some other items in there that may have sentimental value to someone. As you know, I am not a sentimental man.''

Charles nodded and put the painting under his arm before his father changed his mind. He felt relieved and could scarcely wait to show Lise. No, his father was definitely not a sentimental man. If anyone knew that, it was Charles. Not sentimental, not a warm or tender father, not much of an example to a son who was about to become a father, but there he was, the only father he'd ever have, standing in his study, his body ramrod straight, his eyes bright and as alert as ever, offering Charles very possibly the thing he'd come to Rhineland to find.

Charles looked through the paintings of other ancestors he couldn't identify, then came upon a small wooden chest with marble inlays.

"Go ahead, open it. Filled with trinkets, help yourself. Heaven knows how much the thief was paid for it. A pittance, I imagine. In any case, no matter how little it was worth, I didn't want it sitting in some shop for strangers to paw over.''

It was all jewelry, mismatched earrings, pendants of

semi-precious stones and a heavy white-gold ring embossed with one decorative letter—*F*.

"I'll take this, if you're sure you don't want it," Charles said, holding the ring between his thumb and forefinger.

His father shrugged. "It's not worth much, I'm afraid," he said.

"It is to me," Charles said and put it in his pocket. If it was Frederic's it was possible he'd given it to Gabrielle. If not, how had it landed in Rhineland?

Before they left the study, Charles paused to look at a group of framed pictures on the wall. There in the middle was a newspaper clipping of himself accepting the wine-maker of the year award. He didn't see any pictures of Wilhelm. And he wasn't going to look for any. He was surprised his father cared enough to save the picture, let alone frame it and put it on his wall.

"Yes," Jacques said. "That was quite an honor. We… your mother and I…were very pleased, very proud. Naturally there are exceptions to the rule about appearing only twice in a lifetime. Receiving such a prestigious award…this was doubtless one of them."

Charles nodded. That might have been the only time he'd ever heard his father tell him he was proud of him. It didn't make up for the many years of benign neglect, but it taught him a lesson. A lesson he intended to benefit from when raising his own children. Be lavish in praise. It isn't rationed. Neither is love. But be sparing in criticism. A cold, tight knot in his chest he didn't even know was there seemed to dissolve as he stood in his father's study, looking at the face he might come to resemble one day. If only he could avoid resembling him in other ways.

"Thank you, Father," Charles said soberly. He didn't say it but the thanks were for the painting, the ring and for the much belated praise.

He and Lise didn't stay much longer. They made more polite conversation with his parents and said good-bye. Lise saw the painting under his arm and her eyes were bright with curiosity, but she didn't say anything until after his father's chauffeur had deposited them at their hotel.

With a flourish he set the painting on the table in their sitting room.

"It's him," Lise cried, tracing the outline of his bearded face with her finger. "It must be him. But how... why...where..."

He recounted his conversation with his father and they studied the picture under the lamp. There in the corner was the initial G, signed with an elaborate flourish.

"I can't believe it," she said. "If we hadn't run into your father..."

"We wouldn't have found it," he agreed. "It was fortunate timing. I still can't believe he went down to the shop in the old quarter himself. I would have expected him to send someone."

"I got the feeling from talking to your mother he was highly offended that one of his servants would steal from him. Maybe that's what motivated him to get the things back. Because she didn't seem to think it was worth all the fuss. An amateur painting, assorted jewelry that didn't seem to be that valuable. Was that your impression?"

"There was one very valuable landscape. But other than that, no, it definitely wasn't the intrinsic value by any means. He never even reported it to the police. He undertook the search to get the things back on his own to avoid publicity, he said. It's not like him at all. He was always good at delegating authority. He offered me whatever I wanted."

"But what does it mean?" she asked. "If it ended up here in Rhineland, does that mean Gabrielle didn't take it

with her? It would have been hard to explain to a new
husband why you were keeping a portrait of another man,
especially one you'd painted yourself, for yourself so you
wouldn't forget him.''

"Is that what you think?" he asked.

"Yes, but I'm a romantic," she said.

Charles fingered the ring in his pocket. Should he give
it to her now or wait until later?

"Didn't you make dinner reservations for seven?" she
asked.

He put his arm around her. "Hungry again?" he asked
with an indulgent smile.

They had a typical Rhineland dinner at a small bistro.
The first course was fish from the mountain streams, the
second course was venison with a rich mushroom sauce.
They finished with a coupe royale. Lise licked her spoon,
savoring the smooth vanilla ice cream and the dark chocolate sauce.

"That was wonderful," she said.

They'd discussed his parents during dinner. Charles told
her he was no longer bitter about the way he'd been raised.
He realized they'd done the best they could, considering
who they were. The main thing that continued to bother
him was the way they'd treated Lise.

She told him she had determined to put whatever role
they'd played in Wilhelm's divorcing her behind her. Besides, if they'd influenced Wilhelm, she ought to thank
them, because the divorce had saved her from a life of
misery with Wilhelm.

They walked slowly back to their hotel, lost in thoughts
and memories. The cobblestone streets were lit by gas
lamps which intensified the atmosphere of an old medieval
town. Lise was so tired she was grateful for Charles's arm

around her. She was worried about the sleeping arrangements, but so tired she could probably fall asleep anywhere.

One thing disturbed her. She hadn't told Charles, but on the grand piano in the drawing room of the palace, she'd seen a wedding picture of herself and Wilhelm. She had no idea why his parents kept it there, but it had sent a shaft of pain through her. Just when she'd thought she was putting her former marriage in the back of her mind, the picture brought it all back again. She managed to keep smiling and talking to Marianne Rodin, but now that fatigue was creeping up on her, so did the melancholy.

After they collected their key from the front desk and rode up in the glassed-in elevator to the third floor, Charles led the way into their suite.

"Shall I run a bath for you?" he asked.

She nodded, but she didn't know if she'd be able to stay awake long enough. She peeked into the commodious tiled bathroom with its updated shower room that looked like a capsule of tempered glass with a high-tech showerhead and four water jets. She admired the whirlpool bath that Charles was filling with hot water for her.

Then it was time to go into the bedroom to get her nightgown. There was no way to postpone it any longer unless she fell asleep here on the chair next to the tub. There it was. A huge king-sized bed, covered with a canopy. The covers were turned down and there was a Swiss chocolate bar on each pillow.

"They must have known you were coming," Charles said.

She looked at the bed, but didn't say anything. If this were their official honeymoon, maybe then he'd make love to her in this bed under the swaths of filmy fabric, like something out of the Arabian Nights. Or maybe he'd take a bath with her in that huge whirlpool bathtub. Or maybe they'd make love under the shower with the four water jets letting them unwind and deal with any lingering stress. They'd soap each other's bodies until they were so attuned and alive they'd make love right there in the shower. She felt the heat rise up her neck and flood her face. But Charles didn't seem to notice.

Turning this trip into a honeymoon was only in her mind. She'd never mentioned the word in front of him. He'd never mentioned it to her. Her last honeymoon had been spent in Monte Carlo where Wilhelm had gambled with friends late at night and into the morning. She wanted no repeat of that.

"I mean the chocolate," he explained.

"Oh, yes. Well, I'll have my bath now."

When she came out of the bathroom she was wrapped in a towel. She'd completely forgotten her pale green nightgown of shimmering silk, one of those her sisters had given her.

Charles was sitting up in bed reading, his back against the headboard, wearing only silk boxer shorts. She drew in a quick breath, telling herself not to look, not to gaze lustfully at his well-muscled chest or at his legs. But he'd stopped reading and was gazing at her over the edge of the book. She felt his eyes on her and she fumbled with the catch on her suitcase while holding the towel firmly over her breasts.

She went back to the bathroom to change into the nightgown and when she came out he jumped up and went in. Her hopes were dashed. She couldn't sit up in bed waiting for him. Not after she'd told him how tired she was. Once again, they'd missed an opportunity. Of course, he didn't see it that way. He only wanted to make love to her when he was ready to have another child. He'd married her to take care of her, and to have a wife and children. She'd give him all the children he wanted. But what about love? She wanted to give and receive love too. If she wasn't so tired, she'd wait up and tell him so.

But not only was she tired, she was a coward. So she turned off her bedside light and closed her eyes.

Neither Charles nor Lise ever mentioned the word *disappointment* when discussing their trip to Rhineland. How could they, when they'd accomplished what they'd set out to do? They'd found the lost painting. They chose a spot in the informal living room to hang the portrait, which they were convinced had been painted by Gabrielle. Instead of calling on one of the servants, Charles found a hammer and nail in the tool shed and planned to do it himself. It was a warm morning and he was late for work. Each day he went in a little later, finding excuses to stay at home a little longer, to have a leisurely breakfast with Lise and discuss plans for the day, both his and hers.

He turned the frame over and pushed his finger into the back of the painting. Behind the fragile backing, a white paper was folded into a small square and hidden. He fished it out and held it up for Lise to see.

Her mouth opened in surprise. Her eyes widened. She took it from his hand and opened it slowly and carefully.

"Oh, Charles," she breathed. "Look at this." She sat down in an armchair and spread the paper in her lap. He turned on the wall lamp and leaned over her shoulder. "It's not her writing," she whispered. "Could it be his?" She proceeded to read aloud.

My Dearest,
    Do not worry. I will come for you in time. Do what you must do but do not forget me. I love you.
                                        Your devoted F.

"I can't believe our luck," Lisc said. "We have proof positive now that she painted the picture and put his letter behind it. Can't you just imagine how desperate she was to have some memento of him, especially if she was going off to marry someone else?"

"So you really believe she painted it for herself?" he asked.

"How else could she keep his image? She didn't have a camera to take his picture. But we still don't know if he ever did come for her. We don't know how it all turned out. There must be a clue somewhere. I'll call Marie-Claire and see if she'll come with me to the palace today to go through those old trunks."

Charles kissed the top of her head and went to work.

Marie-Claire was delighted to hear from Lise. When Lise told her they'd been in Rhineland and stayed at a romantic old inn, Marie-Claire beamed at her.

"Your honeymoon. You finally had a honeymoon. Which nightgown did you wear?"

"The green silk," Lise admitted. For all the good it did her.

"How did Charles like it?" Marie-Claire asked her, trying to hide a knowing smile.

Lise had no idea how Charles had liked the nightgown. He hadn't said a word. But she couldn't disappoint her sister.

"He thought it was stunning." Lise said. "I don't know where you two do your shopping, but everything you gave me is so beautiful, so lovely, so…"

"So sexy," Marie-Claire continued. "That was our purpose. To replace all those old clothes of yours."

"You mean from my previous marriage."

"Yes, that one," Marie-Claire said, curling her lip with

distaste. ''I'll bet he found it even more stunning with you in it.''

''He could hardly keep his hands off me,'' Lise said. But somehow he had kept his hands off her. He'd only looked. She didn't mind lying about it. It was better than telling her sister the truth. That would have led to a discussion she had no wish to participate in.

Marie-Claire was happy to go with Lise to the palace, especially when they entered the kitchen from the servants' entrance. Just the smell of cinnamon and sugar and yeast bread rising was enough to give both sisters a sense of déjà vu.

''I haven't been in the kitchen for ages,'' Marie-Claire told the cooks. ''I've missed your biscuits and hot buns.''

Lucette hugged Marie-Claire and told her to come more often and bring Ariane. She and Lise promised to bring her next time she was in town. Lise led the way to the attic, glad to have company after the unhappy experience the last time when she'd overheard that disturbing conversation. If it happened again, at least she'd have Marie-Claire to cheer her up and tell her it meant nothing. Her sister was so giddy with her love and her new life with Sebastian she was looking at life through rose-colored glasses.

They sat cross-legged on the dusty attic floor with all the windows open.

''Why are we doing this again when we could be taking advantage of this beautiful spring weather and sitting around the swimming pool at the tennis club?'' Marie-Claire asked, brushing her hands together.

''This is important. Frederic is your ancestor too. You saw his picture on the wall at my house. Don't you want to find out what happened to his affair with Princess Gabrielle of Rhineland? The best thing would be any letters from her to Frederic or the missing pages of her diary, though they'd probably be somewhere in Rhineland.''

''So we don't really know what we're looking for,'' Marie-Claire said blowing the dust off a round-topped metal trunk.

''No, we might be on a wild-goose chase.''

''Does this wild-goose chase have anything to do with you and Charles?''

''Well, maybe. After all, she was married off to a man she didn't love, at least we think she was.''

''And you were married off to Wilhelm. Now I see the connection,'' Marie-Claire said. ''You want to know if her story had a happy ending.''

''There's nothing wrong with that, is there?'' Lise asked her sister.

''Only if you're having doubts about your own happy ending. Are you?''

''Of course not,'' Lise said quickly. But her sister was not fooled.

''What's wrong?'' Marie-Claire asked with a frown.

''Nothing,'' Lise insisted. ''Charles is the most wonderful husband you can imagine, aside from Sebastian, of course. He's kind, generous, faithful....''

''But...'' Marie-Claire prompted.

''But he doesn't love me,'' Lise said softly. She hadn't meant to tell anyone, but the pressure of keeping it a secret was too great for her to keep to herself any longer. Her sister was the only one she could tell, and even now she was afraid to hear the pity in her sister's voice.

''Do you love him?'' Marie-Claire asked.

Startled, Lise looked up at her, tears glazing her eyes. ''I...I...'' Suddenly she knew it was true. She'd fallen in love with her husband. That was what was really bothering her. She didn't know when it had happened. Was it their wedding night? Was it their so-called honeymoon? It had come about so gradually she was hardly aware it had happened at all. But she knew it was true. She loved him not only for what he'd done for her, but for what he was. A good man. A man who'd been in his brother's shadow most of his life, but who had emerged as a man who towered over his brother in every way.

She also loved him passionately. She wanted to be his wife in every sense of the word. She wanted to make love to him and show him how much she loved him. She wanted to have a whole houseful of children with him. But she didn't want to wait to make love until this baby was born. Even if he didn't love her that way, or any way, she would continue to love him and to hope and pray he'd love her back.

"You don't need to say anything. I can see it. I saw it at your party, the way you looked at him. You're in love with your husband. There's nothing wrong with that."

"There is if your husband doesn't love you. Don't tell me he does, I know better," Lise said sadly. "He told me he didn't love me or expect me to love him. He only wants my respect."

"But why did he marry you?" Marie-Claire asked, leaning forward toward her sister.

"To make up for Wilhelm's divorcing me. Because he's such an honorable man. I said no at first. But he insisted. I only gave in because of the baby and the tenuous situation here in St. Michel. With the monarchy in doubt, I feared for our future. Without a husband and his financial support, where would I be?"

"I see," Marie-Claire said. "What are you going to do?"

Lise shook her head. "Nothing. What can I do?"

"You could tell him."

"That would make things worse. Imagine how he'd feel—embarrassed, and worst of all sorry for me. We have an agreement. This was to be a marriage of convenience. If I told him I'd changed my mind, or rather I couldn't control my emotions, it would change everything. No, I can't tell him. I can't do anything but keep it to myself. I trust you not to tell anyone."

"Of course," Marie-Claire said. She reached over to give her sister a hug. "It will all work out, I know it will. In the meantime, we'll find something that will prove there was a happy ending for our Frederic and Princess Gabrielle. Let's get started, then we can get to my club for a swim. I can't see spending an entire beautiful afternoon up here in the attic. You look like you could use some sun, Lise. You're altogether too pale. And you need to stop obsessing about these long-lost ancestors. It's too late to do anything about them."

Marie-Claire was right. What she didn't say was that it was not too late to do something about her own situation. But what? It was easier to think about something in history than to solve her own problems.

After an hour of going through boxes of crinoline skirts and lace bodices, Lise could tell Marie-Claire was running out of patience. Surrounded by piles of old clothes, the smell of mothballs in the dusty air, Lise begged for just one more trunk. Then she'd give in and go off swimming with her sister. Fresh air and exercise, Marie-Claire convinced her that's what she needed.

Inside the ancient dark green trunk with the worn straps were a box of military medals. At last, something that had belonged to a man. A military man. But there were many military men in the history of St. Michel. Then, at the very bottom of the trunk, they came across a packet of letters, held together with string, addressed to Frederic at the front of a battle somewhere in France.

Lise grabbed the bundle and cried out in delight. "Look! This is fantastic. I told you we'd find something."

"Don't get too excited. They could be from his mother, you know."

"Would you keep your mother's letters?" Lise asked, opening the one on top. "Oh, no, you're right. Or you're almost right. It's signed 'your loving father.'" She was crushed. How much more disappointment could she take? It was wonderful having their pictures, but not knowing what had happened to them was like an unfinished book, an unsolved mystery.

"Keep going. Maybe they're not all from his father."

Lise leafed through the letters. "The handwriting looks all the same. But I'll take them anyway. You never know what I might learn. Charles will be so interested. Now we can go. You've been great, Marie-Claire. I couldn't have done it without you." She closed the trunk, stood and closed the windows. At least she hadn't heard any disturbing conversations today. "Marie-Claire, I have to go home. I'll go to your club with you tomorrow. It's Nanny's first day back tomorrow, and I want to get her suite ready."

Lise was looking forward to showing the gardens to Nanny and most especially to sharing the letters with Charles. Marie-Claire was sweet to join her in the search for Frederic's personal belongings, but it was only Charles who would appreciate any information they could find.

Charles found her in the garden, sitting on a bench and drinking a citron pressé. She looked drowsy and slightly sunburned. Her hair was tousled and her eyes matched the color of the summer sky. He stopped and stared at her. His heart banged loudly in his chest. There were times like this he could hardly believe his good fortune. After years of struggling to live up to his family's standards, to out-do his brother, he'd been given more than he'd ever dreamed. The most beautiful wife in the world, a child on the way and a spectacular abode to live in. But the most gorgeous château would be nothing without her. He knew that. He'd known that when he bought the place. If she hadn't agreed to marry him, he would have backed out of the deal. What good would a château be without a wife and children to share it with him? A feeling of complete and utter happiness filled his heart and soul. He wanted to know if she felt the same. If she ever regretted her decision to marry him. But he didn't want to spoil this moment either. So he said nothing.

He asked what she'd been doing and her face lit up. She showed him the packet of letters and he marveled at her good luck in finding them, though he warned her they might never know the end of the story.

"But we have to find out," she said with so much determination on her face, he didn't doubt she would find out somehow, sooner or later.

"I came home early to tell you there's an emergency meeting of the vintners in Burgundy tomorrow. I have to go there to mediate. Tonight I'll write up a proposal, or the consortium I've been working on will fall apart. The French grape pickers are threatening to go on strike. Half of the wineries will support them, the others won't. The whole thing may fall apart anyway, but I have to see what I can do."

"Oh, Charles, that sounds impossible."

"Not impossible, just difficult."

"You let me babble on about Frederic when you were worried about the business," she said. "I'll tell the cook we'll eat early."

Charles was so absorbed in the problems in France, he

seemed to have forgotten about Frederic's letters. Lise didn't want to interrupt his work so she waited up for hours, but the light in his study remained on. From what she could tell, he spent the evening on the phone and on his laptop computer. Lise brought him a cold drink and he barely looked up to thank her. In the morning, he kissed her good-bye on the cheek.

"I shouldn't be gone more than a few days. You have my cell phone number if you need me. Are you sure you'll be all right?" he asked.

"Of course. Nanny is due back today and Marie-Claire wants me to spend my afternoons with her at her club. She says I need the exercise and sun."

"Not too much sun," Charles cautioned, touching the tip of her nose with his finger. It wasn't until he was at the border of France, waiting to go through customs that he remembered he hadn't asked her what Frederic's letters had contained.

Lise stood at the front door watching him drive away. She felt unreasonably sad and low. Her whole body felt heavy though she'd scarcely gained any weight yet. She didn't know what was wrong with her. Many husbands went off on business trips. As she'd told Charles, she had Nanny and her sister for company. He'd only be gone for a few days, for heaven's sake. She had to chalk up her feelings to the mood swings of pregnancy. That was all it was.

She'd hoped to share Frederic's letters with Charles, but when he'd retired to his office to work last night, she'd wandered around the house, listless and out of sorts. The letters were still on her bedside table, unopened and unread. It would have been so exciting to read them together, to discover the truth about what happened. Even if they hadn't discovered anything, they would have done it together. Now he was gone.

She sent the chauffeur to pick up Nanny at the train station, and when she arrived, Lise hugged her, wishing the older woman didn't feel so small and frail in her arms.

"Let me look at you," Gertrude said, holding Lise by the arms. "Yes, you've changed. You're an old married woman now."

Lise sighed. "I'm still the same as I ever was. Stubborn, willful, greedy. Still wanting more than I've got."

Gertrude shook her head. "I don't believe it. Not my girl."

"Come up and see your room," Lise said. "It's a little bigger than you had in the cottage." She led the way to the second floor where she'd furnished a suite for Gertrude simply but comfortably with a few tasteful antiques and a Persian carpet that was worn but that glowed with subdued reds and blues.

"Oh, my, this is grand. Are you sure I deserve all this?"

"All this and more," Lise said. "You'll want to rest after your long trip. Then come down and we'll have lunch together and tell me about your sister's family. I hope they can still get along without you because I can't. I think you'll approve of the cook. Of course she can't make cassoulet the way you do, so you'll have to show her."

Gertrude sniffed. "Hmmpf. I won't be showing anyone how to make it. If you want some, I'll make it myself. That recipe is secret and I intend to go to my grave with it."

"That's what I thought," Lise said, hiding a smile. "Just say the word and I'll clear out the kitchen for you."

Chapter Nine

After lunch Lise met her sister at the country club Marie-Claire and Sebastian belonged to. Lise had never been there before. Her parents had considered such a place too bourgeois for royalty, but it had a certain old-fashioned charm to it with its wide verandas and clay tennis courts and blue-tiled swimming pools. The landscaping was impeccable, with green lawns bordered by begonias in pinks and purples. Marie-Claire ordered fresh-squeezed lemonade for them from the outside bar while Lise changed into a modest two-piece tankini that covered her now slightly rounded stomach. She came out of the dressing room, walked across sun-warmed tiles to the pool, leaned back in a padded pool chair next to Marie-Claire and closed her eyes. The afternoon sun warmed her skin and the scent of roses wafted toward the pool from the bushes along the path.

"No wonder you come here every day," Lise said. "It's a wonderful spot. Remember how we wanted to join the club when we were teenagers, when everyone else we knew belonged?"

"Yes, there's something to be said for being disinherited," Marie-Claire said. "We can act like normal people." She tilted her head to get a better look at her sister. "How do you feel?" she asked with concern.

"Fine. It's just that I don't have any energy. It must be psychological because I'm physically fine. I was just at the doctor's last week and he said I was completely fit. But Charles had to go out of town today and I feel like I've lost my best friend. Actually, I have. Whatever I said yesterday, forget it. He really is my best friend. What more could I want?"

There was a brief silence while Marie-Claire looked like she was going to say something in answer to Lise's question, but thought better of it. "What was in the letters?" Marie-Claire asked.

"I haven't had a chance to look. I helped Charles pack and then…I don't know…maybe I was afraid I wouldn't find anything, so I haven't really gone through the letters." She didn't say that half the fun of solving this mystery was solving it with Charles. No, that wasn't true. Ninety percent of the fun was solving it with Charles. It was a something that brought them closer together.

"I'm worried about you. You seem down in the dumps. I haven't seen you that way since your divorce. Well, I have a surprise for you that will cheer you up," Marie-Claire said, reaching for her beach bag.

Lise's eyes flew open. "You shouldn't," she said, but she sat up straight and fastened her eyes on her sister's bag.

"You won't say that when you see what I found. You'll say I *should* have done it. And I did. After I left you yesterday I got to thinking about Frederic and Gabrielle. And I felt guilty coming here without you. Knowing we'd found something of Frederic's, I thought there might be more there."

"See, I told you it was a fascinating story. Now you're hooked too."

"Maybe, or maybe I couldn't stand to see you so frustrated and disappointed. After the letters, I had a feeling there had to be something more in that trunk. So I thought up an excuse, and went back to the palace. I told the cooks I wanted their recipe for sticky buns and then I sneaked up to the attic again. After emptying the trunk upside down on the attic floor, look what I found." Marie-Claire's eyes were dancing with excitement. She pulled out a rectangular package wrapped in blue velvet and handed it to Lise.

"So, after I found this," she pointed to the package, "I was on my way out through the kitchen, when who should I run into but her majesty."

"Which one?"

"Queen Celeste. She was giving orders to the cooks about how she has to have a special diet and they've been feeding her too much and she's gained too much weight."

"Did she speak to you?" Lise asked.

"She glared at me. Asked what I was doing there. I shoved the…the…what I found for you, under my shirt, and I said I'd come to visit Grandmama. The cooks whispered to me that the big news that really upset her is that Luc Dumont seems to have located the missing heir, Katie and Father's child. Therefore Celeste's own son, if she has a son, may not inherit the throne," Marie-Claire said, her eyes widening.

"What?" Lise said, dumbfounded. "You mean our brother, the future king of St. Michel, has been found and will save us all and our country?"

"That's what they said. I'm almost afraid to believe it. If it's true…" Marie-Claire's voice trailed off.

"It would change everything. It would mean that we have a future here. Not just us, but our children and our children's children. Oh, Marie-Claire, I only hope you're right.''

"Maybe I shouldn't have told you. It may be just a rumor. Oh, I'm so afraid this will be another dead end.''

Lise put her arms around her sister. ''All we can do is wait and see what happens,'' she said.

"You can imagine how upset Celeste was thinking that her son won't inherit the throne after all. She certainly isn't going to even remember that I was in the palace at all. If she does, who cares? What can she do to any of us now?''

"Arrest you for trespassing?'' Lise suggested. ''Or grand theft?''

Marie-Claire shrugged. ''Let her try. I'm sure she didn't notice I had something under my shirt. She was too upset about her weight gain and the possibility of losing her position as future dowager. Well, go ahead. Enough gossip. Open the package.''

Lise was almost afraid to open it. Afraid to be disappointed, afraid it wasn't going to be what she thought it would be. Slowly she pulled the velvet back and turned it over in her lap. She gasped. It was the porcelain plaque with Gabrielle's dark eyes gazing solemnly back at her, her long dark curls cascading over one shoulder and her left hand placed between her breasts. On the third finger of her hand was a large gold ring. It was not a wedding ring.

"Oh, Marie-Claire, it's her,'' Lise said in a hushed tone. ''It's Gabrielle. Where did you find it? Was it with Frederic's things?''

"It was in an officer's mess kit, if that's what they called them in those days. It had his name on it. Captain Frederic de Bergeron. It's in good condition, don't you think? You know better than I. You're the art historian.''

"Yes, oh, yes, it's amazing. The colors are so vibrant. The pink dress and her fair skin, the rose at the waist and her pale skin. What do you make of that ring she's wearing?''

''It looks much too big and heavy for her. It's certainly not a wedding ring, so maybe this was painted before she got married.''

''I can't wait to show this to Charles. Oh how I wish he was home.''

''So what do you make of it being in Frederic's belongings, obviously his military equipment. Did he carry it around from battle to battle? How did she get it to him? Did he never marry? Did she?''

''Now who's curious?'' Lise said with a smile. ''As far as I know he was a career soldier and he never married. I know less about her because she's from Rhineland and I don't have any archives to go to. All I know is she was engaged to someone else, someone she didn't want to marry. I'd give anything to know how it turned out.''

''Then the letters…''

''Yes, the letters. But I want to wait till Charles gets back. It's our project, his and mine.''

''Just promise to keep me informed,'' Marie-Claire said.

Lise did a few laps in the pool. The doctor had given her a list of activities recommended during pregnancy and swimming was high on the list. After drying off in the sun, she said good-bye to Marie-Claire and, because Charles had insisted she do so, she called the chauffeur to come and pick her up.

She'd scarcely settled back on the leather seat with her wet suit in her bag beside her when she was hit with a powerful stomach cramp. She drew in a sharp breath and tried to relax. It was impossible. Instead she leaned forward and gripped the edge of the seat. Another cramp caused her to double up in pain.

Bertrand, the driver, looked at her in the rearview mirror. His face was creased with concern.

"Are you all right, ma'am?" he asked.

Lise couldn't speak. Her mouth was dry and her heart was pounding. She shook her head.

"Shall I call the doctor?" he asked, his eyes wide at the sight of Lise slumped over, her arms wrapped around her waist.

"Just…take me to the…"

"To the hospital," he said. "Yes, ma'am, right away."

The St. Michel hospital was only a few miles away but the ride seemed interminable to Lise. She was doubled up in pain as the cramps continued to attack her one after another. She was cold, then she was hot. She shivered and she was covered with cold sweat. She couldn't be in labor. It was impossible. She didn't know what was wrong with her and she was so frightened she was shaking.

She was hardly aware of being carried into the hospital on a gurney. The blurred faces above her were calm and competent. Their uniforms were crisp and white. They were saying she was going to be all right. But how did they know? They would call her family. How would they know Marie-Claire's number? And how could they call Charles? How would they know where to find him? She couldn't remember his cell phone number.

All she cared about was that they stop the pain. The next thing she knew she was in a hospital bed in a small room that was spinning around. People were coming and going, poking, prodding and turning her this way and that. She tried to protest, to explain, to tell them to call Charles, but she couldn't seem to get the words out. She blacked out and when she came to, mercifully the pain had stopped. She was still shaking with fear and cold.

"How are you feeling, Mrs. Rodin?" the doctor asked. It wasn't her doctor. It was one she'd never seen before.

"What happened?" she asked, pulling the sheet up to her chin.

"You went into premature labor," he said. "It seems to have stopped, but we want to head off any further contractions."

"But why? This is only my fourth month."

"It happens." He sat down on a stool at the edge of her bed with her chart in his hands. "Not usually this early though. No one knows why. What we do know is that we don't want you to deliver this baby now. The good news is the membranes around the baby didn't rupture. Then we might be in trouble. So far so good. The contractions have died down and we're going to do everything possible to keep them from recurring."

"Everything…like what?" she asked.

"Like putting you on bed rest. If that doesn't work, giving you certain drugs and if all else fails, we might have to do a procedure where we stitch up around the cervix so your baby will stay where it belongs for the next five months.

"We haven't been able to notify your husband," the doctor said, getting to his feet. "We called your house but only a woman who says she's your nanny is there. She's on her way here now. If you can give us another number we'll call your husband. I'll send the aide in. In the meantime the nurses will call me if there's any change. I've left word with Dr. Duverger and I'm sure he'll be along to see you. You're not to worry."

Not to worry. Easy for him to say, Lise thought. She couldn't bear the thought of losing this baby. When the aide came in she asked for her purse and got out her cell phone. She called Charles's cell phone but got his voice mail. She tried not to sound alarmed or worried in her message. But she couldn't keep her voice steady. She only told Charles she was in the hospital and passed on the nurse's message not to worry.

"I've had a little problem," she said. "They've got me in the hospital but I'm really going to be fine. Call me." Then she called Marie-Claire. Her sister wasn't there either.

A tear trickled down Lise's cheek as she handed her phone to the nurse. What if she lost the baby? What if bed rest didn't work and they had to stitch her up? Wouldn't she have to be anesthetized? Wouldn't it hurt? What if it didn't work? She hated herself for being such a baby. But she was terribly frightened.

When Nanny came with her nightgown, peignoir, her toiletries and a basket of fruit and cookies, she was able to put on a better face. She assured Gertrude she was going to be fine, and just saying the words helped to make her believe it herself. Nanny wanted to stay, but Lise insisted she go home. She was in good hands.

Then she was alone again, but they'd given her something to make her sleep and she drifted off, too tired to change out of her hospital gown into one of her lovely nightgowns.

Charles got her message when he came out of a meeting with representatives of the vintners. After hours of hammering out a compromise, they'd agreed to sign an agreement with the growers. His sleeves were rolled up, his tie was askew, his hair was mussed and his shirt was wrinkled. He was proud of what he'd accomplished, but when he heard Lise's message, he forgot everything. All he could think of was getting back to St. Michel.

First he called Lise's cell phone, but there was no answer. He broke out into a cold sweat. He punched in the number of the hospital and gripped the phone so tightly his hand hurt. He talked to the nurse on the floor who assured him his wife was resting comfortably and had not had another contraction for at least an hour.

"Contraction?" he exclaimed.

"Didn't you know? She went into premature labor," she explained patiently.

"What about the baby?" he demanded.

"The baby is fine. So is your wife."

"Then why is she in the hospital?"

"Bed rest and observation. If all goes well, the doctor won't have to take any further measures."

"What kind of measures?"

"The doctor will explain everything tomorrow when he makes his rounds."

Charles walked out of the wine-growers' cooperative building without seeing the men who he'd been meeting with, without hearing their words of congratulations for working so hard on the agreement. All he could think of was Lise. Lying in the hospital. Possibly losing the baby. Alone. Frightened.

He got into his car and started driving. He knew there were no flights to St. Michel until tomorrow. It was better to drive. The roads would be empty at night. He could drive as fast as his car would go. And he did. He put his foot on the gas pedal, pushed it to the floor and kept it there. While he drove he thought of her, pictured her alone in a hospital bed, and wished he'd never left her. Not now, not when she needed him.

If she was all right, if the baby made it through the next five months, he'd never ask for another thing in his life. He'd tell her how he felt about her. That he couldn't live without her, that he'd loved her since the first day he'd seen her. Yes, he loved her. He knew it now. He'd always known it, but he hadn't been able to say it, even to himself. He'd been too afraid of being rejected, of coming in second-best behind Wilhelm.

He wasn't afraid of anything anymore, only of losing her and the baby.

Eight hours later he pulled up in front of the hospital. The night-shift nurses were leaving and the day-shift personnel were arriving. He was bleary-eyed and disheveled. Every muscle ached. He didn't wait for the elevator, he took the stairs two at a time to the fourth floor. He paused only long enough to ask for her at the nurse's station.

At the door to her room he almost ran into Dr. Duverger.

"How is she?" he demanded, looking over the doctor's shoulder to see her for himself.

"She's going to be fine. It's good to see you, Mr. Rodin. We've just given your wife a shot to relax the uterus. We don't want any more contractions. As you know, it's way too early for her to be going into labor."

"Why…what caused it?" Charles asked.

"We don't know yet. It could be any number of internal things. Incompetent cervix, abnormal uterus, or nothing serious at all. Don't worry, we have ways of dealing with whatever it is. We start with rest and observation then move cautiously to some therapy. That's the drug I mentioned to you. Your wife is in no danger. It's the baby we're worried about."

Charles paled. "Can I go in?"

Dr. Duverger stepped out of the way. "Of course. She's a little groggy and may not know what's going on, but go ahead. She's been asking for you."

He rushed in and gasped at the sight of her pale face. The doctor said she was in no danger, but she looked so frail. He couldn't lose her now, not now when he knew how much she meant to him and that he couldn't live without her. What if she lost the baby? He couldn't stand the thought. He sat on the edge of her bed. Her eyelids fluttered open and then closed again.

"Lise," he said softly.

"Charles," she whispered. "Is that you?"

"I'm here," he assured her. "I'll never leave you again."

She smiled weakly. "I don't want to lose the baby."

"You won't," he said. "Just relax and go to sleep. You're going to be fine and so will the baby."

He said the words with all the conviction he didn't feel. He was scared, but he couldn't let her see it or hear it in his voice. She had to believe she'd be fine. She had to be fine. She had to keep the baby.

Her eyes closed again.

"I love you," he said. He couldn't hold back the words any longer. "I can't live without you. So get well. Come home. I'll be here."

He moved from the side of her bed to the chair. A nurse brought him coffee. After a sleepless night, he needed it to stay awake. The nurse asked if he wanted to wait in the lounge. She offered to tell him when Lise woke up. He shook his head. He had to stay. He'd never forgive himself for being away when it happened. He might have been able to prevent it. He dozed off and woke up when Marie-Claire came into the room, her eyes red and her forehead lined with worry.

"I came last night but they wouldn't let me see her," she whispered. "I've been sick with worry. How is she? When did you get here?"

"The doctor says she's in no danger, they're just trying to prevent her from going into labor. They've given her a drug that ought to help. We just have to wait and see."

"We went to the club yesterday. She was fine. She went swimming and she called the chauffeur and then...I don't know what happened. Charles, you look awful. Go get some sleep in the delivery-room lounge. I'll stay here."

He let her convince him to go. He slept doubled up on a couch that was two feet too short for him for a few hours and came back to relieve Marie-Claire.

"She hasn't woken up, but she was mumbling something about Frederic and Gabrielle," Marie-Claire told him.

The sound of their familiar names penetrated Lise's subconscious. She tried to open her eyes. The blurred images of her sister and Charles swam into view.

"Charles," she said. "We have the plaque." She tried to smile but her face felt as if it was cracking. What was wrong with her? Why did they look so sad and worried. "What's wrong?" she asked. She looked around at the white walls. "Where am I?"

"You're in the hospital," Charles said. "You..." His voice broke. His jaw clenched.

Fear struck her. She put her hand on her stomach. "The baby?"

Charles found his voice. "The baby's fine. You just relax. You went into premature labor yesterday. But the contractions have stopped now. That's good."

It came back to her. The club, the car and the terrible pain. After that everything was a blank. "How long have I been here?"

"Since yesterday. About twenty-four hours."

Twenty-four hours? Where had they gone? She'd been dreaming. She'd dreamt the most wonderful dream about her and Charles and Gabrielle and Frederic.

"Where are my things? I have to show you the picture of Gabrielle that Marie-Claire found. The one we were looking for." She looked around the room. Marie-Claire opened the drawer of her bedside stand. Lise put her hand on her forehead to try to clear her brain. She had to find it to show Charles. "I had it in the car yesterday, in my bag."

"I'll go ask the nurse where your things are," Marie-Claire said.

Lise fought her way out of a fog to concentrate on Charles. He'd been away and now he was back. She knew that much. "How was your trip?" she asked.

"It was fine, everything went well, until I got your message. You had me worried."

"I'm sorry," she said. "I hope you didn't cut your trip short. While you were gone I had a dream…I dreamed you said you loved me." She smiled dreamily. Her head seemed to be floating above her body. She was looking down on herself and Charles. She was no longer afraid to tell him how she felt about him. No longer afraid to find out how he felt about her. Whether that was due to the pills they gave her or a new outlook on life, she didn't know. She just knew she loved him and she had to tell him. From somewhere above her hospital bed she saw him bend down and kiss her lightly on the lips. It was the warmest, sweetest kiss she'd ever had.

"I did," he said. "That wasn't a dream. I love you, Lise. I've loved you since the first moment I saw you, but I knew I couldn't have you so I fought it. I told myself it wasn't love. But it was. It is. Don't say anything. Don't worry about not loving me back. If it happens…"

She took his hand and pressed it to her lips. She was flooded with a profound sense of happiness. If she was dreaming, she didn't want to wake up. If she was awake, she didn't want to fall asleep. Her eyes filled with happy tears.

"Charles," she said. She had to tell him how she felt. But she couldn't. She was too tired and her lips wouldn't form the words. She drifted off to sleep with his hand in hers.

After three days in the hospital there had been no more contractions and the doctor could find no physical reason for the premature labor and no reason for it to happen again. Lise was bored and cranky and eager to get out. She was especially cranky because she hadn't told Charles she loved him. It seemed they hadn't had a moment alone.

"Please, Charles, take me home," she said, sitting up in her bed. "I want to go back to the château. I can't stand it here another minute. The food is terrible. They wake you up in the middle of the night to poke you and prod you. The lights are on all the time so you can't sleep. I have to get out of here. If you don't take me, I'll call a taxi."

He raised his eyebrows in mock dismay. "That won't be necessary," he said. "I had no idea you felt this way. I'll take you home if you promise to be good."

"Of course I'll be good," she said indignantly. "And I promise I won't overdo. Nanny is there to take care of me, not to mention the servants. And the food. I want Nanny's coddled eggs and the tisane she makes with the herbs from the garden." And I want to be alone with you, she thought. Just the two of us.

"You're in luck," Charles said with a smile. "The doctor is releasing you today. As soon as they bring the wheelchair, we can go. The car is waiting downstairs."

"Thank you," she said. She reached up, brought his face down to hers and kissed him. His eyes warmed to the color of hot chocolate. "Then you can go back to work. You won't have to take care of me. I don't know how you've gotten any work done. Every time I wake up you're here," she said. "Not that I'm complaining."

"You'd better not be," he teased. "Because you're going to continue to see a lot of me. We're way behind on the story of Frederic and Gabrielle.''

"That's not all we're behind on," she muttered. The doctor had told her they had to wait two weeks before resuming "marital relations." In two weeks she intended to put her sexiest nightgown on and seduce her husband. "By the way, what happened to the plaque?" In her hurry to show the doctor she was well and able to leave the hospital, she'd forgotten the plaque.

"Marie-Claire took it to our house. She thought it was too valuable to leave in the hospital. I haven't seen it yet."

"You haven't seen the letters either. I almost forgot. We found a packet of letters to Frederic from his father in the trunk. You see? I have much too much research to do to stay here any longer, too much unfinished business to attend to.''

The most important of which was to tell Charles how she felt about him. She wanted to wait until her head was clear, when she knew she wasn't dreaming, and she wanted to be at home.

That evening she had her chance. After she and Charles had had dinner in her room, the maid cleared their trays. Since she wasn't allowed to resume her "marital relations," Lise put on an old flannel gown that was soft and cozy to the skin.

"Lise," Charles said, sitting on the edge of her bed. "Where did that gown come from? I've never seen you in it before. It's so old-fashioned. So Victorian. It makes you look... It makes me want to take it off you and ravish you." He was gazing at her as if she'd suddenly appeared in a demi push-up bra and thonged panties. "I wish... How long did the doctor say we had to wait?"

She blushed. "Two weeks. But that doesn't mean..."

"That doesn't mean I can't kiss you, hold you, caress you, does it?"

She threw her arms around him and pulled him down next to her. She buried her face in his chest. "No," she said.

They slept together that night in her bed with Lise curled up in his arms. In the next two weeks they found many different ways of having "marital relations" that the doctor would have approved of. Lise was so blissfully happy she almost forgot she hadn't told Charles she loved him.

She told herself she was waiting to find out if Gabrielle and Frederic ended up together. That would be a sign that true love was possible. Not just for them but for their descendants. Yes, Charles had said he loved her, or was that just a dream? In any case, it was her turn now. She knew it and yet...

They sat together in the solarium, having coffee and fresh strawberry-rhubarb pie that Nanny had made with Frederic's letters on the table in front of them.

One morning when she awoke in his bed, the scent of his shaving lotion and the breeze off the river were hanging in the air. It was spring in St. Michel and what a spring. Unseasonably warm weather had caused the daffodils and tulips to pop up early. Charles came out the bathroom wearing only his silk boxer shorts. Would she ever get used to seeing him like this, his broad bare chest with the light dusting of hair, his hair damp from the shower and small drops of water lingering on his shoulders? Would she ever get used to the idea that he loved her? Would she ever get up the nerve to tell him she loved him? So many opportunities had come and gone.

"I have to tell you something, Charles," she said, feeling so nervous the color drained from her face. What if that had been a dream when she thought he told her he loved her? What if she caught him off guard? What if he wasn't ready to accept her love?

She took a deep breath. "I love you. I don't know when it happened. It crept up on me so gradually I didn't know what was happening. For a long time I was afraid to love anyone, especially you. I was looking for a sign that love does exist, that it lasts and endures. I thought if I found out that Frederic and Gabrielle ended up together, that would be the sign I was looking for. But their lives are not our lives. We have to work out our own marriage. So I'm not waiting for their happy ending. I'm going to make my own. With you if you'll have me."

"I'll have you," Charles said soberly. "I've been waiting, hoping, praying you would love me, Lise," he said as he walked to the bed. "Although you couldn't love me as much as I love you."

"Now wait a minute," she said. She was prepared to argue that point.

He didn't wait. He didn't want to argue. He broke into a wide smile, swooped her up in his arms and spun her around. Then very carefully and very gently he put her back in bed, and went to the open window. "She loves me," he shouted to no one in particular and the whole world in general. If the perch in the river were surprised to hear Charles Rodin expressing his feelings so vocally, they didn't know anything about love. But Charles did. Thanks to his princess, he'd learned about love and he wanted the whole world to know. In case anyone didn't hear the first time, he said it again. "Lise de Bergeron Rodin loves me. And I love her."

The next day they decided it was time to read Frederic's letters. They sat together in the solarium overlooking the garden with café au lait and a bowl of fresh strawberries from their garden. They'd hung the plaque with the picture of Gabrielle in there on the wall, and Lise was wearing Frederic's ring, the one Charles had gotten from his father. Lise glanced up at the picture and rubbed the ring with her fingers. Whether they found out anything about Gabrielle and Frederic's romance, she'd always have the ring, always feel the connection, thanks to Charles. It was fitting they should open the letters there in view of the portrait on porcelain. If it was bad news or no news at all, they were prepared. It didn't change their own lives or their own future.

The thin blue sheets of paper were covered with a spidery scrawl. Each one began "Dear son" and ended "Your loving father, Pierre de Bergeron." They skimmed, they scanned and finally they hit pay dirt.

It was Charles who found it. He held it up and gave it to Lise.

"I think this is what you're looking for," he said.

"Dear Son," she read.

I am sorry to hear of your injury on the battlefield, but we are looking forward to your return to St. Michel. I have hired a nurse to take care of you and nurse you back to health. I have explained that you are a bachelor officer and she should have no fears about your moral fiber. She is a widow and a refugee seeking safe haven from these terrible wars which are plaguing our continent. She came to us looking for help with just the clothes on her back and a letter of introduction from someone I know in Rhineland. She is installed in Rosamund's room awaiting your return.

Hurry home to your country and your family.

Your loving father, Pierre de Bergeron.

Lise's eyes filled with tears.

"We may never know any more than that," Charles said.

"But that's enough. We know she married the Greek prince and that he died and that she found a way to get back to Frederic. We know he never married. I have to believe she nursed him back to health and then…they lived happily ever after. I wonder if she ever revealed to anyone here that she was a princess?"

"He knew," Charles said. "That's all that matters." He leaned across the table and kissed her, tasting the ripe strawberries on her sweet lips. "Once a princess, always a princess."

A PRINCE AT LAST!
by
Cathie Linz

CATHIE LINZ

left her career in a university law library to become a *USA Today* bestselling author of contemporary romances. She is the recipient of the highly coveted Storyteller of the Year Award given by *Romantic Times* and was recently nominated for a Love and Laughter Career Achievement Award for the delightful humour in her books.

Cathie often uses comic mishaps from her own trips as inspiration for her stories. After travelling, Cathie is always glad to get back home to her family, her two cats, her trusty word processor and her hidden cache of cookies!

For my senior editor, Mary-Theresa Hussey, for inviting me to participate in this fun project, and for my editor, Allison Lyons, for wining and dining me in New Orleans but especially for being so easy to work with! Many thanks to you both!

Chapter One

"I'm having a bad heir day," Luc Dumont announced with a growl as he walked into Juliet Beaudreau's office.

"What happened?" Juliet hastily shifted a pile of papers to clear a chair for her unexpected visitor.

But Luc ignored the empty seat and paced instead, not easy to do in the tiny room that served as Juliet's office in the lowest level of the tower in St. Michel's de Bergeron Palace. Luc's very presence made the room seem even smaller. He was the kind of man who made an impression.

He'd certainly made an impression the first time Juliet had met him three years ago. Ever since then she always lit up inside whenever she saw him. Tall and lean, with thick brown hair and rakishly carved features, he had the most vivid blue eyes she'd ever seen. Instead of his usual work attire of a perfectly fitted black suit and light-blue shirt with a burgundy tie, he was wearing a black shirt and pants, which made her think he'd literally just returned to the palace from his most recent trip.

IIe was a man of many facets, deeply serious at times, wryly humorous at others. There had always been something slightly smoldering about him, deep beneath his cultured exterior.

At the moment he simply looked gorgeous…and upset.

"What happened?" Luc repeated. "You wouldn't believe me if I told you."

"Certainly I would. Did you finally find the lost heir?" She knew that as head of the country's Security Force, Luc had been assigned the mission of tracking down the missing heir to the throne of St. Michel.

"It looks as if I have." Luc kept pacing.

"You don't appear to be very pleased with the outcome," Juliet noted, coming around the solid oak table she used as a desk to perch on the front corner. While doing so, she briefly wished she was wearing something a little more attractive than a black top and skirt before refocusing her attention on Luc's news. "Who is it? We already know it's not Sebastian LeMarc. His claim proved to be false."

"That was his mother's doing, not his. Mothers can be a deceiving lot sometimes." Luc's voice held such bitterness.

Concerned, Juliet placed her hand on his arm, temporarily stopping his restless pacing. "Talk to me, Luc. Tell me what's going on. You know you can trust me."

It stung slightly that he didn't acknowledge her trustworthiness, but he did begin talking. "I just returned from visiting my father."

Which might explain his unsettled mood. Maybe it had to do with his family and not with the missing heir. "Did the visit go badly?"

"Depends on who you ask," Luc replied cryptically.

"What happened?"

"I have to fill you in on a bit of background first. My mother died when I was six," he said curtly, "and my father remarried after that."

"And your new stepmother was awful," Juliet continued. "And you were sent away to school in England, first to Eton and then to Cambridge."

Luc frowned. "How did you know that?"

Uh-oh. Juliet tried to backpedal. "Didn't you tell me?"

He shook his head. "No. I don't talk about my family life with anyone."

"All right," she reluctantly admitted. "I checked out your resumé, okay? Before he died, King Philippe granted me unlimited access to the royal archives and records."

"To do your thesis on the history of St. Michel, not to go nosing around in my personnel files. And I'm sure they didn't list anything about my stepmother being awful."

"I discerned that much for myself. Are you angry with me?" She gave him her most winning smile.

He wearily shook his head. "No. I'll let you off easy this time. Anyway, since I was sent off to school in England, my father and I haven't spent much time together. Maybe if we had, the lies would have come out sooner."

"What lies?"

"The lies about everything. About the man I thought was my father, the woman who was my mother, about the man I am today." His voice was rough with emotion.

Juliet had never seen Luc so upset. She didn't know if it was due to his English schooling or his work with Interpol before coming to St. Michel, but Luc was always a man in control, a man with hidden depths, a man who maintained his cool and kept his distance.

Juliet suspected it was because of his upbringing, that he had felt like an outsider in his own family once he was packed off to school. She knew the feeling well. As the late king's stepdaughter, she'd never really felt like part of the royal family. Her stepsisters, once the royal princesses, had never deliberately made her feel like an outcast. But she *was* different. She was the dark-haired, shy, bookish one amid all the pretty and popular blondes.

She'd always felt as if she didn't really belong. The one person who had befriended her was Luc. He might be thirty-two to her twenty-two, but she was older than her years. And she felt a special kind of bond with Luc, a bond she'd never dared explore for fear of ruining what they already had.

She knew Luc saw her only as a friend and that was fine, she'd take whatever she got. And she'd be the best darn friend Luc had ever had.

"Whatever lies might involve your father or your mother, I can tell you one thing about the man you are today," Juliet fiercely said. "You're an honorable man."

"You don't know what it's like, finding out your entire life is based on a lie."

"And I'm not likely to know what it's like if you don't tell me exactly what happened." Now her voice was tinged with a bit of exasperation.

"I'm not making much sense am I?" he noted wryly.

"No, but that's okay. Why don't you start at the beginning and go from there?"

"Ah, the beginning. Well, that would be with Prince Philippe's marriage to Katie, the one the young prince was told was invalid because Katie was underage at seventeen."

"Yes, but we know now that that wasn't true," Juliet reminded him. "The marriage *was* legal and valid. That's

PLAY THE
Lucky Key Game

Do You Have the LUCKY KEY?

and you can get

FREE BOOKS
and a
FREE GIFT!

Scratch the gold areas with a coin. Then check below to see the books and gift you can get!

 I have scratched off the gold areas. Please send me the 2 FREE BOOKS and GIFT for which I qualify. I understand I am under no obligation to purchase any books, as explained on the back of this card. I am over 18 years of age.

▼ DETACH AND POST CARD TODAY! ▼

Mrs/Miss/Ms/Mr _____ Initials _____ D3FI

BLOCK CAPITALS PLEASE

Surname _____

Address _____

_____

Postcode _____

🔑🔑🔑🔑 2 free books plus a free gift   🔑🔑 1 free book

🔑🔑🔑 2 free books   🔑 Try Again!

Visit us online at
www.silhouette.co.uk

The Reader Service™ — Here's how it works:

Accepting the free books places you under no obligation to buy anything. You may keep the books and gift and return the despatch note marked 'cancel'. If we do not hear from you, about a month later we'll send you 3 brand new books and invoice you just £4.99* each. That's the complete price - there is no extra charge for postage and packing. You may cancel at any time, otherwise every month we'll send you 3 more books, which you may either purchase or return to us - the choice is yours.

*Terms and prices subject to change without notice.

why you've been searching for their child all these months."

"Yes, well, the search is over."

"And you're having a bad heir day. That's what you said when you came in. And I'm assuming that you were referring to the missing heir, not to a haircut gone wrong."

Luc had wonderfully thick brown hair. At the moment it had an unusually rumpled look about it, due to his shoving impatient fingers through it. "You assume correctly. I was referring to the missing heir."

"And you still haven't told me who he is."

"I know. It's just I'm finding this entire thing a little hard to accept."

"What entire thing?"

"Well, finding out that my father isn't really my father at all for one thing."

Her exasperation instantly melted away. "Oh, Luc."

He tried to shrug it off, but she could tell he was more disturbed than he was letting on.

"My life is turning into one of those American soap operas," he growled in disgust.

"Did your father tell you this news while you were visiting him?"

"No. I went to see him to get to the bottom of this mess."

She was confused. "What mess?"

"I had reason to believe that Albert Dumont might not be my real father. He confirmed it. My mother was married before. And not just once, but twice."

"Did Albert know who your father is?"

"He didn't know at the time, no. All he knew was that my mother was unhappy with Robert Johnson, her previous husband, and that she divorced him. Apparently the lout cheated on her. Albert did business with the corporation Robert Johnson worked for, and he met my mother at some official function. Albert was also divorced and once my mother was free, the two of them married and settled down in France. I was all of two or three at the time. I know my mother's father died shortly thereafter, leaving her with no relatives in America.''

''So Albert thought that you were this Robert Johnson's child?''

''Well, apparently not. Apparently Albert knew that my mother was pregnant with another man's child when she married Robert. She asked Albert to let me believe Albert was my father, even going so far as to arrange for a fake French birth certificate for Luc Dumont, listing Albert as my father and Katherine as my mother.''

Juliet could see why he felt betrayed. The man he thought was his father turned out not to be his father after all. So many lies.

His voice was harsh. ''Luc Dumont doesn't really exist.''

''Of course you do. I'm looking at you, pacing my office like a caged lion.''

''Why did you have to set up shop down here anyway?'' He dropped onto the empty chair and fixed her with an aggravated glare. ''We could have found you a bigger office in the north wing.''

''I love it here.'' She waved a hand at her small but cozy surroundings. The grey stone walls dated back to the 16th century, their irregular surface still showing the marks where they'd been chiseled by hand. Aside from the oak table she'd retrieved from the royal storage room, she had a pair of mismatched Chippendale chairs, a mahogany bookcase and a lady's Victorian chintz armchair all squeezed into the tiny space. A tattered Oriental rug covered the stone floor. "You can see the gardens right outside my window."

She paused a second to enjoy the climbing pink roses that grew along the tower walls, framing her view of brilliant-colored flowering shrubs beyond, including luscious rhododendron and some late-blooming azaleas, graced by a trio of white butterflies dancing in the air. In the distance were the beds of sweet-smelling peonies and vibrant poppies and irises in colors ranging from deep purple to palest white.

She never tired of looking outside and drinking in the natural beauty. It fed her soul. Not that she'd ever tell anyone that. They already thought she was a little strange, a bookish oddity.

"The tower is one of the oldest parts of the palace," she continued. "Since I'm researching the history of St. Michel for my postgraduate work, this is the perfect place for me."

"Close enough to the boiler room that you can hear the pipes clang in the winter."

"True, but it's spring now. And you're trying to sidetrack me." She returned her gaze to him. "It won't work, you know. I have a one-track mind. It's why I'm so good with research. Once I get an idea into my head, I carry it through. So let's get back to you and your family. You said earlier that it all started with Prince Philippe's wedding to Katie. How so? Did Katie know your mother?"

"You don't understand. Katie *was* my mother."

Juliet was stunned. "But...but..." she sputtered. "That would make you..."

"The missing heir." Luc nodded. "Bingo. Now you see why I said I was having a bad heir day. Here I've been chasing all over Europe and America and it turns out *I'm* the missing heir. How ironic is that?"

She didn't know about ironic, but it was certainly freaking her out. She could only imagine how Luc must feel.

When he'd said that his father wasn't really his father, she'd never made the connection between his royal search and his family life. Luc had always been like her—an outsider to the inner circle of royalty, someone with regular rather than royal blood.

But not anymore. Now even that link between them was being broken.

"You're the missing heir," she repeated slowly. "Your father was…"

"King Philippe, who, when he was still a prince, married my mother Katherine, whom he called Katie. I should have made the connection." He was on his feet and pacing again. "I'm a trained investigator, for heaven's sake. But it never even occurred to me. She died when I was so young, I don't remember much about her. The only thing I have is a book on St. Michel she used to read to me. I kept it for sentimental value."

"Who else knows about this?"

"Sometimes it feels like everyone knew but me."

"What are you going to do?"

"How should I know? I'm still trying to absorb it all."

"Queen Celeste will not be pleased." Celeste was King Philippe's fourth and most recent wife, now widow. When King Philippe had died of a heart attack, the country had grieved, but those in power had panicked.

For one thing, according to ancient St. Michel law, the throne couldn't be passed to a female. And when the dowager queen had made her startling declaration that the king had married secretly at the age of eighteen and that a child had resulted…well, the palace had been turned upside down.

"Celeste is still maintaining that the child she's carrying is a boy," Juliet said.

"And I suppose she's still refusing to have an ultrasound to determine the baby's sex, right?" Luc asked.

Juliet nodded. "Correct."

"What a mess."

"You're the heir," she repeated. "The oldest male. The future king of St. Michel. I'm going to have to practice curtsying."

"You do and I won't speak to you," he warned her.

"But it's protocol to curtsy to the king."

"What do I know about being a king?"

"Well, for one thing, you're very good at giving orders," she pointed out with a grin

"Sure. Orders are easy. Reporting what I just found to the prime minister and dowager queen, that is not going to be easy."

"Why not?"

"Who'd believe that I'm the future king?" Luc scoffed. "I'm not a diplomatic man. I don't know anything about governing."

"You can learn. I'm certain the prime minister and the dowager queen will be delighted with this news."

"I brought proof with me," he said abruptly. "Not so much to convince them as to convince myself. It seems my mother left a key to a safety deposit box in Albert's care, to use if I ever came asking about my birth father. Since I didn't know Albert wasn't my father, it was doubtful I'd ever think to ask him anything. Inside the box was a registered copy of my birth certificate. I thought it had to be another fake, but I checked the paper trail, this time using my mother's name and it checks out. Before that I was looking for Katie Graham, her name on the marriage certificate to Prince Philippe. I'd already traced Katie back to Texas and found she married Ellsworth Johnson.''

''I thought you said his name was Robert Johnson?''

''Americans have this irritating habit of not using their proper Christian given names, especially Texans. Robert was his middle name. It was all there in the safe deposit box. Marriage certificates, my birth certificate and a letter from my mother.''

''Really? What did she say?''

''I haven't read it yet.''

''Why not?''

''Because I don't know if I can forgive her,'' Luc said bluntly. ''And I don't think there's anything she could have written in that letter that would justify her lying to me, or letting me live a lie.''

''Maybe she was trying to protect you. She was so young when you were born. Barely eighteen. Pregnant and alone. She tried to provide you with a stable home and father when she married Albert.''

''She married one man knowing she was pregnant with another man's child.'' A muscle flexed in his clenched jaw. ''How honorable is that?''

''You won't know until you read her letter,'' she replied.

''I don't need to read it to know what she did was dishonorable.''

''I realize you feel that way now, but you have to read her letter, Luc.''

''If you're so interested, then you read it,'' he growled, yanking it out of his pocket and tossing it onto her bookstrewn desk. ''I'm not interested. I don't care what it says. Now if you'll excuse me, I have to prepare for my meeting with the prime minister and dowager queen and I need some fresh air to clear my head.''

With that curt announcement, Luc left as abruptly as he'd arrived.

Chapter Two

Juliet stared down at the envelope on her desk as if it were a snake that might lunge out and bite her. Her fingers trembled as she traced the elegant handwriting—*Luc.*

What had his mother been thinking when she'd written his name? Had she hoped that he'd never find out he was heir to the throne of St. Michel? Would she even have known? From what Luc had told her of the investigation, Katie had been told that her marriage to Philippe was illegal.

Which meant Katie would have believed her son to be illegitimate. And she'd have done everything she could to hide that fact from him.

Juliet knew how much legitimacy mattered. The royal princesses had had to weather that storm of controversy themselves when Lise's rotten first husband Wilhelm had sold the story to a tabloid. Once the word was out that King Philippe had had a secret first wife, whom he'd never divorced, the paparazzi had swarmed the de Bergeron Palace like a bunch of locusts, feeding off the scandal.

The princesses had all left the palace now—Marie-Claire had married Sebastian, Ariane had gone to Rhineland and married Prince Etienne, Lise had finally found true happiness with her former brother-in-law, the honorable Charles Rodin. Juliet's own half sister Jacqueline was visiting cousins in Switzerland and protected from most of the scandal while their brother Georges had headed off to the Andes in Peru for a few weeks of summer skiing.

At least things had worked out well in the end for the three older princesses, who had all found the men of their dreams.

Juliet thought she'd found the man of her dreams as well—Luc. Her chances of having him see her in a romantic way had always been slim at best, but now they were impossible.

Juliet turned and caught her reflection in the small mirror propped on top of the bookcase along the opposite wall. She'd placed it there to reflect the view of the garden rather than out of any vanity on her part.

She had nothing to be vain about. Her green eyes were all right, she supposed, but her long dark hair had never behaved properly, and was at this moment falling out of the topknot she'd secured it in with a pencil to hold it in place. Her eyebrows were bushy, or so her roommate in boarding school had once told her, and her mouth was too large to be elegant. She even had freckles, something no princess would ever have.

Of course, she wasn't a princess. She was the ugly stepsister. The smart one, the bookworm, more interested in the past than in her future.

On those occasions lately when she had dreamt about

her future, she'd placed Luc at her side. Her gaze traveled from her reflection to the letter on her desk.

The fact that Luc was the missing heir changed *everything*.

She certainly didn't have what it took to make a king happy. She didn't even have what it took to keep a rich St. Michel businessman's son like Armand Killey happy. Three years ago, Armand had swept her off her feet, telling her he loved her quiet beauty. And she'd bought every word, had, in fact, hungered for someone to love her after her mother had died.

But Armand hadn't really loved her at all. He'd simply been using her in order to get close to the king. Juliet had heard him and his father discussing the plan. She'd been devastated and humiliated, as well as angry with herself for being so stupid as to fall for Armand's slick ways in the first place.

''Did you read the letter yet?'' Luc asked, disrupting her thoughts and once again catching her unprepared. He must have gotten the fresh air he'd said he needed by taking a brief walk in the garden, out of her line of vision.

''No.'' She paused to remove the pencil from her hair and let the dark strands tumble where they may. She'd learned long ago there was no fighting her hair, it always won. If it didn't want to stay up, it wouldn't. Turning to face Luc, she said, ''I did not read it. And I'm not going to until you do.''

''Then you'll be waiting a very long time,'' he retorted, ''since I have no intention of ever reading it.''

''Luc.'' She reached out to cover his hand with hers. ''You're upset right now. Don't make any decisions just yet.''

''Don't make any decisions?'' His voice was harsh, making him sound like a man pushed to his limits as he pulled his hand away. "I have to. I have to tell the prime minister and the dowager queen what I've discovered. I have an appointment with them both in less than half an hour."

Juliet tried not to be hurt by his physical withdrawal from her, reminding herself that he had a lot to deal with. A good friend wouldn't get all sensitive, wouldn't show her pain. She'd be supportive and reassuring. "As I said before, I'm sure they will be pleased with the news."

"And as *I* said before, I know nothing about being a king."

"There is a silver lining in all this you know. At least you won't have to worry about getting along with the new king."

"Trust you to find a silver lining."

She wrinkled her nose at him. "You make me sound like a naive Pollyanna who still believes in happy endings."

"You don't believe in happy endings?"

"My mother never found her happy ending," Juliet noted somberly. "She married Philippe out of a sense of duty, hoping to provide for her children, Georges and I. I don't think she ever truly loved the king the way she loved my father. Which was perhaps a good thing given the fact that the king only wanted one thing from my mother—an heir. In the end she died trying to provide him a son."

"Are you bitter about that?"

His question surprised her. "I try not to let myself be, but it is difficult at times," she admitted. "After the first baby was stillborn, the doctors warned that another pregnancy might be risky. But the king wouldn't listen and my mother went along with his wishes. Jacqueline was born a year later. I think the fact that the pregnancy went so well lulled the king and my mother into a false sense of security. Two years later my mother was pregnant again. This time things did not go as well." Juliet's throat tightened as it always did when she thought of those dark days. "I miss her still. That's why I feel so strongly about you reading this letter from your mother, Luc. Because I know the influence a mother can have, and how that loss leaves a void in you."

"My situation is entirely different. My mother died when I was six. I don't remember much about her."

"Perhaps reading her letter will bring back some memories."

"I don't want to remember," Luc stated bluntly, returning to his earlier pacing. "I've got enough trouble dealing with the present without dredging up the past any more than I absolutely have to. As it is, I'll have to rehash the entire story for the prime minister and dowager queen."

"The dowager queen has always had a soft spot in her heart for you."

"She just has an eye for younger men."

"Luc!" Juliet gave him a startled look before laughing somewhat guiltily. "You shouldn't say such things."

"See, I told you I'm not cut out to be king. Already I'm saying the wrong thing." His words sounded serious but there was a slight twinkle in his eyes.

"Well, the dowager queen is your grandmother so I suppose one could say something slightly outrageous about one's own grandmother."

"My grandmother?" Now Luc was the one who looked startled. "I hadn't thought about that."

"And with Marie-Claire, Ariane, Lise and Jacqueline, you've got four sisters."

"Half sisters," he corrected her. "Three of whom

have all married in the past few months. There must be something in the palace water that's responsible for all these weddings.''

''Your half sisters would disagree with you, I'm sure. They all married for love.''

''A romantic idea to be sure,'' he scoffed.

''You don't believe in marrying for love?''

''It isn't something kings are supposed to do, is it?'' Luc replied, pausing in front of her desk to bestow a brooding look down at the letter still resting there. ''Supposedly King Philippe and my mother were in love, and look where it got them. It seems to have messed up the rest of their lives.''

''It doesn't have to happen that way.''

''Oh, so now you're the expert on royal love, hmm?'' He turned to face her, propping his hip on the corner of the oak table as she had earlier. ''I thought your thesis was on the role royal women played in St. Michel's history.''

''And that role sometimes included falling in love.''

''What about you? Have you ever fallen in love?'' Luc asked her.

''I thought so at the time.'' Then Luc had come to the palace and things had changed. Her feelings for Armand had dimmed in comparison to her awareness of Luc. ''What about you?''

''Love makes you vulnerable and I try not to be vulnerable.''

No surprise there. ''If you're so invulnerable,'' she teased him, ''then you shouldn't be nervous about this upcoming meeting with the prime minister. You should be cool and calm, as you always are. A man in control.''

''Is that how you see me?''

She nodded. It was easier than adding that it was one

of the ways she saw him, that she also sensed something deeper within him.

"Well, I'll take that as a compliment then. Doesn't stop me from being uneasy about this meeting, however."

"Do you want me to help…" Juliet began, before stopping as she remembered that it was the king, not merely Luc, she was offering assistance to. As if a king would need a bookworm's help. "Never mind." She took a step away from him.

"No, go ahead. You were going to offer help with what?"

"Your meeting. By coming with you. A stupid idea."

"Not stupid at all. You've got a quiet way of getting people on your side. But this is one battle I've got to fight on my own."

"Of course," she said formally, taking another step back. "I understand and I agree."

"Why are you doing that?" Luc demanded, noting the change in her voice immediately.

"Doing what?"

"Going all proper and starchy on me, pulling away from me."

"This office isn't large enough for me to move very far away," she pointed out in an attempt to add a little levity.

But Luc wasn't buying her act for one second. Giving her a dark look, he said, "Don't you dare start acting differently now that you know about me being…" He paused and sliced the air with his hand instead of continuing.

"King," Juliet said. "The word you are searching for is *king*. And you can't expect me to act as if nothing has happened."

"I expect you to continue to be my friend as you've been since I arrived at the palace three years ago."

"I will always be your friend, Luc, but this is bound to change things between us."

"Not if we don't let it. And I refuse to let it," he stated. "You must promise to do the same."

She shook her head. "I don't think I can promise that."

"Why not?"

"Because you being the king changes everything. Some things we have no control over."

"The one thing I plan on doing with this situation is maintaining control," Luc stated firmly.

"Some things are beyond our control," she repeated with soft sadness.

Some things…like falling in love with a man who would be king.

"So Luc, I hope the fact that you called this special meeting means you have some good news to report to us," Prime Minister René Davoine said with his customary dignity. Slim and blessed with plenty of pewter-gray hair and a mustache to match, he was the picture of a distinguished statesman. Dressed in a two-piece dark suit as always, he appeared more somber than he actually was.

"I have news, but I'm not certain how good it is," Luc replied.

"Don't mutter, Luc," Dowager Queen Simone instructed him tartly.

Standing before the two of them made him feel like a bug under a microscope. As for the dowager queen, he'd never met anyone quite like her.

Thin and regal, she possessed a presence that filled the

room—and considering they were in the huge Throne Room, that was no small feat. At age seventy-five, she had her short dark hair meticulously maintained so that not one hint of gray or white showed.

Aside from her attitude, her eyes were the most memorable thing about her. They were a piercing blue, not as dark as his own, more the color of a light sabre. They certainly had a way of slicing right through a person who irritated her, which he'd apparently just done.

Queen Celeste had tried to convince anyone who would listen that Dowager Queen Simone was "dotty." And, while the older monarch had forgotten some details of the events that surrounded her son's early marriage, there was no denying that in most cases the dowager queen was still as sharp as a tack.

She was eyeing him with honed intensity. "Those English schools taught you how to enunciate properly."

"I could speak in French or German or Italian, if you prefer, ma'am," Luc retorted.

She waved his words away with an imperious wave of her wrinkled but still elegant hand. On her left hand was the elaborate diamond ring that her husband, King Antoine, had given her upon their engagement over fifty years ago. She'd outlived both her husband and her only son due not only to her strong constitution but also to her iron will. "English will suffice."

"Please be seated, Luc," the prime minister said with a much more inviting wave of his hand.

Luc sat on the Louis XIV chair as if it might collapse beneath him. This sudden attack of nerves was so unlike him. He'd been dealing with the prime minister and the dowager queen for months without any problem. But that had been when he'd been an employee, when he'd been head of the country's Security Force. It was a job he enjoyed, a job he knew how to do, a job he was very good at.

Damn. He should have asked Juliet to come with him when she'd offered. She'd know what to say. While she was shy around large groups of strangers, she had a way of disarming people with her quiet smile and sincere empathy.

"Well, Luc?" The prime minister looked at him encouragingly. "Have you found the missing heir?"

"I believe so, yes."

"You *believe* so?" Simone said. "You mean there is some room for doubt?"

"No, I found the birth certificate for Katie Graham's child, a son."

"A son." The prime minister almost applauded with delight. "Have you located him?"

"Yes."

"I told you Luc would succeed," the prime minister said.

"What is this son like? Is he someone suitable? He's not living in some American trailer park, is he?" Dowager Queen Simone demanded. "Someone who would be a disgrace to the throne and the de Bergeron name?"

"I don't believe he'd be a disgrace, no," Luc replied. "Naturally he's somewhat stunned with the news."

The dowager queen leaned forward eagerly, her thin hands resting on her gold-filigree-topped cane. "Where is he?"

"You're looking at him."

She blinked her laser eyes at him. "I don't understand."

"Katie Graham was my mother."

Luc could relate to the look of astonishment on the

prime minister's face. He'd felt that way himself when he'd first heard the news. He *still* felt that way.

The dowager queen's expression was harder to read.

"If you knew Katie Graham was your mother, then why on earth did you spend the past few months searching for her son?" the prime minister asked.

"I knew my mother as Katherine Dumont," Luc replied. "I had no idea about her...colorful past. It was only as I began the investigation that I started putting the pieces together. Even then, I didn't believe it could really be true. When I went to my father—the man I believed to be my father—and confronted him, he gave me the key to a safe deposit box that my mother had requested I open should I ever question my heritage. It's all here." He opened the manilla envelope he'd brought with him. "The entire paper trail—wedding certificate, my real birth certificate, not the one my mother had Albert Dumont falsify."

"Falsified birth certificates seem to have reached epidemic proportions around here lately," Simone noted tartly.

Luc flinched.

"Not that we're accusing you of any such behavior," the prime minister hurriedly assured him.

"I can understand your skepticism," Luc said. "I considered not sharing this information with you at all, just pretending I never found it."

"Why would you do something like that?" the prime minister asked.

"Because I'm not any happier about this...situation than you are," Luc said in a clipped voice.

"You misunderstand me." Simone put her thin hand on his arm. He was surprised to feel it trembling slightly. "Is it really possible? Could you be...my grandson?"

"According to those papers I am. Even so, I'd still like to get corroborating evidence from an independent source before we proceed any further."

"You sound as if you're not happy with this news, Luc," the prime minister said. "I can tell you that I, for one, cannot think of a more honorable man to take the throne."

Simone was looking almost gleeful. "You know what this means? It means that awful Celeste won't get her grasping hands on the throne. Her baby is due any minute now, and if it's a boy, well, then our ship would have been sunk."

"I don't think Queen Celeste will take the news about Luc very well," the prime minister noted.

"As I said," Luc interrupted them. "No one but the three of us and Juliet is to know about this news just yet."

"Juliet?" Simone raised a perfectly penciled eyebrow. "So you told Juliet. Before you told us?"

Luc refused to squirm in his seat. He was a former Interpol agent, he was not a schoolboy being reprimanded by his headmaster.

"Yes, I told Juliet before I told you." The set of his jaw communicated his aggravation. "Do you have a problem with that?"

"I fear it would do me no good if I did," Simone replied. "I've always liked Juliet. She's a wise little thing. So what did she advise you to do?"

"She didn't advise, she listened." Luc's pointed look indicated it was something that the older woman could learn to do better.

Simone smiled and leaned back in her chair with satisfaction. "Yes, you will do well as the king. Quite well indeed."

"I want you both to swear you won't tell anyone about this information until we can get it confirmed," Luc said. "And the situation with Rhineland also has to be addressed."

The prime minister paused in his close inspection of the material Luc had handed him. "The birth certificate is registered, and the rest of the documents appear legitimate."

"I know someone from Interpol, someone very discreet, who will do some follow-up work," Luc said.

"I understand you were born in Texas," Simone said with a slight shudder. "Thank goodness Katie had the foresight to bring you back to Europe and civilization. Imagine if we'd had to track you down in Texas, as some kind of roving cowboy."

"You've been watching too many movies," Luc said. "Not everyone in Texas is a cowboy." He knew, he'd traveled to Texas during the course of his investigation.

"Some are ruthless businessmen like J. R. Ewing," the dowager queen continued, "on that television show…what was it called? 'Houston'?"

"'Dallas'," Luc corrected her.

"There's no point in worrying over what might have been," the prime minister said. "We should focus on what our next course of action should be. I will need to notify the Privy Council."

"I'm still trying to get information from the French customs agency about Katie Graham's arrival and departure from France. Those records from over thirty years ago are in some warehouse waiting to be transferred onto the computer system."

"What do you hope to gain from those records?" the prime minister asked.

"The date Katie arrived in France to marry King Phil-

ippe and the date she left for the United States,'' Luc
said.

''But you already have so much information from earlier in your investigation,'' the prime minister noted,
opening his own file on the subject. ''The marriage certificate between Katie and Philippe, the birth certificate
of her son Lucas Johnson, the marriage certificate of Katie Graham and Ellsworth Johnson, the divorce certificate
of Katie Graham and said Mr. Johnson and lastly her
marriage certificate to Albert Dumont.''

''I could still be Albert's son, just trying to pass myself
off as the king's.''

''DNA testing would resolve that.'' The prime minister
gazed over the top edge of his reading glasses before
removing them entirely to solemnly ask Luc, ''Would
you be willing to subject yourself to that?''

Luc paused before nodding.

''Ah,'' Simone murmured. ''I understand now. It is not
that you want us to be sure you are the real heir, it is
that you yourself are not sure that you *want* to be the
king. Isn't that correct, Luc?''

Yes, Luc silently noted, the elderly dowager queen was
still sharp as a tack, all right. She'd certainly summed up
his emotions in no time at all.

''Your Majesty?'' the footman whispered to Celeste as
he delivered her lunch to her suite on the second floor of
the palace. ''I have some information for you.''

Shortly after her marriage Celeste had completely re-
decorated the suite in shades of ivory and gold. She
thought the colors complemented her own coloring—the
ivory of her flawless skin, the gold of her perfectly cut
hair.

''Information? It had better be something good,'' she

warned him. "The baby has been kicking me all day and I'm not in the best of moods, Henri."

"I overheard a conversation…"

"Overheard?"

"I was clearing the dowager queen's tea tray from the Ruby Salon, which is right beside the Throne Room."

"I am aware of the location of the rooms in this palace," Celeste said. "Get on with it."

"I happened to be standing next to the closed doorway leading into the Throne Room and happened to overhear the conversation between the prime minister, the dowager queen and Luc Dumont."

"Luc is back from France?"

"He arrived this very afternoon."

"With news I presume?"

"Yes, ma'am. Outrageous news."

"Well hurry and tell me, I haven't got all day. I believe I've gone into labor." Celeste gripped the front of the footman's ornate jacket. "Tell me…and quickly!"

"Luc is claiming that he is the rightful heir."

Celeste's grip on the footman tightened until she was almost choking the small man.

"Of course, I do not believe it," the footman wheezed, struggling for air. "You are our most beloved and beautiful queen."

"And I'm about to give birth to a boy," she said, panting slightly. "A boy who will be the king. Go now. Fetch Dr. Mellion. Get him and no one else. You understand?"

Henri nodded so fast his footman's cap almost fell off.

"And tell no one what you have heard about Luc," Celeste continued. "It is all a lie, a conspiracy by that dotty old woman and her crazy prime minister. Remember, Henri—" she released her grip on him and patted his arm as she smiled her famously charming smile ''—I will reward those who are loyal to me. Reward them *greatly*.''

''Thank you, Your Majesty. My only aim is to serve you.''

Her smile slipped as another contraction hit. ''Then go get Dr. Mellion and be quick about it!''

Chapter Three

"Have you heard the news?" Juliet asked Luc the next morning. She'd come to his office first thing. They were alone, and with the office door closed, assured of some privacy.

Unlike her own working space, his was spacious and possessed every modern convenience—computer, fax machine, a bank of telephones. His desk held a blotter, a penholder and a lamp. No mess, no pile of papers. Everything was neatly in its place, under control. Even the chairs in his office possessed a firm practicality that didn't make them particularly nice to sit in, but she plopped into the nearest one anyway.

"What news?" Luc barely looked up from the file he was studying.

"Celeste had a baby boy at four this morning."

"Oh, that news," he said absently. "Yes, I heard."

He'd reverted back to his usual working attire of a perfectly-fitted black suit and light blue shirt with a burgundy tie. He looked very classy...and very much like a "hottie" to quote her sister Jacqueline's favorite terminology.

Wishing she could just sit here and admire the view—him—Juliet realized she should try to keep her mind on court business and not funny business, like making out with Luc on his smooth desktop. "Did you hear she's proclaiming he's the next King of St. Michel?"

"Celeste has proclaimed a number of things over the past few months. It doesn't mean any of them are true."

Too jumpy to sit still for long, Juliet abandoned the chair for the corner of his desk, where she perched. Luc clearly hadn't noticed the flowing floral skirt she was wearing, nor the gauzy pink camisole top that had required all her nerve to put on. After all, she was visiting the future king. She'd almost put on the nunnish gray dress she wore to chapel. But some spark of rebellion had prompted her to stick to her present attire. "Did you tell her that you're the real heir to the throne?"

"No." Luc closed the file he'd been studying. "She was rather busy last night."

"When do you plan on telling her?"

Getting up to come around his desk and join her on the front edge of the desk, Luc replied, "As late as possible."

Juliet nodded understandingly. "She's not going to be pleased."

"Now there's an understatement," he noted dryly.

"When is the announcement going to be made about you being the true heir? How did the dowager queen and prime minister take the news? And…"

"One question at a time." Luc placed a teasing finger over her lips, effectively silencing her questions while sending her heart into overdrive. His skin was warm against hers. She was suddenly assailed with the urge to draw his finger into her mouth, to taste his skin.

She leapt away as if burned, almost falling from the desk. What kind of wanton was she to have such thoughts? Especially about the future king! She should never have worn this camisole top. It gave a girl ideas, ideas that she was far sexier than she really was, far more confident.

"Something wrong?" Luc asked.

She frantically shook her head, her dark hair tumbling down into her eyes. A pencil wasn't the best hairclip, but it's what she usually used to wrap her hair up into a knot on top of her head, and she'd somehow misplaced all of hers, which wasn't surprising. She often got so engrossed with her research that she lost track of things like pencils. So she'd had to leave her hair loose this morning.

"No, nothing." She wanted to sit down, but now felt awkward doing so while he still stood. All of a sudden the realization that he was the king was overshadowing *everything* else. "Go on with what you were saying, please. I didn't mean to interrupt."

"I don't care if you interrupt."

"It isn't polite."

"Which brings me to my next topic."

He still hadn't answered her previous questions, but she wasn't about to point that out now. Instead she tried to look properly attentive and respectful and not as if she secretly longed to kiss him.

"I want you to do a favor for me," Luc said.

"I'll do whatever I can."

He smiled. "I was hoping you'd say that. Because I want you to give me royalty training."

She stared at him blankly. "Excuse me?"

"I want you to teach me all the kingly things I'll need to know."

When she just blinked owlishly at him, he put it another way. "I'd like you to tutor me on protocol, customs and traditions of the royal family."

"I'm sure the protocol minister would be glad to help…"

Luc cut off her words. "No way am I going to that toady fellow. I dealt with him when I first arrived at the palace and he had the effrontery to tell me not to chew gum in front of the king. What are you smiling at?"

"Your use of the word *effrontery*. A very regal term."

"I don't feel regal," he confessed. "It feels so strange to think of King Philippe as my father."

"I imagine it does. I know none of this has been easy for you."

"And it's not going to get any easier. Which is why I need you to help me quickly learn my way about. You and no one else."

If only that were true. If only he did need her, as a woman rather than as a friend. And if only he wasn't the future king. And if only she were more beautiful and confident. And had bigger breasts. Hey, since she was making wishes here, she might as well wish for the entire package.

"So what do you say?" Luc asked.

"I'm honored that you'd ask me, but I truly don't feel I'm the best person for this job."

"I feel you are."

"There, you're already sounding like a king. You don't need me."

"You're doing it again," he warned her.

"Doing what?"

"Going all strange on me. All distant."

"I'm sorry if I've offended you."

"Oh please." He rolled his eyes at her. "You used to take great joy in offending me."

"I did not!" she vehemently denied. "Name one time when I did that."

"When I told you that men made better leaders than women and you said I was sounding like a chauvinist pig."

"Well, you were. But that was before…"

"I want the two of us to remain as we were before."

Which was part of the problem. He was happy with them just being friends as they'd been before, whereas she wanted so much more. And now those hopes were futile. As king, Luc had to marry someone worthy, someone who had the confidence and polish of the royal princesses, not an ugly duckling like herself. And she knew herself well enough to know that the more time she spent with Luc, the more intense her emotions for him were likely to get. Not a smart thing. And if nothing else, she was a smart woman.

"Come on, Juliet, I can't do this without you."

He could, of course. She knew he could. But it was impossible for her to turn away from the look of teasing pleading in his intense blue eyes. She doubted there were many women on the entire planet who could turn Luc down when he gave them that look—no matter what he wanted.

"Protocol and traditions, right?" she said briskly.

"Right. Piece of cake, right?"

"Speaking of cake, I think we'll begin with royal meals and formal state dinners." She kept her voice coolly efficient. If she was going to be coerced into doing this, she was going to do it her way.

"That sounds fine. There's just one thing. I don't want anyone knowing you're giving me these lessons."

"Why?" Was he ashamed of being seen with her? The thought stung like a cruel barb.

"Why? Because I don't want anyone else knowing yet about my being the future king," he explained. "Not until the corroborating documentation comes in. I figure we have about a week to ten days before that happens."

"So you're not telling Celeste that you're the king until then?"

"That's right. I thought you and I could get together later at night, after everyone else in the palace has gone to bed," Luc suggested. "Would that work for you?"

Work for her? None of this worked for her. Not one single thing. Not him thinking of her as a friend, not him being king, certainly not her spending more time alone with him. But there was no changing reality. And the reality was that she had to help him. "That will be fine." She could only hope that stating it so confidently would make it so.

Bond. Juliet Bond. That's how she felt. As if she were participating in some sort of covert operation.

She was even wearing the appropriate clothing—black, so she wouldn't be seen in the palace's shadowy hallways. King Philippe had ordered a reduction in the electricity used within the palace, and had replaced the light bulbs with low-wattage models that wouldn't need replacing for a decade.

The dim light served her purposes well. So did the fact that most of the servants had gone home to their own beds in St. Michel, leaving only a skeletal staff behind in the palace. A hundred years ago, the staff would have lived on the top floor in the servants' quarters. But things had changed a lot in the past century.

She tried to imagine any of the royal women she was researching sneaking down the hallway toward the Crystal Ballroom to meet the future king. Only one kind of woman did that. A royal mistress. Not that a royal mistress would ever have been caught dead wearing the tailored black slacks and black long-sleeved T-shirt she was presently wearing. Or rubber-soled shoes so her footsteps would be quiet in the marble corridors. Not the sexiest of outfits.

As often happened, Juliet was so caught up in her own thoughts she didn't realize anyone was in front of her until she almost ran smack into him.

At least she didn't shriek in surprise. Instead she emitted a startled *oomph.*

A pair of male arms circled her waist. But even before they did so, she knew it was Luc. Her nose was buried in his shirtfront and she could smell the citrus scent of his soap.

He, too, had changed from his normal working attire. Instead he was wearing the most deliciously silky shirt in a midnight blue that brought out the color of his eyes. She noticed that the minute she looked up. She also noticed the fact that he was smiling at her. Little crinkles appeared at the corners of his eyes.

She'd once spent several hours trying to pinpoint the exact blue of his eyes. She'd even gone so far as to check out a color chart in an old watercolor set from her boarding school days.

She'd been younger then. And foolish.

Foolish enough to believe a man like him might come to have feelings for a girl like her. But now the man was about to become a king, leaving her even further behind.

"Nice outfit," Luc was saying with a grin. "All you need is some face camouflage and you'd be ready for a covert op."

"Since there are no jungles in St. Michel or in the palace, I didn't see the point in wearing camouflage. It's not as though we were rendezvousing in the Palm Room," she noted tartly, not appreciating his comments about her clothes.

"I'd never find you in all those palms and ferns in there. Besides, it's too easy for someone to spy on us."

"Now who's sounding like James Bond?" she countered mockingly.

"I already told you that I don't want anyone else knowing about our meetings."

"And I still say you'd be better off having the protocol minister assist you in this matter."

"Now don't go getting all prissy on me, it's not that I'm ashamed to be seen with you or anything. That's not what you're thinking, is it?" Luc demanded, studying her face. "Because you're dead wrong."

"If you say so, your majesty."

He glared at her. "None of that fancy talk."

"You're going to have to get used to it," she firmly informed him. "So you might as well start now."

"Not with you."

"Yes, with me. At any official function, you're going to have to be comfortable with the way others treat you. And they *will* treat you differently. You must learn to be comfortable with that."

"Or learn to be a damn good actor," he muttered.

"Which will no doubt come in handy as well," she briskly agreed. "Now, one of the royal rules is that no one is to speak to you unless spoken to. I can foresee that this will be a problem since you're so close-mouthed.''

"I am not closemouthed. See?" He pursed his open lips at her.

She was immediately distracted by his actions and by the sensual outline of his mouth—the sculpted curve of his upper lip, the seductive fullness of his lower one. There was little doubt that most women would be fascinated by his smile, fascinated by *him*...period. Even without the title of king. Without any title at all. Without *anything* at all.

Oh my. She raised her hands to her cheeks. Concentrate, she fiercely ordered herself. And not on him! On protocol. Which certainly precluded her having fantasies about him. *Focus on protocol. What were you saying? Oh yes, you were telling him that he was closemouthed, no, don't look at his lips again. Stay focused.*

"You must learn to speak first and initiate a conversation," she continued as if nothing had happened. "Go ahead. Pretend I've just walked into the royal dining room for an official function. What do you say?"

"Whaaatsuuup?" he drawled, like those American beer commercials they saw on satellite television.

She stifled a laugh and attempted to give him a reprimanding look worthy of Mrs. Friesen, the headmistress at her boarding school. Mrs. Friesen was the queen of reprimanding looks.

He lifted a brow. "What's wrong? Not appropriate?"

"Not appropriate," she agreed.

"Do I know you in this scenario? Are you an old friend or someone I've never seen before?"

"You don't know me," Juliet replied.

"Are you from St. Michel?" Luc asked.

"No."

"Then I'd ask you who were, where you're from, what you're doing in St. Michel... Now what's wrong?" he demanded as she sighed and shook her head.

"I said to initiate a conversation, not to interrogate me."

He arched one dark brow at her. "There's a difference?"

"Yes, there's a difference."

"You're talking to a man who spent eight years in Interpol before coming here to be Head of Security. I'm much better at interrogations than I am at conversations."

"You don't seem to have that trouble with me," Juliet pointed out. "You and I have had some wonderful conversations."

"You're different."

She wanted to ask him how she was different, but he answered before she could do so.

"You're a friend," Luc said.

As she'd suspected. She knew he only saw her as a friend and nothing more than that. *Get used to it and get over it.*

"How would you speak to a stranger?" she said.

"The way I just told you."

Juliet sighed. Changing his many years of Interpol training was clearly not going to happen overnight. "All right, we'll come back to conversation later. For now, let's concentrate on royal protocol. As our monarch, you and the highest-ranking foreign dignitary will walk into the dining room together. Your respective spouses will walk behind you."

"So which role are you playing?"

"Excuse me?"

"Are you the foreign dignitary or my spouse?"

While the thought of being Luc's spouse made her

insides melt, the thought of being the king's spouse made her stomach clench. "I'm a foreign dignitary."

"Fine. That means you walk into the room beside me, right?"

She nodded.

"Should I offer you my arm?" Luc asked.

"That's not necessary, no." She didn't want him touching her any more than was absolutely required. Which should be no touching at all.

"It's a little dark in here, isn't it?" Luc noted as they entered farther into the large room.

Juliet reached over to turn on the switch controlling the porcelain hand-painted chandelier. While nowhere near as grand as any of the ones in the Crystal Ballroom, this exquisite one-of-a-kind piece had been a gift from Queen Victoria. But the main focus in the room, aside from the series of Rembrandts hanging on the wall, was the huge table that seated forty easily.

She gestured for him to sit at the table before taking the seat beside him. "Normally the footmen would take care of our chairs, pulling them out and pushing them back in. As you can see, earlier this afternoon I laid out two place settings as if this were a formal dinner."

"There's enough silverware here to choke a horse."

"As the king, you shouldn't say anything about choking a horse," she chastised him. "It could be taken out of context and spread around the tabloids. Next thing you know, you're being portrayed as someone who is cruel to animals. You can ride, can't you?"

"Excuse me?"

"A horse. You can ride a horse, can't you?"

"Yes, although I haven't ridden a lot in the past year or so."

"Then we should stop by the stable for a brush-up

lesson. But back to the dinner. You probably attended some formal functions while you were at Cambridge.''

''Not really, no. As a university student, I drank a lot of Guinness and ate a lot of curry, the hotter the better.''

''Really? Why?''

He shrugged a little self-consciously. ''It's a macho thing.''

The idea of Luc trying to prove his machismo brought to mind more forbidden images of decidedly sensual ways in which he could demonstrate his manhood. Images filled her mind of wickedly tempting options that had him plying her with kisses hotter than any curry. That made her nervous, and, as she did whenever she was nervous, she started talking. ''Usually royals stay away from spicy things.'' She almost tripped over her own tongue as another chapter of images flashed into her mind—Luc and spicy things. Luc *as* a spicy thing. ''Um, I heard that garlic, spaghetti, tomato sauce and shellfish have been banned from the menu when the Queen of England pays an official visit to Italy. And the media has an unwritten rule never to photograph or film her while she's eating. The press has a similar rule here. Blackberries and summer raspberries are also off most royal menus, since having tiny seeds stuck in one's teeth would disfigure a royal smile. Fish and meat are served without bones to avoid a possible choking hazard, as once befell our dowager queen in her younger days. A similar incident occurred with the Queen Mum, Queen Elizabeth's mother, I believe.''

''How do you know all these things?''

''I was babbling, wasn't I? Sorry about that.'' She gave him a sheepish smile. ''My brother Georges often teases me that I'm nothing but a walking encyclopedia of trivia.''

"You're much more than an encyclopedia," Luc noted quietly.

He looked at her, meeting her gaze with a speculative interest that was a bit disconcerting. Her lashes tumbled over her eyes as she quickly shifted her eyes downward to the table.

"Yes, well..." She cleared her throat. "So you're saying that while you were at Cambridge you didn't attend any formal functions of any kind?"

"Only one—the graduation ceremony, filled with pomp and circumstance and traditional robes."

"Well, there you go then. That sounds very regal."

"That was over a decade ago."

"It's probably like riding a bike, once learned not forgotten."

"Aren't you going to ask me if I know how to ride a bike?"

"Bike-riding isn't an often-used activity for a royal."

"I biked a lot when I was in university."

She tried to imagine Luc on a bicycle, but kept seeing him on a big powerful motorbike instead. He'd look wonderful in black leather.

Not good, Juliet sternly reminded herself. Keep your mind off his body and on his protocol.

"Yes, well..." She fidgeted with the array of forks to the side of the china plate, part of a set that had been a gift from the Royal Family of Holland. "Do you know what this is?"

"A fork," he replied helpfully.

"What kind of fork?"

"A silver one?"

"What kind of silver fork?"

"A royal silver fork?"

"It's a fish fork. You can tell by the different tines."

She went on to list each of the eight pieces of flatware. And then quizzed him on each one.

"These people have way too much time on their hands if they're so obsessed with which fork to eat with and when," Luc declared in exasperation after he'd misidentified the first-course fork as the salad fork.

"Do you want to return to conversation 101?" she warned him.

He waved his hand in surrender. "No, no, let's stick with flatware, by all means. I'm simply fascinated by flatware. Tell me more," he invited with a mocking gleam in his devilish eyes.

So he thought this was funny did he? She'd teach him a thing or two. "The first fork was used in the eleventh-century but it took eight hundred years before it was universally used in western cultures." She went on until his eyes glazed over. "Are you getting bored, your majesty?" When he didn't answer, she repeated, "Your majesty?"

"Huh?" he said with a startled oh-you-mean-me look.

"I asked you if you were bored by my lessons?"

"You're a very good teacher. It's just that there's only so much one can comprehend about the tines of a fork before it all becomes hazy in one's mind."

"A king can't afford to allow his mind to become hazy, your majesty."

"I told you to stop calling me that."

"And I told you that you need to get used to hearing it, and to responding to it."

"You know, I think I'm starting to love it when you use that prissy voice on me."

She stood up, straightened her shoulders and said, "That's not an appropriate comment."

"You wanted me to respond, right? Well, I'm responding. Come on, Juliet. Loosen up.'' The next thing she knew Luc had taken hold of her hand and tumbled her onto his lap.

Grinning down at her with devilish sexiness, he started tickling her just beneath her right ribs, where he knew she was particularly vulnerable. But Juliet squirmed just as he reached for her, and his hand brushed her breast instead of her ribcage.

They both froze.

Chapter Four

Juliet's startled gaze flew to his. She was so close she could almost drown in the rich blue of his eyes. Perched as she was on his lap she was all too aware of the intimate differences between male and female. She could feel the magnetism flowing between their bodies.

She couldn't move, couldn't breathe, and certainly couldn't look away. He appeared as caught up in the moment as she was. Her parted lips were mere inches from his. She could feel his warm breath on her mouth. Was he leaning closer?

Desire and anticipation were like a fire dancing over her sensitized skin.

Then she was set back on her feet as suddenly as he'd tugged her onto his lap.

What had just happened? Had he been about to kiss her or had she imagined that?

Luc's smile was sheepish. She knew hers was awkward. The air between them seemed to hum. Each of them hurriedly moved away—retreating to a separate arca of the dining room as if afraid of what might happen otherwise.

Juliet tried to read Luc's emotions from his expression, but his years at Interpol had given him the ability to hide his feelings when he wanted them hid. The only thing she caught was him staring at her as if trying to read her mind. Could he guess that she'd wanted him to kiss her? Was he regretting joking around with her? Was he sorry he'd tumbled her onto his lap? Should she say something? Make a joke? Try and break the ice? Or make a run for it in an attempt to save face?

That last option sounded darn good to her at this point.

"I think we've done about all we can for one evening," she said briskly. "We'll arrange the next tumble…I mean tutorial in the stables."

Tumble in the stables. She tried not to blush at her verbal slipup. Had he noticed?

"That sounds fine," Luc said, his voice as smooth as ever. "I suppose no one would get suspicious if we were to bump into one another there."

"Nothing suspicious at all," she quickly agreed. "You bumped into me earlier."

"Right," he agreed just as quickly. "I bumped into you and there was nothing to it."

"Absolutely nothing," she said with cheerful brightness. "One friend bumping into another."

"With a little horseplay thrown in on the side. The stables would be a good place for that," he said. "For horseplay, I mean."

Smooth, real smooth, Dumont, Luc told himself. This is Juliet you're talking to here. Why this sudden attack of nerves? You weren't this jumpy when you had your first weapons training exam.

But then, caressing her breast had been as explosive as handling live ammunition.

He honestly hadn't been trying to cop a feel when he'd pulled her onto his lap. It hadn't been a premeditated move on his part at all. She'd just been acting all starchy and distant and he'd simply wanted to tease her into remembering that they were friends.

Instead he'd raised an entirely new issue. And that wasn't all he'd raised.

His reaction to her feminine body had not been a platonic one. He wanted to kiss her, and he almost had before he'd come to his senses. He might not have the protocol manual memorized yet, but he was pretty darn sure that seducing Juliet would *not* be deemed appropriate behavior.

Seducing Juliet. Where had that idea come from? Probably from the raging arousal that still held his body in its taut grip. But where had this entire reaction come from? He'd known Juliet for years and had never even placed her and seduction in the same sentence before.

Maybe he'd been too long without a woman. That must be it. He'd been searching for the missing heir for months and that had left him with no time for anything else, including romantic relationships. And the year before that he'd dated several women, but hadn't found one that really held his interest.

His job and the long hours he kept had proved to be a stumbling block as far as long-term relationships with a woman went. And now there was this king thing.

"So I'll meet you in the stables tomorrow," Juliet was saying. "Will three in the afternoon be convenient?"

"Sure," he replied although he had the sudden feeling that nothing about this entire situation was going to prove the least bit convenient at all.

*   *   *

Juliet was in love. She had no doubts whatsoever about that. And what's more, her love was returned tenfold, perhaps even a hundredfold, by the objects of her devotion—two-month-old kittens from the stable cat, Rexxie.

The purring balls of fluff were stretched out on her lap with utter faith in her ability to keep them safe. How wonderful it must be to have that kind of trust. She hadn't felt that way since her father had died. Her mother had loved him so intensely that she'd never quite recovered from his passing.

One of the kittens wiggled and tucked his head under his brother's leg to get more comfortable. Juliet had named the gray-and-white one Mittens and the black-and-white one Rascal. She wasn't allowed to have a pet while she lived in the palace and having one at boarding school certainly hadn't been allowed. While attending her first semester at the Sorbonne in Paris she'd shared a cat named Mignon with her older roommate Cleo, who had taken the cat home with her to Provence upon graduation.

Paris was a beautiful city, but Juliet had become homesick, so she'd transferred to the local university here in St. Michel where she'd completed her degree and graduated with top honors. She was now working on her advanced degree in history.

This morning she'd been in her office supposedly working on reading the diaries and private letters of Queen Regina, but instead had spent much of her time daydreaming about Luc and reliving that moment last night when he'd tumbled her onto his lap.

Why had he done that? He'd just been kidding around, one friend to another, she told herself as she'd done a hundred times over the past fifteen hours. He didn't mean anything by it.

And that moment when their lips had almost touched? When his hand had touched her breast? The kitten stretched and snuggled its silky head against the very same breast Luc had touched. She could still feel the warmth of his hand, as if it had been imprinted through her skin to her very heart.

Looking down, she blushed at the sight of her nipples showing through her white shirt. She'd removed her formal riding jacket so she wouldn't get fur on it while playing with the kittens.

Her appearance in the stables hadn't aroused any suspicions, because she'd been a frequent visitor since the kittens had been born. The stablehands didn't even notice her, which was fine by her. Juliet had never been the kind of female a man noticed.

She'd never minded that before. She was smart and that had always been enough for her in the past. And then Armand Killey had come into her life, with his charming ways, sweeping her off her feet.

But Armand had just been using her. After she'd confronted him about his deception, he'd at first tried to deny it before realizing the game was up. Furious at having his plan backfire, Armand had said some scathing things to Juliet—telling her no one would love her for herself, that she lacked the elegance and class of a true royal, that she was the gangly, ugly stepsister.

He'd hit her where she was the most vulnerable.

Juliet had no royal blood in her veins. The king had only been her stepfather. And she wasn't elegant or gorgeous like her stepsisters, the royal princesses, or adorable and charming like her half sister, twelve-year-old Jacqueline.

She'd thought at the time three years ago that she'd been broken-hearted. Then Luc had come into the palace and into her life. And the longer they knew one another, the more she suspected that while Armand had severely damaged her self-esteem as a woman, he'd never truly touched her heart. Luc, on the other hand, seemed to have the key to her heart. And that made her entirely too vulnerable.

Whereas Armand had hurt her deeply, Luc had the power to destroy her. Not that he ever would intentionally. But the very fact that he was the heir to the throne of St. Michel meant that there were some pretty insurmountable differences between them now.

While Mittens slept on her breast, Rascal woke up and started playing with his own tail, tumbling over backward as he did so. In an effort to save him from falling off her lap, she stuck her legs straight out so he'd roll down her thighs to her knees. The kitten scrambled back up her trousers to the safety of her lap. Luc wasn't as lucky. He tripped over her shiny riding boots and landed face-first in a pile of hay.

Great way to make an impression on a king, she thought to herself as she quickly set the kittens back into their basket and hurried to Luc's side.

"I'm so sorry. Are you okay?"

He got up and plucked the hay from his dark hair, while shooting her a wry glance. "If you wanted to take a tumble in the stable with me, all you had to do was ask."

"It was an accident," she protested. "I had two of the kittens on my lap and one was about to fall off, so I…"

"Tripped me?"

"I put my legs out and you stumbled over them. You should have watched where you were going."

"Me? You're the one who created a hazard."

"They didn't teach you how to avoid falling over

someone's feet in all your Interpol training?'' she automatically teased him as she had many times in the past before remembering who he was now.

As if able to read her thoughts, he cast her a warning glance meant to remind her that they were not alone. Leaning close, he whispered in her ear, ''Don't you dare your highness or your majesty me here.''

His breath was warm against her skin and smelled of coffee. She wondered if she'd taste coffee on his lips. Unable to resist touching him, she pulled a few bits of hay from his hair. ''You look like the scarecrow from the *Wizard of Oz*.'' If the Wizard had been played by a young sexy Pierce Brosnan perhaps.

''Was the scarecrow the one who lacked a heart?''

''The scarecrow lacked courage, which you have tons of. The Tinman was the one who lacked a heart, which you also have.''

''Not everyone would agree.''

''You've definitely got a heart,'' she whispered, sliding her hand down to his chest. ''I can feel it beating.''

Again their eyes met and time stood still. As had happened last night, Juliet was swept up in a wave of sensual awareness. Her surroundings melted into the background, and all her attention was focused on this one instant in time, on this one man in the universe.

She felt the throb of his heart beneath her palm, felt the warmth of his skin through the cotton of his riding shirt. Her own heartbeat was pounding so loudly she was surprised Luc couldn't hear it.

''Luc, I didn't see you there.'' The interruption came abruptly and caught them all by surprise. The stablehand named Pierre appeared disconcerted to have walked in on them. ''Is there something you need?''

What Luc needed was his head examined for allowing

himself to think of Juliet this way. What had come over him? By this morning he'd convinced himself that last night had been a momentary lapse, a freak occurrence never to be repeated.

Yet here it was, just a few hours later and again Juliet was getting to him. His life was complicated enough at the moment, he certainly didn't need a romantic entanglement to further muddle things.

"No, Pierre, I'm fine," he belatedly replied, stepping away from Juliet and, he hoped, from further temptation. "I just thought I'd take one of the horses out for a ride."

"Monarch is feeling frisky today, why don't you take him?"

Luc knew all about feeling frisky. "I'll do that, thanks for the suggestion."

"I've got Annabelle saddled and ready for you, ma'am," Pierre added with a shy smile for Juliet.

"I already told you to call me Juliet," she gently scolded him, her smile brightening her entire face. "Thank you, Pierre."

"Not at all, ma'am, I mean Juliet."

"We'll both be there shortly," she added.

Pierre nodded and reluctantly walked away.

"That young man has a giant crush on you," Luc told her.

"Don't be ridiculous." She scooped up the basket of kittens.

"I'm not being ridiculous, I'm being observant. Didn't you see the way he blushed and tripped over his own tongue when he spoke to you?"

"Pierre is just shy."

Luc reached out to gently rub one of the kitten's ears. It was Mittens, who adored ear-rubbing more than anything except for the cooked chicken Juliet sneaked in from the royal kitchen.

Seeing Luc's slender but large hands on the tiny kitten made her melt inside. His gentleness made her think he'd be good with a baby. It was the first time she'd thought of him and children. She wanted children herself. Only the other day she'd realized that her mother had been married and pregnant by the time she was Juliet's age.

"What are you thinking about?" he asked her.

She could hardly say "your children" so she replied, "Our next lesson."

"We've barely started this one yet," he noted.

"I suspect you'll do fine on a horse." He certainly looked fine in the formal riding attire. The crisp white shirt was none the worse for his tumble in the hay, and the dark jacket and tight-fitting jodhpurs hugged his body like a glove. She quickly looked away before he could practice his eye magic on her, drawing her into his gaze. "Ballroom dancing is next."

He grimaced.

There wasn't time to say anything else until they'd both mounted their horses and begun their ride. Even then, Luc waited until they'd cantered some distance from the palace in the royal park, well beyond the formal gardens, before pulling Monarch to a halt and turning to face her.

"Ballroom dancing?" he repeated.

"Don't tell me you don't know how to dance."

"The last dancing I did was at a Sting concert, and somehow I doubt that the movements will be the same in this case."

"Not unless you were doing a waltz at the concert."

"Waltzing was frowned upon," Luc noted dryly.

"Well, it's not frowned upon at a formal ball. I'll meet

you in the Crystal Ballroom just before midnight to-night.''

"Are you planning on wearing your covert operations outfit again?'' he inquired.

"Now you're planning my wardrobe?''

Luc shrugged. "It's just that if you're going to teach me how to dance in a formal situation like a ball, then perhaps you should dress appropriately.''

"If someone sees me walking down the corridor in a formal ballgown they're bound to get suspicious,'' she pointed out.

"Then let's compromise. Wear that black slinky dress you had on the other week for the ballet gala.''

She frowned. "Slinky? I don't have anything slinky. Oh, you mean that black slip dress? It *is* a favorite of mine. I got it at a vintage clothing store in Paris.''

"Wear that and I'll be a happy man,'' Luc stated.

He might be a happy man, but she'd be a very vul-nerable woman, moving closer to falling even more in love with him with every second.

Juliet looked at the clock for the tenth time in as many minutes. She even went over to the mantelpiece to make sure it was working correctly. After all, the timepiece was almost a hundred years old and had been stashed in the palace attic for most of that time. The glass was missing from the face, but the elegantly painted cherubs dancing around the outer edge were exquisite.

Everything in the two rooms assigned to her—a large sitting room/bedroom and an attached drafty bathroom—had either been rescued from the palace's attic or base-ment.

Junk, Celeste had proclaimed in disdain, preferring her own royal apartments with their ivory chaises and gilded cabinets. But Juliet loved the comfy feel of her surroundings, where nothing was perfect, but everything blended together in a way that made her smile.

Blue was her favorite color, and that showed, from the faded blue damask of an armchair to the delicate robin's-egg blue in a series of watercolors of Venice. Sure the chair had a few lumps; she just sat around them. And yes, the watercolors had age speckles along the edge, but that just endeared them to her all the more.

As in her office, a large Oriental rug covered the floor and books covered almost every available space. A few smaller items on display, like the porcelain figurine of a mother and child, had been purchased by her at some out-of-the-way shop in Paris or St. Michel catering to those who liked unique pieces.

Indeed, her college friend had referred to Juliet's decorating style as "Paris Flea Market" and told her it was all the rage now.

Juliet studied her reflection in the slightly cracked rococo mirror. The black dress Luc had ordered her to wear did go well with her pale coloring and dark hair. But there was no way it was slinky. Was there?

She turned sideways and sucked her tummy in. She even attempted to take a few regal steps before wobbling on her high heels.

Juliet never had mastered the art of walking in these darn things. She was tempted to wear flats, but Luc was right in his assessment that for the lesson to be most beneficial they'd have to recreate the actual atmosphere of a ball as best they could in the circumstances. He was even bringing music. She wondered if he planned on bringing a Sting CD.

She smiled and tried walking again. Better this time.

Not regal by a long shot, but no longer as dorky or book-ish.

Of course, the logical, practical side of her brain was sternly warning her that it shouldn't matter how she looked, what she wore, or how she walked because she was merely tutoring Luc. It wasn't as if they had a date or anything.

Guard your heart, she warned her mirror image, who showed no sign of heeding her words if the grin on her face was any indication. You'd think she'd just been given a huge box of dark chocolates or something, the way her face was beaming.

Her smile faded as she remembered the baby gift that she'd sent to Celeste's apartment that afternoon. It had been returned by the footman Henri, one of the few servants Juliet couldn't warm up to, along with a note from Celeste.

I hardly think a toy giraffe is appropriate for the new king of St. Michel, since giraffes are not regal animals. It is my hope that you were not trying to insult baby Philippe II with your paltry present.

Most of the time, Juliet simply tried to keep out of Celeste's way. After her mother's death, it hadn't taken King Philippe long to find a replacement. Celeste was a beautiful woman, with classy features and lovely blond hair. But the class was only skin deep—and it had nothing to do with the fact that, like Juliet, she lacked any royal blood. No, her commonness had more to do with her behavior than her background.

Not that Celeste couldn't be sweet and charming when the occasion warranted it. She could. And that surface brightness blinded some to her true nature. But not Juliet.

Enough thinking about Celeste. It was almost midnight, the magical witching hour. She had to hurry or she'd be late.

The Crystal Ballroom was located on the main floor toward the back of the palace, facing the gardens. The huge rectangular room got its name from the series of priceless Austrian crystal chandeliers on display—three large examples placed down the center of the long room and three smaller ones at each shorter end of the room. The elaborate design created a tiered waterfall of crystal drops, each one mirroring a rainbow of colors as they reflected the light. The first time Juliet had seen them, she'd felt as if she were standing in the middle of a rainbow.

The famous chandeliers weren't illuminated tonight. Instead Luc had set a series of candles on the sideboard.

It wasn't the first time she'd seen him in a tuxedo, but her breath always caught at how devastatingly handsome he was in the formal attire. The impeccable cut emphasized the athletic fitness of the strong body beneath—the broad shoulders, the lean torso, the narrow waist.

His mouth was quirked into a teasing smile as he murmured, "Well, do I pass inspection?"

"You'll do," she replied a tad breathlessly. "I see you brought the music." She nodded toward the portable stereo system on the Italian marble floor. "Is it Sting?"

"No, it's Strauss. I borrowed some CDs from the prime minister. He has an amazingly vast and diverse collection, everything from Mozart to Duke Ellington to the Beatles."

"Strauss is good for waltzing."

"So is that dress," Luc noted approvingly. "I'm glad you took my suggestion and wore it tonight."

"Suggestion?" she repeated with a lift of one brow. "An order was more like it."

"Does that mean I'm sounding more kingly already?"

"I told you from the very beginning that you were already a pro at giving orders."

"Yes you did, and I appreciated the vote of confidence."

"That's what friends are for," Juliet replied with deliberate cheerfulness. The look he'd just given her when he'd commented on her dress a moment ago was still making her heart hum. Nerves were clearly fueling her imagination, because she could almost have sworn that a smoldering sexual interest had been present in the depths of his gorgeous eyes.

Hah, that'll be the day, she thought to herself. Luc looking at her as anything other than a buddy.

What about the other night? that nagging voice in her brain demanded. *What about the almost kiss? Or that moment in the stables when his eyes met yours...?*

Get real, she ordered her fanciful thoughts. You can't afford to get caught up in this fairy-tale moment. Don't do it. Don't play the fool the way you did with Armand.

"All right then," Juliet said crisply, as she did whenever she started a lesson with Luc. "Let's get started. I'd like this lesson to be more productive than the one on dining. We never did get around to things like olives."

"Olives?" Luc lifted one elegant eyebrow at her in a gesture she recognized and was coming to love.

"Yes, olives. One must always take olives with a spoon and never a fork. Here, I've written up a list for you." She handed him a neatly folded piece of paper.

"I suppose I mustn't drink my soup, either, hmmm?" he teased her.

She flushed. "You asked me to help you."

"So I did and I truly appreciate the help. I'll look over your notes later when I'm in bed."

She could picture him in bed—his bare chest with a tantalizing whirl of dark hair leading down to his navel, the white sheets gathered down around his narrow hips, barely covering him.

Suddenly the ballroom was unbearably hot. She would have fanned herself with a sheet of paper, but she'd just handed it over to Luc and she wasn't about to grab it back again. She'd just have to pretend nothing was happening, that her hormones weren't going into overdrive.

"Yes, well…" She cleared her throat and began again. "As I mentioned earlier in the stables, I believe you'll find the waltz the most useful dance. We'll start with the basic position, your hand curved around my waist, your other hand clasped in mine."

"What about white gloves?" Luc suddenly said. "I'm not going to have to dance in white gloves am I?"

The mental image of him dancing in white gloves and nothing else had her stumbling over her own two feet.

"Steady there," he murmured, catching her in his arms.

"I'm not that good a dancer," she said, embarrassed by her inability to focus. "You'd do better with someone else."

"I don't want anyone else," he said.

If only that were true. If only he really did want her as something other than a friend.

"And don't even think about turning me over to the protocol minister," he warned her. "Can you see me dancing with him?"

Juliet had to smile. "No. If you don't like the protocol minister, there's always the Privy Council."

"Not one of whom is a day under seventy."

"I'm sure the prime minister is."

"Yes, but any group that makes the prime minister look like a spring chicken isn't a group I want to dance with. *Capiche?*"

Her smile had turned into a full-blown grin by now. "*Capiche.* Your fluency with so many languages will serve you well as…"

Luc placed his finger over her lips as he had the other night. "The walls have ears," he warned her.

She firmly moved his hand away from her mouth. She was not about to succumb to temptation tonight. She was going to be practical from the get-go. "I still don't see why you have to be so secretive about this news."

"Remember what happened with Sebastian? The tabloids were all speculating that he was the heir and the announcement was almost made that he was. I don't want something like that happening again. Which is one of the reasons I wanted independent confirmation of everything I learned in France about my true heritage."

"And what's the other reason?"

"The Rhineland situation needs to be addressed plus I wanted some time to learn the royal ropes, so to speak."

"Speaking of which, we should resume our dancing lessons. We don't have all night."

"Why not? Do you have someplace else you have to be?" he demanded.

"Yes," Juliet teased him. "I've got a hot date waiting to pick me up outside the palace walls."

"You'd better not," Luc growled, surprising her with the intensity of his voice.

"Why not?"

"Because of this…" Without further ado, Luc kissed her.

Chapter Five

Juliet didn't know who was more shocked—herself or Luc. She did know that being kissed by him was better than she'd ever imagined, and she'd imagined it very often in vividly sensual detail.

But none of those fantasies had prepared her for the sheer pleasure of the real thing. The candlelight flickered against the walls, showing their shadows merged together. She closed her eyes and focused on his mouth, returning his kiss with fervor.

His lips were warm and unexpectedly soft. They were also seductively hungry and erotically intent.

Tilting his head in the opposite direction, he targeted her mouth again, his lips parting hers in a sensual dalliance that made her knees melt.

He slid his arms around her, his hands burning through the thin silk of her dress as he clasped his fingers at the base of her spine and tugged her closer. She felt the smooth material of his tuxedo jacket beneath her fingertips, smelled the burning candles.

She felt as if she, like those candles, was going up in flames. She had known with a feminine instinct that he was destructive to a woman's reason, but she had no idea how powerful a distraction he could be—wiping out all thought of propriety or common sense and replacing it with sheer sensation.

Flickers of desire soared upward from the depths of her body. She felt the thud of his heart against her breast and knew her own nipples were rubbing against the fine material of his jacket. She should be outraged, she should be embarrassed, but she was neither. He made her shiver and burn at the same time with a powerful response that she couldn't control.

His mouth promised an ecstasy beyond belief, while his tongue tempted hers to come play an erotic game of hide-and-seek. Her lips parted even farther. He quickly accepted her invitation, his tongue darting inside to explore the dark recesses of her mouth even as his hands explored the curve of her derriere.

She was intoxicated with pleasure, gasping for breath as he shifted his kisses along her face to nibble at her ear.

The moment's respite was all it took for reality to reassert itself.

"What are you doing?" she whispered, whether to herself or him she couldn't be sure.

"Kissing you," Luc whispered in reply, his voice as hazy as hers.

"You shouldn't."

"Why not?"

"Because you're…you and I'm…"

"You're Juliet," he murmured against her lips. "You smell like lemons and taste like heaven."

"Do you say that to all your friends?"

Friends. The word doused Luc like a bowl filled with ice water. He had no business kissing her this way. He immediately released her and stepped away.

"Sorry," he said curtly, turning away so she wouldn't see the effect she'd had on his body. "I don't know what came over me."

Liar, he silently mocked himself. He knew damn well. Ever since he'd tumbled Juliet onto his lap the other night, he'd known she was getting to him. He wasn't sure why. Why now? Was it fate's way of laughing at him? Of turning every single corner of his life upside down, including his friendship with Juliet, a friendship he'd come to rely on strongly. The idea of ruining that friendship was one of the few things that truly scared him.

But this newfound sexual awareness of Juliet as a woman was also more than a tad disconcerting. She was ten years younger than he, and much more inexperienced. He had to be the responsible one here. He should have been the one to come to his senses first, instead of her questioning his motives.

She'd been right to call a halt to things when she had, before they had gotten completely out of hand. In the middle of a ballroom, for heaven's sake.

It had to be the candlelight and the music. He marched over to the portable stereo and leaned down to hit the Stop button with so much force the electronic equipment skidded on the marble floor.

There, that should be better. He turned to face Juliet. "Again, I'm sorry about that."

Juliet was at a loss for words. What could she say? That she wasn't the least bit sorry? That she'd loved every minute of it? That would be an understatement.

"You were just trying to be a friend by helping me out here," he continued, "and I took advantage of that."

A friend. That dreaded word again. Juliet wished she could obliterate it from their vocabulary. But if she did that, what was she left with?

"Do you want to continue the lesson or would you rather call it quits for tonight?" he asked her.

"What do you want?" she asked in return.

Luc looked at her for a moment, his sensually brooding gaze seeming to indicate that he wanted *her,* before he turned away from her.

"I want my life back," he said, his voice harsh. "I just want my damn life back."

"I demand to speak to the Privy Council!" Celeste angrily informed the prime minister first thing the following morning.

"No one is allowed to speak to the Privy Council, aside from the king and he is no longer with us."

"My *son* is the king," Celeste declared.

"The Privy Council would have to make that determination," the prime minister calmly replied.

"Which is why I must speak to them. It's been nearly a week since my son Philippe II was born, yet still they refuse to make the proclamation declaring him king."

"And you know the reason why. You are aware of the fact that King Philippe was married to Katie Graham and that together they produced a child—possibly the heir to the throne."

"I know that the dowager queen has been telling such stories, but that is all they are. Stories. Figments of her imagination."

"It is more than imagination. We have documentation."

"I can supply experts who will say that your documentation is a forgery," Celeste countered, narrowing her eyes. "There is already talk that you and the dowager queen concocted this story to keep my child from the throne. Is the Privy Council aware of this fact?"

"I will inform the Privy Council of your concerns."

"Of course you will," she mocked him.

"If you doubt my word about speaking before the Privy Council, you have only to read the Royal Charter of St. Michel. It is all there. In the case of questionable succession, the Privy Council will meet and discuss the situation. No member of the royal family is allowed in on those discussions. The Privy Council includes the prime minister and four noblemen whose families have held the position for hundreds of years."

"I also know that it states in the Royal Charter that if there is no male heir then St. Michel reverts back to Rhineland."

"That is not going to happen," the prime minister firmly declared.

"And it's not going to happen because *my* son is the male heir, the only son of King Philippe."

"The Privy Council is waiting for me. I must go, ma'am."

"Oh, you'll be going all right," Celeste muttered as she watched him walk away. "Right out the palace door, the minute I'm in charge of things. I don't need you or your musty old Privy Council. I've got more powerful allies than you'll ever know."

Juliet spent the entire morning immersed in the early 1800s. It was better than dealing with her own life in the present day.

Luc's kisses last night had left her tossing and turning all night. No matter how she tried, she couldn't get the memory out of her mind. The texture of his lips, the taste of his mouth, the tantalizing swipe of his tongue against the roof of her mouth. All these things and more took control of her senses, put her in danger of *losing* her senses.

She'd come to work early, determined to make some major headway in her research reading. She'd fallen behind schedule because of Luc.

She had completed one section of Queen Regina's diaries and was ready to move on to the next volume when something outside caught her attention. The sun was shining as it often did this time of year in St. Michel, and the flowers in the garden basked in the light. The irises were past their peak glory but still put on a colorful display—from pale yellow to darkest purple. But it was the woman who'd just entered the garden who made Juliet pause. She appeared distressed as she hurried across the path toward the gardener's quarters at the back of the palace. It was Yvette, the head gardener's wife.

Perhaps she was just in a hurry to return home. Juliet knew that Yvette had recently had a baby, and she had meant to give her a baby gift. She had one wrapped in her quarters all ready to go, but all her spare time was spent preparing lessons for Luc—or lusting after Luc. The bottom line was that Luc had distracted her.

She was also distracted by the sight of something shiny out of the corner of her eye. Turning, she saw that it was a large foil box of candy and it was being held by Luc. Actually, he was waving it as if it were a white flag of surrender.

"I come bearing gifts." Luc took a few steps into the room, as if to gauge her reaction before deciding to proceed further. Apparently deciding it was safe, he came in and elegantly propped himself on the corner of her desk. He waved the now-open box practically under her nose. "Chocolate, to apologize for my behavior last night. I was in a strange mood and had no right venting my frustrations on you."

His words stopped her in midreach for a dark chocolate truffle. "Is that what kissing me meant to you? Venting a few frustrations?"

"No, I meant afterward. When I said I wanted my life back and called off the lesson."

"And went storming off, don't forget that part."

He didn't hesitate. "And went storming off." He paused as if unsure what to say next.

He looked so awkward that Juliet had to say something to break the ice. "So you kissed me to avoid dance lessons, is that it?"

He smiled. "Yes, that's it."

They both knew it wasn't, but there was a certain shared relief in falling back on old familiar friendship patterns. She took a chocolate. "You're a devious man."

"A devious man with chocolate."

"Which makes you all the more dangerous." She popped the truffle into her mouth before closing her eyes in ecstasy.

"And hard to resist?" he asked hopefully.

"Impossible to resist," she said. "How did you know these are my favorites?"

"I know a lot of things about you."

"Like what?"

"Like the fact that you lose pencils at an alarming rate, that you have a weakness for vintage clothing and kittens. And a talent for looking beneath the surface dents to see the real beauty beneath."

She wondered if that was a talent he had, to look beneath her bookworm appearance to the real her.

"Other people see junk," Luc said. "You see... possibilities."

She had the feeling that they were no longer talking about furniture here. "Because I see the possibilities in you?"

He nodded.

"I'm not the only one, Luc. The dowager queen and the prime minister both admire you so much."

"The Privy Council is meeting again today."

She nodded. "I know. I still have that letter from your mother, if you're ready to read it."

"I'm not," he said curtly.

She knew he would be, someday. And when he was, she wanted to be by his side.

The Privy Council wasn't known for moving quickly. Glaciers were speedier than this noble body of elders. Today's meeting had lasted the entire day and well into the evening. It was days like this that made retirement look very pleasant to Prime Minister René Davoine.

While the prime minister had gone to his office to check on the day's business, the Privy Council had taken an early and extended dinner break before returning to the Privy Council Meeting Room for after-dinner cognacs and cigars.

Opening the ornately carved heavy wooden door, René had to wave his hand in front of his face to clear some of the cigar smoke from the room. It was so thick he couldn't even see the series of dour portraits hanging from the dark paneling along the walls. Peering through the stale air he could just make out the other four members of this elite group. All wore heavy red velvet robes and matching white wigs dating back to the eighteenth century.

Prior to the present situation, St. Michel hadn't had a meeting of the Privy Council since 1866, when it had been alleged that the oldest son had been borne to the king's mistress and that the rightful heir was the second son. The Privy Council had met then to look over the documents and make a decision. It had taken them four years.

Today's members showed a similar inclination to be snail-like in the speed of their decision-making. They had first come together after King Philippe's death and had hit several bumps in the road since then. This was not a crowd for bumpy roads.

Baron Severin was the oldest and therefore the self-proclaimed leader. White-haired and a bit hard of hearing, he had the upright bearing of a military man. By contrast, the Duc de Montreaux was noticeably bow-legged, caused by his lifelong enthusiasm for riding. Sir André DeVallis and Count Baptiste Rivaux looked very much alike. Both men were balding with florid faces and very rotund builds. Neither did much talking.

"Gentlemen," René said. "I'm here to see if you have reached a decision about Luc Dumont's claim to the throne."

"*Eh?*" Baron Severin bellowed, having refused to wear his hearing aid because it interfered with the fit of his wig. "Luc's on the phone?"

"His claim to the throne," René corrected, speaking succinctly and as close to the older man's ear as he could. "Has the Privy Council reached a decision?"

"These things take time, my boy."

Baron Severin was the only one who would think that at age sixty René was a boy.

"I fear that Queen Celeste may be about to make trouble," René warned them.

"That confounded woman has been trouble since the moment King Philippe got engaged to her," the Duc de Montreaux proclaimed.

"It's a shame the days when the Privy Council had to approve a royal engagement are over," Baron Severin said.

The other three solemnly nodded their agreement.

René tried to get them back on track. "Be that as it may, gentlemen, may I remind you that you still need to make a decision regarding Luc Dumont."

"Fine fellow," Baron Severin said.

"Excellent head of security," Duc de Montreaux agreed. "I say we keep him on."

René sighed, gathering his tattered patience before reminding them, "We have the birth certificate stating that he is the son of King Philippe and Katherine, also known as Katie Graham."

"Well, now, it wouldn't be the first birth certificate we've seen proclaiming someone to be their son, now would it?" Baron Severin in turn reminded him. "We're still awaiting confirmation from the authorities in France that the documentation is indeed true and accurate. You cannot hurry these things along, my boy."

"St. Michel needs its king, gentlemen. We have been without a monarch long enough," René said.

"You really think this Luc is the one?" Count Rivaux asked, speaking for the first time.

"I do," René replied.

"And you believe he will carry the de Bergeron family name with dignity and honor?" Baron Severin asked.

René nodded. "I do. Luc is a serious man. He isn't one to take duty lightly. I do not believe there is a frivolous bone in his body, in fact."

"Is that so?" Duc de Montreaux said from beside the window. "In that case, what is he doing slipping out the back of the palace with that young filly Juliet in tow?"

Chapter Six

"Where are you taking me?" Juliet demanded breathlessly as Luc hurried her down a garden path, away from the palace.

"To a carnival," he replied. "We've been working hard, it's time we took a break."

Luc was casually dressed in black jeans and a black T-shirt. He was the epitome of a sexy cat burglar, moving with an elegant smoothness and speed. Pulled along behind him as she was, she had the most tempting view of his body, his slim waist tapering to lean hips and long legs. And his derriere…even thinking of it as a royal posterior didn't slow down her racing heart.

She had to say something to break the sexual tension building within her. She focused on his dark clothing.

"Are we going on some kind of covert mission?" she inquired with what she thought was an admirably good example of friendly cheerfulness.

"Let's just say I'd rather not announce my presence to the paparazzi."

"They've been hounding the palace ever since that rat Wilhelm sold the story about King Philippe's marriage to Katie to that tabloid."

"I know." Luc led her to the edge of the formal gardens. "That's why I tightened security around the perimeters of the grounds."

She paused, cautiously eyeing the thick forest before them. "If you're planning on walking through the woods to avoid detection, I have to warn you that I'm not dressed for it." She waved a hand down at her vintage 1950s black sundress. "You should have told me to wear slacks."

"There's no need for that." Luc wasn't about to admit that he liked looking at her legs. "We're not going through the woods." He paused before a huge oak tree on the edge of the woods, walking around it to pull out…a gleaming motorcycle.

Juliet eyed it distrustfully. "I'm not dressed properly to ride on the back of that thing."

"Yes, you are," he assured her. "Come on, hop on. We're not going far. You can tuck your dress around your legs."

"Easy for you to say," she muttered.

"Do you want me to help?"

"No, you stay where you are," she ordered him, resting her hand on his shoulder as she daintily mounted the motorcycle.

Luc felt her wiggling against him as she arranged the skirt of her dress. Her breasts brushed against his back, and her legs bracketed his.

A familiar fire smoldered within him. It wasn't the kind of flame that flared to life the instant he saw her; it was the kind that grew in intensity each time they were together. Instant lust he could deal with, but this overwhelmingly powerful attraction was something else entirely.

"I should have worn black leather," he heard her mutter, and almost groaned aloud at the sexy fantasy of her dressed like a biker babe—her thighs barely covered by a short skirt, her breasts pushing against a tight T-shirt. His body responded to the hot images, forcing him to shift position, which only made her thighs rub against his even more.

When had his sweet innocent friend Juliet turned into a sultry sex kitten?

"I'm ready," she informed him.

He was ready, too, so ready that his body was about to explode. A flick of his wrist and the well tuned engine roared to life.

"Hang on tight," he told her and she obeyed, plastering herself to him.

The night air was deliciously cool against his flushed skin as he drove down the path leading past the stables to a little-used service road. He nodded at the guards on duty before stepping on the throttle and letting the Harley have its way.

Juliet pressed her face against his back and closed her eyes, not in fear but in pleasure. Now she could concentrate on the enjoyment of being so close to him. She could smell the fresh scent of his soap, could feel the warmth of his skin through the cotton of his T-shirt. She had her arms wrapped around his flat stomach, her hands gripping his sides. She could feel him breathing.

Her lips automatically pursed in a tiny kiss before she realized what she was doing. Turning her face so that only her cheek rested against his back, she opened her eyes and tried to focus on the passing scenery but it was going by too quickly.

"We're almost there," Luc yelled over his shoulder, as if sensing her sudden restlessness.

He might have sensed it, but he couldn't know the reason for it. Reality had reared its ugly head once again in her mind. A king on a Harley. The days when Luc would be able to take off like this were limited. She knew that would be very hard for a man like him, a man who valued his independence and freedom.

She would be there for him, she vowed. To help him adjust.

And then what? The taunting question demanded an answer. Then do you sit by like a good little girl while he marries some gorgeous princess?

Oh, do be quiet, she silently ordered her wayward thoughts. Let me just enjoy this evening for what it is, a night out with Luc.

Luc stopped the Harley on the carnival grounds a few minutes later. The colorful lights of the various rides reflected off the metal of the motorcycle as he dismounted with ease and turned to help her. Her skirt had somehow hiked up during the ride, and was now at the mid-thigh mark. Before she could rectify that matter, Luc put his hands on her waist and lifted her from the back of the bike as if she weighed no more than a feather.

When she'd given him the first lesson in the royal dining room, and he'd talked to her about biking to classes at Cambridge, she'd fantasized about him riding a gleaming motorbike. And here he was. Her fantasy come to life, grabbing her by the hand and hurrying her along to the carnival's entrance. There might be flashing clown faces instead of cherubs, but to Juliet this was heaven, sheer heaven.

A large arch lit their way, flashing lights perched on top in a garishly cheerful illumination. This was no classy night at the ballet, Luc silently noted. He hoped Juliet wouldn't be disappointed.

The place was crowded, mostly with young people. Teenage girls in shorts, tank tops and body glitter roamed in packs, pausing to giggle and whisper whenever they saw a group of their male counterparts. Teenagers in St. Michel were the same as teenagers in the rest of the world. Out to have a good time.

Luc could relate to that. He had the same goal tonight. To have a good time and not think about the future.

The midway was lined with rides that tilted, rolled or shook. But it was the Ferris wheel that caught his eye. "Let's go on that first."

"I'm not very fond of heights," Juliet warned him.

"Just hang on to me," he replied.

That she could do, having perfected "hanging on" while sitting behind him on that motorcycle. As she boarded the Ferris wheel with Luc at her side, Juliet wondered how many more fantasies of hers would be fulfilled tonight.

The ride started gently enough. It was only as they were lifted higher and higher, that a flutter of anxiety hit her.

"Don't look down," Luc advised, taking her chin in his hand and gently lifting her face skyward. "Look up. Look at all those stars."

It was a glorious spring night. The dark sky was dotted with sparkling pinpricks of light, a divine necklace strung together across the heavens. And there, just above the horizon, a golden full moon was rising. It truly was a magnificent sight.

"It's magical," she breathed.

"Magical," he agreed, looking at her instead of the sky.

The ride ended too soon, and Juliet insisted on taking another before Luc laughingly demanded they move on to the next one.

An hour later they stopped at the food tent for a meal of sausage and crisp *pommes frites*—french fries—which they washed down with chilled red merlot from one of the many local vineyards. St. Michel was well-known for its wines. For dessert they had freshly made cotton candy wrapped around paper cones.

As they left the eating area, Luc happened to see a father with his small son. The man held the boy's hand, and the child looked up at his father with awe and delight.

The scene reminded Luc of when he was that age. Had he ever looked up at Albert that way? Was that why he felt this stupid ache in his chest?

Or was it because the man he had believed to be his father all these years wasn't his father after all?

Not that Luc had spent a lot of time with Albert. Once Luc had reached the age of eight, school had become his home—first Eton then Cambridge. While at university, Luc had become good friends with Jeremy Landing, the son of a high official in Interpol. Luc had spent several summer vacations with Jeremy and his family. He'd preferred doing that to dealing with the tension between Albert and his second wife, feeling like an outsider in what was supposed to be his own home.

Jeremy's father, Spencer, had been impressed with Luc, who spoke five languages fluently and had excellent grades in all his subjects at Cambridge. Spencer had been the one who'd suggested that after leaving university, Luc should consider a career in Interpol.

It seemed like a great idea to Luc. Interpol, an international police force, was an appropriate home for someone who felt that he belonged nowhere in particular.

Luc still felt that way, as if he belonged nowhere in particular. This despite the fact that he now had blood relatives—a grandmother, several half sisters, a baby half brother.

But he couldn't seem to get comfortable with the idea that he was no longer on his own. And he couldn't seem to get comfortable with the idea of his future being locked into the strict codes and traditions of royalty.

This was where blind passion had landed them all. In a carnival house of mirrors—where nothing was as it seemed. His mother and King Philippe hadn't been able to be practical and control their emotions, so they'd run off and married. And now look at the convoluted mess they'd left behind.

Luc gave the father and son a brooding look, angry at the tug he felt at his heart, the tug of a little boy who'd had a father and then lost him to a second marriage. He'd rightly told Juliet that he avoided love because it left you feeling too vulnerable. Not giving a damn was a much saner, a much more sensible way.

His gaze shifted to Juliet. He didn't seem to be able to be sensible about her. Yet sometimes it felt as if she was the only sensible and solid thing left in his life. During this past week she'd been his Rock of Gibraltar. When it had felt as if everything else in his life had been turned upside down, Luc had only to look at her and feel better.

The trouble was that looking at her didn't merely make him feel better. It also made him want her. So, in a way, even his relationship with Juliet had changed. Because in the past few years, while he'd always considered her to be a good friend, he'd never gotten sexual ideas about her. But all that had changed.

Now he thought about her when he restlessly tossed in

his bed at night. He dreamt about her, about that kiss they'd shared in the Crystal Ballroom the other night.

Luc felt as if he were a man on the run from his own destiny, a destiny not of his own choosing. So here he was tonight, playing hookey like a kid who'd run off to join the circus.

"Everything all right?" Juliet asked him.

"Yes. Come on, let's try our luck at one of the booths."

"Win a tiara for the lady!" a burly bald man invited with the feigned cheer of a natural-born salesman. "Come on then, sir, win a bright and shiny bauble for your pretty sweetheart."

"What do you say?" Luc turned to ask Juliet. "Wouldn't you like a tiara of your own?"

"Doesn't every girl long for a tiara of her own?"

She'd just been kidding, but Luc took her seriously. "Here." He handed over some money to the vendor who quickly counted it.

"This will give you ten chances to hit the red center of the target with one of these balls," the vendor said.

"I won't need that many," Luc confidently replied.

In the end he was right. He hit the target on his fifth try. The vendor grudgingly handed over the prize before turning his attention to more customers.

Luc led Juliet to a small stand of trees that afforded them a bit of privacy before turning to her and bowing. "Your tiara, m'lady." He placed it on her head before standing back to admire his handiwork. "It looks good on you."

She laughed and shook her head, making the tiara slip to one side. "I find that hard to believe."

"Why is that?"

"I'm not the royal type."

"Neither am I," he noted quietly.

"Luc, I'm sorry." She placed a hand on his bare arm. His skin was warm beneath her fingers. "I didn't mean to bring that up. I know you're trying to forget it all tonight."

"That's not as easy to do as I thought."

"I'm sorry," she repeated, reaching up to remove the tiara.

"No." His hand stopped her. "It does look good on you. You look good."

She laughed self-consciously. "I'm sure I have mustard on my chin and there are probably remnants of cotton candy on my cheek."

Luc cupped his hand beneath her chin and lifted her face. Leaning down to study her closely, he declared, "No mustard. Not a trace. The cotton candy claim may need further investigating, however."

He completed that investigation with his lips, tasting his way from her left cheek across her lips to her other cheek and back again. "Mmm," he murmured against her mouth. "Sweet, very sweet."

It *was* sweet—and hot and tempting. And when he leaned away to grin at her, Juliet wished they weren't just pretending, wished they really were just a man and a woman out for an evening of fun. Instead she worried about him getting into trouble for being out with her.

He's the king. Who's going to yell at him?

Yes, Luc would be in charge, but he would also be expected to behave in a certain way and required to conform to rigid standards. Kissing her at a carnival did not conform. She was not suitable. She was no European aristocrat, she had no royal blood of her own. She was just a commoner who was falling in love with a king.

Not a wise move, to be sure.

"Come on," Luc said as he had all evening, once again grabbing her by the hand. "There are still a few sights we haven't seen yet."

He headed them toward the other side of the midway, pausing in front of a fortune teller's tent. "Let's see if she says there's a crown in my future," Luc said with that contagious smile of his.

The interior of the tent was so dark Juliet had to pause to get her bearings. In the center was a woman seated at a table, with a bright light shining down on a crystal ball and a deck of tarot cards. The fortune teller had a brilliantly patterned scarf wrapped turban-style around her head. Large gold hoop earrings hung from her ears and a pair of gold front teeth flashed in her mouth as she gave them a huge smile. "Welcome, come in, sit. Let me tell you about things to come. I am Magda and I do it all—read palms, tea leaves, tarot cards, the crystal ball. Which would you prefer?"

"Which one has the highest degree of accuracy?" Luc asked as he held out one of the chairs for Juliet before taking the other for himself.

"Ah, for you, I think reading the palm would be best." Magda quickly reached for his hand and turned it over to study it closely. "Hmmm, very interesting. You have a split life line here. Which means that you will be leading two lives, each one very different from the other. And your love line is interesting, too. I see conflict and confusion here. Your health line is good but has several fractures, times when you have been in great jeopardy. I see a time like that approaching you. Wealth is coming to you soon as well, a great deal of wealth. But it is uncertain whether it will bring you happiness."

Luc snatched his hand away. "Do my friend's hand now."

Juliet tried to ignore her irritation his calling her a friend had caused. Magda took Juliet's hand and said nothing for the longest time. "You are very smart, and you see more than most. You have one great passion in your life. He is tall, dark—"

"—and handsome," Luc supplied.

"And in danger," Magda corrected him. "The outcome is still unsure at this point." Looking Juliet in the eye, Magda added, "But I sense that you are an old soul and are prepared to fight for your future. I wish you luck, miss, and I fear you will need it."

After paying Magda and going back outside, Luc said, "Well that went as expected."

"You expected her to tell you that you're in danger?"

"I expected that tall, dark and handsome would come up. I hoped in your reading and not in mine," he added with a roguish grin.

But Juliet couldn't smile. The fortune teller's words had unsettled her. "She said you were in danger, doesn't that bother you?"

"Not really. It wouldn't be the first time I was in danger. Listen, all that hot air made me thirsty. Let's go get a drink."

And he was off again, this time leading her to a small concession stand that had been set up to one side. The striped red-and-white colors made it easy to spot, and it was the only place to get a drink on this side of the midway.

Luc sat Juliet at a nearby bench while he stood in line. When he finally placed his order, they were all out of everything except for the local beer. The vendor indicated a barrel filled with ice and told him to pick out his bottles.

Luc did so, turning his back to the metal pole holding up
the tent canopy.

A moment later the heavy metal pole crashed down on
him.

Chapter Seven

"Luc!" Juliet cried, leaping to her feet and running over to the fallen concession tent.

The collapsed canopy covered everything now, preventing her from seeing him.

"I'm okay," Luc's voice was muffled by the heavy canvas.

The vendor came scurrying around from the back, apparently not caught up in the collapse. "I am so sorry, so sorry," he kept repeating as he enlisted the help of some passing men to lift the remnants of the heavy canopy and free Luc.

When she finally saw Luc emerge, she almost cried with relief.

"Are you sure you're okay?" she demanded, running her hands down his arms as if needing to verify for herself that he hadn't broken anything.

"I'm fine. It would take more than a stupid canopy falling on me to hurt me."

"Luc, that heavy metal supporting pole narrowly

missed you and believe me that was capable of doing plenty of harm had it connected with your head or your back.''

''But it didn't. It was just one of those stupid accidents, like almost getting hit by a piece of falling masonry from the palace the other day.''

His words made her go cold in the gentle warmth of the night. ''Whaa…at?'' Her voice sounded as shaken as she felt.

''You know where they've recently set up that scaffolding along the edge of the south wing to do some repair work? Well, I was walking by when half a gargoyle or something fell down, narrowly missing me. The thing must have weighed a ton. It shattered on the pavement.''

''Why didn't you say anything?'' she demanded, infuriated by his nonchalant attitude about his own safety.

''I gave the construction foreman a fiery lecture about on-the-job safety.''

''I mean to *me*. Why didn't you say anything to me?''

He raised one dark brow, indicating his surprise at her vehemence. ''Because it wasn't important.''

''Of course it's important. There's a pattern here. Twice in the past few days you've almost been seriously injured.''

''Oh, please.'' He rolled his gorgeous rich blue eyes at her. ''This incident tonight is nothing. A gust of wind probably knocked the canopy down.''

She wasn't buying that for one minute. ''There isn't a spit of wind tonight, it's completely still.''

''There's no way someone would have known I would be standing beneath that particular canopy on this particular night.''

She hated it when Luc used that logical tone of voice on her. "They would if you were being followed."

"You really do have a vivid imagination."

She hated it even more when he didn't take her seriously. "Stop acting so nonchalantly about all this. I'm worried about you."

"I can see that. It's the first time in decades that anyone has worried about me. But there's no need."

The thought of no one worried about him for years and years made her heart ache. His mother had died, his stepmother was worse than useless, and his father had apparently forgotten about him once he'd shipped him off to boarding school.

At least Juliet had her older brother Georges to depend on, and her younger sister Jacqueline. But Luc had grown up with no one—no one to fuss over him, no one to worry about his well-being, no one to love him.

Her thoughts were interrupted by the agitated voice of the vendor offering them free beer, before he realized that the fallen canopy had knocked over the barrel filled with beer bottles and smashed them all.

"That could have been you," Juliet said, pointing to the smashed debris that the men had just uncovered.

"But it wasn't. I can't live my life with could-have-beens. Especially not now."

She wasn't about to let him off the hook. "Now is when you have to be especially careful, Luc. There are people who will not be pleased with your...discoveries about your past. People who have a lot to lose. And there are still some dissident Rhinelanders who want St. Michel annexed to their country so they can have river access. Who knows what they might have planned? You can't be cavalier about your safety, Luc. I couldn't bear it if anything happened to you."

"Nothing is going to happen to me," he promised her. "Nothing at all."

"Did you do it?" Celeste whispered to her lover Claude Guignard as she welcomed him into the private apartment she'd rented in St. Michel. No one at the palace knew about this place, located near the river, where she let her sensual side have free reign—red velvet couches and chairs in the living room, a leopard-print bedcover and mirrored ceiling in the bedroom. This pied-à-terre was where she plotted her future. "Have you killed him yet?"

"It's not that easy to make it look like an accident."

She pulled away from him to bestow an icy look of disapproval. "Which means no, you haven't killed him."

Claude cringed as if dreading what she might do or say next. "The falling masonry should have worked. I followed him tonight to the carnival and successfully collapsed a tent on him."

"A tent?" she repeated, mocking him. "A lethal weapon to be sure."

"There was a heavy metal pole that almost made a direct hit, but he turned at the last minute."

Her cold expression was warmed by a sudden smile and a thoughtful expression as she drifted into the living room. "There may be a better way. Killing him was perhaps a tad too obvious. We may still be forced to do that, of course. But I'm exploring other options."

"Other options?"

"Yes. I've arranged for a top secret meeting here and have invited a very important guest."

"Who is it?"

There was a discreet knock on the door. "Ah, that

should be him now. You'd better open it, the queen shouldn't be seen doing something so menial.''

Claude did her bidding, as he always did.

Celeste had her most gracious smile in place as she greeted her visitor. ''I'm so glad you could make it here this evening.''

''Your invitation was too intriguing to refuse, Your Majesty,'' Berg Dekker replied, taking her hand and bowing over it before kissing it with just enough flirtatiousness to make Claude's brown eyes flash with jealousy.

Berg was a tall man with ice-cold features. He'd earned the nickname Iceberg because he so coldly went after what he wanted in business, regardless of who or what got in his way. The environmental fanatics claimed his petroleum and chemical plants were major polluters. Celeste really didn't care. The important thing was Berg's enormous wealth and influence. He gave buckets of money to his pet charities, cultural foundations and political causes. His power joined with hers would make a formidable alliance.

''Claude, you know Berg Dekker, one of Europe's most powerful and successful businessmen. And, as you know, Berg, Claude is St. Michel's deputy energy minister.''

''If this is about that money that changed hands several months ago...'' Claude began nervously.

''Do be quiet, Claude,'' Celeste chastised him. ''This meeting isn't about the bribes you've been taking from Berg for years.''

''It isn't?'' Claude almost sagged with relief.

''No, of course not. I admire you and Berg for making an arrangement that was beneficial to you both. Claude, do get our guest some wine.''

He did as she ordered.

"A toast." Celeste raised her crystal wineglass. "To a mutually prosperous future."

When Berg touched his glass to hers, she saw the interest in his pale blue eyes. She sank onto the couch, striking an elegant pose in her designer outfit—a chic Valentino cocktail dress that showed off her great legs. "Do sit down." She patted the couch on either side of her. Berg chose to sit at her right, Claude got the seat that was left over. "The matter I wish to discuss is much larger than a few bribes here and there. Berg, I know how passionately you have supported the cause of Rhineland annexing St. Michel. And I know that while you have patriotic reasons for your views, you also have practical reasons. You are in the lucrative petrochemical business—refining and transportation. This business would be made easier and less expensive if you were to have access to the St. Michel River, leading to and from the North Sea, correct?"

"Correct."

"Then I have what I hope will be an irresistible proposal for you."

"Everything about you is irresistible," Berg murmured in a charming voice.

"You are being too kind." Celeste fluttered her eyelashes at him before crossing her legs, showing a generous amount of thigh. "I fear I'm not looking my best after having given birth to the heir to the throne a mere week ago."

"You are looking ravishing with that special glow that only a new mother could display." Berg lifted her hand to his lips. "The best paintings by Raphael and Rembrandt pale in comparison to your beauty. And I should know, as I have rather an extensive collection of artwork, one that would put the royal collection of St. Michel to shame.''

"It is a shame that St. Michel was taken from Rhineland,'' Celeste murmured.

"That is my view,'' Berg agreed. "For hundreds of years we ruled this area. Then some rabble-rousers demanded independence and forcibly took our rightful heritage from us.''

"That was way back in the sixteenth century,'' Claude pointed out in an affronted voice. "And some would say that the group Rhinelanders for Annexation are a bunch of rabble-rousers,'' he added, clearly unhappy about the fact that Berg still held Celeste's hand.

"Of course, anyone who said that would be wrong,'' Celeste stated with a warning look at Claude. "My proposition is one that would benefit us all. I've learned that you have quietly been supplying a great deal of the funding for Rhinelanders for Annexation, Berg.''

"There is no law against that.''

"Of course not. But I think you and I can work together to get what we both want.''

"Why would you want to make a deal with us?'' Berg asked. "You have a son, a healthy baby boy. There is no threat of St. Michel returning to Rhineland due to a lack of a male heir.''

"Actually the problem we have is that we have too many male heirs,'' Celeste said. "I trust that this meeting and everything that is said here will be held in the utmost confidentiality?''

Berg nodded. "You have my word.''

"Mine, too,'' Claude hurriedly added.

"Good.'' Her smile reflected her pleasure. "It would not be in any of our best interests for word of this conversation to get out.''

"What did you mean by saying there are too many male heirs?" Berg asked.

Celeste leaned closer. "You have no doubt heard the ridiculous story about King Philippe's youthful marriage to that American girl named Katie Graham."

Once again, Berg nodded. "Yes. And I know that Luc Dumont has been searching for the child they are rumored to have had together."

Celeste appeared surprised. "I wasn't aware that that was public information."

"It isn't, but I do have my sources."

"The story, of course, is a total fabrication." She waved her hand dismissively. "A way for Prime Minister Davoine to hang on to power. He knows that the moment my son becomes king, I will fire him for being an incompetent fool, and replace him with someone like Claude here. Someone loyal to me."

"I'm assuming then, that Luc found someone he believes to be the heir?" Berg noted astutely.

"Yes, but that's not important. As I said, the entire story is a fabrication. However some people may be fooled by these lies. So I need a way of uniting the people of St. Michel. If I were to present the country with a solution to the vexing Rhineland problem, then naturally they would all support me in their gratitude."

Berg's pale blue eyes narrowed suspiciously. "What kind of solution?"

"I propose that we share the rights to the river. That way you would save millions in shipping costs, since you would no longer have to pay the local taxes and tariff. We would also be more lenient in our regulations on the cargo sizes of your barges and the number of barges you can use at any one time. I understand the current regime has been making life difficult for you, shutting down your operations because of pollution concerns despite Claude's best efforts to look the other way. That would not be a problem if we were to enter into a partnership—a silent, secret partnership.''

Berg's expression went from suspicious to calculating. "What exactly is it you want from me?''

"I want your support, as leader of Rhinelanders for Annexation, for my plan.''

"I am not the leader,'' Berg protested. "I am merely one of many patriotic souls who feel our country has been wronged.''

Celeste smiled. "Come now, there's no need for any false modesty here. You are the power behind the organization. Those men they arrested a few weeks back were merely the figureheads. *You* possess the real power.''

Berg's icy eyes showed a flash of admiration. "Not many have figured that out.''

"Like you, I have my sources.'' She shifted against him, subtly brushing her body against hers. "So what do you say? Do we have a deal?''

Berg smiled. "Yes, Your Majesty, it appears that we do.''

"Shhhh,'' Juliet cautioned Luc with a giggle. "You're going to wake everyone up.''

"I'm not the one making noise, you are. How many of those free beers did you have?'' The vendor had insisted on treating them, sending his son to get another case of beer to make up for the unfortunate incident involving the tent canopy.

"None. I'm drunk on life.'' Juliet smiled as she dreamily danced her way down the garden path leading to the palace, which looked romantic in the moonlight with its golden sandstone walls and towers creating a fairy-tale silhouette against the night sky. Most of the many windows were darkened at this time of night. But the Cheval de Roi fountain was illuminated, its trio of rearing horses seeming to hover above the water. "Wait."

"What for?"

"I want to make a wish." She dug into her purse. "Did you know this fountain is rumored to have magical properties?"

"I think after that fortune teller at the carnival, we've had enough magic for one night."

"No, this is different. I've been reading the diaries of Queen Regina and she writes about it there. The horse in the middle represents King Philippe's great-grandfather's prized stallion. And the two females flanking him were thought to represent his wife and his mistress."

"The stallion's?" was Luc's mocking reply.

"No, the king's. And once the fountain was up, no horse from the royal stables ever lost a race. The fountain became known as a lucky place, a place to make dreams come true. You can't look at the horses when you make your wish, you have to turn away from them in deference."

"Fascinating, I'm sure."

"It is. Which is why I'm going to make a wish." She removed a coin from her purse and, turning her back to the fountain, quickly tossed it over her left shoulder where it fell into the fountain's water with a distinct plop. "Here, I'll give you a coin to make a wish, too."

"I don't make wishes—" Luc began when Juliet interrupted him.

"Oh no!" she wailed.

"What's wrong?"

"The coin! That was my special lucky coin. One my

mother gave me that I carry with me all the time. I didn't mean to use that. I need it back.''

"You can't get it back.''

"Yes, I can. I'm going after it. You stand guard and make sure no one from security comes by.''

"I *am* security.''

"Then close your eyes. I'm going in.'' She kicked off her shoes and carefully waded into the fountain. ''My goodness, that stallion is certainly well-endowed,'' she noted as she bent beneath it to get to the center of the fountain.

"Stop eyeing the equestrian private parts and get your fanny back here,'' Luc ordered her.

"Not until I get my lucky coin.'' She plodded through the water, raising her skirt even higher to avoid getting it wet.

"Oh, for heaven's sake,'' he muttered in exasperation. ''It's dark out here. You can't see what you're doing.''

"I can, too. The fountain is lit. Oh, I think I see it!'' She leaned forward eagerly, a tad too eagerly as it turned out, because an instant later she lost her balance and fell onto her derriere.

"I didn't realize you'd be doing a water ballet tonight.'' Luc's voice was filled with laughter. ''Or is it synchronized swimming you're performing? If so, I'm going to have to mark you down for a lack of finesse in your landing.''

"I'll give you a lack of finesse.'' Juliet reached out to swipe her hand along the water, creating a giant splash that doused Luc and left him blinking at her in surprise.

Noting the dangerous gleam in his eyes, she quickly started scooting away. ''Now, Luc, you started it by insulting my lack of finesse. What are you doing?'' She eyed him suspiciously. "Why are you taking off your shoes?"

"Because I don't want to ruin them when I come in there after you."

"You don't have to come in. I've got my coin." She held it aloft and stood up, her cotton dress clinging to her like a second skin. "I'm coming out. As soon as you take a few steps away from the fountain. Not *into* the fountain." He showed no signs of obeying her. "Luc, be sensible."

"I am being sensible. As head of security I found a strange and unauthorized object in the fountain. It's up to me to remove it."

Juliet placed her wet hands on her equally wet hips. "Luc Dumont, you get out of this fountain this instant!"

"Now, Juliet, you know how that prim voice of yours drives me wild."

"I mean it, Luc." She backed up until she was up against one of the equine statues' flanks and could go no farther.

"I'm sure you do."

"It was your own fault you got wet. You taunted me. And you know how I hate being taunted."

"Yes, I know. I also know that you're rather fond of this." He wrapped his arm around her waist and tugged her to him. Leaning down, he brushed his lips across hers.

"Mmm, that is rather nice," she murmured against his mouth.

"Nice?" He drew his head back to give her a reproachful look that melted her knees. "Only nice? Clearly I'll have to try harder."

Wrapping both arms around her, he lifted her against him as he devoured her mouth with a hotly sensual kiss that had her parting her lips and greeting his tongue with her own. The splashing sound of the fountain's water mimicked the beating of her heart in her chest. The wet material of her dress provided little protection as her thighs were pressed against his, making her very aware of his arousal.

She felt her nipples tingle and firm. He dabbled the wet point of his tongue along the roof of her mouth as his right hand shifted to cup the soft swell of her breast.

Looking down on them from a window on the second floor, Baron Severin tsk-tsked disapprovingly and told the prime minister, "René, I fear this Juliet girl may not be a good influence on our future king. I think it's time the dowager queen had a talk with those two."

Luc found the summons waiting for him when he arrived at his office just after sunrise. He hadn't gotten much sleep after kissing Juliet in the fountain last night. He got hot just thinking about it. He couldn't believe he'd made out with her like some randy teenager.

The sound of one of the palace guards beginning his nightly rounds had finally brought him to his senses last night. He'd helped Juliet scramble out of the fountain, then watched her as she grabbed her shoes and ran barefoot into the palace without saying a word to him.

And now he found a message on his desk announcing that the dowager queen wanted to see him the moment he came in. Knowing she was an early riser, and knowing she liked having her breakfast served in the sunny Emerald Salon just outside her rooms, he figured he might as well get this over with.

"Ah, Luc, how nice to see you." She smiled and gestured to the chair beside her. "Come, join me for breakfast."

"Some coffee would be nice. Black, please," he requested of the footman.

The dowager queen allowed him two sips before starting her inquisition. "I hear that you and Juliet were cavorting in the fountain last night."

It was all he could do not to spew his coffee all over the priceless tablecloth.

The dowager queen patted him on the back with surprising strength. "There now, we can't have you choking. Not after all this work went into finding you." Turning to the footman, she dismissed him before returning her attention to Luc.

"Your highness..." he began.

She interrupted him. "You may call me Grandmother. Some of the girls call me Grandmama on occasion, which I find endearing, but I thought Grandmother would be more comfortable for you."

Luc couldn't think of one comfortable thing about this entire situation.

"Baron Severin from the Privy Council was a little...chagrined, shall we say, when he saw you two last night. The man doesn't have a romantic bone in his entire body."

"What was he doing spying on me?"

"Actually he was just looking out of the palace window. He had no idea the wild scene he'd be witnessing."

"You make it sound as though we were indulging in some kind of orgy or something," Luc protested.

"Were you?"

"Of course not! Juliet isn't that kind of woman."

"What kind is she?"

"You've known her longer than I have."

"In years, perhaps. But Juliet has always kept her distance from me. I have the impression of a bookish young woman who is more comfortable reading about the past than living in the present.''

"She was living in the present last night," Luc said.

"Apparently so." The dowager queen's blue eyes sparkled as she pinned him with one of her piercing stares. "I'll make you a bargain. If you promise to call me Grandmother, and to have tea with me every day this week, then I'll assure the prime minister and Baron Severin that there's nothing to worry about, that you and Juliet were merely having fun in the way young people today do."

He set down his coffee cup with a distinct clink. "That's blackmail."

"How else am I to get to know my grandson better?"

"You could try asking. A strange concept for a monarch maybe," Luc noted in irritation. "But an effective one nonetheless."

"Asking? Hmmm." She sipped her tea before gracefully returning the delicate china cup to its matching saucer. "An interesting concept, to be sure. All right then, Luc. Will you have tea with me this week?"

"No," he said without hesitation. "Not *every* day. But I will spend some time with you. Providing you don't try to interrogate me about my private life again."

She bestowed a regal stare upon him. "My dear boy, had I wanted to interrogate you, you'd know it, believe me."

"I'm fairly good at interrogations myself," Luc warned her, not the least bit intimidated.

Her smile widened. "I do believe I'm going to enjoy having you as my grandson, Luc."

Chapter Eight

Juliet noticed the furtive looks Yvette, the head gardener's wife, was giving her before the morning's weekly staff meeting began. She prayed it wasn't because Yvette had seen her with Luc in the fountain last night.

Oh, but it had been divine. Standing in the moonlight, held in Luc's arms and kissed the way a man kisses a woman he wants. But was it the way a man kissed a woman he *loved?*

She knew she loved him. She'd suspected it for ages, had been inching closer with every breath she took. But last night, when Juliet had returned to her rooms, she'd known. She loved him.

The thought of Luc being hurt by one of the accidents that had befallen him lately was enough to make her sick at heart. And angry. Furious, in fact. No one was going to hurt the man she loved. She'd do whatever it took to protect him.

Which is why she was speaking at the staff meeting this morning. Everyone—from the lowest of housemaids to the valets and footmen to the palace steward and the royal chef himself—gathered in the staff dining room just off the kitchens.

The air was still filled with the warm aroma of the cinnamon buns that had been freshly baked that morning, and a small vase of freshly cut roses adorned the spotless table. Alistair, the palace steward, had previously worked at Buckingham Palace and he prided himself on the small finishing touches.

"Thank you all for allowing me to speak to you during your meeting," Juliet said. She knew almost all of them by name.

"As you are aware, things have been very stressful since the king's death. I don't have to tell you all how volatile the situation could easily become. There are some in Rhineland who avidly support annexing St. Michel. Now, our security is in excellent hands with Luc Dumont. He looks after the safety of us all. I just thought that during these difficult times, we could repay the favor by helping him out a bit."

"How can we do that, miss?" Andrea, one of the housemaids, asked.

"By keeping our eyes and ears open, by reporting anything suspicious to Luc, no matter how inconsequential you might think it is."

"We like Luc," the chef declared on everyone's behalf. "He doesn't put on airs like some people."

"He gave a big contribution when my daughter needed that surgery last year," one of the footmen said.

"And he gave my son a stern lecture when he was getting into trouble," another said. "Turned him right around, our Luc did. My son is doing just fine now, getting good grades."

"Of course we'll help out Luc, in any way we can," Alistair promised. "You can count on us."

The stories and their support warmed Juliet's heart. She had no idea Luc had quietly been helping those in need. Luc, of course, had never said a word. He wasn't the type to go blowing his own horn, to brag about his accomplishments or his generosity. He was a doer, not a talker.

Which boded well for the people of St. Michel. They would soon have a wonderful new king. But their gain would be Juliet's loss.

Although, if she were honest with herself, she'd have to admit that there was a tiny part of her that had started to secretly hope once again. It wasn't logical and it wasn't practical but… Those looks he'd been giving her, and more important those kisses they'd shared. Their relationship was at a new crossroads. The problem was that each path ahead held its own dangers.

Luc could do worse than to marry her. The rebellious thought chased its way across her brain. Certainly no one would love him more than she did—no one could.

But Luc wasn't looking for love. He'd said as much himself. Which meant he'd be looking for someone compatible with his new lifestyle. And while Juliet certainly knew her way around the palace, it wasn't the same as having a royal bloodline. There was simply no substitute for that. Plus there was the matter of hating to be in the spotlight, another strike against her in the royalty department.

"Juliet, the dowager queen asked me to give you this." One of the footmen held out an envelope on a silver tray for her.

She took it with some trepidation. Why would the dowager queen be writing her? She opened the wax seal and removed the fine parchment paper. "Your presence is required for tea this afternoon. I've decided it's time you interviewed me for your paper on the history of St. Michel's royal women."

Generally speaking, Juliet tried to avoid the dowager queen as she tried to avoid Queen Celeste, albeit for entirely different reasons. Queen Celeste had never appreciated Juliet's presence in the palace. After all, Juliet was the child of her husband's former wife. But since Juliet was no threat, either in her beauty or her need for attention, Celeste usually ignored Juliet.

The dowager queen, on the other hand, had a way of intimidating not just Juliet but almost everyone she came in contact with. Lately, Celeste had been promoting rumors that the dowager queen had gone "dotty" in her old age. Juliet wasn't buying it.

The dowager queen possessed the type of regal presence that was hard to find these days. It dated back to Queen Victoria's time, when monarchs were monarchs and no one questioned their authority. In Victoria's case, this meant that she forbade new servants to look her in the face. Instead they had to keep their eyes firmly on the floor at her feet.

Juliet would have been glad for such a ruling in the de Bergeron Palace, because the dowager queen had the most piercing blue eyes she'd ever seen. They weren't rich and filled with depth like Luc's. They had a way of taking you apart inch by inch and finding all your faults.

Not that the older woman had ever voiced any criticisms. She didn't have to. One look from her said it all. Which left Juliet wondering what the dowager queen would be saying to her this afternoon.

Teatime arrived all too soon. Juliet had tried to bolster her sagging confidence by wearing a lovely dress with a

Liberty print of tiny flowers. The dress was made for a
tea party. Well, not really. She'd gotten it in a little shop
during a visit to London. But it did have the look of a
tea party somehow. At least in her mind. And, she hoped,
in the dowager queen's as well.

She'd restrained her hair into a French braid with help
from one of the maids and had taken special care with
her makeup, which had to be discreet but not nonexistent.

She'd brought a notebook and pen with her, to take
notes. The dowager queen had promised to tell her story,
and Juliet was hoping she could add the information to
her own research.

The dowager queen's apartments were in the south
wing, on the sunny second floor overlooking the fountain
and the gardens at the back of the palace. The rooms all
possessed a stately elegance and none more than the
White Drawing Room where they were having tea.

Juliet paused for a moment to simply appreciate her
surroundings. Straight ahead were ceiling-to-floor French
doors, which opened onto a terrace. In front of them
stood graceful marble statues and tall lapis lazuli vases
overflowing with irises. In one corner of the room was a
French Florentine cabinet inlaid with panels of semi-
precious stones. And in the other corner was the dowager
queen.

"Ah, there you are, child. Well, don't just stand there.
Do come in."

Juliet performed a brief curtsy as her mother had
shown her when they'd first moved to the palace.

The dowager queen beamed at her in approval. "Your
mother taught you well. No one knows how to curtsy
properly these days. It's not taught at school any longer,

and it should be. Where would the world be without civility and manners, I ask you? In my day, things were very different. Why, when I married King Antoine, the women all curtsied when I walked down the aisle. And the event certainly wasn't filmed the way they are these days. That bad trait started with Princess Grace allowing her wedding to be filmed.'' Her expression turned disapproving.

Juliet was a longtime admirer of the beautiful actress who had become a princess. "I've read that she only did that in order to dissolve the remaining seven years on her movie contract with MGM.''

"Perhaps, but those Grimaldis have always been a wild bunch. The de Bergeron family is much more traditional. My father was a grand duke, so I was raised in the ranks of St. Michel's aristocracy and taught the rules of protocol and propriety from birth." She paused a moment to give Juliet a thoughtful look even as she indicated with a royal wave of her hand that Juliet should be seated beside her. "Perhaps it's wrong of me to have you curtsy. After all, I am almost family.''

That one word, *almost,* created a huge gulf. One that, for the first time in her life, Juliet was glad of. Otherwise, she would have been related to Luc, and that would have been more than she could have borne.

"Jacqueline is my granddaughter and you are her half sister. Do you take sugar or milk in your tea?''

"Milk, no sugar, thank you, ma'am.''

The dowager queen handed Juliet a cup of tea in a delicate china rimmed with roses. Quickly setting her notebook and pen on her lap, Juliet took the teacup and prayed she wouldn't spill anything.

The dowager queen tilted her head regally, her short dark hair meticulously in place, her powder-blue suit just a shade darker than her piercing eyes. "Jacqueline is due back from Switzerland soon, isn't she?"

"Next week."

"She's a handful, that girl is."

"As are many of the de Bergeron women," Juliet felt compelled to point out. She might only be Jacqueline's half sister, but she loved her dearly and wasn't about to let anyone speak badly of her.

With a nod of her head, the dowager queen indicated that the footman on duty was to offer Juliet a selection of tea sandwiches and goodies from a three-tiered serving dish.

Juliet paused to admire the swan-shaped dainty bit of frosted sponge cake as well as a huge strawberry dipped in white and dark chocolate to resemble a tuxedo.

"Take one of the strawberries, they're delightful this time of year." The order was implicit even if the older woman's tone was aristocratically charming.

Juliet did as she was told.

"So you're writing a paper on the de Bergeron women." A new level of interest had entered the dowager queen's voice.

Juliet set her plate on a side table. She couldn't eat and speak at the same time, not with someone as overwhelming as the dowager queen. During all their previous meetings, other family members had always been present, mitigating the impact the older woman had.

"Yes, ma'am. Actually I'm doing a thesis on the role of women in St. Michel's royal history. I've just been reading the journals of Queen Regina who, as you know, lived in Queen Victoria's time. She had eight children and, like Victoria, she saw them all well married to the heads of other royal houses across Europe. When her husband the king had a stroke, she took on his duties herself and ran the country quite successfully. She was a wise and compassionate queen.''

"The power behind the throne, eh? No doubt that's what Celeste was hoping for.''

"I wouldn't exactly describe her as either wise or compassionate.'' The words were out of Juliet's mouth before she could stop them.

The dowager queen cackled with laughter. "Well said. So you're not as quiet and sweet as one might think. Good. I like a person who speaks her mind.''

"Then, if I may be so bold, might I ask why you invited me here for tea today?''

"I called you here today because I wanted to get to know you better. I understand you've been spending a great deal of time with Luc.''

"Luc and I have been friends for a long time.''

"That's all? Just friends?''

"Yes.'' Juliet prayed that lightning wouldn't strike her for telling a bold-faced lie to the dowager queen.

"Hmm.'' The older woman subjected her to one of her piercing stares, her light-blue eyes slicing right through her. "As you know, Luc's station in life will soon be changing dramatically.''

"I'm aware of that, ma'am.''

"I know. Luc said that he'd told you about it even before coming to the prime minister and me.''

"He only did that because—''

She waved Juliet's words away with an imperious wave of her elegant hand. "You don't have to defend him to me, child. Although it's admirable that you'd want to. It's not my intention to interrogate you about your private relationship with Luc. As his grandmother I'm merely trying to learn more about him.''

"Then you should really speak to him.''

"I've tried to." The dowager queen leaned forward in agitation, her thin hands resting on her gold-filigree topped cane. "The impudent young pup says he doesn't have time for tea with me."

"I'm sure he meant no disrespect, ma'am."

"Oh, he came nicely enough yesterday morning and sat on the very chair you are in now, looking all elegant and handsome. He does have the most divine eyes, doesn't he?"

Juliet had to smile. "Yes, ma'am. He does."

"And the most stubborn nature. How do you deal with him?"

"By letting him be himself," Juliet replied, "and accepting him for who he is."

"I'm well aware of who he is. Although he insists no one else know until that confounded paperwork comes through from the French authorities. It should come any moment now. The two independent investigators that Luc also insisted we hire have told us they'll have their final report within the next forty-eight hours with Luc's DNA results."

"So soon?" Juliet's stomach clenched at the thought of how little time they had left.

"St. Michel has been without a king long enough. Celeste has been agitating to have her infant son named as the heir. The impudence of the woman! When there have been rumors for months about her having an affair, even before my poor son passed on. Who knows if her child is really my son's? She refuses any DNA testing for the infant. That woman will never rule St. Michel, not as long as there's breath left in my body!"

The flush on the older woman's cheeks concerned Juliet, as did her labored breathing. "It can't be good for you to get so upset, ma'am. Would you like me to call someone?'' The footman who had served them earlier had departed.

"No, no, I'm fine.'' The dowager queen patted Juliet's hand. "There's no need for concern. I'm not about to…how do those Americans put it? Ah, yes, I'm not about to kick the bucket just yet.''

"I certainly hope not, ma'am.''

"I intend to stick around for some time yet. After all, I've got a new grandson and I want to see him crowned as our next king. And I want to see him married and have children of his own to aggravate him.''

"Luc would be an excellent father,'' Juliet murmured, remembering how gentle he'd been with the kittens out in the stable.

"I heard he took you to the carnival. Don't look so surprised, very little occurs in this palace that I'm not aware of.''

"He just needed a bit of time away from all this.''

"It pains me that he is having trouble accepting the changes in his life.''

"He needs time. His entire life has been turned upside down,'' Juliet gently reminded her.

"I understand that. What I don't understand is why he won't speak to me about it.''

"Luc has never been the talkative type,'' Juliet replied. "He's not one to share his deepest feelings easily. That's not to say that he doesn't have heartfelt emotions, he does even if he doesn't always want to. But he believes that emotions get in the way.''

The dowager queen nodded her approval. "A proper royal attitude to be sure.''

Juliet boldly gathered her courage. "I hope you won't try and change Luc. He needs the freedom to be himself.''

The dowager queen gave an imperial shrug. "A certain amount of freedom is lost when you are of royal birth, there is no getting around that fact."

"I realize that. But I'd hate to see Luc turn into an emotionless and distant man. I don't want that for him."

"What *do* you want for him?"

"His happiness," Juliet said simply. "I just want him to be happy."

"Ah, that may be harder to achieve than you think."

"I'd do anything in my power to make him happy," Juliet fiercely vowed.

"Would you now, child? That's admirable." The dowager queen's smile turned slightly melancholy. "But I fear that making Luc happy may be something that is beyond either of our abilities to control."

Juliet flopped down on her bed with a sigh of relief. She'd survived tea with the dowager queen. Not only had she survived but she'd struck gold—coming back with several pages of notes about the older woman's life, including her recollections of her mother and herself as a young woman accompanying the royal family to London, where they lived in exile throughout the 1940s and the worst of the Second World War.

At the time, St. Michel had an active resistance movement, like the French Resistance, and most of the men of the aristocracy joined forces with their fellow countrymen. King Philippe's grandmother had carried top secret messages with her to give to the British authorities. Another case of a royal de Bergeron woman stepping forward to act courageously.

A sudden pounding on her door interrupted her thoughts. She was surprised to find Luc standing in the hallway. Looking sexy and agitated, he strode past her without even waiting for an invitation to come in. Juliet barely closed the door before he began speaking. "I heard you were commanded to appear before the dowager queen."

"She invited me to tea."

"What for? Did she try and pump you for information about me? What did you tell her?"

She put her finger on his lips as he'd once done her. "One question at a time. Do you remember when we had that protocol lesson in the dining room? When I talked about the difference between interrogation and conversation? This would be a prime example. You're interrogating me."

"I most certainly am." He relaxed his tense stance and began seductively nibbling her finger. "And I make no apologies for that."

"For what?" Her voice was breathless and distracted.

"For interrogating you. I'm attempting to get the facts here."

"And did you think you could nibble them out of me?" She would have sounded righteously indignant were it not for the hint of laughter in her voice.

"I thought it might be fun to find out."

Fun? That was putting it mildly.

"So what did the dowager queen want?"

Juliet couldn't speak coherently and be seduced by him at the same time.

Taking a step away from him allowed her to resist the temptation Luc provided. "She said she wanted to get to know me better."

"She's known you for years. You came to live here at the palace when you were what—four?"

"We spent most summers and many vacations with my father's family so that my mother could focus on bearing Philippe a son. When I was here, I tried to be as quiet and inconspicuous as possible so I wouldn't be sent away again. Not that we didn't have a wonderful time with my father's family, we did. But I missed my mother when I was away from her.''

"Of course you did. That's no way for a child to be treated.''

"You weren't treated the way a child should be treated, either, being sent off to boarding school so young.''

"Something we both have in common, eh?'' He brushed his fingers across her cheek while gazing at her with his rich blue eyes. "Mothers who selfishly went after what they wanted and damn the consequences.''

"Or mothers who thought they were doing what was best for us in a difficult situation.'' She captured his hand and held it in hers. "Have you thought about reading the letter your mother left you?''

"I've thought about it.''

"And?''

"And I'm not doing it. Don't give me that look. There's nothing she can say that would change what she did.''

"I agree that nothing can change *what* she did, but her letter might explain *why* she did it.''

"You've always got an answer to everything, don't you?''

"I just want what's best for you, Luc.''

"This is what's best for me,'' he murmured lowering his head to brush his lips over hers. "Being with you.''

She felt a ripple of anticipation slide up her spine as he tasted and tested the corners of her mouth, sliding across the full softness in between before lingering. The kiss grew and expanded from one delicious caress into an intimate seduction. Lost in the intimacies of his tongue moving against hers, she was further enthralled by the passage of his hands over her body.

The demure floral dress she'd worn to the dowager queen's tea was turned into a temptress's gown in his able hands. The soft cotton material magnified his every caress, allowing her to feel each one of his fingers as they glided from her back to her breast.

His embrace became a passport to a world of wondrous sensations as he teased the roof of her mouth with his tongue and claimed her breast in the palm of his hand, his fingers closing over her warm and willing flesh. He brushed her firm nipple with his thumb, making her burn with forbidden pleasure.

Her knees became weak, and she welcomed the feel of a soft mattress beneath her. His lips never left hers as he followed her down, blanketing her with his powerful body.

Rolling onto his side, he pulled her closer. She melted against him, caught up in the magic of his touch.

His knowing fingers gained entrance to the front fastening of her bra. Her highly sensitized nerve endings vibrated when she felt his warm breath on her now-bare skin. Luc didn't hurry as he caressed and nibbled, kissed and paid homage to every delectable inch of her breasts—running his tongue from the upper line of her ribs to nuzzle the firm underside. Then he traveled up and over, his evocative tongue wickedly trailing along, following the passage of faint blue veins against the creaminess of her flesh until he reached the sensitive peak. His thumb ventured closer, guiding her into the warmth of his mouth.

Juliet moaned with pleasure and arched her back. His wet heat surrounded even more of her now, even as his lower body throbbed against hers. The hard ridge beneath his trousers fitted with exquisite precision against the aching secret juncture of her body. The stroking contact was more arousing and exciting than anything she'd ever known before.

The temptation to experience the full possession of this man, to be just once wholly his, was overwhelming. As he settled even more of his weight over her, she greedily welcomed him—his powerful body, his creative seduction. She wanted more.

He slid his fingers beneath her dress, caressing the back of her knee before moving upward to her thigh and increasingly closer to the one spot that wept with need. By now the friction of his body moving against hers had become a delicious torment, one he huskily promised to remedy.

Passion prevailed as her mind was completely monopolized by her body's urgent desire to merge with his, for the two of them to become one. Urging him on, she opened herself to him.

But before his seductive fingers could gain access, they were interrupted by the arrival of thirty-six sharp claws scrambling across their partially clothed bodies.

"Ouch!" Luc exclaimed.

"Be careful, it's the kittens," she warned him, fearing he might toss them aside. "Don't hurt them."

"I would never hurt them, but they can't say the same for me." He held out his arm, which now showed a bright red scratch on it.

"I'm so sorry. I know I'm not supposed to have the kittens in the palace, but I was afraid Mittens and Rascal would get trampled by the horses if I left them in the stables. So I sneaked them inside yesterday." Juliet stopped her self-conscious refastening of her clothing to gaze at him. "I'm so sorry they hurt you. Shall I kiss it better?"

His eyes met hers, and he spoke to her without saying a word, making her breath catch and her heart race. The undisguised passion she saw reflected in their blue depths was overwhelming. His gaze ranged over her now-covered curves with the erotic knowledge of a man who'd touched her intimately, who'd taken her to the very threshold of passion's gate.

Her body still vibrated with that awareness.

Before Luc could speak or act on the fiery desire etched on his face, they were interrupted again as the door bounced open. This time it wasn't kittens, it was her younger sister Jacqueline.

"So, what are you two up to...or shouldn't I ask?" the precocious adolescent inquired with a wicked grin.

Chapter Nine

"**J**acqueline!" Juliet leapt from the bed as if propelled by one of the medieval catapults on display in the palace dungeon. "What are you doing here? And why is your hair purple?"

"More important what are you and Luc doing on your bed?"

"Nothing." Juliet frantically smoothed her hair, which had come loose from the French braid. "I was just showing him the kittens."

"I don't think that's all you were showing him," her impudent sister drawled.

Juliet frowned at her. "I thought you wouldn't be back until next week."

"I missed everyone in St. Michel too much to stay away any longer."

"Well, I'd better get back to work." Luc was clearly eager to avoid getting stuck overhearing a sisterly heart-to-heart conversation.

"You might want to wipe the lipstick from your cheek before you do," Jacqueline advised him.

"She's just kidding," Juliet hastily assured Luc. "There is no lipstick on your cheek."

Jacqueline showed no remorse. "Only because my bookish big sister doesn't wear any."

"Nice having you back, Muffin," Luc told her with a grin.

"Nice being back, Spyman." Seeing Juliet's startled look, the twelve-year-old added, "That's my nickname for him. Didn't you tell her, Luc?"

He shook his head, which tumbled more of his dark hair onto his forehead. Had she messed up his hair? Juliet had hazy memories of running her fingers through the surprisingly silky dark strands as he caressed her bare breasts with his seductive mouth and tongue.

"No, I didn't tell her," Luc was saying. "Some things are meant to be top secret, Muffin."

Jacqueline nodded with a maturity beyond her years. "Understood, Spyman. See you around."

Juliet waited until Luc had left before turning to her sister. "Jacqueline, you really can't go calling Luc Spyman any longer."

"Why not?"

"Because...well..." She floundered a moment, remembering that Luc didn't want anyone else knowing about his true background just yet. "I can't tell you all the details right now, but believe me when I say that there are very good reasons."

"You mean because he may soon be king?"

Juliet almost swallowed her tongue. "Where did you hear that?"

Jacqueline shrugged and dropped into a nearby comfy

chair, flinging one leg over the arm. "Grandmama told me. I stopped by to see her before coming here."

The dowager queen was indeed Jacqueline's grandmother. Her sister was able to straddle both worlds—the royal world of her father the king and the real world of their mother. All this and she was only twelve.

Still stunned, Juliet was not expecting her sister's next observation. "So, Luc has turned out to be quite a hottie, huh?"

Juliet blushed a brilliant shade of red.

"Oh, so you think so, too?" Her sister practically chortled with delight.

"I think that purple hair better be temporary. And you should have changed clothes before seeing the dowager queen." Juliet tugged her sister to her feet. "Why are there holes in your jeans? That top is much too skimpy. And what is that in your navel?"

"It's not permanent. It's a navel gem. And the girls at school love my clothes, they think I look like Britney Spears."

"Not a goal of mine, I admit. And it shouldn't be one of yours, either. She is an entertainer, you are—"

"The daughter of a king," Jacqueline cut in. "Yeah, I've heard it all before. And for your information, Grandmama loved my outfit. And my hair. She told me so herself. She said if she were a decade or two younger, she'd be wearing a navel gem herself."

Juliet had to laugh at the idea of the proper dowager queen ever showing her navel.

"You should show more skin yourself," Jacqueline advised her. "You usually dress as if you were Grandmama's age."

"Thank you for those kind words," Juliet noted dryly.

"I wasn't trying to be insulting, I was just telling the

truth. Isn't that what you are always after me to do? To tell the truth?''

''When it's appropriate.''

''And when it's not?'' Jacqueline instantly demanded.

''Then if you can't say something nice, say nothing at all.''

''I like your kittens. That's something nice, isn't it?'' She scooped Rascal up and dropped back into the chair. ''So tell me, why were you and Luc making out?''

''Jacqueline!''

Her younger sister blinked up at her, making Juliet realize that she was wearing glittery eyeshadow that matched her purple hair. ''What?''

''That is not an appropriate question. Not that Luc and I were making out.'' First lying to the dowager queen earlier that afternoon, now lying to her sister. What was happening to her? Juliet wondered. She used to be a very honest person, wrapped up in her books and research. Not at all the kind of woman who'd make out with a sexy man like Luc.

''Now who's not telling the truth?'' Jacqueline sent a very pointed look at the rumpled bedcoverings.

Juliet was about to resume her defensive posture when an inner voice advised her to wait a minute. Her younger sister was not her keeper. Juliet was the older, the wiser, and the more conservative one. Usually. ''I don't have to explain myself to you.''

''Why not?'' Jacqueline's mutinous expression was pure adolescence. At times like this, Juliet fervently wished their mother was still alive to help guide them both. ''I always have to tell you everything. It's not fair.''

''Life isn't always fair,'' Juliet noted quietly. ''I suppose it's time we both learned that.''

* * *

"Ah, Luc, I'm so glad you decided to join us," the dowager queen said as she welcomed him to the White Drawing Room.

Luc knew this was the room where the dowager queen had hosted tea with Juliet earlier that afternoon, before he'd almost seduced Juliet in her own bed. His body still hadn't recovered. He was a man accustomed to being in control—of his life, of his future, of his emotions. All that had been blown sky-high the past few weeks and he was left with chaos. He did not like chaos.

This was neither the time nor the place to brood over what had happened—not to mention what had almost happened—in Juliet's private apartments. His thoughts were too jumbled to make any sense at the moment anyway.

"I'm joining you because you practically ordered me here."

"You're the king." She gave him an arch look. "No one should be able to order you to do anything."

"That's the first good thing I've heard about this job," he growled. "So what's the emergency?"

"You do have a way of getting right to the point, don't you?" She didn't make it sound like a compliment, and her laser gaze indicated her displeasure.

"So I've been told."

"By Juliet?"

"You and I had an agreement about my private life being off-limits, remember?"

"We had an agreement that you would call me Grandmother, remember? And that you would spend more time with me."

Luc sighed. "I spent time with you yesterday morning, Grandmother. That's when you promised not to interfere in my private life, remember?"

"I promised not to interrogate you again. I didn't say anything about not interrogating Juliet. But that's besides the point. I called you here today to discuss St. Michel's national security."

"Then why isn't the prime minister here?"

"The poor man came down with a touch of tummy flu. Too many hours spent with the Privy Council if you ask me."

"What is this matter of national security you're talking about?"

"I think Ariane and Etienne should tell you themselves. Ah, here they are now. Right on time."

Prince Etienne of Rhineland had the aristocratic bearing of a man born into royalty. Wearing a superbly tailored suit, he possessed the confidence of a ruler.

Not that Luc wasn't a confident man. He was. But a ruler? The jury was still out on that one.

Like her husband, Princess Ariane also had that regal manner down pat. A petite woman with blond shoulder-length hair and blue eyes, she had an adventurous nature that sometimes got her into trouble. For instance, there had been the time she'd decided to go to Rhineland to spy on the royal family in an attempt to learn more about the rumored plot to take over St. Michel. She'd learned that the royal family had no part in it, and then she'd fallen in love with the prince.

To his surprise, Ariane came right up to him and hugged him. She grinned at his stunned expression. "It's so good to see you again, Luc. I've always wanted a big brother."

Luc glared at the dowager queen who merely smiled back at him. "I thought we agreed not to tell anyone," he reminded his grandmother.

"Ariane isn't *anyone*. She's my granddaughter."

Luc shot a look at Etienne, who merely rolled his eyes as if to say it's no use fighting these two.

"Is that why you called for me?" Luc demanded. "Because Ariane is here for a visit?"

"Because she and Etienne have something important to tell you."

"We have news regarding the extremist faction known as Rhinelanders for Annexation, or RFA," Etienne said.

Luc nodded. "I'm familiar with the organization."

"We've long suspected they had a plan to overthrow the monarch and the government here and annex St. Michel to Rhineland. As you know, my family does not approve of any such move and has made an official statement to that effect. But this group is very good at playing on the strong nationalistic feelings of my countrymen. They excel at bringing out the worst in people."

"I'm familiar with that type of modus operandi." In his years at Interpol, Luc had dealt with various extremist groups who took violent action to have their agendas met.

"We arrested two of the group's leaders several weeks ago, but suspected that they were merely the front men for the organization. We had no idea who was really pulling the strings."

"And supplying the money," Ariane added.

"A great deal of money," Etienne agreed. "We just arrested Berg Dekker when he returned to Rhineland earlier this morning."

"Berg Dekker?" Luc shook his head in amazement. "I've heard of him, of course. He's a frequent target of the regional environmental groups because of his practices." Luc had long wondered how Dekker got approval to use St. Michel River to ship his petroleum products to and from the North Sea. Other European countries had turned him down, citing his poor record in abiding by local shipping restrictions and his goal of putting profits above all else.

Luc had never been in a position to question Dekker's business dealings before. It was just hitting him that he now was. "What do you have on Dekker?"

"Our authorities have been following an elaborate paper trail of hidden trusts and dummy corporations, following the money that Dekker took in and where it went. He illegally funneled a lot of it into the Rhinelanders for Annexation group. We also uncovered his plot to destabilize the economy of Rhineland to unseat the monarchy so that he could run as the country's savior."

"How does this affect St. Michel?" Luc asked.

"Luc is a bottom-line sort of man," the dowager queen said apologetically.

He glared at her. It stung his pride to have someone apologizing for his behavior.

"That's what will make him such a great king," Ariane declared. "He'll cut through all the cow dung and get right to business."

"Ariane!" The dowager queen fixed her with a disapproving look before cracking a slight smile. "A royal does not refer to cow dung."

Ariane was not intimidated. "Would you prefer I call it by one of its more vulgar names?"

"I'd prefer you not mention it at all. Now where were we? Ah, yes, Etienne, you were about to tell us more about how this Dekker fellow relates to St. Michel."

"In addition to his plot to destabilize Rhineland, he also planned to move forward and annex St. Michel. At least that was his plan until he met with Queen Celeste."

"He met with Queen Celeste?"

"So he claims. We have no proof that the meeting took

place. But Dekker swears that Celeste came to him with an offer.''

''I knew that woman was a hussy!'' the dowager queen declared.

''Not a sexual offer,'' Etienne quickly clarified. ''A business offer. Dekker says she promised him unlimited access to the St. Michel River in exchange for his supporting her infant son's claim to the throne.''

''Of all the nerve!''

''Now, Grandmother…''

''We have no proof,'' Etienne reminded them. ''Celeste denies the meeting ever took place. She claims that Dekker is merely trying to make trouble for her, to destabilize St. Michel just as he planned to destabilize Rhineland.''

''I don't believe a word she says,'' Ariane declared. ''Etienne and I came here today to warn you, Luc. To warn you about Celeste. She clearly plans on doing whatever it takes to put her baby son on the throne. Perhaps it's time to tell her you are the rightful heir.''

''If she's as devious as you say she is, then she probably already knows. Which is why…''

''Why what?'' Ariane asked.

''Nothing.'' Luc shook his head. ''It's just that Juliet was suspicious of a few strange occurrences.''

''What kind of strange occurrences?'' Ariane demanded.

Luc briefly told them about the falling gargoyle and the collapsing tent at the carnival. ''Clearly not the work of a professional. If Celeste wanted me dead, there are definitely more effective ways of trying to assassinate me.''

''Don't underestimate her,'' Ariane warned him. ''Just

because she's been foolish so far doesn't mean she won't turn deadly at the drop of a hat."

"Or the drop of a crown. There's a lot at stake for her," Etienne said. "I agree with my lovely wife. Don't underestimate Celeste."

"They've arrested Dekker!" Claude entered Celeste's riverfront apartment and then collapsed on her red velvet settee.

"Do stop hyperventilating, Claude."

"Didn't you hear me? Dekker was arrested the moment he returned to Rhineland this morning. It's on all the news reports. They're saying that he tried to overthrow the government."

"What government?"

"In Rhineland."

"Then we're fine. We're not involved with the government of Rhineland."

"No, but we just negotiated a deal with Dekker a few days ago. He's bound to tell the authorities that."

"He has. And I've already denied it." She studied her perfectly manicured nails before giving Claude a reprimanding stare. "You really should learn not to panic. It's not an admirable trait by any means."

"How could I not panic? The man we made an illegal deal with was just arrested."

"There was nothing illegal about our deal with him. And even if there was, no one else need know about it. The main problem here is Luc."

"Luc?" Claude was clearly bewildered.

"Do try and keep up," she told him tartly. "Luc is about to be named heir to the throne. We can't let that happen."

"So we're back to the plan of killing him?"

Celeste sighed. "It would appear so."

* * *

"So how does this royalty thing work?" Luc voiced the question from his office chair.

"Pretty well from my perspective," Etienne answered from the chair across the room.

They'd spent the past few hours reviewing the case against Dekker, going over the intelligence files Etienne had brought with him from Rhineland. Then Luc had brought out a bottle of fine brandy and the discussion had grown a bit more personal.

"Yes, well you were born into the job, so to speak. And speaking of jobs, I suppose I'm going to have to find a new head of security soon. Damn." Luc rubbed his forehead. "I really liked this job, this office."

"You could move the throne in here."

"The dowager queen would have a fit."

"She's more resilient than you think."

"It's not her resilience I'm worried about, it's mine." Luc jumped up and started pacing. "How do you manage to have a private life? You married a princess. But what about someone outside of the royalty business?"

"Wait a moment, marrying Ariane was anything but a no-brainer. We certainly had more than our fair share of troubles."

"Yes, but she *is* a princess. She, like you, grew up in this world."

"Are you talking about marrying a commoner?"

"I'm not talking about marriage at all."

"Then what are you talking about?"

"Damned if I know," Luc muttered, walking over to his window to stare down at the fountain where he'd kissed Juliet.

"Do you have a certain woman in mind?"

"All the time. She's in my mind all the time."

"And you don't think she'd be someone suitable?"

"She's very suitable. For me, Luc. But she wouldn't just be getting involved with me. She'd be getting involved with the King of St. Michel."

"Involved but not married?"

"I don't know." Luc shoved his free hand through his hair before taking another healthy swig of brandy. "I can't seem to think very straight these days."

"I've had almost thirty years to become accustomed to my title," Etienne said. "You've had what...a few weeks? Give yourself time."

"I've run out of time. The dowager queen told me tonight that the Privy Council will be approving my claim to the throne within the next forty-eight hours or less."

"Not much time left to get your thoughts in order."

When Etienne left a short while later, Luc returned to his desk, intending to clear up some outstanding paperwork. If someone else was going to take over this job, then he wanted everything in tip-top shape when they came in. Someone else sitting in his chair, at his desk. The thought irked him.

Maybe he should bring the pieces of furniture with him to wherever it was that the king did his daily job. Luc wasn't even sure what room in the palace it was. He should know that. As head of security, he no doubt did know it at one time. A time when he'd been a sane man with a fairly normal background. Until this king thing.

He snapped another file folder closed, and, as he did so, something caught on the edge of the paper before slipping to the floor. Picking it up, he realized that it was the letter from his mother. Juliet must have left it here that morning she'd come to perch so seductively on the corner of his desk, the morning he'd first asked her to help him by giving him lessons on how to be a king.

Read it Luc. He could almost hear Juliet's voice. *Read the letter.*

He tore open the envelope.

To My Dearest Son,
If you're reading this letter it means Albert has already told you the facts about your heritage. I need to tell you the *reasons,* to tell you why I had to deceive you.

I know you're probably angry with me for never telling you who your biological father was, but I didn't want you saddled with the stigma of illegitimacy. When Philippe's parents told me that the marriage wasn't valid because I was underage, something inside me just crumbled and withered. Perhaps I should have been stronger, perhaps I should have done things differently.

I can only say that I have always loved you, from the second the nurses put you in my arms. Know that you are and always will be my beloved son, the light of my life. And please forgive me.

Your loving mother.

The last few words were a bit smeared, as if they'd got wet at one point. Had his mother cried as she wrote the letter?

Something inside him, an invisible inner wall, cracked—allowing a trickle of emotion through. His fingers clenched around his empty brandy glass as he stared at the letter until his eyes burned. *My dearest son…you are and always will be my beloved son…your loving mother.* The words shifted and blurred.

A muscle in his jaw clenched. His mother had died without ever knowing her marriage to Philippe was indeed legal. The injustice of it all hit him with the power of a fist.

"Luc?"

For one fleeting instant, he thought the tentative woman's voice was that of his mother. He blinked before identifying her. The dowager queen.

"Are you all right?" She came forward into his office.

"Why?" He drilled her with his fierce gaze. "Why did you tell my mother the marriage wasn't valid?"

"Ah." She slipped into a nearby chair, looking as old as her years for the first time. "I was wondering when that would hit you."

"She left me a letter."

"I see." Her face seemed to age even more. "And did she curse me in it?"

"No." Luc's harsh voice caught. "She asked me to forgive her."

"And do you?"

He paused a moment before nodding. He could forgive his mother now that he'd read her words.

"Good. But now you're not sure about forgiving me, correct?"

"Correct."

"Ah, Luc. I wish I could tell you how it was. Katie's father was only a middle-management employee of an American corporation. They had no money and no social standing. Three decades ago, that was a major thing. Her father was here in St. Michel on business for three months. Katie had plenty of time to explore the area. She met my son, and they fell in love. She became pregnant, and, without telling anyone beforehand, they went to France and were secretly married in a civil ceremony.

My husband, King Antoine, told Philippe that the marriage wasn't valid because Katie was only seventeen. I
didn't know whether that was true or not. But in my
mind, King Antoine was the absolute ruler, the final word
on any subject. If he said it wasn't valid, it wasn't valid.
King Antoine also informed Katie's father that if they
told anyone about this scandalous affair, he would pressure her father's employer to fire him. The king gave
Katie's father a substantial sum of money, without her
consent or approval. I'll never forget the look on her face
as her father whisked her away.''

The dowager queen had to pause to regain her composure before continuing. ''Do I wish that we hadn't interfered in our son's life? Without a shadow of a doubt.
I believe that Philippe spent the rest of his life trying to
find the kind of love he shared with Katie and that he
went to his grave loving her.'' Her voice trembled with
emotion. ''I wish we had brought Katie home to the palace with us, that I'd been there to hold you when you
were born, to lavish you with attention as I did my granddaughters while they were growing up. But I wasn't. I
can't undo the past, Luc. I can only look ahead to the
future. Your future. The King of St. Michel's future.''
She held out her thin elegant hand, wrinkled with age.
That's when Luc realized that the lavish diamond King
Antoine had given her was no longer sparkling on her
left finger.

''Where's your ring?'' His voice sounded rusty even
to his own ears.

''I put it in the vault. I no longer choose to remain tied
to my husband and the bad choices he made and I went
along with. I want to make a new start. Granted, seventy-
something might be a tad late to start fresh, but I'm game
if you are. What about it, Luc? You told me that I should

try asking instead of ordering. So here I am." Her out-stretched hand trembled and her laser-blue eyes were filled with deep-seated pain and uncertainty. "Ask-ing...no...*begging* you for forgiveness and the chance to start anew."

Luc took her hand in his. A second later he was around the desk, kneeling before her with his arms around her surprisingly slight frame.

"Welcome home, my boy." He could almost hear his mother's voice repeating his grandmother's refrain. *Welcome home, Luc. Welcome home, my dearest son.*

Chapter Ten

Juliet was up with the sun the next morning, taking an early-morning walk in the palace gardens to clear her mind. She hadn't been able to sleep much at all last night. The erotic memory of Luc's lovemaking had kept her awake—her body still thrumming from the unresolved passion of their heated embrace.

She'd always been a firm believer in waiting until after marriage before giving her virginity to the man she loved. That resolve had never been tested before, not even with Armand. But Luc was different. He had a way of overwhelming her common sense and going right to her heart.

The fact that she was intensely attracted to him wasn't the reason they'd almost made love yesterday. Hormones alone didn't rule her actions, *love* did. And that potent combination had proven too powerful to resist.

What would have happened if the kittens and her sister hadn't interrupted them? Would Luc have made love with her? Did he know she was a virgin? Would that matter to him? It wasn't anything they'd ever discussed, not being a topic that was easy to include in everyday conversation.

Juliet had no doubt that Luc was accustomed to women with more sexual experience than she had. But that hadn't seemed to bother him yesterday. He'd groaned with pleasure when she'd returned his kisses. His hard body had throbbed with desire for her. His voice had been husky with need as he'd whispered in her ear, and his blue eyes had blazed down at her with smoldering passion.

The memory alone was enough to make her weak at the knees. As she sank onto one of the rustic benches lining the winding path, she tried to distract herself by focusing on her surroundings. It promised to be another gorgeous late-spring day, with only a few billowy cumulus clouds to add a bit of interest to an otherwise intensely blue sky. Not the blue of Luc's eyes, however. They were darker than sky blue. She'd long ago given up trying to put an exact color on them—they were simply his eyes and they were awesome because they were *his*.

Her gaze wandered over the gardens themselves. The irises were almost through blooming and the rest of the roses were about to burst into color. With their fragrant blossoms and beautiful displays, they were a favorite of hers. Climbing roses in a delicious shade of apricot clambered alongside deep purple clematis over the ten-foot arbor surrounding her.

It was so peaceful here. Birds chirped as they hopped from branch to branch on a nearby tree. A huge bumblebee droned lazily right over her head as it meandered from flower to flower. Then Juliet heard something else, something not as serene as the natural symphony of the birds and the breeze rustling through the leaves. It sounded like someone softly sobbing.

Juliet left the arbor and followed the heartwrenching noise to the back end of the garden. There she found Yvette, the head gardener's wife, sobbing while attempting to till the small vegetable garden beside the gardener's house. Her infant was apparently sleeping in a wicker bassinet on the bench by the back door.

"What is it, Yvette?" Juliet put an arm around her trembling shoulders. "What's wrong?"

The other woman kept crying.

"Is it the baby?"

Yvette's crying increased.

Alarmed, Juliet said, "I'll go fetch the royal physician."

"No!" Yvette stopped her sobbing to grab Juliet's arm with desperate hands. "No, you mustn't."

"If the baby is sick, then we have to have a doctor check her out."

"She's not sick."

"Then what's wrong? You've been acting strangely for days now, Yvette. I've heard about postpartum depression caused by the hormonal changes after pregnancy. Why don't we have the physician check you out just to be sure?"

Yvette wiped the tears from her cheeks and stared at Juliet with a miserable expression in her brown eyes. "I know what's wrong with me and it has nothing to do with hormones."

"Then what is it? You know you can trust me, Yvette."

"I don't know what to do." Yvette plucked at her apron. "I swore I wouldn't tell anyone ever, but I can't live with what I've done."

"Is it your husband?" Juliet prompted gently. "Your marriage?"

"I didn't want to do it." Yvette's tears started to roll again. "I told my husband that it was wrong, that no amount of money could make up for what we had done."

Juliet patted her on the back sympathetically. "Go on."

"My husband's mother is ill and needed expensive medical treatment available here in St. Michel. The debts began to mount. That's when she came to us. With an offer."

"Who came to you?"

"Queen Celeste. Or rather one of her representatives."

"A man or woman?"

"A man. Dr. Mellion."

Juliet had never liked Celeste's physician. He had an arrogant way about him.

Yvette continued. "He presented us with an offer, enough money to pay for all the medical bills and much more as well."

"In exchange for what?"

"For my baby." Yvette whispered the words.

Juliet was stunned. "He wanted to buy your baby daughter?"

"No, he wanted to buy my baby son."

Now Juliet was confused. "But you ended up having a girl."

Yvette nervously looked over her shoulder. "Perhaps I shouldn't be telling you any of this."

"Most definitely you should tell me everything," Juliet stated firmly. "Did the doctor say why he wanted to buy your baby?"

"It was only in the event that Queen Celeste had a baby girl."

"But she had a boy and you had the girl. So the deal fell through, right?"

Yvette shook her head, her short dark curly hair bouncing in the slight breeze. "No, it did not fall through. I wish it had. I wish with all my heart that it had. But it did not."

"What do you mean? What are you saying, Yvette?"

"That I sold my baby boy to the queen."

"And the baby girl you have?"

"Is the queen's," Yvette confessed in a hushed, frightened voice.

"But how…?"

"Dr. Mellion switched the babies shortly after they were born. When it was discovered that Queen Celeste had given birth to a daughter, her doctor and his assistant came and took my son. I'd given birth a few hours before. I barely had time to see him, to hold him before he was taken from me. Ripped from my arms. I begged them not to take him." Tears streamed down Yvette's flushed cheeks. "But they took him anyway. They gave me a baby girl instead."

Juliet was stunned by this news. She'd always known that Celeste was a schemer but she'd never expected her to go this far, to steal another woman's baby and try to pass it off as her own. The suspicions had been that perhaps the child wasn't really the king's, that it was the result of a liaison with a lover. But no one had suspected that Celeste wasn't the mother. That was too wild a scenario for anyone to have come up with. Anyone but Celeste.

"Oh, Yvette." Juliet hugged her. "I'm so sorry that they put you through this."

"We made a bargain with the devil, it is right that we pay. But it isn't right that these two innocent babies pay as well. I want my son back."

"I know you do. Don't worry, we'll get him back for

you. There now, dry your tears. We'll go to Luc and tell him everything. He'll take it from there.''

"We'll be sent to jail." Yvette's voice trembled with fear.

"No, you won't. The doctor may well go to jail, but you won't.''

"But I sold my baby.''

"It was not your idea. Your husband agreed to the plan because he was in dire need of money for his poor sick mother. No one will blame him for that, although they may question his judgment in agreeing to this plan. But it is Celeste and the doctor who are to blame here. They are the ones who initiated this devious plan.''

"You really think we can get my little boy back without going to jail?" For the first time, a faint glimmer of hope shone in her dark eyes.

"I'm certain of it. Come now, dry those tears.'' Juliet paused at the sound of her name being urgently called. "Here, I'm here.''

Henri, one of the footmen, came rushing into the vegetable garden, crushing the tender vegetation beneath his feet. "We have been searching for you everywhere, Miss Juliet. You must come at once. There has been an accident.''

The hairs on the back of her neck prickled and she went cold all over. "An accident?''

"Yes. It's Luc Dumont. He's asking for you. I was told to bring you to him immediately. Come, we mustn't wait. Every second counts!''

"What happened? How badly is he hurt?''

"The injuries are serious,'' Henri replied. "Life-threatening.''

Juliet's heart stopped. She couldn't breathe. Luc, seriously hurt. It was her worst nightmare come true. Talons of panic clawed their way through her.

"You, there." Henri pointed at Yvette. "I fear Miss Juliet is going to need comforting when she sees how badly off Luc is. You must accompany us."

"But I can't leave the baby," Yvette protested.

"Bring the infant with us," Henri said, "but hurry. Or we shall be too late. There's a car waiting to take you to him."

Dazed and terrified for Luc, Juliet nodded for Yvette to do as Henri said. Moments later they were in a dark sedan rushing from the palace. It was only then that she realized they weren't alone in the sedan. Claude Guignard, St. Michel's deputy energy minister, was in the car with them. He patted her hand with commiseration. "It doesn't look good. I'm sorry."

"Were you with Luc? What can you tell me about the accident?"

"There was an explosion. I was sent to get you."

Please God, let him live. Don't let him die!

Juliet kept repeating that prayer over and over again, as they raced through the city of St. Michel. "Wait, your driver missed the turnoff to the hospital."

"Luc isn't at the hospital."

"Why not?"

"He was injured near the warehouses down by the river. They fear moving him before his condition has been stabilized. To do so would guarantee his death."

Cold terror gripped every part of her body, making it hard for her even to breathe.

What had Luc been doing at a warehouse by the river? Had he been following a lead about the Rhinelanders for Annexation group? Had they caused his accident? St. Michel had never had to worry about terrorist activities in the past, but the world was a different place these days. If the deputy energy minister was involved, then it must have something to do with petroleum? At one of the loading facilities along the river perhaps?

"We'll be there in a minute or two," Claude assured her.

True to his word, the sedan pulled to a halt beside one of the warehouses. Juliet was out of the car in an instant. "Hurry! Take me to Luc!"

"Follow me." Claude led them inside.

The difference between the bright sunshine outside and the darkness of the warehouse had Juliet pausing for a moment as she frantically tried to scan the room. "I don't see him, Mr. Guignard. Where is he?"

"In the small storeroom ahead." He stood aside to let them go ahead of him.

Juliet and Yvette had no sooner stepped into the room than the door was slammed behind them.

The light in there was even dimmer, provided only by a small and dingy barred window located up near the ceiling. There was no sign of Luc, or of anyone else.

Juliet was getting a very bad feeling about this. She turned to the closed door. "Mr. Guignard, open the door." She was rather proud of the command in her voice, using her best dowager queen impersonation. "Open the door this instant!"

"I'm afraid I can't do that, Juliet."

The baby started to cry.

It was all a ruse. Juliet realized that now. "Luc isn't hurt at all, is he? You said that to get me here. Why?"

"Because I overheard Yvette spilling her heart to you, the stupid fool. I had to do something before you went to Luc and told him everything."

"Now, Claude, you don't want to do this." Her voice

was more empathetic now. Obviously the commanding
stuff hadn't worked. Besides, it wasn't a natural for her.
"You're not thinking clearly."

"Of course I'm not thinking clearly!" he shouted in
return, making the baby cry all the more. Yvette was also
starting to sob quietly.

Juliet refused to give in to fear or panic. Too late, she
recalled rumors linking Claude with Celeste. "You can't
just keep us locked up here."

"I can and I will until I figure out what to do next.
Don't bother screaming, both warehouses on either side
are deserted this time of year. No one will hear you."

"Luc will come after me. He'll find us."

"No, he won't." Claude's voice sounded dangerously
confident. "I'll make sure of that."

The door to the White Drawing Room swung open and
bounced against the wall. Luc automatically assumed a
defensive posture. He never sat in a room with his back
to the door, part of his security training. When he saw it
was only Jacqueline, he relaxed. Then he tensed up again
at the possibility that the precocious adolescent had come
to tell his grandmother about finding Luc and Juliet together on her bed yesterday afternoon.

He tried to read the girl's expression, but all he got
was panic. Which meant what? In Jacqueline's case it
could mean anything from a clothing crisis to a rumor
about one of her favorite boy bands calling it quits. She
looked like something from an MTV video with her
denim miniskirt and her stretchy top covering only one
shoulder. And then there was her purple hair.

"A princess never runs into a room as if she were on

fire, *mignon*," the dowager queen reprimanded her. "I've told you that before."

"Have you seen Juliet?" Jacqueline's chest was heaving as if she'd been running. It made the sparkling blue gem in her navel dip and ripple.

"No," the dowager queen replied, not the least bit flustered by her granddaughter's garish appearance.

"She's missing!" Jacqueline exclaimed.

The dowager queen wasn't impressed. "What are you talking about? You really must curb that dramatic streak of yours, Jacqueline."

But Luc took her words seriously. "When was the last time you saw her?"

"Last night. She left a note on my door at six this morning saying she was going to go for a walk in the gardens. That was hours ago."

Luc was instantly on alert. "Have you had the guards check the gardens?"

Jacqueline nodded. "Yes, and I've checked the palace as well. She's not in her office or her quarters. And none of the servants have seen her, either. Alistair already asked everyone."

"Did you check the stables? There were kittens there…"

"I checked. No one there has seen her at all today."

"I'm sure she's fine," the dowager queen said.

"Then where is she?"

"Come on, I'll help you find her," Luc said.

"But, Luc!" the dowager queen protested. "What about Celeste? You are supposed to be going to an emergency meeting with the prime minister about the situation."

Luc's reply was curt. "Celeste and the prime minister can both wait. Juliet is more important."

"What other songs do you know, Yvette?" Juliet stood perched on an overturned storage box as she tried to reach the tiny window. This was one of the few times she was glad of her height. Just a few inches more and she'd be able to at least look outside, see if anyone was about. Meanwhile, she needed Yvette to keep making noise as she joined her in loud choruses of everything from Broadway show tunes to French lullabies to Madonna's songs. There was always a chance that some passerby might hear them. Screaming for help for almost an hour had only increased their panic and left their voices hoarse. That's when Juliet had come up with the singing idea.

"I can't sing any longer, miss."

"Certainly you can. You mustn't give up, Yvette."

"We are doomed!" the other woman wailed. "Didn't you hear them talking about us? That man plans on putting us in the cargo hold of some river barge and shipping us off to South Africa. I'll never see my baby boy again."

"Now, Yvette…"

"They're going to win! They're going to kill Luc and have my son take over as the ruling king. Queen Celeste is going to win."

"Stop that." Juliet jumped down from her makeshift ladder to grab Yvette by the shoulders. "Look at me. And listen to me. No one is going to hurt Luc. He's had years of training as a security specialist. He knows what he's doing. He will find us. And until he does, we have to stay calm and be smart. Do you understand?"

Yvette nodded.

"Good. Now, how about a Britney Spears song?" Juliet started restacking the boxes. "She's my sister's favorite."

"Now do you believe me that Juliet's gone?" Jacqueline demanded after they'd scoured the gardens and found no sign of her.

Luc was trying to stay calm. "The junior gardener said he saw Juliet heading toward the head gardener's cottage early this morning."

"I know that. I was standing right beside you when he told you. But there's no one at the cottage now. We've been standing here pounding on the door for ages. And you even climbed in the open window to check things out and saw nothing suspicious. Right?"

"Right." No sign of forced entrance or of anything amiss. Spotting a child at the cottage next door, Luc motioned the boy over. He seemed more interested in Jacqueline's navel jewelry than Luc's questions. "Do you know Juliet Beaudreau?" Luc's voice was sharp.

The boy, who looked to be about nine or ten, nodded and swallowed nervously. "Have you seen her today?" Luc asked.

The boy nodded again.

"Do you know where she is?"

"A man came and took them away." The boy's voice quivered. "He took the gardener's wife and Julie."

"What man?"

"Henri, the footman."

"Celeste's favorite footman," Jacqueline declared. "Come on, let's go find him."

"You go stay with your grandmother. I'll deal with Henri alone."

"He's probably already left the palace," she warned him. "If he has, go find Celeste."

Luc was about to inform Jacqueline that he didn't need a twelve-year-old with purple hair telling him how to run an investigation, when he saw the fear in her eyes—eyes so similar to Juliet's. "Don't worry, Muffin. I'll find her." He gave her a brief hug.

"You'd better, Spyman." Her voice was jaunty but her smile was shaky. "Juliet is one of a kind. We can't lose her."

Luc deposited Jacqueline in the dowager queen's safe care before calling Alistair, the palace steward, on the palace phone. As Jacqueline had suspected, Henri had gone missing as well. Luc wasted no time, going directly to Queen Celeste's quarters.

He pounded on the door once before opening it.

"How dare you enter my quarters without my permission!" Celeste stood before him, dressed in an expensive designer suit and dripping in priceless jewels, the epitome of royal outrage. "Who do you think you are?"

"I'm the King of St. Michel and I want to know what you've done with Juliet."

"You're not the king yet." Her smile was more smirk than anything else.

"Is that a threat? Threatening the monarch is an offense punishable by life imprisonment, Celeste. I don't think you want to spend the rest of your days in a prison, now do you?"

Her confidence waned as the hard edge of his voice finally got through to her. "I don't know what you're talking about. I didn't threaten you. I'm a mere woman, still weak from birthing the king's child.''

''You haven't had a weak moment in your life.''

She actually preened at his comment. She placed a conciliatory hand on his arm. ''Perhaps we should work together, Luc. To unite St. Michel. If you were to marry me, then the people would be sure to accept you as their leader.''

He stepped away from her in disdain. ''I wouldn't marry you if you were the last woman in the universe. So you can stop batting your eyes at me and keep your hands to yourself. I'm not buying the *femme fatale* routine.''

For the first time, Celeste looked at him with a hint of fear. Good. He had his war face on, the one he used with terrorists and hardened criminals, the one that warned them that he'd just as soon stomp on them as talk to them. His voice turned as deadly as his expression. ''You have ten seconds to tell me what you've done with Juliet. And if you've hurt her, I swear you'll pay with your life.''

Celeste backed away from him, her eyes wide. ''It wasn't my idea,'' she shrieked. ''It was all Claude's fault.''

''Claude?''

''Claude Guignard. He panicked, and he took Juliet.''

''Took her where?'' Luc loomed over Celeste as she sank back onto the ivory-and-gold pillows of her lush sofa.

''I don't know.''

''I'm not buying that. Your ten seconds is just about

up,'' he growled. "Don't make me force you into telling me what you know.''

"The warehouse,'' Celeste babbled, her upper lip dotted with sweat. "He took her to an abandoned warehouse...by the river...you'll find her locked up there.''

"You'd better pray that I do find her and that she's unharmed. You'd better pray real hard, Celeste.''

Luc left her cowering on the couch.

A second after he closed the doors, he heard her furious curses followed by the sound of something—a vase perhaps—smashing against the wall. "Don't let anyone in or out,'' he ordered the two guards he'd posted at either side of the entrance. "Under any circumstances.''

Chapter Eleven

Luc heard Juliet before he saw her. He heard her singing a Sting song. At the top of her lungs.

He and the rest of his security force broke down the locked door into the warehouse as well as the one in the storage room. And then he had her safe in his arms.

She insisted on trying to tell him something about Celeste's baby, but he didn't care. All he cared about was Juliet.

He cupped her dusty face with his hands. "Are you all right? Did he hurt you?"

"I'm fine. I'm so glad you're here." She touched his cheek as if to confirm he was indeed real.

Luc took her into his arms again, kissing every inch of her face.

"Luc, I'm trying to tell you something important. Celeste switched babies with Yvette. Her child is actually a girl. This girl." She pointed to the baby in the bassinet.

"She screams almost as loudly as Celeste," he noted ruefully.

Juliet laughed unsteadily. "Her diaper needs changing. The baby, I mean. Not Celeste. I'm babbling again; aren't I? I knew you'd come, I kept telling myself you'd come. I'm so thirsty."

Luc quickly handed her a chilled bottle of water even as he nodded to his security officers to assist Yvette and her baby.

"Let's get you out of here and back to the palace." Luc kept his arm around Juliet as he guided her to his waiting car, complete with a driver.

"Did you hear what I said about Celeste swapping babies?" Juliet asked as the sedan sped through the streets to the palace, led by a police escort that cleared the way through busy late-afternoon traffic.

"Yes, I heard." In the back seat of the large sedan, Luc tucked Juliet's head onto his shoulder and rested his chin atop her head, his arm remaining firmly around her as if he were afraid she might disappear at any moment.

"I promised Yvette you'd get her baby boy back for her."

"I will." He ran his fingers through her hair, smoothing it out.

"You don't seem surprised by the news."

"Nothing Celeste does surprises me any longer."

"So now you believe me? I told you she was up to something."

"Aside from swapping babies, she also conspired with Berg Dekker to overthrow the governments of Rhineland and St. Michel."

"Oh, my." Juliet blinked in surprise. "She has been busy. Where is she now?"

"Under house arrest at the palace."

"So it's over?"

Touching her chin, he gently lifted her face to his. "One chapter is over, but the next is just beginning."

Thinking about the future made her stomach do somersaults in an unpleasant way. Juliet nervously swallowed a lump in her throat. "The dowager queen told me that the Privy Council would be meeting soon to declare you the king. I imagine that will be done even faster now."

Luc nodded, his expression growing more solemn. He might have said more, but they had arrived at the palace and his attention was required as he was bombarded with questions and demands from the prime minister the moment they stepped out of the sedan.

Juliet and Luc were separated by the crowd of servants and government workers who'd gathered to welcome them back to the palace. "Juliet!" Luc shouted.

"She's being taken care of by the dowager queen," the prime minister assured him, urgently tugging on his arm. "No need to concern yourself, your majesty. There's much to be done if we are to make the announcement of your impending coronation to the people of St. Michel in the morning."

Your majesty. The prime minister had just called him your majesty. For the first time it really sank in. This was it. No more time for adjusting. No more dress rehearsals or protocol lessons. This was it.

"Are you ready for the gala ball this evening?" the dowager queen asked as they took tea together in the White Drawing Room two days later.

"Yes, ma'am," Juliet dutifully replied, lying through her teeth.

"I told you to call me Simone. Or Grandmama, as Jacqueline does."

"Yes, ma'am, Grandmama." Flustered, Juliet set her

teacup down before she dropped it. Her fingers trembled. Nothing about her life seemed real anymore. She hadn't seen Luc since the prime minister had whisked him away almost forty-eight hours ago. Not in person, anyway. She'd seen him on the television as he'd addressed the nation. The dowager queen had been at his side, as had the three princesses. But not Juliet. Once again she was the outsider.

"She's nervous about the party tonight," her sister declared. The purple dye had washed out and left Jacqueline's hair its usual dark-blond color.

The dowager queen appeared surprised by this revelation. "Why should you be nervous, Juliet? You've attended royal functions before."

"Tonight is different," she replied.

"She wants to look her best for Luc."

"Jacqueline!" Juliet was tempted to throw the tray of scones at her sister. But then her emotions had been on edge ever since she'd been parted from Luc.

As promised, he'd reunited Yvette with her infant son. Yvette had stopped by to tell her the news, along with the information that Celeste had climbed down a drainpipe outside her apartment window and had escaped from the palace along with her lover Claude.

The baby girl that Celeste had actually given birth to was in the safekeeping of a nanny at the palace while DNA testing was done to confirm the little one's paternity. Should Claude turn out to be the biological father, then Yvette had offered to raise the baby along with her own son. Otherwise, if she truly was King Philippe's daughter, Luc had vowed to take care of the little girl.

Juliet could understand that with all that going on, he'd had his hands full. But he could have called her, written her an e-mail, something. He was in the same palace, having moved into the king's apartments. If it weren't for the servants, she wouldn't know anything. What did it say about her that she felt closer to them than to the royal family?

"Daydreaming about Luc?" Jacqueline teased her.

Juliet's fingers itched to reach for the scones and toss a few in Jacqueline's direction, but she valiantly restrained herself once again. "No, I was thinking about the festivities this evening. It's been a while since we've ever had such a grand party. Queen Regina once had a garden party and invited every citizen of St. Michel to come. I believe four thousand attended that event."

"Well, we haven't gone quite that far, but everyone who's anyone will be there tonight. Not just the aristocracy, but the business and education leaders as well." The dowager queen took a sip of tea. "The event is meant to introduce the country to their new king. As you know, the coronation will take place at the end of the week."

"Two days from now. I had no idea you'd be able to arrange everything that quickly."

"We've had the procedure in place for hundreds of years. And we've been waiting since my son's passing to crown the next king. It promises to be a joyous occasion."

"So, Juliet, are you wearing that revealing Versace gown like the one Jennifer Lopez wore to the Grammy Awards?" Jacqueline's eyes gleamed with devilish humor.

"No, *I'm* going to wear that gown," the dowager queen replied, without batting an eye.

Juliet and Jacqueline both burst into laughter—Jacqueline with delight, Juliet with guilty pleasure. Putting her hand to her lips, Juliet eyed the older woman uncertainly before relaxing upon seeing the dowager queen's smile.

"And I'm sure you'll look lovely in it…Grandmama," Juliet said.

"Thank you, Juliet. And what about you? What are you wearing this evening?"

"Something that covers her from head to toe probably," Jacqueline replied on her behalf.

"Since the infamous Versace gown is already taken—" Juliet shared a grin with the dowager queen "—I guess I'll have to make do with something else."

"Something else that covers her from head to toe." Jacqueline's voice was gloomy as she reached for another tea cake, this one shaped like a flower.

"You don't have to make do with anything," the dowager queen told Juliet. With a tilt of her regal head she motioned to the footman on duty, who opened the doors and ushered in a chic-looking woman dressed in a gorgeous suit the shade of periwinkle. "This is Madame Chantille, the most talented dress designer in all of Europe."

"You are too kind, your highness."

"And these are my granddaughters. Do you think you can fix them up a bit for tonight's party?"

Madame Chantille studied them for a moment before nodding emphatically. "Leave them in my capable hands, ma'am, and I'll transform them into the belles of the ball."

Luc tried not to sigh impatiently as his valet slipped on his jacket for him. He'd been putting on his own jacket for more than twenty years, but now that he was a king he was no longer allowed that luxury.

The royal attire featured the deep blue and red of St.

Michel's national colors. The military-style jacket was filled with medals along the right breast pocket, each one indicating some special point in the country's history. Luc hadn't had time to learn the names of all the medals yet, he'd been too busy trying to memorize his lines for the coronation on Sunday.

The Privy Council had performed a private ceremony with only themselves present so that Luc could assume his duties immediately. And what a mountain of paperwork had awaited him! He'd had nonstop meetings with the cabinet members of the government and had hardly slept since returning to the palace, but what irked him most was that he had yet to see Juliet.

He'd sent her a corsage for tonight and told her to save him the first dance. He'd also assigned a guard to watch her, wanting to make sure she was safe even though Celeste and Claude had fled the continent and were on their way to South America, to a country without an extradition agreement with St. Michel. He did take some pleasure in knowing that the royal jewels she'd taken with her were fakes, replaced by the dowager queen when her son had first announced his engagement to Celeste.

It was easier for Luc to think of King Philippe as the dowager queen's son than as his own father. In his heart of hearts, Albert would always be his father. Albert had sent his regrets that he couldn't attend the festivities tonight, but said he'd be there for the coronation ceremony on Sunday.

The promise of seeing Juliet tonight was the one thing that had kept Luc going. His valet placed the rich red satin royal banner across Luc's chest and pinned it in place with the Cross of St. Michel. Luc looked in the mirror…and saw a king.

Twenty minutes later Luc looked across the crowded Crystal Ballroom…and saw Juliet.

Juliet had never seen the Crystal Ballroom look love-lier. Except perhaps for that night when she'd attempted to give Luc dancing lessons, when he'd lit candles and played Strauss waltzes on a boom box. The first time he kissed her. Tonight a string quartet provided the music and the priceless Austrian crystal chandeliers were all lit up, showering the room with mini-rainbows dancing off the numerous tiers of faceted crystals.

The mirrored walls reflected the beautiful people in their gorgeous gowns and elegant tuxedos. Footmen, at-tired in their most formal livery of red jackets and pants, were stationed around the perimeter of the huge ball-room, ready with silver trays of slender Bohemian crystal fluted glasses filled with St. Michel's best champagne.

Juliet also caught sight of the three de Bergeron sisters. The romantic Marie-Claire was with her aristocratic busi-nessman husband Sebastian, who could give George Clooney a run for his money. At one point in the search for the missing heir, Sebastian's manipulative mother had claimed that he was Katie's child. Juliet could only imag-ine how upset that must have made Marie-Claire, who was already half in love with him. The truth had come out, and Sebastian had gone on to marry Marie-Claire in a lovely ceremony.

Ariane, the middle sister, was laughing at something her husband Prince Etienne of Rhineland had just said to her.

The eldest princess, Lise, was gazing up adoringly at her new husband Charles Rodin. Lise, several months pregnant, had that wonderful glow about her. Juliet had never seen her look happier.

All three woman looked stunning with their blond hair and light eyes. Juliet was certain that the dowager queen didn't have to call in a specialist to help any of them. They all knew what to wear, how to look gorgeous naturally. It had taken a team of five to make Juliet look this good.

But she did look good. Even she was willing to acknowledge that much. In fact, she looked almost beautiful.

Catching a glimpse of her reflection in the mirrored walls, she almost didn't recognize herself. Madame Chantille had chosen a magically divine dress in white and silver that shimmered with every step Juliet took. The strapless top hugged her body, showing off her bare shoulders, while the rich drape of the material added grace to her appearance by its sheer elegance as it curved in at her waist before flaring out in a full-length skirt. Her hair, behaving perfectly for once, was arranged in a cascade of curls falling from the top of her head.

She hoped Luc recognized her. She had yet to catch sight of him.

The ceiling-to-floor French doors were open to the large terrace leading down to the gardens, allowing the fragrance of old-fashioned roses to perfume the room. Juliet paused to smile and chat with one of the footmen who'd recently become engaged.

Her sister tugged on her arm. "Did you see Luc? Talk about a hottie!"

Juliet didn't even bother reprimanding her sister. "Where is he?"

"On his way over here. Ten people have stopped him to talk with him, so it's taking him a while, but he's almost here. Hey, Spyman, how's it going?"

Luc smiled. "I haven't spilled anything yet, Muffin,

so I'd say it's going okay. Better now that your sister is here. You look breathtaking, Juliet.''

She shyly lifted her gaze to his. ''Thank you.''

His vivid blue eyes searched her face, then wandered over her body in a visual tour that was as seductive as a touch. The surrounding crowd seemed to fade into the background as Juliet's entire focus was fixed on him.

He looked incredibly good in the formal attire of the King of St. Michel. Still, she'd always have a special affection for him wearing his biker black jeans and black T-shirt. And then there was his classy sophistication in a tuxedo. Tonight he had a regal bearing that suited him well but made her very aware of his newfound position.

''I see you're wearing the corsage I sent you.'' His voice was husky.

''Yes.''

''You two are just a fountain of dazzling conversation,'' Jacqueline mocked them both. ''I'm off to find a drink. A soft drink, so you can relax, big sister. Did you know she could look this good, Spyman?''

''She always looks good to me,'' Luc replied.

His smile made Juliet feel like Cinderella at the ball. But she didn't have long to bask in the moment before the prime minister interrupted them.

''There you are, your majesty. It's time for you to speak to the crowd. Actually, we're already ten minutes behind schedule.'' With his pewter-grey hair and mustache, the normally dignified statesman appeared a tad agitated. ''We can't delay any longer.''

''Wait for me,'' Luc told Juliet. ''I'll be back.''

As the two men made their way to the decorated dais at the corner of the ballroom, Juliet heard the comments from the women around her—comments about Luc's good looks and his being proclaimed Europe's most eligible bachelor in the tabloids that morning.

As the crowd moved forward to hear Luc's official statement welcoming everyone to the palace tonight, Juliet chose to stay by the cooling breeze wafting in through the open French doors. She was admiring how well Luc held himself, how confidently he spoke to the huge crowd, when a man's voice from her past interrupted her.

"Still spending your time daydreaming, Juliet?"

"Armand!" Her stomach dropped as she turned to face him. "What are you doing here?"

"I'm an invited guest, just as you are."

Clearly his way of making her feel like an outsider in the palace. Looking at him now she was astonished that she'd ever thought him good-looking. Not that he'd changed that much. But she had.

She was older and wiser now. She could see the lines of weakness in his tanned face, the meanness beneath his surface smile, the self-absorption of his entire attitude. He had light-brown hair perfectly cut and a square jaw that suited a male model. But there was no one inside the pretty outer shell.

Luc had more sex appeal in his little finger than Armand could ever have. She'd been lucky to have discovered Armand for the shallow man he was before it had been too late.

That didn't mean she wanted to have a conversation with him now, or at any other time for that matter.

"Nice dress," Armand casually noted. "Someone must have helped you pick it out. I always told you that you needed an image consultant."

Bull's-eye. A direct hit on her self-confidence. And he said it with such charm, too.

Keeping his eyes on Luc, Armand said, "Quite a story,

the missing heir turning out to be right under our noses all this time. The press is having a field day with it all. In order to restore credibility to the throne our new king will need a *real* royal to show him the ropes. There are a number of European princesses who could be excellent candidates. Already tonight, Wilmena of Saxony has made some inroads, but the young princess from Liechtenstein may well give her a run for her money. Some of my associates tell me that they've already started a betting pool regarding the identity of our future queen. So far Wilmena is the odds-on favorite. She comes from an old and prestigious family.''

The more Armand talked, the more inadequate Juliet felt. She had to get away from him. ''Excuse me, but I must go check on my sister.''

''Oh, your *half* sister, you mean. Don't let me keep you.'' Armand's smile was a double-edged sword that cut even further into her dwindling confidence. It was as if he knew that it had taken a team to make her look like Cinderella at the ball, and that at midnight she'd return to what she always had been—the nondescript dark-haired woman lost amid her beautiful blond sisters.

Juliet walked away, but knew she needed a break entirely from the ballroom, so she slipped out the next set of French doors to the terrace, down the wide steps to the gardens that had always given her peace. She'd no sooner settled on a bench then she was joined by someone.

''Ah, Mademoiselle Beaudreau, just the person I was searching for.'' The proclamation came from none other than the head of the Privy Council, Baron Severin.

Juliet knew the history of the Privy Council, about the combination of ancient European aristocratic titles—one earl, one duke, one count and one baron.

Baron Severin was the only person who scored higher on the intimidation scale than the dowager queen. He possessed the upright bearing of a military man and had a thick head of white hair. While not wearing his ceremonial robes this evening, he still looked as powerful as he was.

She couldn't imagine why he'd be looking for her, but she didn't think it could be a good sign. Unless he had some sort of historical question about the coronation on Sunday?

She tried to think positively.

"I won't beat about the bush, young lady. I saw you frolicking in the fountain with young Luc. That kind of unsuitable behavior is not befitting our new King Luc. Things are different now. More is expected of him. His every move will be closely monitored, by the press and by the people of St. Michel. While that kind of common behavior may be acceptable for you, it is not for him. We must be certain that his past mistakes aren't repeated. His associates have to be of the highest calibre. Surely you understand what I'm saying?"

She nodded. Baron Severin was saying she was a mistake, a bad influence on Luc. She sat motionless, caught in the grip of an anguish too deep to manage.

"He'll be expected to make a royal marriage, uniting the de Bergeron family name with one of equal stature from within the aristocracy of Europe."

"I understand," she whispered.

"I thought you might. An intelligent girl like yourself had to realize the damage you were doing."

His words were like poisoned arrows piercing her soul. Armand's earlier comments had opened the lid on her self-doubts, but the baron had just put the nail in the coffin, killing any hope she might have.

Everything he'd said was true. Unlike Armand, the baron wasn't trying to hurt her, wasn't trying to make trouble. He was simply pointing out the facts.

She'd become a liability to Luc. There was only one thing to do. Leave. Immediately.

Chapter Twelve

Inside her private rooms, Juliet didn't bother changing clothes. Instead she tossed a few things into a bag, her hands quivering as she grabbed her belongings without any sense of order. She stopped as she reached for the black sundress she'd worn when Luc had taken her to the carnival.

Remembering that night made her crumple onto the bed, silent tears pouring down her cheeks. As her pain increased, so did the need to get away. She left the rest of her things behind, including that dress. She could always have some things shipped to her later. When she decided where she was going.

She hastily scribbled a disjointed note to Jacqueline saying she needed to get away and apologizing for missing the new king's coronation. She was sure they'd all get along without her.

Including Luc.

She knew Luc had feelings for her—feelings of friendship, perhaps even more than that. But because she loved him so much, she couldn't be the one to bring dishonor upon him. He had a path very different from hers.

She had to set him free. And she had to do it now, this very moment, while she still had the courage, while the baron's words still burned in her soul.

If she saw Luc again, she'd weaken. She couldn't say goodbye, couldn't even leave a note for him. She had to cut it off entirely. It was best this way.

Her heart was breaking, but she was doing the right thing. That knowledge should have made her feel better, lessened her anguish in some small way. But it didn't.

Grabbing her belongings, she hurried down the deserted marble hallways. The joyous sounds of music and people laughing drifted up from the ballroom, mocking her as she made her silent escape. She raced out a side entrance of the palace, past a startled Alistair. Her compact car was just as she'd left it, parked outside the royal garages, unfit to rub bumpers with the exclusive Mercedes and BMWs inside.

It only took her a moment to stow her things. As she gathered the skirts of her dress and slid behind the steering wheel, she vowed that she'd return the dress to the dowager queen the next day, sending it by insured shipper. She needed to start making a list of things she had to do.

Staying focused on that prevented her from crying. The insides of her eyelids felt like gritty sandpaper from keeping the tears at bay. But that was a good thing, because it meant her vision wasn't blurred, and she could drive away from the palace without further delay. She refused to even allow herself one final look in her rearview mirror.

She had to be strong. She'd known this moment was coming. She'd always known she hadn't quite fitted in.

Close, but not close enough. Always an "almost." Never good enough. There was no changing that.

She'd been foolish to think otherwise. Fairy tales didn't come true for girls like her. The privileged and gorgeous de Bergeron daughters—they were the heroines in the classic tales, the ones who got their happy endings.

Juliet should have stuck to her books. That was the world she belonged in, the quiet peaceful world of history and academic work. Maybe she'd become a professor of history.

She should add that to her list. Right after Find a place to live away from St. Michel, and Return ballgown to the dowager queen. She doubted the older woman would want her calling her Grandmama any longer.

"You did a wonderful job with your welcome speech, Luc," his grandmother, the dowager queen, congratulated him.

"Thank you." His attention quickly wandered over the crowd. "Have you seen Juliet? I asked her to wait here for me."

"Already ordering the girl about, are you?"

He smiled a bit sheepishly. "She's accused me of being bossy in the past."

"She's a good girl."

"She's more than that." Luc wasn't certain when the first realization had come that he loved her. That night he'd kissed her in this very ballroom? The night he'd whisked her off to the carnival? When he'd almost made love to her? Or when he'd almost lost her to Celeste's evil plot?

The awareness of his emotions hadn't struck him like a thunderbolt out of the blue. Instead it had crept up on him like a gentle breeze, infiltrating his very soul until

he knew that his life lacked all meaning without Juliet.
It might seem as if one day she'd been just a friend and
the next she was indispensable to him, but in the past
few weeks his feelings for her had been undergoing a
powerful transformation.

"So you have special feelings for her?" his grandmother asked. "Beyond friendship?"

Luc nodded.

She gave him one of her laser stares. "And your in-
tentions toward her are honorable?"

"Yes. But I don't know that she'll want me. I'm no
prize."

"You're a king!"

"A definite handicap in her book," Luc noted dryly.
"Juliet has no desire for life in the limelight. And if she
marries me, she will be thrust into the spotlight."

His grandmother placed a reassuring hand on his arm.
"Juliet is stronger than you give her credit for."

"I know she's strong. I also know that none of this—"
He waved his hand at the surrounding crowd "—is her
idea of a good time. She'd much rather be reading a good
book."

"She'd much rather be in your arms," his grandmother
said with a sparkle in her eyes. "Go on, go find her and
tell her how you feel. Life is too short to wait, you need
to grab your happiness and follow your heart. I'll support
you, Luc. I won't make the same mistake I made with
my son, I promise you that."

"Thank you, Grandmother." He kissed her cheek.
"You have a heart of gold after all."

"Just be sure you don't let anyone else know about
that. I have a reputation to uphold, you know." She play-
fully smacked his hand with the painted fan she'd used
to cool herself with all evening. "Now be off with you!"

* * *

Juliet had brought the kittens with her in a cat carrier placed on the floor of the passenger seat. Their mews made her feel guilty for taking them, but she'd needed them. She was leaving everything else she loved behind. Surely she could be forgiven for taking Mittens and Rascal?

Tears threatened again but she bit her lip to keep them away. There was no time for weakness now. She'd think about everything later, when she was safely away. At the moment she was heading toward France, and she'd stop whenever she got tired. She'd always wanted to take a road trip, have the freedom to come and go as she pleased. This was her chance.

She turned on the car radio, not too loud so as not to scare the kittens, but when Sting's song "Brand New Day" came on, she had to turn it off again. Luc liked Sting's music. Too many memories there.

She'd driven several kilometers from the palace when she heard the sound of a police siren. Glancing at the speedometer, she muttered under her breath as she realized she'd been going over the posted speed limit. Sure enough, the police car pulled her over to the side of the road.

Sighing, she turned and reached into her purse for her license. "I'm sorry. I know I was going a bit too fast," she began apologizing when she looked up at the official standing at her car door. It wasn't any ordinary St. Michel police officer.

It was Luc. Still wearing his royal uniform.

She was stunned. "What are you doing here? How did you know where to find me? How did you even know I'd left?"

"My grandmother saw you driving out. I had a security car trail you until I could get here and take charge of things myself. You are in serous trouble. You've been accused of stealing the King of St. Michel's heart.'' His voice and expression were stern, but his eyes—his eyes positively ate her up. ''Do you have anything to say in your own defense?''

''Yes.'' No matter how he looked at her, she had to be strong. ''I'm not the kind of queen you need.''

''You're the *woman* I need,'' Luc fiercely interrupted her, yanking open the car door and tugging her into his arms. ''You're the woman I *love*. I'm nothing without you.''

She blinked her tears away. ''You're the King of St. Michel.''

''I'm Luc and I love you. Marry me. Help me. Laugh with me. Love me.''

''Oh Luc, I already do love you! That's why I had to leave. Don't you see?''

''All I see is you.''

''That's the problem then. You're too close to me to see the situation objectively. Baron Severin isn't.''

Luc frowned. ''What does he have to do with anything?''

''He talked to me tonight, pointed out some things that I already knew.''

''Like what?''

''Like the fact that you need someone of royal blood, as you are.''

Luc swore under his breath. ''The baron is dead wrong. The dowager queen has already given us her blessing.''

''The baron told me that I was hurting you by frolicking in the fountain with you,'' she countered unsteadily.

''The only thing that could hurt me is your leaving

me.'' She could see his pain in the clenching of his jaw, in the stormy anguish reflected deep in his blue eyes. ''Promise me you'll never do it again. Promise you'll marry me.''

''Luc, you haven't thought this through—''

''Of course I have.'' He tilted his head at her, lifting one dark eyebrow in that way she loved. ''I always think things through, you know that about me.''

''I thought you didn't believe in love, that it made a man vulnerable.''

''It's certainly made me vulnerable.'' He placed her open palm on his chest right over his heart. He stared down at her, his compelling blue eyes smoldering with passion, desire and most important…love. ''Do you feel that? My heart is beating for you. If being king means I can't have you, then I'll refuse the position, call off the coronation.''

''You can't do that!''

''I certainly can. And I will if you don't marry me. Because I'm not ruling as king without you by my side as my queen.'' His voice was suspiciously hoarse, making him sound like a man at the end of his emotional rope.

''Oh, Luc.'' She lifted her hand to his face and stood on tiptoe to place a tender string of kisses across his beloved face. ''I love you so much. I was just trying to do the right thing.''

''The right thing is marrying me. Will you be my wife?''

Here it was. That fork in the road of her future. Which should she take—the safe path that kept her life quiet or the risky one that kept her with Luc? In the end, the decision was inevitable. Knowing he loved her was the missing key. She couldn't leave him. ''Yes. Yes, I will.''

"Thank God." Luc lowered his mouth to hers for a kiss of dedicated passion and lifelong commitment.

"We'll just add a wedding ceremony to the coronation," he murmured against her lips as he trailed kisses across her face. "Everybody is already gathered together, we might as well kill two birds with one stone.

"Kill two birds, hmm? How romantic," she teased him with a laugh. "Is this what I have to look forward to for the next fifty years together?"

"The next *seventy* years, and I'll show you what you have to look forward to." He kissed her again, this time incorporating all their joy and laughter.

A short while later, they transferred her belongings and the kittens into the back of the police car he'd commandeered, leaving her car by the side of the road for a member of the security force to drive back. On their way to the palace, Juliet voiced her concerns. "Are you sure about this? A wedding in two days?"

"I'm positive." Luc flashed her a smile of utter confidence. "How difficult can it be?"

"You want to do *what?*" his grandmother practically shrieked as she sat in the White Drawing Room and stared at Luc and Juliet in disbelief.

"You heard me. I want to marry Juliet right before the coronation. You told me you approved," Luc reminded her.

"Of marrying her, yes. Of doing it on Sunday, no. I never said that was a good idea."

"Perhaps we should wait," Juliet said hesitantly.

"I'm not going to be crowned king without her," he said curtly, with a warning look at his grandmother.

She met his gaze head-on and impatiently tapped her

foot on the floor for good measure. "Luc, you're bullying the girl. Have you asked Juliet what she wants to do?"

"He's not really bullying me, ma'am," Juliet earnestly assured the dowager queen. "I wouldn't let him get away with bullying me. He's just being his regular bossy self."

"I told you to call me Grandmama." She smiled at Juliet. "Now, what made you take off from the ball this evening?"

Luc answered on Juliet's behalf. "That old windbag Baron Severin came after her tonight and fed her a load of garbage about her not being fit because she's not royalty. I want the man banished from the country."

Juliet had to laugh.

"What?" Luc turned to frown at her. "The man insulted you. He made you run away from me. He's lucky I don't toss him into the dungeon."

"He didn't insult me, he was just concerned about my suitability to be your wife. And he didn't make me do anything. It was my own insecurities that made me leave. But that was before I knew you loved me." She squeezed his hand, which had been clasping hers since they'd arrived at the palace. "Now nothing could make me leave your side."

"Not even the entire Privy Council throwing a hissy fit?"

She grinned at him. "Not even that."

"I told you she was a good girl," his grandmother said rather proudly. "Now, about setting a date for the wedding…"

"We're getting married on Sunday," Luc repeated.

"Is this agreeable to you, Juliet? It's your wedding day, too. Most brides want time to plan their special day."

"I've already got the dress," Juliet confessed.

"That slinky black one?" Luc asked hopefully.

The dowager queen's voice was horrified. "She is not getting married in black!"

"No, it's based on Queen Regina's wedding dress," Juliet quickly inserted. "A friend of mine in Paris made one up for me several years ago. She was a fashion design major and had to do a wedding dress…so I had her do this one. I always thought it was too lovely to actually wear."

"Do you have it here at the palace?"

Juliet nodded. "I was going to use it as part of my thesis presentation."

"I think you'll be putting it to a much better use this way," the dowager queen stated.

"I agree." Luc put his arm around Juliet and hugged her to his side.

His grandmother eyed them both doubtfully. "But still, we have less than forty-eight hours…."

"No wedding, no coronation," Luc stated.

His grandmother threw her hands in the air. "All right, all right. I didn't say it would be impossible. Just difficult."

Luc leaned down to kiss her. "You can manage 'difficult' with both hands tied behind your back."

"You charming sweet-talker, you. All right, leave it to me," his grandmother stated in her most regal voice. "We'll have your wedding on Sunday."

"I really don't need a bridal shower," Juliet was telling the dowager queen the next evening.

"Nonsense. It's tradition. My granddaughters have a lovely evening planned for you. Come, it's time to open your gifts. We all worked together on this."

"Before we start, there's something I've been meaning

to say.'' Ariane stood to face Juliet. ''I know that throughout the years, while you never actually said anything about it, you've never quite felt as if you fit in, and I feel badly that I never did more to make you feel welcome.''

''Me, too,'' Marie-Claire said.

''And I do, as well,'' Lise agreed.

Juliet blinked away the tears. ''Thank you. That's so sweet of you all. I realize now that my feelings of insecurity were rooted within me and weren't caused by any of you deliberately trying to make me feel like an outsider.''

''Maybe so, but we could have done more, included you more. We were too self-absorbed,'' Ariane said.

''We were princesses, it was our job to be self-absorbed.'' Marie-Claire grinned.

''Anyway, as Grandmama said, we all got together in planning our gifts for you,'' Jacqueline continued. ''Not that you gave us much time, but we like a challenge, or so Grandmama tells us. Our theme, of course, is something old, something new, something borrowed, something blue.''

''Open this one first.'' Ariane handed her a large box, beautifully wrapped.

Inside, Juliet found a gorgeous antique veil. ''It's the veil I wore at my wedding,'' the dowager queen said.

''And I at mine,'' Marie-Claire said.

''Then I wore it at my wedding,'' Ariane said. ''Now we would love for you to wear it.''

Nothing could have indicated more their intention to include her as family, and nothing could have touched her more. For the first time in her life she really felt at home with these women. Juliet blinked, the tears in her eyes right on the verge of rolling down her cheeks. ''I don't know what to say," she whispered, "except thank you so very much."

"I get to wear the veil after you," Jacqueline said. "As my something borrowed."

Juliet laughed. "I hope not for a few years yet."

The presents continued—a lovely string of pearls from Ariane for something new, a beautiful set of antique cameo earrings from Lise for something old, a racy pale-blue lingerie set from Marie-Claire, and, from the royal jewels, a stunning sapphire bracelet from the dowager queen as something blue. The bracelet matched the ring that she and Luc had selected from the many rings in the royal collection.

And from Jacqueline came a ring box. "It's not sapphires or anything like that," she warned, a bit self-consciously. "It's our mother's ring. With posies all around it. It's very small, but I thought you'd like to wear it as a pinkie ring when you get married. Do you like it?"

Juliet responded with a huge hug. Their mother hadn't had much jewelry, because when she'd married King Philippe, he'd insisted she give it all away and start fresh. This ring was the only thing she'd kept. "Thank you." Looking over her younger sister's head, she told everyone, "Thank you all!"

"Well, now." Juliet could almost have sworn she saw a shimmer of tears in the dowager queen's eyes as she announced, "It's after nine. I fear that Jacqueline and I will have to leave now. We need our beauty sleep."

"Me, too," Lise said. "A pregnant woman needs her rest."

"So do I," Juliet said. "After all, I'm getting married in the morning."

"No, you stay a little longer," the dowager queen told

her. "Ariane and Marie-Claire have something else for you."

Ariane waited until they'd left before turning to Juliet. "Given the premise that less is more, I've arranged for a little entertainment for us this evening."

"Did you get the Dauberville String Quartet?" Juliet inquired.

Ariane shook her head. "No, they weren't available. Alistair," she addressed the always reserved palace steward, "is the entertainment ready?"

Alistair fixed her with a disapproving look before donning his customary look of blandness. "Yes, your highness."

"Good. Tell them to proceed. Come sit down, Juliet. Right here on this couch. Yes, that should give you a good view."

View? Of what? A second later Juliet had her answer as the door to the Ruby Salon burst open and a quartet of men marched in

"I told you to get good-looking men for this job," Marie-Claire hissed to her sister.

Ariane shrugged. "They were all booked. Regular Joe Party Boys Incorporated were all that was left at such short notice."

Juliet stared in disbelief at the out-of-shape, middle-aged men who were gyrating madly to the sound of "I'm Too Sexy." Then they ripped open their shirts, revealing bulging bellies. She felt like sinking under the couch.

Just when she thought matters couldn't get any worse, as the men finished their production number by prancing in thongs, revealing a row of pudgy behinds, Luc walked into the room.

Juliet sent him a silent plea to rescue her from this fiasco, but he just grinned at her. "Sorry to interrupt. I

can see you ladies are busy at present. I'll come back a
bit later.''

"No, Luc, wait!" Juliet called out, but he was gone.

Ten minutes later the exotic dancers, as they called
themselves, had completed their act and departed. Ariane
and Marie-Claire were still wiping tears of mirth from
their eyes, and Juliet had had to giggle a time or two
herself at the men's deliberately outrageous moves.
They'd clearly been laughing at themselves and enjoying
every moment of it.

"Now can I go to bed?" Juliet asked the sisters.

"Not quite yet," Alistair surprised everyone by saying.
"There's one more item on the agenda this evening."

"Did you arrange this?" Ariane asked Marie-Claire,
who shook her head.

The music this time was Carly Simon's classic "Simply the Best." Alistair stepped out of the room and the
door opened. Juliet, Ariane and Marie-Claire all gasped
simultaneously.

For in walked three sexy men dressed in flowing white
shirts and well-fitted jeans. And they weren't just any
three men—they were none other than Marie-Claire's
husband Sebastian, Ariane's husband Prince Etienne, and
Juliet's fiancé Luc.

Of course, Juliet only had eyes for Luc. "We heard
you ladies were looking for a little entertainment this
evening," he drawled, his smoky blue gaze fixed on Juliet.

A moment later, they ripped off their shirts and let
them drop to the floor. Juliet's heart raced at the sight of
Luc wearing nothing but a wicked grin and jeans that
hung low on his lean hips, revealing his sexy navel.

Coming closer, Luc held out his hand, inviting her to
join with him in a royal version of salsa dancing that was

more like swaying to the music while wrapped in each other's arms, his thighs pressed between hers.

"Never let it be said the de Bergeron girls don't know how to throw a bridal shower!" Ariane and Marie-Claire laughed as they and their husbands danced their way out of the room.

"And never let it be said that their men don't know how to keep them on their toes and make them happy," Luc added with a wicked smile.

The only thing Juliet remembered about her wedding the next afternoon was Luc looking incredibly handsome as he said his vows to her. The Victorian-style wedding dress Juliet's friend had made looked wonderful with the dowager queen's veil and the jewelry her sisters had given her.

Juliet felt part of a strong bond as she smiled at the sisters, who were her bridesmaids Jacqueline, Ariane, Marie-Claire and Lise. All were lovely in ivory gowns shimmering with beadwork. Once again, the dowager queen's favorite dressmaker Madame Chantille had come to the rescue. And Juliet's brother Georges had flown in from summer skiing in South America to give Juliet away.

It was a perfect day.

The coronation ceremony would begin immediately following their wedding. The body of the St. Michel Cathedral was packed. Invitations were at a premium and overflow accommodation was provided in the gallery above the east door. Some sixty European royals were there, filling the pews. Television cameras covered the ceremony while reporters waited outside.

But, just as last night, Juliet only had eyes for Luc. She said her vows with the utter confidence of a woman marrying the man she loved. And when the priest said, "You may now kiss your bride, your majesty," Luc lifted the veil from her face and took Juliet in his arms.

Her happiness was complete, not with this happy ending but with this happy beginning of the rest of her life—a life shared with Luc.

Epilogue

One year later...

Juliet sadly shook her head at King Luc of St. Michel. "I never thought you'd leave me for another woman."

"I didn't leave you," Luc denied as he climbed back into bed with her. "I just went to change Michelle's diaper."

Juliet sighed. "She's a gorgeous baby girl, isn't she? And I'm not just saying that because she's my daughter."

"Of course not."

She gazed at him earnestly. "I mean, other babies are cute. Yvette's two little ones, Anise and Paul, are cute." DNA testing had confirmed that Celeste's baby girl had indeed been sired by her lover Claude and not by King Philippe. Yvette had renamed her son Paul and, as promised, was raising both children as her own with assistance from the palace. Luc had said, rightly so, that it wasn't fair to burden Yvette with the extra cost of another child without providing financial help.

"Yes, they are cute and a handful now that they are over a year old."

"And Lise's little girl is adorable, as is Ariane's newborn son. And Marie-Claire told me just yesterday that she's pregnant."

"First you girls all get married within a few months, now you all have babies." He shook his head.

"We're a close family," Juliet noted with a grin. "But our Michelle is special."

"Of course she is. I'm sure she smiled at me while I changed her diaper tonight."

"She probably was showing her appreciation, not only for the changing of her diaper but for the changing of the constitution, allowing females to inherit the throne of St. Michel."

Luc shrugged modestly. "It was nothing. It was time for St. Michel to join the twenty-first century."

"It was a big thing, Luc."

"Want me to show you another big thing?" he murmured seductively, snaring her in his arms.

"Why, you wicked man, you!" She pulled him even closer.

"I was referring to my smile. What did you think I meant?"

Juliet just grinned at him. "I love you so much, Luc."

"Show me," he whispered.

She did, with great enthusiasm. She'd found her prince at last and he was the king of her heart.

* * * * *

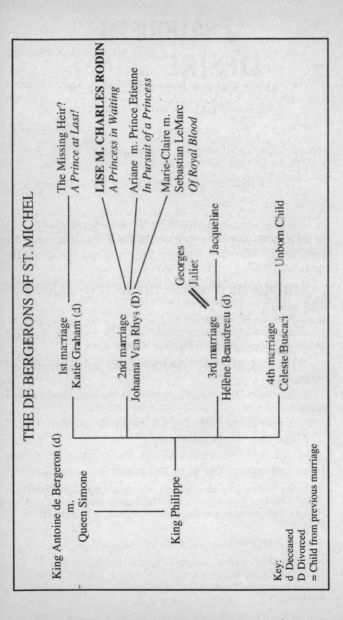

THE DE BERGERONS OF ST. MICHEL

King Antoine de Bergeron (d)
m.
Queen Simone

1st marriage
Katie Graham (d)

The Missing Heir?
A Prince at Last!

LISE M. CHARLES RODIN
A Princess in Waiting

Ariane m. Prince Etienne
In Pursuit of a Princess

Marie-Claire m.
Sebastian LeMarc
Of Royal Blood

2nd marriage
Johanna Van Rhys (D)

Georges
Juliet

Jacqueline

King Philippe

3rd marriage
Hélène Beaudreau (d)

4th marriage
Celeste Buscari

Unborn Child

Key:
d Deceased
D Divorced
= Child from previous marriage

SILHOUETTE®
DESIRE™ 2-IN-1
AVAILABLE FROM 20TH JUNE 2003

HER ROYAL HUSBAND Cara Colter

Crown and Glory

Jordan's long, hot summer with handsome Ben ended when he returned home, not knowing that she was carrying their child. But when they meet again, she learns *his* secret—he's really a prince…

THE PRINCESS HAS AMNESIA! Patricia Thayer

Crown and Glory

A jet crash left Princess Anastasia with amnesia, and an undeniable attraction for her handsome rescuer, Jake. But as her memory returned, would their love vanish…or become strong enough to supersede the demands of duty?

THE PLAYBOY MEETS HIS MATCH Sara Orwig

Millionaire's Club

Retired FBI agent Jason Windover had a new assignment—to keep feisty redhead Meredith Silver out of trouble. But would his electrifying kisses keep her sufficiently distracted?

THE BACHELOR TAKES A WIFE Jackie Merritt

Millionaire's Club

Millionaire Keith Owens loved his bachelor ways—until elegant and sophisticated Andrea O'Rourke came back. Years ago, she'd left town, swearing to forget him…but this time he swore she wouldn't escape…

THE SEAL'S SURPRISE BABY Amy J Fetzer

Returning home fifteen months after one perfect night with Melanie, Navy SEAL Jack Singer was shocked to discover that he was a father. He knew that marriage was the solution—but could he persuade Melanie?

ZANE: THE WILD ONE Bronwyn Jameson

Julia's world was rocked when rebel Zane returned, with his raw sensual power that tempted her deepest desires. But what would happen to their love when he learned about the child their passion had created?

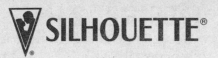

Available from 20th June 2003

Available at most branches of WH Smith, Tesco, Martins, Borders, Eason, Sainsbury's and all good paperback bookshops.

0703/081/SH55

Maitland Maternity

SILHOUETTE®
DESIRE™

invites you to enter the exclusive world of

The Millionaire's Club

**where five seriously powerful and
wealthy bachelors set out to find a traitor in
their midst…and maybe encounter
true love along the way.**

May 2003
THE MILLIONAIRE'S PREGNANT BRIDE
by Dixie Browning
(in a two-in-one volume with A Man of Means by Diana Palmer)

June 2003
HER LONE STAR PROTECTOR
by Peggy Moreland
and
TALL, DARK…AND FRAMED?
by Cathleen Galitz

July 2003
THE PLAYBOY MEETS HIS MATCH
by Sara Orwig
and
THE BACHELOR TAKES A WIFE
by Jackie Merritt

0503/SH/LC60

0203/SH/LC54

SILHOUETTE® DESIRE™

is proud to introduce

DYNASTIES: THE CONNELLYS

Meet the royal Connellys—wealthy, powerful and rocked by scandal, betrayal...and passion!

TWELVE GLAMOROUS STORIES IN SIX 2-IN-1 VOLUMES:

SILHOUETTE® SENSATION™

presents

ROMANCING THE CROWN

The Royal family of Montebello is determined to find their missing heir. But the search for the prince is not without danger—or passion!

0103/SH/LC50

SILHOUETTE® SUPERROMANCE™

is proud to present

THREE GOOD COPS

by
Janice Kay Johnson

The McLean brothers are all good,
strong, honest, men. Men a woman
can trust…with her heart!

HIS PARTNER'S WIFE
May 2003

THE WORD OF A CHILD
July 2003

MATERNAL INSTINCT
September 2003

0503/SH/LC64

SILHOUETTE® SPECIAL EDITION™

proudly presents

CROWN AND GLORY

*Where royalty and romance
go hand in hand...*

April 2003 - Silhouette Special Edition
The Princess Is Pregnant! by Laurie Paige

May 2003 - Silhouette Special Edition
The Princess and the Duke by Allison Leigh

June 2003 - Silhouette Special Edition
Royal Protocol by Christine Flynn

July 2003 - Silhouette Desire 2-in-1
Her Royal Husband by Cara Colter
The Princess Has Amnesia! by Patricia Thayer

September 2003 - Silhouette Desire 2-in-1
Searching for Her Prince by Karen Rose Smith
The Royal Treatment by Maureen Child

November 2003 - Silhouette Desire 2-in-1
Taming the Prince by Elizabeth Bevarly
Royally Pregnant by Barbara McCauley

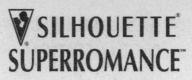

SILHOUETTE®
SUPERROMANCE™

proudly presents

Men of Maple Hill

a heart-warming new trilogy from

MURIEL JENSEN

Meet the men of this charming
Massachusetts town and the
women who come into their lives.

Man with a Mission
February 2003

Man with a Message
July 2003

Man with a Miracle
December 2003

*Emotional stories with a sense of
humour and lots of family!*

0203/SH/LC53

SPECIAL EDITION™

Vivid, emotional, satisfying romances—

These stories capture the intensity
of living and loving and creating a
family in today's world.

INTRIGUE™

Danger, deception and suspense.

Breathtaking romantic suspense,
full of mystery, deception and
dangerous desires…

FREE

2 BOOKS
AND A SURPRISE GIFT!

We would like to take this opportunity to thank you for reading this Silhouette® book by offering you the chance to take two more specially selected titles from the Desire™ series absolutely FREE! We're also making this offer to introduce you to the benefits of the Reader Service™—

- ★ FREE home delivery
- ★ FREE monthly Newsletter
- ★ FREE gifts and competitions
- ★ Exclusive Reader Service discount
- ★ Books available before they're in the shops

Accepting this FREE book and gift places you under no obligation to buy; you may cancel at any time, even after receiving your free shipment. Simply complete your details below and return the entire page to the address below. **You don't even need a stamp!**

YES! Please send me 2 free Desire books and a surprise gift. I understand that unless you hear from me, I will receive 3 superb new titles every month for just £4.99 each, postage and packing free. I am under no obligation to purchase any books and may cancel my subscription at any time. The free books and gift will be mine to keep in any case.

D3ZEI

Ms/Mrs/Miss/Mr ....Initials...........................
BLOCK CAPITALS PLEASE

Surname...

Address..

....

....Postcode ....

Send this whole page to:
UK: FREEPOST CN81, Croydon, CR9 3WZ
EIRE: PO Box 4546, Kilcock, County Kildare (stamp required)